Dear Reader:

There are some romances that never lose their sense of enchantment: books from the authors you love but have never been able to find, or stories that you read long ago and still resonate in your heart. Here at Pocket Books, we know how special those books are, so we decided to create Pocket Classics. These beloved books have been tested by time and emerged the winners, and we've made them available once again in brand-new editions.

Is there any author more versed in the romance of the American West than Linda Lael Miller? Whether portraying life and love in a small frontier town, across the ranchlands of the 1890s, or with the modern-day cowboy in all his rough-hewn sexiness, this #1 *New York Times* bestselling author keeps readers spellbound with novels like *My Darling Melissa*. With its proud, determined heroine and irresistible man's man hero, this favorite from her Corbin brothers series captures a time and place where passions ruled the heart.

We love this book just as much now as we did when we first published it, and we hope that you will, too.

Happy reading!

Books by Linda Lael Miller

Available from Pocket Books

Linda Lael Miller

MY DARLING MELISSA

POCKET BOOKS

New York London Toronto Sydney New Delhi

Pocket Books
A Division of Simon & Schuster, Inc.
1230 Avenue of the Americas
New York, NY 10020

This book is a work of fiction. Any references to historical events, real people, or real places are used fictitiously. Other names, characters, places, and events are products of the author's imagination, and any resemblance to actual events or places or persons, living or dead, is entirely coincidental.

First Pocket Books paperback edition February 1990

POCKET and colophon are registered trademarks
of Simon & Schuster, Inc.

For information about special discounts for bulk purchases,
please contact Simon & Schuster Special Sales at 1-866-506-1949 or
business@simonandschuster.com.

The Simon & Schuster Speakers Bureau can bring authors to your
live event. For more information or to book an event, contact the
Simon & Schuster Speakers Bureau at 1-866-248-3049 or visit our
website at www.simonspeakers.com.

Manufactured in the United States of America

20 19 18 17 16 15 14 13 12 11 10 9

ISBN 978-0-671-73771-9
ISBN 978-1-4516-5528-5 (ebook)

For Debbie Macomber,
loyal friend,
walking partner,
and yarnspinner *extraordinaire*

ℕ One

She appeared out of a driving rain, a spirit of the storm, clutching the skirts of her billowing white wedding dress in her hands and running for all she was worth. A circlet of bedraggled flowers graced her dark hair, which hung in sodden ropes to her waist. Her gown was most definitely ruined, and her dainty slippers were muddy and wet.

Quinn Rafferty stood fascinated on the platform of his private railroad car, heedless of the rain and the keening of the train whistle that signaled imminent departure. The nymph had gained the tracks now and was charging toward him.

Quite a lot of her trim but womanly bosom was visible from Quinn's vantage point, and he was charmed. When the train lurched into motion and began to clatter and clank he saw the bride set her beautiful jaw and burst into even greater speed.

"Damn you, h-help me!" she gasped, holding up one hand.

Quinn was stunned to realize that she'd actually caught

up to the train. Like a man moving in a dream he reached down, gained a hold on her, and hauled her aboard.

Her small, nubile body slammed against Quinn's, and although the impact was slight, for a moment he was as breathless as though he'd been buried alive in a high-country snowslide.

The sprite was spitting mad and panting from her flight and her fury. Her azure eyes snapped. Quinn recovered himself enough to grin and tip the brim of his hat with insolent good manners. He allowed his gaze to slide down over her, and again he had that sensation of being crushed beneath some invisible, elemental substance.

"This is so sudden," he quipped, to hide his distress at being so violently affected by this little snippet of a girl in a muddy wedding dress and a crown of drooping petunias.

She was looking back on the town of Port Hastings now, a certain dismay in her round eyes. A flock of disgruntled wedding guests had gathered at the tracks, peering after her through the drizzle, shouting and waving their arms.

"Forgive me," she whispered. And then she lifted delicate, gloved fingers to her lips and blew a kiss to the throng.

Three men towered in the forefront of the crowd. The one wearing a clerical collar lifted his hand in farewell and smiled sadly, but the other two looked as though they could uproot railroad spikes with their teeth and chew them like peppermint sticks.

Quinn wondered which one was the spurned groom. While he'd never been afraid of any man—save his own father—he was glad he didn't have to give an accounting of this episode to either of those two. And that very relief nettled his pride.

"Shall we?" he asked with biting politeness, extending an arm.

The lady took the offered arm, full of disdainful dignity, and allowed Quinn to escort her into the car.

She looked around her, clearly unimpressed with the luxury Quinn had worked all his life to acquire, and plopped her sodden bustle down on a velvet-upholstered bench. She was peeling off her spoiled slippers while Quinn went to the liquor cabinet and poured healthy doses of brandy for himself and the runaway bride.

"What's your name?" he demanded, fairly shoving a crystal snifter into her hand.

She accepted it without the maidenly reluctance Quinn had anticipated, her incredible azure eyes fixed for the fraction of a moment on something above and beyond his right shoulder. "Pullman," she said, after that brief and patently disturbing hesitation. "Melissa Pullman."

He took a long draught of his own brandy before sitting down in a nearby chair and ran one hand through his light brown hair. "Well?" he prompted when, after several long sips from her glass, Miss Pullman had not volunteered her story.

"Well, what?" she countered testily.

Quinn sighed, turning his snifter between his palms. "I'd like an explanation," he responded tautly. "I think you owe me that."

She sighed, and her straight little shoulders stooped just a bit as she pondered the amber depths of her brandy. "I suppose I do," she conceded, and Quinn found himself feeling sorry for her.

The sentiment was of short duration.

"I'm not sure I'm going to tell you anything, though," she added. She eyed him in an appraising fashion. "You are a man, after all."

"Thank you very much."

"Not at all," came the immediate retort. "It wasn't a compliment. And your name, sir?"

"Rafferty," her host allowed, annoyed. "Quinn Rafferty." Even though he was indisputably the best poker player in four counties, Quinn found that he couldn't keep a straight face. What he was feeling was more than mere idle curiosity; it was a driving, vital need to know. "Which one of those three giants was supposed to be your husband?"

A smile curved her lips, and Quinn was struck with a piercing awareness of her loveliness. God in heaven, even in that dirty, water-spotted wedding dress, with her hair dripping and her face wet with rain and, Quinn suspected, tears, she was the most beautiful woman he'd ever seen. "None. They were my brothers."

Quinn searched his memory for a trio of Pullman brothers based in Port Hastings and came up dry. "And the groom?"

"I doubt that Ajax would stoop to running after me." She made the admission with a small sigh. "He's practically royalty, you know. His family goes back to the time of William the Conqueror."

Quinn shrugged, irritated by that kind of pretension. "We all go back to Adam and Eve, don't we?"

To his surprise, she smiled. "You're right, Mr. Rafferty. You're absolutely right." She shoved the snifter at him. "Might I have more brandy, please?"

Quinn was about to refuse—it was powerful stuff, that brew—when he knew a certain stab of sympathy. The poor little sprite had run out of a church, through a pounding rainstorm, and been wrenched aboard a railroad car by a complete stranger. Despite the cocky act she was putting on, Quinn was convinced that Melissa Pullman was nervous and afraid.

He rose and refilled her snifter, and when he handed it back she took a great gulp. After a few more such swallows she seemed more receptive to sensible conversation.

"Why did you leave Ajax at the altar?" Quinn asked kindly.

Melissa smoothed her skirts, ignoring their hopeless condition, and avoided Quinn's eyes. She bit down hard on her lower lip for a moment, then tossed back the last of her brandy. "I didn't love him," she stated shakily, and in a hoarse voice, after a very long time.

Quinn had his doubts as to her sincerity. "Wouldn't it have been simpler to say so?" he prompted in a gentle tone.

"I couldn't have faced him," she said.

"Then why didn't you just tell your brothers how you felt? Surely they would have understood."

Melissa hiccuped and set her snifter aside on a table that, like all the other furniture in the car, was bolted to the floor. She shook her head. "As far as they're concerned, I'm a spinster," she confided. "I'm sure they thought Ajax was my last chance."

Moments before, Quinn had been glad not to have to deal with the Pullman brothers. Now he longed to confront them. "Bull—balderdash!" he muttered. "How could you be an old maid? You're on the sunny side of twenty or I'm a donkey's first cousin!"

She gave a pealing, slightly drunken giggle and gingerly removed her halo of flowers. "I'm twenty-two, and your family heritage would explain your stubbornness, wouldn't it?"

Quinn knew that he should have been insulted—in essence, she'd just called him a jackass—but the truth was that Melissa's presence filled him with a peculiar, suspenseful kind of joy. "How do you know I'm stubborn?" he demanded to know.

Melissa yawned, delicately covering her mouth with one hand. "It's written in every line of you," she answered. And then she toppled unceremoniously to one side and closed her eyes with a sigh that wrenched at Quinn's insides. "I'm very tired," she explained.

Quinn went to the bed, hidden beyond an ornate partition, and came back with a lush, furry lap robe that was usually put to more adventurous uses. He covered Melissa, who made an endearing little snoring sound, and then turned away.

It was at that moment that his gaze found the word "Pullman" stenciled discreetly near the arching roof of the car. Quinn Rafferty knew then that he'd been bamboozled, and the humiliation robbed him of every whit of tenderness he'd drummed up for the would-be bride sleeping on the bench.

He wished he'd never laid eyes on Melissa whatever-her-name-was, let alone hauled her into his railroad car like that.

His instinct told him he'd made a disastrous mistake—the kind that could change the course of a man's life.

Quinn Rafferty liked his life just the way it was.

It was dead dark when Melissa awoke, confused and a little scared. Noise and motion combined to assure her that she was aboard a train bound for God only knew where.

She remembered the events of the preceding day in bits and pieces—her family and friends gathered at the church, the confession Ajax had made so offhandedly, the terrible hurt that had driven her to flee, unable to explain to anyone.

Before that pain could catch hold of her again Melissa shifted her thoughts to the man who had lifted her off the tracks and onto the platform of the railroad car just before her strength would have given out. He was a handsome one, Mr. Rafferty was, with his golden brown hair and eyes the color of caramel, and he had good, sturdy white teeth as well.

She supposed he was in his mid-thirties; and, since he had use of this luxurious railroad car, he was most certainly well-heeled, probably successful. . . .

Melissa stifled a sob. She didn't give a damn about Quinn Rafferty or what he'd achieved in life, and she never would.

It was Sir Ajax Morewell Hampton that she loved, and trying not to think about him was a hopeless task.

If Melissa had had a pillow, she would have buried her face in it to muffle the outpouring of grief she could no longer stem, but she had none. She covered her face with both hands and let go of her despair, wailing as the force of it carried her, like some unseen river, beyond the far borders of her pride and into a place where there was no such vanity.

The light of a lantern flared, showing red-gold between Melissa's fingers; there was a muttered exclamation, and then Mr. Rafferty sat down on the bench and drew her awkwardly into his arms.

His chest was broad and strong; being held by Rafferty was like being held by one of her brothers, and yet strangely different.

"You do love him," Rafferty said quietly.

"No!" Melissa lied with all the strength she had, shuddering in his arms. "I hate him—I swear I hate him!"

Rafferty made no reply to that. He simply held Melissa, and she was grateful, for she felt in that moment as though she would fly apart if it weren't for his tight grasp holding her together.

After a long interval he cursed.

Melissa's sobs had subsided to sniffles, and she gazed up at him in the lamplight, alarmed. "What is it?"

Instead of answering, Rafferty got to his feet—he was wearing a silken robe with a dragon embroidered on the back—and stormed around a partition. He returned moments later, carrying a linen shirt.

"Put this on," he ordered, flinging it at Melissa.

She swallowed hard, staring at him. A heartbeat before he'd been comforting her; now he was demanding the unthinkable.

Rafferty went to the liquor cabinet and helped himself to a drink. This time he didn't offer Melissa refreshment, and she hadn't the nerve to ask for it. She couldn't make out the diatribe he was muttering, except for the word "stupid," which was woven throughout.

Melissa finally found her voice. "I won't," she said clearly.

The caramel eyes scanned her with angry impatience. "Look at you—you're wet to the skin from the rain. If you die of pneumonia before morning, it'll be no fault of mine."

Melissa was profoundly aware, all of a sudden, of her damp, cold gown. Although discomfort had niggled at her in her sleep, she had been too exhausted, and too drugged with brandy, to be concerned. She glanced toward the partition.

Quinn spread his hands. "You can have the bed, minx, and I'm not going to be peering around the wall at you while you change. Get on with it, so a man can get some sleep."

Melissa scrambled around the barrier, as much out of curiosity as cold, and was struck to encounter a bed of nothing less than decadent proportions. A brief investigation proved that the sheets were silken ones, and the blanket was chinchilla.

Giving a long, low whistle of exclamation through her front teeth, Melissa set aside her heartbreak over Ajax and began straining to unfasten the many buttons at the back of her gown. Only that morning Mama and Banner and Fancy and Tess had been there, doing them up by turns and joking that it was too big a job for one woman but perfect for one man.

Tears sprouted in Melissa's eyes, but she forced a smile into her voice. "You live a shamefully self-indulgent life, Mr. Rafferty," she called out.

Rafferty ignored the observation. "Tell me what that bastard did to you, to make you run away and then cry like that."

Grateful for the wall that hid her from his view, Melissa squirmed and struggled with those dratted buttons for several frustrating moments, then answered, "You won't believe it, Mr. Rafferty. You truly won't believe it."

"Try me," prompted Mr. Rafferty.

It would be a relief to confide in someone, Melissa decided. Someone objective, someone unimportant in the general scheme of her life. "He had a mistress," she confessed in a very small voice, as though the sin of that were somehow her own. "He'd brought her all the way from Munich and installed her in a house in Port Hastings and then had the gall to invite her to our wedding!"

There was silence from beyond the partition, the still kind that precedes a violent storm. But instead of exploding, Mr. Rafferty came around and began helping Melissa with the buttons of her gown.

The motions of his fingers were awkward and slow, but there was something so tender in the gesture that Melissa felt fresh tears smarting in her eyes. Lord knew she'd done her share of crying that day, and then some. It was time to stop, to get a hold of herself, to go on with her life.

She lifted her chin and sucked in her breath.

"Where exactly is this train headed?" she asked.

"I wondered if you were ever going to get around to asking about that. It's on its way to Spokane."

Melissa's mouth fell open, and she whirled, clutching the bodice of her dress to her bosom with both hands so that she wouldn't further disgrace herself. "Spokane! That's on the other side of the state!"

The look in Quinn Rafferty's brown eyes was completely at variance with the gentle solicitation he'd shown moments before. It was, in point of fact, arrogant and quite smug. "What do you care—Miss Pullman?" he drawled.

Melissa's cheeks smarted with heat and color. She could not afford to offend this man. She was alone with him in a railroad car that looked as if it had been decorated by a spendthrift madam. It was night, and they were in the middle of nowhere.

"My name isn't Miss Pullman," she confessed, lowering her eyes.

"No!" he cried in mock surprise, laying one hand to his breast.

Melissa stamped one foot. "I'm Melissa Kate Corbin," she announced, infuriated. "Do you know what that means, Mr. Rafferty?"

The expression of surprise was transformed into one of theatrical horror. "No. What, pray tell, does that mean?"

Melissa was stumped. Under the circumstances, she wasn't sure it meant anything.

"Never mind," she finally said.

Rafferty chuckled at that, finished unfastening her dress, and then left her to her privacy.

"You're better off without this Ajax character," he observed after some time, when the lamp had gone out. By then Melissa was cuddled deep between the silken sheets of Mr. Rafferty's bed, clad only in his ruffle-fronted shirt. He was probably sleeping on the narrow bench where she had reclined before.

Melissa sighed. "I suppose so."

"I still don't understand why you had to run away. You could have explained the whole thing to your family—"

"But I couldn't have," Melissa argued. "Mama and I had had words about Ajax on more than one occasion—she never liked him, you know. And if I'd told my brothers—well, Keith would probably have been civil enough—he's a preacher, after all—but Adam and Jeff? It doesn't bear considering. Heaven only knows what they might have done to Ajax."

Mr. Rafferty let out a long sigh, as if to show an infinite capacity for suffering. "So you decided to jump aboard the first train out of town," he said.

"Of course not. I was just running, that's all. And I ended up in the railroad yard, so—"

A richly masculine chuckle sounded in the darkness.

"Do you live in Port Hastings?" Melissa asked, wanting to change the subject. "I don't remember ever seeing you there before."

"I make my home on the other side of the peninsula, Miss Corbin. In Port Riley."

Melissa settled deeper into the silken sheets. There was a certain rivalry between the two towns, and that added a spark to an already provocative situation. She sighed. "My brothers say that Port Riley will be a ghost town in five years."

"Oh, they do, do they?"

"Yes. To use Jeff's own words, there's one piss-ant saw-mill grinding out two-by-fours, and that's it for industry."

"'One piss-ant sawmill'?" It was obvious that Melissa had touched a nerve. "I'll have you know that '*piss-ant* sawmill' is mine, Miss Corbin, and I own one of the biggest timber operations in this state. There are four banks in Port Riley, along with a cannery and a library and a hospital. Until six months ago, there was a newspaper." He paused and drew a deep breath before finishing grandly, "Further-more, there are seventeen saloons."

"Oh," Melissa chimed, with prim airiness. "That changes everything. Any community with seventeen saloons is cer-tainly worthy of its position on the map."

"Go to sleep, Miss Corbin. Tomorrow will be a long day."

Melissa didn't want to think about the next day—or all the tomorrows that would follow it. And she wasn't ready to go to sleep.

"What happened to the newspaper?"

Rafferty gave an exasperated sigh. "What newspaper?"

"The one Port Riley had until six months ago."

"It was burned out."

"By accident?"

"On purpose. Somebody had a difference of political opinion with the publishers."

"Who?"

"I have no idea, Miss Corbin."

"Well, that's a fine thing. Don't you have a United States marshal in your town?"

"Yes, we have a United States marshal in our town," Mr. Rafferty mimicked. "I think he has his suspicions, but he never came up with any proof. Now, if you'll just shut your lovely little mouth, Miss Corbin . . ."

"I need to talk."

Rafferty sighed again. "I think Sir Ajax Whoever may have missed out on a fate he richly deserved."

"What is that supposed to mean?"

"Nothing. Nothing at all. Forgive me," Mr. Rafferty said wryly. "I lost my head for a moment."

"Why are you going to Spokane?"

Mr. Rafferty groaned. "I have business there."

"What kind of business?"

There was a short, deadly silence, but the answer, when it came, was quite reasonably stated. "I mean to deposit you in a hotel, then contact your family and let them know that you're all right. After that I will meet with some business partners of mine—"

"I am not going to be 'deposited' in some hotel like a runaway child," Melissa, sitting bolt upright in bed, informed him. In that moment she knew that she could never go home—her pride wouldn't let her—until she'd accomplished something real and lasting all on her own. Otherwise the family would fuss over her ever after, as if she were an eccentric spinster.

The prospect was alarming; the reality would be unbearable.

She got to her knees and moved aside the window blind to peer out at the passing countryside. The moon bathed the barren country of central Washington State in an eerie light. "I can look after myself," she said, hiding all her uncertainties in a bright tone of voice.

And then she lay down again, closed her eyes, and slipped into a fitful sleep.

When Melissa awakened the car was filled with sunlight, and an elephant seemed to be balancing on one foot on her

11

chest. Her nose was clogged, and the heat emanating from her body was so intense that it threatened to smother her.

A stranger with a bristly white mustache and a stethoscope affixed to his bald head was bending over the bed. "You'll be just fine, miss," he told her.

Melissa was certain that she was dying of some mysterious plague the likes of which had never been documented before. She started to croak out her last words and found they wouldn't come.

"Lots of lemon juice, that's what she needs," the doctor said jovially. And then he turned away.

Accommodatingly, Quinn soon brought her a steaming mug. He looked damnably handsome and damnably healthy in his clean, well-tailored clothes. Melissa could see the ridges left by a comb in his still-damp hair.

Despite her proximity to the hereafter, she managed to drag herself to a sitting position and reach out for the mug. The lemon juice had been liberally laced with liquor.

"Sorry about your new start in life and all that," Quinn said merrily. "Guess you'll just have to go on with the old one."

Melissa narrowed her eyes at him. The moment she arrived on the other side she'd get permission to become a ghost. And then she meant to haunt Mr. Rafferty until all his hair either turned white or fell out.

Rafferty laughed as though he could read her impotent thoughts and patted her fever-hot cheek. "If you're very good, I'll bring you a present," he condescended to say. "Mind Eloise now, and rest yourself."

Eloise, a dour woman in black sateen, appeared at the end of the bed. She was holding a Bible to her bosom and peering through the tiny square lenses of her glasses. It was clear that she had the wrong idea entirely about who Melissa was and what she was doing in Mr. Rafferty's railroad car, sick unto dying or not.

Melissa closed her eyes. They must be in Spokane, she realized, too ill to care what it was she'd meant to do there.

The day was a difficult one. Melissa slept deeply at intervals, but then the fever and her fiery throat would awaken her, making her toss and turn in abject misery.

She was delighted when Mr. Rafferty arrived at nightfall. He brought a present, just as he'd promised, and sent Eloise away.

With the last shreds of her failing strength—she was sure to be dead by morning—Melissa clawed the wrapping paper from the gift Quinn had laid in her lap. It was a book, and Melissa would have laughed if she'd been able to, because she'd written the opus herself—under a pseudonym, of course.

Her eyes sparkled with more than fever as she looked questioningly at her benefactor.

"They're bringing beef stew from the dining car," he said, undoing his tie beside the bed. His glance fell again to the book. "Pure trash, according to the bookseller," he said, "but women love it."

He looked completely baffled when Melissa hurled the volume at his head.

ℰℬ *Two*

Quinn dragged a chair to Melissa's bedside, determined to lend comfort whether it was wanted or not, and sat down to read from the book she had just thrown at him. Wearing the same serious expression she'd seen on her brother Adam's face when he was perusing a medical journal, Mr. Rafferty turned to the first page of chapter one and read soberly, "'Phoebe Millikin was a woman bound for destruction.'" He stopped and gave the book's cover a pensive look, then cleared his throat and went on.

Melissa settled into her pillows, all ears. Despite the fact that she'd written *Phoebe's Dangerous Decision* herself, she was intrigued. The carefully chosen words sounded different falling from Mr. Rafferty's lips. More august, somehow.

He'd covered only about two pages when there was a respectful rap at the railroad car's inner door. Quinn got up to answer it, leaving the book in the seat of his chair.

The beef stew had arrived. Quinn allowed Melissa the use of the tray while he sat on the edge of the bed, holding his bowl in one hand and his spoon in the other.

"Mind your manners," he warned, waggling the spoon at

Melissa. "I can overlook having a book thrown at me, but stew is another matter."

In spite of herself and all her miseries, Melissa smiled. She tasted the stew and found it as savory as any Maggie McQuire might have concocted for the family back home.

Quinn was frowning at her; he had yet to take a bite of his own food. "We have a problem here," he said, as though that were some great revelation.

"We have a number of problems," Melissa pointed out in a scratchy voice that hurt her throat.

Rafferty took in the wrinkled linen shirt she had been wearing since taking off her wedding dress. "You haven't got a damned thing to wear," he said. "This is a scandalous situation—the kind of fine how-do-you-do that could ruin a lady's reputation."

"What about your reputation, Mr. Rafferty?" It pained Melissa to ask.

He grinned, showing those flawless white teeth of his. "It can only be enhanced," he said.

Melissa considered crowning him with her bowl of stew but in the end refrained. She was ravenously hungry—it appeared that death was not imminent after all—and wanted every morsel of her food. She said nothing.

Quinn's glance strayed to the book sitting in the seat of the chair he'd occupied a few minutes before. "I'm sorry you didn't like your present," he told Melissa.

Melissa chewed thoughtfully and swallowed with great care for her sore throat before replying, "It wasn't the present itself, Mr. Rafferty. It was what you said about it."

He looked genuinely baffled. "What was that?" he asked.

"You called my book 'trash,'" Melissa answered reasonably. "I worked long and hard on the manuscript, and while Phoebe is admittedly no Emma Bovary or Jane Eyre, she does represent my best effort."

Quinn's mouth sagged open; Melissa resisted an urge to thrust a spoonful of stew into it. Again, it was greed that stopped her.

"You wrote that book?" Rafferty finally managed to ask.

Melissa finished her stew and fell back against her pillows, weary from the effort of eating. "I did indeed. That one and three others, if you count the dime novels I wrote as Marshal S. Whidbine."

"I'll be damned," Quinn muttered.

"Probably," sighed Melissa, "but that's no concern of mine." She yawned widely, closed her eyes, and tipped her chin at an imperious angle. "Read on," she ordered.

"I will not," Quinn said flatly.

She heard dishes clatter together on the tray and felt it lifted from her lap but did not open her eyes. After a while she slept.

The renewed motion of the train awakened her; she sat up in bed. They must have begun the journey back west. The car was dark, except for a splash of golden light fringing the partition. "Quinn?" she called in a small voice.

When he didn't answer she scrambled shakily out of bed and peered around the wall.

Quinn was seated at a desk, Melissa's novel open before him. He looked up at her and shook his head in dour amazement.

Melissa felt a blush climb her face. Though she couldn't think why, she wanted Quinn to like her work, even to admire it. Obviously, it was more of a curiosity to him.

"You might have mentioned that we were leaving Spokane," she said as the floor shook under her feet. "It just so happens that I wanted to stay there."

Quinn shrugged. There was a parcel on the corner of his desk, and he tossed it somewhat cavalierly to Melissa. "Here. Compliments of your devoted nurse."

Melissa caught the flying bundle in both arms; it was quite heavy. "What is it?"

One of Quinn's powerful shoulders moved in a shrug. "Some evidence of her Christian charity, I would imagine. She and the doctor were very concerned for your soul."

Melissa had already learned that Eloise was the sister of the doctor Quinn had summoned to the railroad car that morning. She was almost afraid to look inside the parcel. "I suppose I should go back to bed," she remarked lightly, feeling lonesome.

"I suppose you should," Quinn answered, closing the book with a telling slam and standing up. "I think I'll go to the club car myself. Play a hand or two of poker."

Melissa's knees were a bit shaky, and she made her reluctant way back to bed. "I know how to play poker," she volunteered hopefully. It was going to be downright dismal in that car if Mr. Rafferty went away and left her.

She heard a drawer open and close, and then Quinn was standing in view of the bed, his hand on the door that led to the next car.

"Get some sleep," he said, giving her an indulgent grin, and then he was gone.

Melissa's eyes burned with tears; she dried them with her palms and valiantly refused to shed more. The devil with Mr. Rafferty, if he didn't want to play a hand of poker with her. He was probably an easy mark anyway.

After a few moments of true despair Melissa forced her attention to the package Eloise had sent. It was wrapped in brown paper and bound tightly with twine, and it took a good deal of concentrated effort to open it.

Inside were two dull, prim calico dresses, along with two pairs of muslin drawers, two camisoles, one oft-mended petticoat, and a dark woolen shawl. There was also a pair of black high button shoes that looked a shade too big for Melissa's feet.

She sat stunned, teetering between fits of laughter and wails of outrage. She was a member of one of the richest, most powerful families in the state and had never expected to be the recipient of Christian charity.

Melissa bit down on her lower lip and held herself steady. The plain truth was that, even though she had access to a fortune, even though there wasn't a gown in all the world so expensive that she couldn't afford to buy it, she needed these clothes. The only other garment she had on hand was a mud-stained wedding dress with a tear in the hem.

She blinked back more tears, sniffled, and then uttered a forlorn little chuckle. A person couldn't start a new and independent life in a dirty wedding gown.

Melissa got out of bed and tried on the dresses. They fit

well enough, but the shoes were a bit too large. She was striding back and forth, trying to get the hang of keeping them on her feet, when Quinn reentered the car with a rush of cold air.

"What are you doing?" he demanded, scowling. It was plain enough that he'd lost at poker.

"I'm practicing," she answered. "If these are going to be my shoes, I'd just better learn to walk in them."

"A cryptic statement if I've ever heard one," Quinn replied, rounding the desk and opening a drawer. He took a wallet from the inside pocket of his tailored suit coat and dropped it inside. An expression of polite horror crossed his face as he took in her worn calico dress. "Great Scott, that's ugly."

Melissa curtsied, though she was beginning to feel weak again. "Thank you so much, sir," she said.

Quinn took her firmly by the arm and led her back to the bed, where he sat her down. "Get back into bed," he ordered when he'd divested her of both her shoes. "A porter will be along soon with more hot lemon juice."

Seeing that Quinn had turned his back, Melissa squirmed out of her charity dress and crawled back under the covers. She was wearing muslin drawers and a camisole now instead of Quinn's shirt.

"I've got it all figured out," she announced, assuming an optimism she did not feel. "I'm going to prove to my family that I can take care of myself."

The porter brought the lemon juice in a crockery teapot. When he was gone Quinn poured the juice into a cup and handed it to Melissa. Only then did he comment, "I can't wait to hear your plans, Miss Corbin."

Melissa took a noisy sip of the hot drink. "I'm not going to touch my trust fund, nor will I charge so much as a paper of pins to my mother's accounts."

A wry grin twisted Quinn's lips; by now he was settled in the bedside chair again. "Drastic measures," he commented.

"I do have a little money that I earned myself, though. From my writing, I mean."

Quinn sighed. "What does your family think of your—er—literary pursuits?"

Melissa lowered her eyes for a moment. "They don't know," she confessed. "Except for Banner, that is."

"Banner?"

"My sister-in-law." Melissa was proud of Adam's wife, and she could not contain her enthusiasm. "Banner, who's married to Adam, is a doctor—not a midwife or a nurse, mind you, but a real doctor. Jeff's Fancy was once a magician, and Keith's wife, Tess, takes the most remarkable photographs."

Quinn gave a low whistle to prove that he was impressed and then ruined everything by saying, "The lady doctor probably has a face ugly enough to stop a grizzly bear's heart."

Melissa took a great gulp of her lemon juice. "I'll tell my brother you said so," she purred.

A slow, insolent smile touched Quinn's mouth. "Do that. I'm not afraid of your brothers, Melissa."

She returned his smile. "All that proves is that you're foolish," she replied lightly. "But that's neither here nor there. Is this train going to stop in Seattle, Mr. Rafferty?"

He arched one eyebrow and then rubbed his chin before answering. "Briefly. Why?"

"The money I mentioned is in an account there."

Quinn cleared his throat and sat forward in his chair, looking earnest and impossibly pompous. "Listen, Melissa—I think this whole idea calls for some careful reconsidering on your part. After all, you're only a woman, alone in the world—"

She smiled sweetly as she interrupted him. "But I'm not alone in the world. I have you, Mr. Rafferty."

"Me?" Mr. Rafferty echoed, looking stricken.

Melissa nodded. "Even though you have in effect compromised my good name, I am in your debt. I'm going to Port Riley with you. I'm going to rent a room, land a job, and make something of myself."

Quinn was aghast but finally managed a raspy "You can't do that!"

Melissa deliberately widened her eyes. "Why not?" A horrible possibility struck her in that instant, and she gasped out, "You're not married, are you?"

"God, no," Rafferty breathed. "But there is a woman. . . ."

That admission injured Melissa, although she realized, of course, that Mr. Rafferty's personal life was none of her affair. She bit her lip and willed tears into her eyes; it was a gambit that always worked with Jeff and Keith.

"Gillian would never understand."

Melissa sniffled. "Gillian?" she whispered miserably.

Quinn shot out of his chair so fast that it nearly overturned. "Damn it, stop that! Stop looking like that, stop sounding like that—"

"I can't go home," Melissa reminded him.

Quinn flung his arms out from his sides. "There's always Seattle," he suggested, with a note of wild desperation in his voice.

"I know too many people there."

"I see that as an advantage!"

Melissa stuck out her chin. "Well, it isn't. Word would get back to my family, and I'd be in Port Hastings before I knew it, tatting doilies and warming my feet by the parlor fire!"

Quinn let out a long, ragged sigh and pushed back one side of his coat to shove a hand into his trouser pocket. "Listen to me," he implored. "I'm an innocent bystander here. I was standing out there on that platform, minding my own damned business, when you came running out of the rain." He paused and drew a deep breath. "Melissa, I've tried to be a gentleman about this whole thing. I gave you my bed, I saw that you were taken care of when you fell sick, and I never once took advantage of you as a lot of men would have done. But I draw the line at letting you ruin everything I've worked for."

Melissa squinted at him, her heart beating fast. "How could I possibly do that?" she wanted to know.

"I told you a minute ago that I don't have a wife, and that's true. But I do have a fiancée, Melissa. Gillian and I plan to be married this summer."

The news shattered Melissa, although she couldn't think why it should. "I see. And what does marrying this Gillian woman have to do with whatever it is that you've worked so hard to build up?"

"We have a—business alliance, Gillian and I. Our combined holdings—"

Melissa held up one hand. "Please. Don't go on—I understand quite clearly. You're marrying this woman for her money."

Quinn started to speak and then fell silent, turning away from Melissa and disappearing beyond the partition.

Even though she knew he was only a few feet away, Melissa felt thoroughly abandoned. She snuggled down into the covers, wondering what she was going to do now.

She had a thought. "If you want money," she called out, "you could marry me. I have a lot of it."

Quinn's voice was tight with anger. "Thanks, but no thanks."

Oddly, the pain Ajax's betrayal had caused her seemed slight beside what she was feeling then. "I'm a virgin," she pointed out in spite of herself.

She heard him sigh, once more the soul of long-suffering forbearance. "Hog-tying a husband won't prove a damn thing to your family, Melissa."

Melissa's lower lip trembled. "You're quite right, of course," she called back. Then she closed her eyes and, with immeasurable difficulty, went back to sleep.

When she awakened again she felt much better. She got out of bed and called out, "Quinn?"

There was no answer, so Melissa dashed to the cubicle in the corner of the car, where the facilities were. When she came out a tub had sprouted in the middle of the floor, filled to the brim with steaming hot water.

Melissa looked at it with longing.

"It's all yours," Quinn said with an indulgent chuckle.

Realizing that she was dressed only in her underthings, Melissa gasped and dodged back into the water closet.

There was a rap at the door. "We'll be in Seattle in an

hour," Quinn said after a moment. "If you want a bath, I'd suggest you get on with it. I'll be in the dining car, having breakfast."

Melissa's stomach rumbled. She could only hope that Quinn would find it in his heart to bring her something to eat when he came back. She waited until she heard the outer door close and then crept out.

The car was empty, and Melissa quickly stripped and stepped into the bathwater. It felt wonderful, soothing her achy muscles, seeming to warm her very spirit. But she dared not linger.

She was wearing one of her two calico dresses and toweling her ebony hair when Quinn returned to the car. It was interesting, she thought, that he didn't knock, and there was an odd, surprised look in his eyes when he saw her.

"I suppose you're hungry," he said accusingly, after a moment of awkward silence.

Melissa had appropriated Quinn's hairbrush, and she began grooming her wild, flyaway mane. "If I am, it's no concern of yours," she said. "We'll be in Seattle soon. After I've stopped by the bank I'll buy myself something to eat."

"Melissa." He was leaning against the partition, watching as she began weaving her still-wet hair into a heavy plait. It would be a horror when she unbraided it, but there was no helping that.

"What?"

"I'm not marrying for money."

Melissa dared to look at him directly, although where she got the courage she did not know. "It's a love match, then," she said. "You love Gillian, and she loves you."

Quinn cleared his throat and looked away. "Not exactly."

She felt a strange exultation. "You don't love her?"

"I like her a lot."

Melissa wanted to smile but managed not to. "Ummm," she said.

"What the hell is that supposed to mean?" Quinn demanded.

"I hope you and Gillian will be very happy together," she lied, but now she allowed herself a smile. "You like her, she likes you. You'll probably both like your children as well."

Quinn's neck flushed red, and he clamped his jaw shut tight for a moment. Then he opened his mouth to speak, but before he could get a word out the whistle shrilled and the train began to slow. Water splashed over the sides of the tub, the walls and floor shook, and Melissa and Quinn just stood there, staring at each other.

Melissa recovered first. She tied her braid with a bit of ribbon taken from her wedding dress and rolled the costly gown and her spare calico into a bundle of sorts. "Well," she said, with a brave lift of her chin, "I'm off to make a name for myself."

"That's what I'm afraid of," Quinn grumbled. His brown eyes seemed to simmer with agitation. After a moment he looked calmer, if still more grim, and he sighed. His hands were strong on Melissa's shoulders. "You don't need to prove anything to anybody. Go back to your home and your family, little one—it's a big, brutal world out there."

"Do you think I'm a child? I have a university education, Mr. Rafferty, and I was almost someone's wife!"

Again anger flared in his eyes, and he laid one hand to his chest. "I keep forgetting what a paragon of sophistication you really are!"

Just then the train stopped, hurling both Melissa and Quinn backward onto the bed.

Melissa was breathless, but Quinn burst out laughing and rolled onto his side, looking down into her rosy face. As his gaze swept her features, however, his expression turned somber.

"Damn," he muttered, and then he lowered his mouth to Melissa's unwillingly, as though some invisible hand were pressing at the back of his head.

When their lips touched a hot tremor went through her. As the kiss deepened a soft, despairing moan escaped her. Her body ached for the weight of Quinn's with an intensity that was just short of true pain while, at one and the same time, her spirit rebelled.

The moment Quinn lifted his head she slapped him and began squirming and struggling to be free.

He stared at her in bewilderment. "What—?"

"Let me up!" she yelled.

He immediately complied. "My pleasure," he responded, and somehow that made Melissa angrier than she would have been if he'd held her captive on that bed all afternoon.

Her face flushed violently pink. She sat up, smoothed her hair, and grabbed for her bundle. "Thank you very much," she said, storming toward the end of the car, "and good-bye!"

She wrenched open the door and stepped out onto the platform.

The railroad yard was a busy, noisy place. A strange mingling of smells and sounds and sights clamored for Melissa's notice, but she strode staunchly into the Seattle depot, through the lobby, and out the other door onto the street.

She hadn't gone half a block before Quinn fell into step beside her, taking her elbow firmly in one hand. He smiled down at her from beneath the rounded brim of an elegant black hat.

"The least you can do, Miss Corbin, is let me buy your breakfast. After all, I'm the man who saved you from your family's undying pity and then almost single-handedly dragged you back from death's door."

"I don't want anything from you, not even breakfast," Melissa muttered through her teeth, but she smiled at passersby lest they think something was wrong. "Go away and leave me alone before I have you arrested!"

"You wouldn't do that." They'd reached a hotel, and Quinn thrust Melissa through the door and into the lobby. She had to take long strides to keep up with him. His voice dropped to a companionable whisper. "If you did, I'd be forced to explain to the police that your celebrated family is probably searching high and low for their precious darling. In fact, I wouldn't be surprised if they were offering a sizable reward."

Melissa thought back to the time her brother Keith's first wife was killed. He'd disappeared in a fit of grief, and Adam and Jeff had established a reward and gotten posters printed within the space of a few days. She looked imploringly at

Quinn as he escorted her into the dining room and smoothly seated her near a window.

When he joined her at the table he smiled warmly. "I've been thinking," he announced, "about your offer to marry me."

Melissa's cheeks flamed, and she was glad Quinn couldn't know how rapidly her heart was beating. "I wasn't serious," she said. She couldn't help remembering the kiss they'd shared on Quinn's bed, nor could she stop the rush of sensations the memory unleashed. If she were Quinn's wife, she would have a legal and moral right to explore the strange delights his body had promised to hers.

"I think you were," Quinn argued affably.

A waitress came, bringing coffee and taking Melissa's order, and then they were alone again.

"I've changed my mind," Melissa spat, as though there had been no break in the ridiculous conversation. "I'd sooner marry a woolly African ape than you, Quinn Rafferty!"

He had the brazen effrontery to take one of her hands in his. The way he chafed the inside of Melissa's wrist with his callused thumb caused a tender blossoming sensation deep within her. "Marry me," he said in an audacious undertone.

Melissa nearly upset her coffee, so swiftly did she pull her hand free of his grasp. "How fickle you are!" she whispered furiously. "What about Gillian?"

"I told you. That was just business."

"Whereas you harbor a deep and undying affection for me, I suppose," Melissa taunted.

"I sure as hell feel something," Quinn responded blithely. "Might as well find out what it is."

If they hadn't been in a public place, and if people hadn't already started to look, Melissa would have slapped Quinn again. She lowered her eyes to the plate of ham, eggs, and biscuits the waitress brought to her and concentrated as best she could on her meal.

As hungry as she was, Melissa could barely eat, her emotions were in such a tangle. She'd truly loved Ajax, or thought she had, but he'd never made her feel such anger, such tenderness, such frustration.

"I won't marry you," she said firmly when she'd eaten what she could. "I couldn't think of tying myself down to a man who merely liked me."

"Who says I like you?" Quinn countered.

Melissa slammed down her fork and made to stand up, but Quinn stopped her by taking a hard but painless grip on her wrist.

"Finish your breakfast," he ordered.

Although she longed to defy him, Melissa found herself obeying.

Three

The hotel dining room was filled with conversation and the cheery clatter of good china. Melissa gazed at Quinn over the rim of her coffee cup, having made short work of her breakfast.

Quinn wasn't sure why he wanted to argue for marriage, when all his life he'd been firmly opposed to the institution. Even his engagement to Gillian Aires had been entered into with an eye to bailing out again if the waters got too rough, but here he was, ready to do his damnedest to persuade a total stranger to become his wife.

"Look at it this way," he said smoothly. "You won't get a chance to prove anything to anybody if your brothers come to Port Riley and drag you back home."

Those fantastically blue eyes of hers widened, then dodged away. "That's true enough," she admitted in a small voice.

Quinn ventured to reach across the tabletop and take her hand in his. In that instant of their touching, innocent as it was, he knew why he was willing to marry Melissa Corbin.

He wanted her. Desperately.

He spoke huskily when he went on. "If you married me, you would become my—ward, so to speak."

"I would become your wife," Melissa said flatly, pulling her hand from his. "And you would have rights that I don't wish to grant you, Mr. Rafferty."

Quinn knew that having this delectable little chit for a wife and not being able to bed her would be an early consignment to hell, but he was confident of his ability to win her over. No woman had ever found him wanting when it came to the art of lovemaking.

He spread his hands, the personification of nonchalance. "I haven't thrown you down and had my way with you so far, have I?"

A rich blush glowed in her cheeks; she lowered her eyes and bit her lip.

"It should be obvious to you," Quinn proceeded to say when she remained silent, "that I'm a man of honor."

She met his gaze squarely. "I'll grant you that," she said.

"And it's true that I won't be able to accomplish anything at all if my brothers find out where I am—even though they'd be outside the law if they forced me to go back home, no one would think of stopping them. Marriage would be my only real protection. But what do you stand to gain from this union, Mr. Rafferty? Money?"

Quinn sighed. "Not exactly. I'm a wealthy man in my own right. What I need is—collateral."

"Collateral?"

"I'm planning to—er—expand my holdings. Frankly, a connection with your family would give me unlimited borrowing power. I could accomplish my purposes without ever touching a cent of your money."

She was tapping her chin thoughtfully with one finger. "Unless, of course, your ventures were to fail."

Quinn set his jaw. "That is out of the question," he said. It was damned fortunate, in his view, that he wasn't some unscrupulous rounder. Melissa Corbin would be all too easy to dupe.

In the next moment she searched his face in a way that made Quinn wonder if he'd made a mistake in adding her up. Although Melissa was naïve, she was also formidably intelligent. "I will never love anyone but Ajax as long as I live," she announced, "but we both know that I can't have him for a husband. Therefore, it doesn't make much difference whom I marry, does it?"

Quinn was unaccountably wounded by this reasoning. "I wouldn't go so far as to say that," he began, but Melissa immediately cut him off.

"Provided you're willing to agree to a few basic terms, Mr. Rafferty, I see no reason why you and I shouldn't make an—arrangement."

Rafferty's sense of injury had turned to pure, patent irritation. "What terms?" he practically snarled, snatching the check from the waitress's hand when she dared approach the table.

Melissa waited primly until they were alone again. "I will not share your bed until such time as I'm ready to have a child," she said, "and I certainly won't be the conventional wife, waiting by your chair to stuff a pipe in your teeth at night and all that rubbish. I still want to make my own way in the world."

Quinn arched an eyebrow. "If it's not too much to ask," he said dryly, "will you at least live under my roof?"

"Of course I will," she replied. "If I didn't, my brothers would never believe that we were really married."

Quinn swallowed, thinking of how Gillian was going to react to this news. Worse, he'd be the laughingstock of Port Riley if his wife was out trying to make something of herself every damned day of the week. Suppose, for example, she wrote another one of those outlandish books?

"H-How long do you think it will be before you decide you'd like to be a mother?" he dared to inquire.

Melissa shrugged. "Who knows?"

Quinn glared at her as he tossed a bill down on top of the check the waitress had brought and pushed back his chair. Melissa waited, primly ladylike, until he drew hers back. "Thank you, Mr. Rafferty," she said sweetly.

Quinn rolled his eyes.

$\cdot$ $\cdot$ $\cdot$

Evidently Quinn Rafferty was a man of no small influence. Before the train pulled out of Seattle, bound for the peninsula, he'd not only secured a special license, he'd followed through and married Melissa.

The whole thing had happened with dizzying swiftness, and Melissa Corbin Rafferty sat in that fancy train caboose when it was all over, staring down at the shiny golden band on her finger and wondering what had possessed her to sell herself into veritable slavery. Tears of awe and fear brimmed in her eyes when she realized the full scope of what she'd done.

She was alone, blessedly, since Quinn had gone to the club car the second they'd returned. No doubt he was drinking, gambling, and carousing at that very moment.

Melissa paced the car, still wearing her oversized shoes and ugly calico dress, a wail of desperation gathering in her throat. If things had gone as they were supposed to, she would have been safely married to Ajax by now, happily honeymooning.

She dashed away her tears with the back of one hand and sniffled. There was no point in pining away for Ajax, for nothing could ever come of her love for him. The only thing to do now was make the best of the situation.

She would go ahead with her plans, just as though there had been no hasty wedding in a judge's chambers, and make a life for herself. Even being a wife in name only would be better than having the whole family fussing over her for the rest of her days.

Having decided all this, Melissa flung herself down on the chinchilla-covered bed and sobbed with despair.

Quinn sat in the club car, enshrouded in the smoke of cigars and cheroots, and threw back a double shot of rye whiskey. He was married, by God, and he had no rights. No rights at all.

What the hell had gotten into him?

He snapped his fingers, and a fresh glass of whiskey appeared in them almost magically. He was seated beside one of the windows, having no desire to join in the rousing poker game going on a few feet away. He'd lost his limit the night before.

Someone dropped heavily into the seat facing his. "You look like a man with a problem," a familiar voice observed.

Quinn looked up to see Mitch Williams, his lawyer and best friend. Blond and blue-eyed, Mitch was a favorite with the women and a fair hand in a fight. Quinn was so surprised to see him that he nearly choked on his whiskey. "What the devil are you doing here?"

"Got on in Seattle, like you."

Quinn let out a long breath. "So you saw her?"

Mitch grinned and held out one hand, palm down. "Little smidgin of a thing, about this big, with blue eyes the size of saucers?"

Quinn nodded.

"Haven't seen her," Mitch said, and then he laughed at the expression on his friend's face. After several moments had passed he asked patiently, "Who is she?"

Quinn swallowed. "My wife."

"Your *what?!*" Mitch choked out the words.

Gazing miserably at his friend, Quinn answered, "You heard me, damn it. Don't make me say it again."

"You actually married that woman?"

Again Quinn nodded.

"Why?" Mitch snapped, rapid-fire.

"I don't rightly know."

Mitch let out a long, low whistle. "Gillian will have your teeth made into piano keys," he said.

Quinn gave him an acid look and held up his empty shot glass. It was replaced in a moment, and he swallowed the contents in a desolate gulp.

The lawyer was leaning forward in his seat, squinting, his voice low. "What happened, Rafferty? Did you have a few too many and marry a dance hall girl, or what?"

For the first time since he'd known him, which was some twenty years, Quinn wanted to knock Mitch Williams on his ass. "She isn't a dance hall girl," he hissed, too loudly. All over the car heads were turning.

"Have you consummated this marriage?" Mitch demanded in an undertone.

"Don't you think that's kind of a personal question?" Quinn shot back. He could feel his neck heating up and swelling to make his collar too tight.

Mitch shrugged. "It all depends on your answer, my friend," he said coolly. "If you're having regrets, and if you haven't taken any real liberties, the marriage can be annulled."

"Annulled?" Quinn echoed stupidly. For all his second thoughts, that avenue hadn't occurred to him.

Mitch nodded.

Quinn spat out an abrupt "No!"

A smug grin crossed Mitch's face. "This has all the earmarks of a real yarn. What the Sam Hill's going on here?"

Quinn drew in a deep breath and sighed it out again. "It all started in Port Hastings," he began. Mitch's eyes got wider as the story went on, and when it was over he swore in exclamation.

"So you carried the Corbins' baby sister off on a train and married her for her money, did you?" Mitch paused, shook his head in awe, and then chuckled. "You're either bone-stupid or the bravest man I ever knew."

A drunk in the next booth voted for stupid.

Glaring, Quinn leaned forward in his seat and demanded of his friend, "Do you know her brothers?"

"I do for a fact," Mitch confessed. "I grew up in Port Hastings, remember?"

Quinn rubbed his stubbled jaw. He needed a shave, a hot bath, and a good meal.

And Melissa.

Before he could respond to Mitch's remark, however, there was a stir at the back of the club car, followed by a spate of delicate coughing. Quinn whirled, full of dread, and sure enough, there was Melissa in that infernal calico dress of hers, waving away the smoke with one hand.

Quinn cursed roundly while Mitch laughed.

"Oh, Mr. Rafferty!" Melissa called out sweetly, standing on tiptoe to peer over the heads of half a dozen shocked poker players. "Mr. Rafferty!"

Quinn shot out of his seat, muttering, and stormed over to Melissa, maneuvering her along the windy little walkway leading into the next car, where a few diners were lingering over lunch.

She stared up at him with wide eyes. "Did I do something wrong?"

Quinn realized that he'd taken a hard grasp on her arm and relaxed his fingers. Annoyed as he was, the last thing he wanted was to hurt Melissa. Ever. "Women aren't allowed in the club car," he informed her in a tight whisper.

"Oh," she replied lamely. "I forgot." Her whole countenance brightened like a Christmas tree with all the candles lit. The scent of Quinn's brandy indicated that she'd been fortifying her courage during their brief separation. "And there was no harm done, after all, was there?"

Quinn wasn't so sure about that. "Melissa," he began in a low, impatient voice. "What do you want?"

She beamed up at him, and he saw rainbows in her eyes. "I've decided that I'm ready to have that child we talked about," she announced.

Several forks clattered against plates around the dining car, and Quinn would have been willing to bet that more than one wine glass had been overturned. "What?" he asked, feeling and sounding as though she'd just clasped both her hands around his neck and squeezed with all her strength.

When he saw she was about to repeat herself, he hastened to cover her mouth with one hand and pleaded, "Don't!"

The azure eyes looked baffled, but when Quinn lowered his hand Melissa was quiet and obedient.

"Go back and wait for me, Melissa," he said, feeling bold in the face of her docile acquiescence. "We'll be in Port Riley in an hour or two, and then we can talk about this notion of yours—"

"We'll talk about it now," Melissa broke in, and even though she was smiling, she was talking through her small, white teeth. She grasped Quinn's hand and all but dragged him through the dining car.

In the privacy of their quarters Melissa stood beside the

bed, flung her arms out wide, and toppled over backward onto the mattress. "Let's get started," she said cheerfully.

Quinn stared at her in absolute wonder for a few moments, and then he began to laugh. It started as a chuckle and quickly advanced to a roar that stole his wind and made his sides ache.

And still Quinn could not stop laughing.

Melissa was stunned, filled with shame. She'd offered herself to her husband, and he was laughing at her.

She raised herself up on her elbows, too proud to cry, though she was sure she'd burst if she didn't find a way to give vent to all the confusing emotions clamoring inside her.

Quinn finally recovered himself, collapsing into the chair where he'd sat reading to her only the night before. "I'm—sorry," he gasped out, rubbing his eyes with a thumb and forefinger.

Melissa knew full well that he was not sorry, that he'd had a good laugh at her expense, and she sighed. "Don't you want me?" she asked.

Quinn's expression was instantly and completely serious. "Very much," he said gruffly.

"Well?"

He brought one booted foot to rest on his knee, took a cheroot and a match from the pocket of his jacket, and commenced to smoke. After an excruciatingly long time had passed he said in a pensive tone, "You're simply not ready."

"Don't you think I should be the judge of that?"

"Not after the way you fell spread-eagle on that bed, I don't."

Melissa was mortified. It wasn't as if she didn't understand what went on between a man and a woman, because she did. And she'd certainly sensed the strange electricity that arced between her brothers and their wives.

Quinn reached out and collected Melissa's novel from a nearby table. "Tell me," he began wryly. "Do you write from experience?"

Melissa wanted to slap him. "I told you that I am a virgin," she hissed.

"I didn't believe you," he immediately answered. "Not until a few minutes ago, anyway."

Embarrassed anew, Melissa sat up very straight and smoothed her skirts. She could not have spoken for anything.

"What made you decide to give yourself to me, Melissa?" Quinn asked gently, after a long time.

She sniffled, unable to look at him. "I was remembering when we—when we kissed this morning. I developed all these strange feelings."

Quinn chuckled. "Then there is hope," he said, so quietly that Melissa almost missed the words. Then, more loudly, he added, "Why don't you lie down and rest until we arrive? You're still not completely well, you know."

Melissa looked at him imploringly. "Will you lie down with me?"

He was silent for a moment, and very, very still. But then, without a word, he came to the bed, and he and Melissa stretched out on it together.

His body was long and hard, but his muscular shoulder pillowed Melissa's head comfortably. She snuggled against him and wondered at the low groan this elicited. It came from the depths of his chest, like some subterranean rumble.

"Melissa," he muttered, and the word rang with despair and hope and reprimand.

Melissa had hoped to be ravished; instead she awakened, sometime later, feeling rested and strong. Quinn had long since left the bed, apparently, for he was standing in front of the bureau mirror, wearing clean clothes and freshly shaven.

He turned and grinned at Melissa as the train whistle shrilled. "Well, Mrs. Rafferty," he said when the ear-piercing sound had died away, "we're home."

Melissa felt a strange mingling of panic and brash eagerness. "So to speak," she said primly. Now that she'd napped and gathered her forces she was glad that her husband hadn't taken her up on her brazen offer.

She sat up and began wriggling back into her shoes, and when she'd finished lacing the first one she raised her eyes to Quinn's face. He was watching her with a frown.

"The first thing you'll have to do is get yourself some decent clothes," he said.

Melissa was taken aback. "I will," she answered patiently, "as soon as I've gotten myself a job or started some sort of business."

Quinn turned and grasped the brass bed railing in his hands for balance as the train began its long, shuddering stop. The whistle was blowing again, punctuating his words. "No wife—of mine—will be seen—dressed like that!"

"May I remind you of our agreement?" Melissa shouted, trying to be heard over the whistle. "I'm going to take care of myself!"

The train came to a final and jarring halt, and Melissa and Quinn were still glaring at each other, speechless with vexation, when the door of the car opened and a sunny female voice sang out, "Quinn, darling, I've missed you terribly!"

The woman was tall and blond, and she swept into the car, her violet eyes dancing with mischief and merriment. She was older than Melissa, and clearly more sophisticated, and the two women disliked each other within the instant.

Melissa had already deduced that this was Gillian; she enjoyed the advantage that knowledge gave her, however briefly.

"Who is this?" Gillian trilled, giving her closed parasol a pretty little spin with her fingers. It was pink and ruffled, to match her pink and ruffled gown. To Melissa's mind, all the woman needed was a lamb and a hoop and she'd look exactly like Little Bo-Peep.

Quinn cleared his throat, looking patently miserable. "This is—"

Melissa bounded off the bed, hand extended. "I'm Quinn's wife, Melissa," she said happily. "So glad to make your acquaintance."

The parasol fell to the carpeted floor of the railroad car with a discreet little thump. "Wife?" Gillian echoed.

"I can explain," Quinn said quickly.

Melissa's high spirits were fading. It was obvious that Bo-Peep's opinion was important to Quinn, and that was not a good sign. If he thought he was going to keep a mistress while she was his wife, he was sadly mistaken.

"No, he can't," she argued. "He can't explain. There isn't a single thing he could say—"

"Shut up," Quinn warned.

Gillian turned in a swirl of pink skirts and swept toward the back of the car. "I don't have to stand here and endure *this!*" she cried with pathos.

"Gillian!" Quinn yelled.

"My, but she hates you now," Melissa said sweetly, her hands folded in her lap.

Quinn gave her a look that would have set a less sturdy soul to quaking and then hauled her roughly to her feet. "Go home and stay there!" he shouted.

"I can't," Melissa responded with equal spirit. "I don't know where we live!"

For a moment Quinn looked as though he might do her bodily harm. His nostrils flared, and his eyes narrowed, and his breathing was quick and shallow. In the end, however, he only marched Melissa to the door and outside.

The weather was springlike and sunny, though recent rains had turned the ground to mud. Port Riley was a busy, bustling place, and from the depot platform Melissa could see the dancing blue waters of the Strait of Juan de Fuca.

There were stores and neat white houses set close together, and in the far distance, on a rocky point, the white column of a lighthouse towered against the blue sky.

Melissa drew in a deep breath, enjoying the frankly curious stares she and Quinn were getting from passersby. It seemed that Gillian's dramatic exit had not been wasted.

A mud-splattered carriage drawn by two mud-splattered horses was waiting at the end of the platform. Quinn opened the door before the driver could do so and fairly flung Melissa inside.

He remained in the street himself, his hands on his hips, and spoke brusquely to the driver. "See my wife safely home."

Aware that she was about to be abandoned, probably so that Quinn could make amends to the disgruntled Gillian,

Melissa struggled with the handle of the carriage door. The vehicle was well underway when she finally got it open. She never made the decision to leap, for the choice was taken out of her hands. While she was gauging her chances of making a safe landing one foot slipped, and she went tumbling unceremoniously into the mud.

Nervous laughter greeted her from the sidewalk, but Melissa was unconcerned. Two booted feet were striding toward her through the muck as she raised herself. When Quinn reached her and grasped her by her shoulders, Melissa twisted to be free.

Quinn cursed and then lifted her into his arms. His neck and the lower part of his jaw turned crimson as he strode back to the carriage and put Melissa inside, much to the amusement of the townspeople, which was plain to hear. This time he joined her.

"I ought to blister you!" he raved in a ferocious undertone when they'd settled on opposite sides of the carriage.

Melissa was inspecting her filthy calico dress. "I wouldn't advise that," she said calmly.

Quinn folded his arms across his chest. "Well?" he prompted.

"Well, what?"

"You got your way—I didn't send you home alone. Just what exactly did you hope to accomplish by embarrassing me in front of half the town?"

Melissa sat as straight and regal as a princess on her way to a ball. "We made certain agreements when we decided to marry, Mr. Rafferty. Your panting after Gillian was not part of the bargain."

He looked truly insulted. "Panting? I was merely trying to—"

"You will not keep a mistress, Mr. Rafferty," Melissa went on as though he hadn't spoken. "Not as long as you are married to me."

"Fine. Then we'll dispense with the separate bedrooms, and you'll settle yourself in mine—Mrs. Rafferty."

Melissa shook her head. "I'm sorry, that isn't possible," she said stiffly.

Quinn stared at her. "What happened to my eager bride?" he asked. "Are you or are you not the same woman who hurled herself backward onto my bed and demanded that I get on with it?"

Melissa's aplomb was crumbling. The scene they'd made in front of the Port Riley depot had been bad enough. "Keep your voice down!" she ordered in an angry whisper.

"I will not keep my voice down!" Quinn bellowed. "And I'll thank you to stop telling me what to do and how to do it, woman!"

In that moment Melissa came undone. Perhaps it was the strain of the past few days; perhaps it was the realization that she'd been incredibly rash. Whatever prompted her, she flung herself at Quinn Rafferty like a hissing, clawing cat.

He wrestled her into submission with a strange mingling of strength and gentleness, and she found herself lying face up across his lap, her wrists caught in his hands, her sodden, muddy skirts gathered around her thighs.

Quinn glared at her for a moment, and she thought the amber fire in his eyes would consume her, but in the end it was his mouth that did that. It fell to hers, fiercely tender, threatening to draw the very soul from her.

She struggled, but then one of his hands closed over her breast, and the kiss deepened. Melissa had lost all desire for battle; she was a willing captive.

Four

Quinn's house was large and white, with an English air about it. There was a bay window on the first floor, and dormers lined the second. At one end of the structure was a turret, similar in shape to ones Melissa had seen on castles in Europe.

Under other circumstances Melissa would have been charmed. As it was, she imagined she'd end up imprisoned in that tower like some fairy-tale princess. The fiery kiss they'd exchanged in the carriage had done nothing to change Quinn's mood—he was coldly, recalcitrantly furious.

Melissa felt strange and disgruntled and achy. She wished that things could be different between herself and her husband, but she had no idea how to bring about such a change. When she'd tried to seduce him aboard the train he'd laughed at her. When he'd wanted to chase after his mistress, and Melissa had exhibited normal jealousy, he'd gotten angry.

Melissa didn't have the first clue how to please Quinn. For that matter, she wasn't certain that he deserved to be pleased. She held her chin at a regal angle while he helped her down from the carriage and led her up the walk by one hand.

The late afternoon sun was blazing, making a spectacle of itself in the western sky. Melissa philosophized to herself that it was always brightest just before dark.

Quinn's front door was so beautiful as to be a work of art in itself. It was made of some rich, dark wood, intricately carved, and the huge oval window in its center was a design in multicolored stained glass. Melissa peered at it in interest, but before she could ask a single question Quinn turned the knob, opened the door, and fairly hurled her through it.

A tiny, white-haired woman wearing a housekeeper's somber sateen garb was waiting in the entryway, hands clasped together in front of her, lips pursed, dark eyes wide.

"Mrs. Wright," Quinn began somberly, his hand gripping Melissa's elbow now, "this is my wife."

Mrs. Wright took in the state of Melissa's hair and attire with barely hidden horror, but she executed a half curtsy all the same and said, "Welcome, Mrs. Rafferty."

Melissa nodded in response. "Mrs. Wright," she said.

Without allowing her so much as a glance at any of the rooms on the first floor, Quinn dragged his bride toward the graciously curving stairs. They had reached the landing when Melissa looked back and saw the muddy tracks they'd left on the carpeting and the expression of despair on Mrs. Wright's small, wrinkled face.

First Gillian, now the housekeeper. She wasn't exactly widening her circle of friends.

Quinn pulled Melissa down the hallway to a room sealed with towering double doors, which he flung open. The room was large enough to accommodate a massive bed of carved teak, two armoires, and a desk. At the far end was a fireplace with two barrel-back chairs and a long settee facing it, and beside the window stood a liquor cabinet. On the opposite side of the chamber was a door that she supposed must lead to a private bath.

Melissa grasped the implications only too well. "This is your room," she said, folding her arms across her chest.

Quinn had gone directly to the liquor cabinet. He poured

himself a drink and took a restorative sip before he bothered to comment. "That it is, Mrs. Rafferty," he said, lifting a crystal snifter in wry salute.

"We agreed—"

"I know what we agreed," Quinn broke in. He paused long enough to take another gulp from his brandy. "But when we struck that particular bargain, Mrs. Rafferty, you hadn't taken a stand against my having a mistress."

Melissa suppressed an urge to stomp one foot in outrage. Control. She must learn to control her emotions. "You might have guessed how I felt—I told you why I left Ajax."

Quinn spread his hands. "This is not a love match, Melissa—we both know that." Behind him, through one of the room's three large windows, Melissa saw the red-gold glow of the sun on the bare and gaunt limbs of the trees that stood in his front yard. "Why do you care what I do?"

Melissa's lower lip trembled. She was tired and hungry, and she didn't feel well, and now she was expected to carry on this irritating conversation. "I won't be shamed, Quinn Rafferty," she answered in a near-whisper that was nonetheless sharp with warning. "I won't have people snickering and saying that I can't hold my husband."

He smiled and availed himself of more of the brandy. "Ah, so it's pride that motivates you. I should have known." He paused and gestured toward the bed, which was the biggest Melissa had ever seen, graced, unless she was mistaken, by a coverlet of mink. "The choice is yours, my love."

Melissa knew that he was offering fidelity in exchange for the rights she'd vowed to deny him, and she blushed hotly. "You know what we agreed!"

"You were willing enough this afternoon," Quinn reminded her lightly.

Melissa's imagination, ever active, was supplying her with ideas of what it might be like to lie naked on that fur coverlet and allow Quinn free access to her body, and a wave of heat washed through her, leaving her weak. She no longer felt bold enough to follow through, however. She needed time, and a much surer knowledge of Mr. Rafferty's character. "I've changed my mind since then," she said lamely.

"That's a pity," Quinn replied, and his hot, brazen brown eyes moved over her. After an inspection that was sweet agony for Melissa he seemed to lose interest, turning away to set his empty snifter down on a small table beside the settee. "I have things to do, Mrs. Rafferty. Feel free to use the bathtub."

With that—he didn't even look at her again—Quinn left the room, closing the doors neatly behind him.

Melissa was confused and furious, but she was also exhausted. Assuming that, since Quinn had abandoned her here, he was conceding the master chamber for her private use, she decided to take him up on his generous offer concerning the bathtub.

Just to be on the safe side, however, she rummaged through the desk until she found a key, and then she locked the outer doors.

The bathtub, made of the finest black marble and practically big enough to swim in, impressed even Melissa, who was something of an enthusiast when it came to such sweet luxuries.

She spent nearly an hour in the tub and came out feeling languid and sleepy. She was wrapped in a towel, her hair hanging down in squeaky-clean tendrils, when a crisp knock sounded at one of the doors.

"Who—who is it?" Melissa called out, trembling a little. It was chilly in the room.

"It's Mrs. Wright," the housekeeper replied brightly. "I've brought your dinner."

It had been hours since Melissa had eaten, and she was hungry. After only a moment's hesitation she turned the key in the lock and then dashed back into the bathroom to hide her state of undress.

She heard a serving cart rattling cheerfully in the suite, and her stomach rumbled in anticipation.

"Are you all right, Mrs. Rafferty?" the housekeeper called out. She sounded sincere in her concern.

"I'm fine," Melissa replied, feeling silly. "It's just that I haven't a wrapper."

Moments later Mrs. Wright handed a ruffled robe of pink

taffeta around the door of the bathroom. "There you are, dear," she said.

When Melissa ventured out, clad in the beautiful robe, Mrs. Wright had finished setting out her dinner on a table near the window and had gone to light a fire on the hearth.

"Thank you for lending me your robe," Melissa said, trying to walk at a moderate pace as she approached her supper. In truth, it was all she could do not to hurl herself on top of it.

Mrs. Wright chuckled happily. "You're most welcome, ma'am, but that isn't my wrapper."

Melissa sank into a chair and delved hungrily into the roast beef dinner that had been brought for her. "Mrs. Wright, I've had a long, hard day. Please don't tell me that my husband likes to wear pink taffeta and ruffles of an evening."

The old woman chortled again. "No, ma'am, he doesn't. He's not that sort."

Melissa decided to drop the subject. While the other possibilities weren't as alarming as the one she'd raised, they weren't comforting to think about. An image of Gillian wearing that very robe did arise in her mind, but she chased it away immediately. "This is a wonderful dinner."

Mrs. Wright nodded cordially in Melissa's direction. A fire was popping on the hearth, casting warmth and a cozy copper glow into the room. "Thank you," she said, and then, after inquiring whether there was anything else Mrs. Rafferty needed, she slipped out.

Melissa felt incomprehensibly lonely. She wondered where Quinn was, and what he was doing, and then decided that she was better off not knowing.

When she'd finished her meal she went to sit before the fire for a while. By then her thoughts had turned to her family in Port Hastings and the ordeal of worry they were probably enduring. She would send them a wire first thing in the morning and let them know that she was safe and sound—and married.

She turned her thoughts to Ajax and was jarred to realize that she could barely remember what he looked like.

His features, so distinct in her mind only a few days before, were now only a haze. She was still pondering this phenomenon when a maid came in, gathered up Melissa's dirty dishes, and wheeled them out again on a serving cart.

Snapped out of her reverie, Melissa hurried over and locked the doors again. Then, with a yawn, she went into the bathroom to clean her teeth and brush her hair.

Minutes later she crawled between Quinn's silken sheets and tumbled, end over end, into a sleep as deep as a desert well.

When she awakened the next morning she was both relieved and disappointed to find herself in bed alone. She scrambled across the impossibly soft coverlet and padded into the bathroom.

Although she'd gone to bed with wet hair, Melissa was unprepared for the sight that greeted her in the bathroom mirror. She looked like someone she'd once seen in a sideshow—the wild woman of Borneo.

She gave a startled little cry, grabbed for Quinn's brush, which she'd appropriated the night before, and began trying to subdue her person into some presentable state. She'd succeeded, to a minor degree, by the time she crept back out of the bathroom again, wondering if Mrs. Wright had, perchance, brought up her spare calico dress. Her thoughts thus occupied, she was completely surprised when she realized that Quinn was seated by the fireplace, drinking what appeared to be a cup of coffee.

He greeted his wife cordially, with a smile, a lift of his cup, and a low "Mrs. Rafferty."

Melissa glanced wildly toward the doors, which she'd so carefully locked the night before. "How did you get in here?" she ventured to ask.

"I used the spare key," he replied with an offhand shrug. "It seemed simpler, if less dashing, than breaking down the door."

Melissa hugged herself, trying to remember if she'd been ravished or not. Surely an experience like that couldn't pass unnoticed, no matter how tired a person might be. . . .

Quinn laughed abruptly, as though reading her mind. He

needed a shave, Melissa deduced on closer examination; his clothes were rumpled, and his eyes had a glazed look that indicated sleeplessness. "That wrapper becomes you," he said hoarsely.

They were mundane words, but for some reason they affected Melissa like a spate of the most romantic poetry. They weakened her, warmed her, made her tremble.

She pulled the robe more closely around herself and took a step backward in unconscious retreat. "I was relieved to learn that it's not for your use," she said, in an attempt to hold up her end of the conversation.

Quinn chuckled. "Did you sleep well?"

Melissa took refuge in the distance formality would afford her. "Like a rock, Mr. Rafferty," she replied.

Quinn thrust splayed fingers through his glossy brown hair and shook his head at some private wonder. When his weary eyes came back to Melissa's face they betrayed a strange tenderness. "I'm glad someone did," he said. "What are you going to do today?"

"Find my dress and shoes, first of all," Melissa answered practically, going about the search in nervous haste. "One can't very well seek a position in this wrapper."

"That would depend," Quinn retorted evenly, "on what kind of position one wanted to be in."

Melissa kept her back to him, anxious to hide the crimson throbbing in her cheeks. She opened the door and peered out into the hallway.

Sure enough, her shoes were there, freshly polished, and the dress she'd worn the day before was draped over a chair. Melissa snatched up her things and ducked back inside, meaning to make a dash for the bathroom. Instead she collided hard with Quinn, who steadied her by grasping her upper arms in his hands.

"Melissa—"

She reflected on where Quinn had probably spent the night and why he looked as though he hadn't slept in a week, and it was all she could do to refrain from kicking him in the shins. "Let me go," she said coldly.

He made no move to release her. "Not until you listen to

me. Melissa, this is all wrong—we can't spend our lives like this. It just won't work."

Suddenly an unexpected terror gripped her, holding her much more tightly than Quinn did. He was about to send her away. He'd probably already had the marriage annulled on the grounds that he had never been intimate with his wife.

Her eyes widened, and she swallowed, staring at him in stricken silence.

His eyes narrowed in puzzlement. "Good Lord, what is it? What's the matter?"

Melissa's lower lip wobbled. "I don't want to go, Quinn. Please don't send me away."

He pulled her close and held her, and his lips moved at her temple. "I won't," he promised gruffly. "I couldn't."

She drew back. "Then what—?"

He cupped his hands on either side of her face and kissed her, very lightly and very briefly, on the mouth. "Melissa," he began, "I spent last night in hell. Give me a chance to be a normal husband to you—please."

So that was what he wanted. Melissa stepped back, wounded to the quick but hiding the true state of her feelings as well as any actress could have done. "While you were in hell, Mr. Rafferty, did you say hello to Gillian?"

For a moment Quinn looked as though she'd slapped him. Then he cursed furiously and turned away from her, again running the fingers of his right hand through his hair.

"I haven't seen Gillian since yesterday afternoon," he said when at last he faced Melissa again. "After the gracious way you informed her of our marriage, I'll probably never see her again."

"Isn't that a pity?" Melissa crooned, hugging her shoes and her calico dress to her bosom.

Quinn gave her a scalding look and then stormed over to one of the armoires and wrenched out clean trousers, a linen shirt, and a jacket. "I don't have to put up with this!" he bellowed. "This is my house, damn it, and you're my wife!"

Melissa would have dodged into the bathroom, but he got to it before she did. She dressed hastily, braided her hair, and wound it atop her head in a coronet, then hurried out.

She didn't have the strength for another nonsensical argument with Quinn.

On the stairs she encountered a maid carrying a tray of food. A folded newspaper lay beside a covered plate, and Melissa appropriated it without a word of explanation.

Downstairs she slipped into a large room filled with books and brass and the scent of pipe smoke, curled up in a chair, and opened the newspaper eagerly.

A drawing of her own face stared at her from the front page of the *Seattle Times*. Beneath it was a lurid headline . . .

HEIRESS FLEES WEDDING, LEAVES HEARTBROKEN GROOM BEHIND

Melissa gave a cry of annoyance and read on. According to the reporter who had written the story, the Corbin family was desperate to find their "little lost lamb" and willing to pay a reward for her safe return. Jeff was quoted as saying that he and his brothers would leave no stone unturned until they found their sister. Of course, Ajax had had to put his two cents in, too. He attributed his bride's defection to nerves and feminine instability in general.

Still simmering, Melissa wadded the newspaper into a huge ball and hurled it across the room. They'd made her sound like an utter idiot, the family had, and in front of half the state, too.

She thrust herself out of her chair and began to pace. She had to send a wire to Port Hastings immediately, and that would take money. She'd left the small sum she'd withdrawn from the bank in Seattle aboard Quinn's railroad car, hidden away under the mattress.

Resolutely, Melissa snatched up her shawl, walked out of the house, and started off in the direction of the railroad depot. When she reached it she found that the train had gone, but Quinn's car had been shunted off onto a side rail. Melissa strode over to it, climbed up on the platform, and tried the door.

It was soundly locked.

"Damn," she whispered, lowering her head for a moment.

"Is there a problem, Mrs. Rafferty?" The unfamiliar masculine voice made Melissa draw in a deep breath and gather her dignity about her. She looked down and saw a tall, handsome man standing nearby. He had fair hair, like Ajax's, and his eyes were a dancing, merry blue.

"How do you know my name?"

"Everyone does," the man answered with a sideways grin. "You're famous now, ma'am." In that moment he remembered his manners and moved toward Melissa with one hand extended in greeting. "Forgive me—my name is Mitchell Williams, and I'm your husband's friend as well as his attorney."

Melissa thought the name sounded vaguely familiar, but she didn't linger on the fact. She had other things on her mind. "I've got sixty-four dollars and seventy-two cents hidden in this railroad car, and I can't get in to fetch it," she complained after shaking Mr. Williams's hand.

If the lawyer wondered at this odd turn of events, he gave no indication of it. "That's easy," he said, taking his wallet from the inside pocket of his suit coat. "I'll advance you the money now, and you can repay me later."

Melissa hesitated—she certainly wasn't in the habit of taking money from strange men. On the other hand, this situation called for extraordinary measures. "Well . . ."

Mr. Williams had already counted out sixty-five dollars, and he was extending the money to Melissa. With great reluctance she accepted it.

"Thank you," she said, averting her eyes. Then, after a moment, she made her way down the platform steps to the ground, assisted by the very gentlemanly Mr. Williams.

He touched the brim of his hat. "No trouble, Mrs. Rafferty," he said, with just the hint of a smile touching his lips. "Out to do some shopping, are you?"

Melissa drew a deep breath and let it out again. "Actually, I was going to send a wire to my family. Is there a Western Union office in town?"

Mr. Williams held out his arm. "Right down the street," he said smoothly. "Please allow me to escort you."

Melissa reflected that Quinn could learn a few things from his friend about manners and the proper way to acquit oneself with a lady. She took the offered arm and smiled. "I'm looking for work, too," she announced.

The lawyer looked surprised, but only for a moment. "Work?" he echoed.

Melissa leaned a little closer to confide, "Mr. Rafferty and I have an agreement, you see."

His blue eyes twinkled. "Do you, now? I don't mind telling you, I can't see Quinn sending his wife out to hold down a job."

"Oh, he's firmly opposed," Melissa replied. "But we made a bargain, and he has to honor it."

Mr. Williams cleared his throat and looked away for a moment. They had reached the Western Union office, but he hesitated outside, forcing Melissa to linger, too.

"The cannery's down that way," he said, gesturing toward the shore. "They're usually looking for help."

"Thank you," Melissa said warmly, letting go of his arm. "For everything."

There was a gentle expression in his eyes when he looked at Melissa again. "Go home to your brothers, little one," he said softly. "You don't have the first idea what you're letting yourself in for."

Melissa gaped at him for a moment, then demanded, "What do you mean? What am I letting myself in for?"

Williams only shook his head, touched Melissa's cheek briefly with one hand, and walked away.

Melissa went into the telegraph office, took up a pad and pencil, and began composing her message to her family. It proved to be a far more difficult task than she'd expected. The things she'd planned to say sounded silly or too verbose.

In the end she wrote:

> NO NEED TO WORRY ABOUT ME. I'M NO LONGER
> A SPINSTER. I'M DISCOVERING LIFE. LOVE, MRS.
> QUINN RAFFERTY (MELISSA).

She directed the wire to Keith, considering him the most charitable of her brothers, paid for the service, and left the office.

The walk to the cannery was longer than Melissa had expected, and it led past several of the seventeen saloons Quinn had bragged about, as well as a suspiciously ornate rooming house or two.

Melissa was relieved when she finally reached the noisy factory on the waterfront. After asking directions of a man who stared at her and repeatedly cleared his sinuses, she picked her way through discarded oyster shells and cigar butts to a little office building that stood separate from the cannery itself.

Her knock brought a brusque summons, and she opened the door and went in.

A small man with a rim of bright red hair ringing his balding pate sat behind a desk, half-buried in papers and all but hidden by a fog of cigar smoke. He smelled of rancid sweat, and Melissa was instantly repelled.

"Yes, yes, what is it?" the little man sputtered as Melissa hovered in the doorway, ready to flee.

"I'm looking for a job," she said politely.

"What do you do?" was the impatient retort.

"A great deal, or nothing at all," Melissa replied bluntly. "It all depends on your point of view."

The fellow behind the desk looked her over and made a harumph sound. "Ever shuck oysters?" he asked, and it was clear from the way he put the question that he expected her to say no.

"Yes," lied Melissa. "Many times."

"Let me see your hands."

Melissa stepped gingerly into the messy, close little room and held out both her hands.

"You've never done any real work with those mitts, lady." There was a small sign, nearly buried in the litter that covered his desk, that indicated his name was John Roberts.

Melissa bit her lower lip and kept her peace. She had no idea what to say now that she'd been caught out as a liar.

Mr. Roberts gave a sort of snuffling chuckle, a sound filled with amusement, indulgence, and no small measure of contempt. He slapped the newspaper that lay in the middle of his desk with one palm. "You're the pretty little piece those Corbin people over Port Hastings way are advertising for, aren't you, miss? I could get a nickel or two for telling them where you are."

Melissa squared her shoulders. "They know where I am, Mr. Roberts. I sent them a wire."

He looked disappointed. "Oh." Like quicksilver, the flow of the conversation changed. "Shucking oysters is miserable work, young lady. They got hard, hoary shells, sharp as razors. I've seen grown men that couldn't handle the job."

"All I'm asking for," Melissa said bravely, "is a chance."

Mr. Roberts thrust himself backwards in his chair, regarding Melissa in a way that made her most uncomfortable. "Don't say old John wasn't kind to you, missy. Don't you ever say that."

Melissa suppressed a shudder. "Does that mean I'm hired?"

Roberts scrawled something on a piece of paper and shoved it at her. "See this fella. He'll give you a knife and bucket."

So began Melissa's first day of employment.

**~~~~** Five

Never in her wildest imaginings had Melissa suspected that physical work could be so grindingly hard.

She sat where she was told to sit, beside a bin full of oysters in a noisy, ill-lit room, crowded between two other women. She was given a bucket of water and a tool, and soon she was busily prying at rock-hard shells.

After an hour her right hand ached so badly that she had to work with her left. She was awkward and slow, and often the knife slipped, gouging her. Saltwater from the bins got into the cuts on her hands and set them afire.

"You'd better hurry it up," commented the woman on her right, along about noon, "or they'll show you the road."

Melissa looked longingly at her coworker's leather gloves, wishing that she'd known enough to purchase a pair. She tried to pick up her pace and promptly punctured herself again.

A deafening whistle shrilled, and all labor suddenly stopped. The worker on Melissa's left, an Indian woman of indeterminate age, smiled at her, revealing several missing teeth. "Dinner time," she said.

Her friendliness encouraged Melissa a little. She returned the smile. "How long do we have?"

"If I were you," announced the other woman, with the gloves, "I wouldn't be worryin' about no dinner hour. You'll be lucky if you still got a job once old Rimley sees that you can't handle the work."

"Leave the girl alone, Flo," interceded the Indian. "You weren't doing so much better on your first day— remember?"

Flo, a plain woman with blond hair and a strong jaw, rose, pulling at her gloves as she moved. She made a harumphing sound, fetched her dinner pail from beneath the long bench where the shuckers sat, and walked away.

"I'm Rowina Brown," said the woman who remained, holding out a friendly hand. Like Flo, she wore gloves.

"Happy to meet you," Melissa said, and inwardly she was laughing at herself. She'd sounded like a guest at a tea party in somebody's rose garden. "My name is Melissa." She flinched at Rowina's grip on her sore hand.

Gentle curiosity flickered in Rowina's dark eyes, but she didn't ask any questions. She retrieved her own pail, still bearing the label of a lard company, from under the bench and stood up. "Come along then, Melissa. I'll be happy to share what I have with you."

Melissa felt shame at having to accept a part of this poor woman's meal, but she was desperately hungry, since she hadn't bothered with breakfast or thought to bring along a sandwich or a piece of fruit. She put aside her pride and nodded. "Thank you," she said quietly.

Rowina led the way out of the shucking shed and down the beach. It was mild for a March day, and the two women sat down on a gnarled, whitened log to enjoy the weather and a meal of cold meat and plain barley bread.

"That's rabbit," Rowina said pleasantly, with a nod toward the meat Melissa was holding in one hand. "My boy Charlie shot it just yesterday."

Melissa thought of Hershel, the rabbit her sister-in-law Fancy had once used in her magic act, and gulped. The creature had escaped into the woods behind the family home in

Port Hastings a few years before; perhaps this was one of his descendants.

"Is something wrong?" Rowina inquired.

In that moment Melissa decided that Hershel's progeny would have to fend for themselves. "Oh, no, of course not," she answered quickly, taking a firm bite. The rest of their short respite from work was tinged with homesickness, though, because Melissa kept thinking of her family. She adored them all, even though a few members—three, to be exact—could be completely impossible on occasion.

"You can get good gloves at Kruger's Mercantile for seventy-five cents," Rowina said as they began their afternoon's work.

Melissa made a mental note to stop at Kruger's directly after she left the cannery, provided she had the strength for such an errand. She was praying for the sound of the whistle long before it blew.

Port Hastings

Katherine Corbin, a blond woman with indigo-blue eyes and a trim figure, surveyed the sullen crew gathered in her study for a meeting.

Adam, her eldest, was as big a man as his father had been, broad in the shoulders and possessed of a lethal intelligence. His hair was dark, as Daniel's had been, but he had Katherine's blue eyes. At the moment he was pacing in front of the bay window overlooking the rose garden. His wife, Banner, a doctor just as he was, and a red-haired, green-eyed beauty who had long since won Katherine's admiration, watched him serenely from a chair near the fireplace.

Jeff, Katherine's second son, was as tall and blue-eyed as Adam, but he had his mother's fair hair. He was bent over a map he'd rolled out on a nearby table, studying it and occasionally shoving one hand through his hair. His annoyance and frustration were evident in every line of his body. His wife, Fancy, was at home on that chilly spring night, recovering from the recent birth of their fourth child.

55

Katherine was secretly worried about Jeff and Fancy; although they tried to put an encouraging face on matters, there was a certain strain between them. Something was very wrong.

Catching herself up short, Katherine redirected her attention to the matter at hand: Melissa's disappearance. Although she was, of course, very concerned about her youngest child, she was not nearly as upset as her sons were. Melissa was twenty-two years old, after all, and she'd been to college and traveled in Europe as well as the United States. Although Katherine knew that her daughter could be impulsive—her flight from the church on Saturday had been evidence enough of that—she was also convinced of Melissa's native good sense.

The door of the study opened, and Keith came in. Katherine gave her youngest son a fond look. Here was her handsome diplomat, her soft-spoken peacemaker. She'd ceased making comments like that aloud long ago, for Adam and Jeff had invariably looked at her askance and remarked that their little brother had a hell of a right hook for a parson.

At his entrance there was a brief silence and then an eruption of energy.

Adam stopped his pacing, and Jeff let the map roll shut, forgotten. Banner sat up a little straighter in her chair and exchanged a beleaguered look with Katherine.

Keith had called this meeting, and he was taking his sweet time in explaining why. He took off his plain black hat, revealing a head of glossy light brown hair, and then removed his coat and gloves. All the while a smile lurked on his lips.

"Melissa's fine," he finally announced. "Just like I said she would be." He took a folded piece of yellow paper from his coat. "When I got home this wire was waiting for me."

Keith carried the missive across the room and laid it on the surface of Katherine's desk. She opened it immediately and read aloud, "'No need to worry about me. I'm no longer a spinster. I'm discovering life. Love, Mrs. Quinn Rafferty (Melissa).'"

"Mrs.—?" Adam bit out, glaring at Banner as though

all of this were somehow his wife's fault. "Who the hell is Quinn Rafferty?"

"I'll tell you who he is," Jeff boomed out, fairly shaking the light fixtures with the force of his fury. "He lives in Port Riley and runs a piss-ant sawmill!"

Both Katherine and Banner flinched slightly.

"And he married my sister!" Jeff raved on. "The bastard— I'll break his knees! I'll use his eyeballs for marbles!"

"Shut up," Keith said gently. His eyes met with his mother's for a moment, twinkling. He was enjoying this.

Personally, Katherine thought that this Rafferty fellow couldn't be any worse than Ajax, but she kept her opinion to herself.

Banner got out of her chair. "I think I'll go over and look in on Fancy," she said, by way of excusing herself. She gave Jeff a tentative, questioning look as she passed him but went out without another word.

Adam had snatched up the wire the moment his mother laid it down, scanning it as though he thought she'd made some mistake in reading it the first time. "What else do you know about this Rafferty?" he asked Jeff.

"I know he'll soon be walking with his feet pointing in the same direction as his ass" was Jeff's immediate response.

Keith grinned at that image and gave his mother a reassuring wink. He perched comfortably on the edge of her desk and folded his hands. "Now, if everybody has expressed his shock and concern, maybe we can talk about what we're going to do."

Katherine wondered what any of them *could* do, if Melissa was actually married to this man, but she spoke up. "I won't know a moment's peace until I'm satisfied that Melissa is safe," she said.

Adam waved the wire in a delayed fit of agitation. "What the devil does she mean, 'I'm discovering life'?"

Keith held up both his hands, palms out, and order was momentarily restored. "I think," he began calmly, "that Mama and I should take tomorrow's train over to Port Riley and find out what's going on."

Jeff was standing at the liquor cabinet. He poured himself a brandy, which was appropriated by Adam before he could raise it to his lips. After giving his elder brother a scorching look he filled another glass. "This is no job for Mama," he said. "After all, she's a woman."

Katherine felt the beginnings of a headache throbbing in one temple. "Jeffrey," she replied, "I will not be treated to one of your idiotic masculine diatribes. If you cannot assist us in our dilemma, then kindly leave this room."

Jeff sank into the big barrel-back chair that had been his father's favorite. He looked most put-upon, but he held his tongue.

"What Jeff was trying to tell us, in his awkward way," Adam pointed out with wry sarcasm, "is that he wants to be there when Melissa explains this mess she's gotten herself into. And so do I."

Jeff nodded somewhat sullenly and took a sip of his brandy.

Katherine sighed. "Good heavens, if you all go storming over there, you'll overwhelm her," she said, rubbing her temple with the fingers of one hand. "Not to mention her poor husband."

"Husband." Jeff huffed the word out in a mockery of the very idea.

Keith spread his hands. "We know where Melissa is, and that she's all right. The rest is academic."

"I intend to find that out for myself," Jeff insisted, and he still sounded surly. He'd been patently impossible lately, and Katherine wished that he could be transformed back into a little boy again, just for a few minutes, so that she could spank him.

Adam was still glaring down at the telegram. "'Discovering life'?" he repeated.

Katherine stood up, feeling weary. At times like this she missed Daniel all the more poignantly. "It's settled," she said. "We'll all travel to Port Riley on the morning train."

With that she left the study.

•   •   •

At the end of the day Melissa still had a job, although just barely, if the lecture she'd gotten from Mr. Rimley was any indication. She was so tired that she stumbled off in the direction of Quinn's house, and if she hadn't had to pass Kruger's Mercantile on the way, she would surely have forgotten to buy gloves.

When she arrived at home Quinn met her in the middle of the walk. He was wearing no tie or coat, and his shirt was open halfway down his midriff. "Where have you been?" He bit out the words.

Melissa lifted her gaze from the matting of dark gold hair on his chest to the snapping annoyance in his eyes. "I've been working," she answered, almost too tired to say the words. "You were right—it's very hard."

His manner softened at her answer, and he muttered her name in a tone of despairing frustration before reaching out to take her hands. When she winced in pain he drew back far enough to look at them, and a soft but explosive curse word escaped him.

"I'm all right," Melissa said woodenly, starting around him.

Quinn shook his head in bewildered wonder and ushered her quite solicitously toward the front door. Once inside he led her into that exceedingly masculine room where she'd planned to read the newspaper that morning.

Seating her in a chair near the fireplace, where a blaze was burning low, he turned up the lamp and then knelt at her side to take a closer look at her injured hands.

Melissa felt an inexplicable, wounding tenderness; she longed to bend down and kiss the top of his head.

"My God," he breathed as he rose to his feet and went over to a cabinet to begin rummaging through drawers and along shelves. "What were you doing?"

"Shucking oysters," Melissa responded sleepily as he came back to her again, carrying a white metal box in his hands. She was touched to see that it was a first-aid kit.

Quinn dropped to his knees again and began cleaning the cuts on Melissa's hands with a gentle deftness that twisted her heart. When he'd treated them with disinfectant he lifted audacious brown eyes to hers and said, "You don't have to do this."

Melissa's eyes burned with tears. "Yes, I do," she answered. "My brothers—"

Quinn shot suddenly to his feet. "Damn your brothers!" he bellowed. "Your brothers have nothing to do with what we're talking about!"

Melissa lowered her head, and a teardrop fell on one of her hands. "You're right," she confessed in a small, broken voice. "It's myself I've got to prove something to, not them."

He sighed heavily and shoved a hand through already rumpled hair. "I'm trying to understand," he told her raggedly. "I'm doing my damnedest to understand."

"I know that," Melissa said softly.

His manner and the sound of his voice were still brusque. "Just sit there," he ordered with a halfhearted gesture of one hand. "I'll go and get you some tea or something."

"Thanks," Melissa sniffled. She would always remember that it was in that homely, ordinary moment that she realized what had happened. By some strange turn of fate, some miracle, she had fallen in love with Quinn Rafferty.

A pile of ledger books on his desk indicated that he'd been going over his accounts, and Melissa smiled to herself. She was married to this man, for heaven's sake, and had no idea what he did for a living.

It was obvious from her sumptuous surroundings that Quinn had more going for him than the single sawmill that Jeff held in such contempt.

She stiffened as another possibility occurred to her. Quinn had told her outright that her fortune would give him almost unlimited financial power. No doubt his desk was strewn with ledgers because he was planning that expansion he'd mentioned.

Despair swept over Melissa as the full import of her situation struck her. She loved a man who had married her for her money.

She looked down through a blur of tears at her mended

hands. Any tenderness Quinn showed her was probably just business, not real affection.

Just then he reappeared holding out a glass of white wine. "Here, love. I think this will serve better than a cup of tea."

Melissa was torn between conflicting needs—one compelled her to slap the glass out of his hand, the other made her want to hurl herself into Quinn's arms and beg him to hold her close.

In the end she simply thanked him, reached for the glass, and took a small sip of the wine. It was a good chablis.

Quinn had noticed the change in her manner, she was sure of that, but he made no comment on it. Instead he built up the fire and went back to his desk.

Melissa expected him to be bent over his accounts again, but when she looked up she saw that he was leaning back against the edge of the desk, his powerful arms folded across his chest, watching her.

"I've been going over this in my mind for the last five minutes," he said gruffly, "looking for a way to say it without setting off that formidable temper of yours." He paused, drew a deep breath, and let it out again in a weary rush. "I don't want you to go back to the cannery. In fact, I forbid it."

Melissa took a gulp of the wine. "It would probably have been better if you'd left off the part about forbidding me," she said calmly.

Quinn chuckled ruefully. "My life was so simple before you came along. I didn't have to pick and choose my words, or rack my brains figuring out what devilment you might be up to—or sleep alone."

Melissa glanced toward his desk and took another draught of the wine. "And you didn't have the means to—how did you put it—'expand your holdings.'"

There was a terrible silence, then Quinn asked, in a low and bitter voice, "What's the matter, Melissa? Were you enjoying my presence a little bit? Maybe thinking that you might not have made such a terrible mistake after all?"

Melissa set her wine glass aside and rose slowly to her feet. Her leather gloves, bought to protect her hands while she shucked oysters, slipped, forgotten, to the floor. "I didn't make a mistake," she said coldly, "and neither did you. We both knew exactly what we wanted."

A look of sad frustration moved in Quinn's handsome face. "Melissa—"

"You wanted collateral, and I wanted a chance to prove that I can make my own way in the world." She squared her shoulders. "I'm very tired, and I'm due at the cannery early tomorrow morning, so I believe I'll have my supper and retire. Good night, Mr. Rafferty."

"Good night," Quinn responded, his voice as rough as gravel, and he returned to his ledgers and his plans.

Quinn ate a light meal at his desk, served by the disapproving Mrs. Wright, and the clock on the mantelpiece was just striking eight when there was a knock at the front door.

Admitted by the housekeeper, Mitch entered the study with his hat in his hand and a baleful, sympathetic expression on his face. "Having trouble, old friend?" he asked, glancing at the ledgers before he took a chair near the fire.

The word "trouble" brought Melissa immediately to mind, but Quinn realized soon enough that his friend hadn't been referring to her or to the attending situation. It had more to do with the account books. "You're not thinking that I'm having financial problems, are you?" he ventured.

He was getting tired of people making him feel like a social-climbing pauper when he owned a thriving timber operation, numerous stocks and bonds, and half interest in the new hotel being built at the end of Simpson Street.

Mitch cleared his throat, obviously embarrassed, and looked down at his boots for a moment. "This morning your wife asked me for money," he said miserably. "She was wearing a dress that looked like it came out of a rag bag and trying to get into your railroad car."

Quinn let out a long breath and sat back in his swivel chair. The nape of his neck ached savagely. "She asked you for money," he marveled, glaring up at the ceiling.

"She said she had some, but it was locked up inside the car."

Nodding wearily, Quinn opened the top desk drawer on the right and took out a cash box. "How much?"

"Sixty-five dollars. It isn't that I'm worried about the money, Quinn—"

"I know." Quinn counted out three twenties and a five and handed them to Mitch. "Stop worrying," he said. "I'm still solvent."

Mitch tucked the currency into his wallet without counting it. "I hope you're not just saying that to preserve your pride or something. I'm your friend, and if you're in trouble, I want to help you."

"I'm in a lot of trouble," Quinn admitted wryly, "but it doesn't have much to do with money. Want a drink?"

Mitch nodded and went to the liquor cabinet to help himself. "How about you?" he asked, holding up a bottle.

Quinn shook his head. "I've had more hooch since I met that woman than in all the rest of my life combined. She's driving me crazy."

Mitch grinned as he poured himself a shot of Scotch and returned to his chair. "Here's to true love," he said, lifting his glass as he sat down.

Quinn gave him a look, then cupped his hands behind his head and kicked his feet up onto the desk. "She's got a job shucking oysters," he said.

A sigh escaped Mitch. "I'm afraid that's partly my fault," he said. "She asked me where she could find work, and I pointed her in the direction of the cannery, thinking she'd find out how hard it was and come home."

Quinn closed his eyes. "You should see her hands," he despaired. "They're all swollen and cut. And she's so tired she can't see straight."

"But she's going back tomorrow," Mitch guessed.

"That's right."

"They're bound to give her the sack," Mitch said. "No way she could keep up."

Quinn opened his eyes again. He was exhausted himself— God, what he wouldn't give to make love to Melissa and then sleep for a solid week. "I know," he agreed. "I'm worried about what that's going to do to her, even though I'd be happy as hell if they showed her the road. Do you think I should pay them to keep her on or something?"

"No," Mitch answered immediately. "I figure if you interfere in this, one way or the other you're going to be sorry."

Quinn knew that his friend was right, but he hated sitting back and watching Melissa take a blow like that. It was easy enough to see that things had gone her way all her life.

After a few more minutes of quiet, companionable conversation Mitch set aside his glass and left.

Quinn was drawn to Melissa, but he forced himself to stay in his study until the numbers in his ledgers began to blur in front of his eyes. When Mrs. Wright came in to collect his supper tray he couldn't refrain from asking, "Has my wife eaten?"

"Oh, yes, sir," Mrs. Wright answered without hesitation. "She's had her supper and her bath and fallen sound asleep. I haven't seen a body so tired since that flume collapsed last fall and you spent a week up on the mountain seeing to it."

Quinn allowed himself a half smile. Overseeing the repair of a flume was simple stuff compared to dealing with Melissa. "She's got a job," he confessed.

Mrs. Wright looked embarrassed. "Yes, sir," she said in a hushed voice. "I know." It was clear that the old woman found Melissa a consuming mystery, and she wasn't alone.

"I want everything done for her comfort," Quinn said, sliding back his chair and stretching. "Make sure, if you will, that she has a good breakfast and something to eat at midday."

The housekeeper nodded and went out.

Quinn looked up at the ceiling. More than anything he wanted to go to Melissa, take her into his arms, and teach her all the sweet pleasures he knew she'd enjoy. There was no way that he could do that, however, and he knew he wasn't going to be able to sleep even though he was worn out. With both these avenues cut off, Quinn was at a loss as to how to spend the rest of the evening.

Gillian came into his mind, but his blood didn't heat the way it used to, nor did his heart rate pick up speed. It amazed him that things could change so quickly, but his

whole world had turned around the moment he'd hauled
Melissa aboard the train. He'd desired her in the most desperate way ever since.

With a sigh Quinn took the spare key to his bedroom
from the corner of a desk drawer and flipped it into the air,
catching it in his palm. One day—one day soon—he was
going to have to win Melissa's trust.

He glanced up at the ceiling again and swallowed hard.
He had a feeling that he was going to have to crawl through
that doorway when the time came, rather than walk.

Presently Quinn dropped the key back into its drawer.
He'd go out for a while, and when he came back he'd let
himself into the bedroom and collapse on the sofa, just as he
had the night before.

GB *Six*

Jeff had hoped that Fancy would be asleep by the time he got home; instead, she was sitting up by the parlor fire, talking with Adam's wife, Banner.

The conversation ceased the instant the women noticed he was there. Jeff felt hurt by that, but he didn't have to ask what they'd been talking about; he knew only too well.

Fancy's soft violet gaze touched his face briefly and then skittered away. "Banner tells me you've found Melissa," she said.

Jeff shoved a hand through his hair, distracted. A twisting sweetness moved painfully within him as he looked at Fancy; though much was wrong between them, he loved her as desperately as he ever had. "Yes," he finally replied. "She's—er—discovering life or something."

Banner was preparing to go; she set aside her teacup, got out of her chair, and reached for her cloak. She was looking at Jeff. "I suppose it's too much to hope that the three of you have decided to stay out of this and let Melissa live her own life."

Jeff sighed, searching his soul for that quality that seemed to elude him more with each passing year: patience. "She needs looking after," he said flatly.

Banner and Fancy exchanged one of those looks of theirs, and Jeff felt his temper heating up.

"Melissa's a grown woman," Banner protested, tying the ribbons of her fancy green bonnet beneath her chin. "She can take care of herself."

"Yes," Fancy agreed, glaring at Jeff as though it were his fault that Melissa didn't have the sense God gave a brass spittoon.

Jeff glanced at the cradle beside Fancy's chair where the new baby lay sleeping and struggled to keep his voice low. Caroline was his only daughter, and she occupied a special place in his heart. "It's been four days since Melissa ran out of the church," he reminded the two women evenly. "Since then she's married a total stranger, and God only knows what *else* she's done. Don't tell me that my sister can take care of herself."

"There's no sense in trying to tell you anything," Fancy said.

Banner hastened toward the door. "Don't bother offering to see me home, Jeff," she told him with sarcastic sweetness. "I brought the buggy."

As much to spite his sister-in-law as to ensure her safety, Jeff escorted Banner down the front walk and helped her into the waiting rig. Though the lights of gas-powered street lamps glowed all around them, the shadows beneath the bonnet of the buggy rendered Banner all but invisible.

She surprised Jeff by reaching out to take his hand for a moment. Her voice when she spoke was soft and earnest. "You do love Fancy, don't you, Jeff?" she asked.

He was affronted. "You know I do," he replied hoarsely.

"Then let Katherine and the others handle this problem with Melissa. You've got enough trouble right here."

Banner had spoken with such cryptic import that Jeff was both alarmed and annoyed, but he had no chance to question her. She was gone in an instant, disappearing with the familiar horse and buggy into the foggy mist.

Jeff went slowly back into the house, still puzzling over

Banner's remark. Sure, he and Fancy had problems—every married couple did—but it wasn't as bad as his sister-in-law had made it sound.

Was it?

He went back into the parlor and stood before the fire with his back to Fancy, thinking.

"I've ordered a set of twin beds," Fancy announced with prim suddenness, and Jeff whirled to face her.

"What?" he demanded in a gruff whisper.

Fancy idly rocked Caroline's cradle, all the while avoiding Jeff's eyes. "I don't think we should sleep together for a while," she said.

Jeff's frustration and fury knew no bounds. "You can't be serious," he burst out. "Good God, woman, you're my wife!"

The baby started in fright and then began to shriek.

"Now look what you've done!" Fancy cried, sweeping the baby up into her arms and starting toward the stairs.

Jeff hesitated for a few moments, too stunned to move, then hurried after her. She was striding along the hallway toward their bedroom when he caught up with her. Caroline was still screaming; at this rate, the boys would soon be awake, too.

The place would be bedlam.

"I'm sorry," he told her.

Fancy gave him a look that said he should be sorry and crossed their room to enter the adjoining nursery and pace the floor with Caroline.

Jeff ached at the lack of understanding between himself and his wife, but he didn't know how to cross the breach. He wasn't even sure exactly what was wrong, but it had all started when Fancy had begun to share Banner's consuming interest in the suffrage movement.

He sat down on the edge of the bed he and Fancy had shared so happily and buried his head in his hands. The baby was settling down by fits and starts, and after several minutes had passed Fancy returned from the nursery, her arms empty.

"What's happening to us?" Jeff asked miserably, and she

looked away for a moment, gnawing at her lower lip, her dark violet eyes brimming with tears.

"I don't know," she answered after a long time.

Jeff rose and crossed the room to lay his hands gently on Fancy's shoulders. He kissed her forehead and then said sadly, "We'd damned well better find out, hadn't we?"

"Will you be going to Port Riley tomorrow about Melissa?" Fancy looked up at him with a plea in her eyes.

Jeff was at a loss as to whether she wanted him to stay or go; in the end, he had to risk being wrong.

"No. Somebody told me tonight that I have troubles enough of my own, and I think they were right."

Fancy rested her cheek against his chest. Her back moved in a small, quivering sigh beneath his hands, and Jeff never knew if his choice had been correct or not.

Keith was standing by the fireplace in the study when Tess joined him there. Her wild mane of brown hair fell freely about the shoulders of her wrapper.

"You're very late," she said, putting her arms around him from behind and rising on tiptoe to kiss the nape of his neck. "And I'm absolutely furious."

He turned in her embrace, resting his hands on her hips and favoring her with an insolent half grin. "Is that so?" he intoned, kissing the tip of her nose. He gave her a little squeeze. "Can't think why you'd be the least bit put out. After all, a woman's place is in the home, and here you are, right at home."

Hazel eyes dancing, Tess gave her husband a poke in the stomach. "You," she accused, "have been talking to Jeff again."

Keith sighed and shook his head. Suddenly his expression was serious. "What's going on between him and Fancy, do you know?"

Tess held Keith a little tighter for a moment and then stepped back. "Fancy feels that she and Jeff have enough children now, and she wants to take a more active part in community affairs—"

"The suffrage movement," Keith put in.

Tess looked at her husband warily. He was in favor of granting women the vote, but he was also a Corbin, strongwilled, with a tendency to dominate at times. His preferences, where a wife's behavior was concerned, weren't always in alignment with his political ideals.

She nodded. "Jeff's solution is to keep Fancy pregnant, and therefore out of trouble."

Keith chuckled and shook his head. "That would be his logic." He shrugged. "Change seldom comes quickly, Tess. And that approach has served men well for a long, long time."

Tess felt a self-conscious blush climb her cheeks. She and Keith had only two children, whereas Jeff and Fancy had four, and so did Adam and Banner. She wondered if her husband felt cheated.

Keith curved a finger beneath Tess's chin and lifted. "What?" he asked softly. Insistently.

There was nothing to do but confess, and Tess knew it. "I was thinking that maybe you wish you'd married a different wife—one who could give you a houseful of children."

His eyes were so gentle that Tess feared to lose herself in their soft azure depths. "Ethan and Mary Katherine *are* a houseful of children," he told her with a grin. Before he could kiss her, however, or even say that he loved her, there was a frantic hammering at the front door.

Tess steeled herself, knowing that this would be one of those nights. Someone in Keith's parish needed him; in a few minutes he would be gone.

The caller was a man who worked in the shipyard; his young wife had delivered a stillborn child only an hour before. Now, in her grief, she wanted the comfort only her pastor could give her.

Tess hurried to fetch Keith's battered old Bible while he shrugged into his coat. "I'll be home as soon as I can," he promised, giving her a brief kiss.

And then the door was closing behind him.

Melissa had expected her second day of work to be better than the first; instead, it was worse. While the gloves she'd bought at the mercantile protected her hands, they also slowed down her efforts. Throughout the morning, whenever Mr. Rimley passed, he counted the oysters in her bucket with his lips moving and then glared at Melissa and shook his head.

"They're going to fire me," she despaired at noon, when she and Rowina sat down on their favorite log to eat lunch. With the kind cooperation of Quinn's housekeeper, Melissa had provided that day's repast of roast beef sandwiches and cherry pie.

"You don't know that for sure," Rowina argued, but she looked worried all the same. She hesitated for a moment, then ventured to ask, "You're that heiress they wrote about in the paper, ain't you? My Charlie read the whole piece out loud to me last night."

Melissa nodded, looking down at her half-eaten sandwich instead of meeting her friend's eyes.

Rowina's tone conveyed a slight sense of betrayal. "You don't need this job," she grumbled, watching Melissa out of the corner of her eyes. "What are you doing here, anyway?"

Melissa wasn't sure how to explain. Her reasons for wanting to accomplish something on her own sounded reasonable, even noble, when she ran them through her own mind. To Rowina, who lived in the hard, real world, they would seem frivolous.

"Well?" Rowina prompted.

"You wouldn't understand," Melissa said softly.

The Indian woman fell silent and ate no more of the food Melissa had packed so carefully in Quinn's kitchen that morning. Clearly, Rowina's feelings were hurt.

"I didn't mean that the way it sounded," Melissa explained after a few awkward moments had passed.

"How did you mean it, then?"

Before Melissa could answer that question Flo appeared, picking her way daintily over rocks and shells to approach.

A smug expression flickered in her pale green eyes as she looked at Melissa. "Well, here's the princess herself," she taunted. And then she made a curtsy and added, "Mr. Roberts sent for you. You're supposed to go straight to his office."

Melissa knew what was coming, and she was crushed, even though she still had her career as a writer. After all, she couldn't tell anyone about *that*. And, for the moment, she was more concerned with Rowina's feelings. "Good-bye," she said quietly, touching the other woman's hand briefly with her own.

Mr. Roberts, the squirrelly little man who had hired her the day before, was waiting for Melissa in his messy shed of an office. He regarded her through a cloud of cigar smoke. "No work for a lady, shucking oysters," he said.

Melissa swallowed. "I know I'll be able to work faster once I've had just a little more practice."

Roberts shook his head. "I've got strong lads who'd like your job, missy. Don't know why I hired you in the first place, except that I could never resist a pretty face."

"I'm fired?"

"You can stay till the end of the day" was the generous response.

Melissa was faced with a decision: walk away with her chin in the air or stay and finish what she'd started. She was tempted to hurry home, do her crying, and forget that the cannery had ever existed, but her pride wouldn't let her leave that way.

As Daniel and Katherine Corbin's daughter, she'd been taught to hold her head high, to keep trying when things looked their worst. She'd done that when she'd first tried to sell her stories, and no one wanted them, and she could do it now.

She lifted her chin and went back to her bench to shuck oysters for another five hours.

By quitting time she was not only tired but broken in spirit as well. The shame of incompetence brought her shoulders low and took the fire from her eyes. Her brothers had been right in thinking that she needed to be sheltered and fussed over, she reflected sadly. She was nothing but a failure.

Katherine Corbin gazed out at the main street of Port Riley through the window of the hotel dining room. So far she hadn't touched her tea.

She and Adam had spent the afternoon making discreet inquiries without turning up a trace of Melissa or that mysterious husband of hers. Mr. Rafferty, it seemed, was on the mountain, where his loggers were felling timber. The maid who'd answered the door at the Rafferty household had averted her eyes and claimed she had no idea where the mistress might be.

The girl had been lying, of course.

Just then Katherine was wrenched back to the here and now. She pushed back her chair when she saw Melissa passing by on the sidewalk and slowly rose to her feet.

Katherine could feel Adam's curious gaze, but she didn't look away. "Oh, dear God," she whispered, stunned at the change a few days had wrought. "My poor little girl!"

Melissa was wearing a crumpled calico dress, a shapeless dark shawl, and shoes that belonged on someone else's feet, but it wasn't her daughter's clothing that had stunned Katherine. It was the stoop of Melissa's shoulders and the forlorn, bereft expression on her face.

She looked as though the world had just come to a violent end and she'd been left to wander through the rubble alone.

By then Adam had spotted his sister, and he stood with considerably less hesitation than his mother had.

"Let me talk to her alone," Katherine said quickly, and Adam sank back into his chair with a sigh.

Snatching up her handbag, Katherine hurried toward the door and out onto the sidewalk. She started to call out to Melissa and then stopped herself, walking faster instead. Soon she'd fallen into step with her daughter.

Melissa looked at her without recognition at first, and then a sort of dull surprise dawned in her hollow eyes. "Mama," she said softly, stopping and turning to face Katherine.

Both women were oblivious to the noisy traffic in the roadway and the people moving past them on the sidewalk. Katherine took Melissa's shoulders in her hands. "Darling, what's happened?"

Melissa suddenly looked around her like one just rising from a sound sleep. "Are—are you alone?"

Katherine shook her head and allowed herself a brief smile. "Adam is with me. Jeff and Keith planned to come along as well, but in the end they couldn't get away. Melissa, we've all been very worried."

Melissa dropped her eyes to the sidewalk. "I'm sorry," she said in a barely audible voice.

Katherine took her daughter's arm gently. "Won't you come inside and talk with me?"

"Just you?" Melissa asked hopefully. "I'm not up to one of Adam's lectures."

Katherine nodded to show that she understood and led her daughter into the hotel and up the stairs to her room. It was small, and since there was only one chair, Melissa sat on the edge of the bed.

"I can't come home," she announced before giving a word of explanation about her flight from the church, her personal appearance, or her hasty marriage to a stranger.

Katherine's patience had reached an end, although the loving tenderness she felt for her daughter had not. "Melissa, why did you run out of the church that way? If you'd changed your mind, you had only to tell any one of us."

Melissa looked small and miserable and much younger than her twenty-two years. "I was so hurt—I didn't want to explain. . . ."

Katherine simply waited, her hands folded in her lap.

Melissa's eyes were filled with remembered pain when she lifted them to meet her mother's gaze. "Ajax has a mistress, Mama. He actually invited her to our wedding."

Rage filled Katherine at the thought, but this was no time to remind her daughter that she'd disliked Ajax from the first, so she kept her peace.

The story spilled out of Melissa in a sudden rush. She told of riding in a railroad car with Quinn Rafferty and of their impulsive wedding and explained her need to accomplish something worthwhile. She'd gotten a job shucking oysters the day before and lost it today, she blurted out, and now she was going to have to start all over again.

Katherine leaned slightly forward in her chair. "What

possessed you to marry a man you didn't know?" she demanded quietly.

Melissa's eyes filled with tears. "It seemed like such a good idea at the time," she answered. "He's kind, and he's very good-looking."

With a sigh Katherine rose from her chair and went to the window to look out on the main street of Port Riley. "Do you love him, Melissa?"

"Yes," came the immediate response. "I think I do."

"And how does he feel about you?"

This time the answer was not so prompt. "I—I have hopes that Quinn will come to care for me s-someday."

Katherine ached inside, for this was so much less than she'd wanted for her child, but she kept her voice light. "Then you won't be coming home with us?" she asked.

"No," Melissa replied. "I'm sorry, Mama, but I can't live in my brothers' shadows anymore. I've got to make a life for myself."

Her heart in her throat, Katherine turned to face her youngest child. There was a very special bond between them, because Melissa was her only daughter. "I'd like to meet your husband," she announced, leaving all her misgivings and worries unsaid.

"I'll arrange it," Melissa promised, rising to her feet. She embraced Katherine, her eyes shining with tears. "Thank you for understanding," she said.

"I didn't say I understood, pumpkin," Katherine answered briskly. She longed to weep, just thinking what a mess Melissa had gotten herself into, but she'd been mothering too long to make a mistake like that. Much as she hated it, she had to let go of her daughter and allow her to live her life in the way she saw fit.

Melissa glanced nervously toward the door of the room. It was clear that she'd been expecting her brother to appear at any moment. "Are the boys angry with me?" she asked.

Katherine smiled. "It's nothing they won't get over," she said. She knew her concern showed as she took in Melissa's clothes and the cuts and bruises on her hands, but she couldn't help it. "Go home and get some rest, darling. We'll talk again later."

Melissa gave her mother another kiss and a weary hug, then left the room.

Katherine immediately sat down, struggling to keep her composure. She longed for the comfort and reassurance of a loving partner, but it wasn't Daniel Corbin who filled her thoughts. It was Harlan Sommers, a rancher she'd met two years before in California.

She sighed. Harlan was pressing her to marry him, and Katherine truly wanted to be his wife, but it seemed that there was always some crisis in the family demanding all her attention. She hadn't even mentioned the man she loved to her children.

Katherine touched the hair at the nape of her neck to see if it was falling from its pins. Harlan held that in a family such as hers there would always be nothing but crises, and it did appear that he was right.

Quinn was in his study when Melissa hurried into the house. He was wearing rough-spun trousers, a flannel shirt, and work boots, and he needed a shave.

Melissa came up short when she saw him. Her husband looked exhausted and smelled like an old bear, but as always, the sight of him had a powerful impact on her.

"I was fired today," she burst out breathlessly.

The expression on Quinn's face was a guarded one. "Oh?" he said, and he turned his attention to the blaze snapping on the hearth.

Melissa would have liked a little sympathy or perhaps some concern for her state of mind, but she didn't pursue those objectives. There were more pressing matters to be dealt with. "My mother and one of my brothers are here. They're staying at the State Hotel."

She had Quinn's full attention now.

He turned to face her squarely, studying her face for a moment, then reached for his coat, which was lying over the back of a leather-upholstered chair. Melissa was finally forced by his silence to speak again.

"Where are you going?"

"To meet your family," he replied. "I won't have it said that they had to come looking for me." His eyes touched her briefly, then glanced away. "It's too much to hope, I suppose, that you were wearing something else when they arrived?" he asked pointedly.

Melissa didn't want to hear Quinn's opinion of calico. "You're a fine one to talk," she said, letting her gaze move over his filthy work clothes.

Quinn allowed her remark to pass unchallenged. "I want to meet them tonight," he told her. He paused to give Melissa a light, nibbling kiss that awakened all her nerve endings. "Sleep well, Mrs. Rafferty."

Melissa grasped at his arm. "Let me go with you," she said, knowing from the moment she opened her mouth that this was something Quinn wanted to do alone.

He shook his head, held her close for a long and deliciously torturous moment, and then strode out of the house.

Melissa had ever been one to do exactly as she pleased, but the truth was that she was very tired that night, and very dispirited. After all, she'd lasted but forty-eight hours at the first real job of her life.

She ate her supper before the parlor fire, reflecting on her situation as she tucked away the meal. Maybe, she reflected, she should think in grander, more sweeping terms than shucking oysters.

She remembered a conversation she'd had with Quinn in his railroad car. He'd said that Port Riley had had its own newspaper until six months before, when it had been burned out.

Excitement filled Melissa, restoring her energy, buoying her spirits. Mrs. Wright came in to collect her tray and was startled by her mistress's exuberant "What this town needs is fearless journalism!"

"Oh, dear," said Mrs. Wright, nearly dropping the tray. "Fearless what?"

Quinn walked into the lobby of the only inn in Port Riley, all too conscious of the impression he was going to make on

Melissa's family. He hadn't wanted to take the time to bathe and change clothes; now he wished he had.

A practical man, Quinn could see no point in mulling over a decision that had already been made. He shifted his thoughts to the State Hotel, which was old and a little on the seedy side. Chances were it wouldn't last long once his new hotel was finished.

He approached the desk and explained that he was looking for the Corbins.

The clerk, who would soon be coming to work for Quinn at the other hotel, smiled obsequiously. "The lady's in her room upstairs, Mr. Rafferty—number twenty-three. The gentleman's in the bar."

Quinn took off his hat and left it at the desk. The saloon adjoining the hotel was a small one, and it was easy to pick out his brother-in-law. He stood a head taller than the other patrons and was obviously engaged in his own thoughts.

Quinn paused for a moment to gather his forces, then cleared his throat almost inaudibly and approached the dark-haired man standing at the bar.

Melissa's brother spotted him in the mirror and turned to face Quinn. His expression was solemn as he assessed the man who had carried his baby sister off in a private railroad car.

"Rafferty?" he finally demanded.

Quinn put out his hand and nodded.

"Adam Corbin," was the response. A handshake was exchanged.

Quinn ordered a drink, and the two men retreated to a table in the corner. They were both seated, with a glass of whiskey in front of them, before either spoke.

"I only caught a glimpse of my sister," Corbin began, his dark blue eyes fairly pinning Quinn to the wall. "I will say, however, that I've seen her looking better."

Quinn sighed and took a sip of his whiskey. "I don't suppose it will come as any surprise to you if I say that Melissa is a stubborn woman. She looks the way she does by her own choice, for her own reasons—the primary one being that she loves to annoy me."

Adam's ominous expression gave way to one of amusement. He chuckled and nodded his head. "That's Melissa," he said.

Quinn cleared his throat and shifted uneasily in his chair. It wasn't that he was afraid—for big as Corbin was, he was no larger than Quinn himself—but that he'd never had to explain the virtual abduction of a lady before.

There was no precedent for that.

Seven

Melissa felt the mattress shift and looked up, blinking, to see Quinn bending over her, his hands resting one on either side of her on the bed. Morning sunlight glimmered in his caramel-colored hair and gave his clean white shirt a pristine glow.

"This life of leisure is turning you into a derelict," he commented with a wink.

Melissa sat up so rapidly that their heads would surely have crashed together had it not been for Quinn's quick step backward. "What are you doing here?" she demanded in a testy whisper. "What time is it?"

Quinn folded his arms, showing no sign that he planned to give so much as an inch of ground, and arched one eyebrow. "To answer your first question," he began evenly, "I'm here because this is my room. As for your second, it's time you were out of bed, that's what time it is."

Suppressing an infantile urge to put out her tongue, Melissa sat up, being very careful to keep the covers pulled to her chin. She ran one hand nervously through her tangled hair. "How did your interview with my mother go?" she asked, her jawline set at an obstinate angle. "Is she going to have you shot, horsewhipped, or fed to the dogfish?"

Quinn grinned at her, and Melissa wondered if the rascal knew how greatly that enhanced his charm. "Why don't you ask her yourself? She's downstairs right now, having breakfast with your brother."

Melissa's eyes went wide.

Bending suavely, Quinn laid an impudent index finger to Melissa's chin. "I can see that you're too overcome with joy to speak," he teased.

"They like you?" Melissa breathed, stunned.

Quinn shrugged, looking obnoxiously pleased with himself. "It seems they think I'm the best thing that's ever happened to you, dear heart."

Melissa's mouth dropped open. She immediately closed it.

"Your brother is of the opinion that a husband's firm, guiding hand might just bring you around," Quinn went on.

Fury rose in Melissa's throat, practically choking her. *"'Bring—me—around?'"* she repeated in a disbelieving sputter. Then she flung back the covers, shot to her knees, and yelled, "'Bring me around,' is it? Why, that arrogant, pompous meathead! I'll box his ears!"

Quinn laughed and hooked his thumbs into the pockets of his silk brocade vest. "My darling Melissa," he said, "how I love your sweet-natured ways."

Melissa flung one pillow at him and then the other. "Get out!" she screamed.

He didn't move. "This is my room," he reiterated. "If anybody's going to be thrown out, it's you." His dark eyes moved idly over the thin camisole and drawers she'd worn to bed, leaving a heated ache wherever they touched. "However," he eventually went on—and now his voice was very low—"I could be persuaded to let you stay."

After giving her husband one glaring look Melissa made her way to the opposite side of the bed on her knees, then got hastily to her feet. She snatched up the pink wrapper Mrs. Wright had given her and covered herself with it, wrenching so tightly on the ties that she cinched her waist

81

painfully. "I will repeat myself, Mr. Rafferty," she said coldly, "once and only once. Leave this room immediately."

Instead of accommodating her, Quinn came around the end of the bed and stood so close to Melissa that she could feel the heat and hardness of his body. Although she was trembling with anger, she was also stricken by the strange effect his nearness produced. It was as though she'd been lifted up and dropped from a great height.

Bold as you please, he untied Melissa's wrapper with one hand, and with the other he smoothed it away. She trembled and closed her eyes—longing to rebel but unable to speak or move—as his hand passed gently over her breast.

Quinn's finger encircled a nipple thinly veiled in muslin, and it peaked in instant obedience to this silent command. Melissa groaned helplessly as he rolled the flesh between his thumb and forefinger.

He had the temerity to chuckle at this.

Melissa opened her eyes and glared at him even as he brought down the front of her camisole and bared her bosom entirely. She could make no move to stop him—her body had betrayed her so completely that she was capable only of reflexive responses—but she wanted him to know that this was not a willing surrender.

He didn't seem to care whether his victory was an honorable one or not. With a low, rumbling groan of his own, he rasped out, "So—beautiful—" and then bent to sample Melissa's bounty with his mouth.

She stiffened with violent, brutal delight and was at last able to move, if only to entangle her fingers in the richness of his hair and hold him closer. She hated Quinn Rafferty in that moment, sincerely hated him, and yet she wanted him to go on loving her this way forever.

Melissa whimpered and let her head fall back in submission as Quinn moved to pleasure her other breast. Her knees melted, and Quinn supported her by grasping her bottom in his hands.

Feeling as though she'd plunged into a wild and raging river, Melissa struggled for some grasp on good sense, but she was lost. During those treacherous moments she would have allowed Quinn almost any liberty with either her body or her soul, but the tender plundering ceased as suddenly as it had begun.

Between one heartbeat and the next Quinn freed Melissa and stepped back. She sat down heavily on the edge of the bed, unable to stand. She had absolutely no pride and, in that instant anyway, no inhibitions.

"Make love to me, Mr. Rafferty," she said.

He was avoiding her eyes as though he was ashamed of what he'd done. "This isn't the time," he said in a raw voice. And then he went to the liquor cabinet. Although his back was turned to her, Melissa saw him lift a bottle and then resolutely set it down again.

Melissa had recovered enough to reach for one of the calico dresses and scramble into it. She was trembling so badly that the task of buttoning up the back frustrated her completely.

When she felt Quinn's fingers at the buttons, however, she twisted away and glared at him. "I can take care of myself!" she sputtered.

Quinn spread his hands in silent concession of the point and strode out of the bedroom, slamming the door behind him.

By the time Melissa entered the dining room, buttoned into the calico dress, her hair braided into a single ebony plait, nearly fifteen minutes had passed. Everyone had finished eating, it appeared. They were waiting for her.

Both Quinn and Adam stood when she came in, but Melissa snubbed them completely, going to her mother's chair, bending to kiss Katherine's upturned cheek.

"Good morning, Mama," she said. Then she went to the sideboard, where scrambled eggs and sausages were warming in a large copper chafing dish, and began filling her plate.

She heard chair legs scraping along the hardwood floor, and when she came to the table Adam and Quinn were seated again and involved in an enthusiastic conversation. Something about a resort hotel overlooking the water.

Katherine glanced periodically from Melissa's face to Quinn's, and Melissa knew her mother was perplexed.

"That dress is positively horrid," the older woman finally remarked, and both the men fell silent.

Quinn gave Melissa a look of sheer vexation, and she was delighted to have displeased him in even a small way. It would be a long time before she forgave him for that little exhibition of lust he had elicited from her upstairs.

"Isn't it?" Melissa responded warmly.

There was a short silence, and then Katherine sighed and began again. "Perhaps I was too blunt. . . ."

Melissa chewed a mouthful of link sausage very thoroughly before answering. "No, it is a horrid dress," she reflected. "But it's mine."

Katherine's indigo eyes were snapping. As though they sensed something coming that they didn't want to witness, Quinn and Adam excused themselves, took their coffee cups, and left the room.

Quinn even went so far as to close the dining room doors behind them.

"You are making a foolish mistake, Melissa," Katherine said moderately, refilling her teacup. It was very quiet in the room after this pronouncement had been made.

Melissa sighed. She wanted solace and affection from her mother, but she suspected that she was going to get a lecture instead. She met Katherine's gaze steadily and asked, "How do you mean?"

"Yesterday you told me that you love Quinn. Were you lying?"

Melissa swallowed hard and shook her head. Her body relived the attentions he'd paid it earlier, and her cheeks went pink with embarrassment.

"No, Mama," she managed to say after several long moments had passed, "I was telling the truth. I do love him— very much."

Katherine's dark blue gaze took in the bodice of the give-away dress with pointed dispatch. "Then why do you insist upon humiliating him before the entire town?"

Melissa was stunned. In the first place, it had never occurred to her that Quinn could be shamed by the clothes his wife wore. In the second, it did seem that Katherine Corbin, long a champion of female independence, was leaning toward the adversary's position.

"Well?" Katherine prompted when her daughter was silent too long.

"I thought I had explained this," Melissa said quietly. "If I use my trust fund or allow Quinn to buy clothes for me, I won't be taking care of myself, will I? I won't be truly independent."

"You're not independent now," Katherine pointed out, spreading her hands in exasperation. "You're living under the man's roof, eating his food—"

"Insofar as I can," Melissa interrupted respectfully, "I'm looking after myself. I have a little money from—from another source. If it will make you happy, Mama, I'll buy a dress."

"Never mind making me happy," Katherine hissed. "We're talking about making your husband happy!"

Melissa raised both eyebrows. "Mama, is that you sitting over there? Or have we an imposter in our midst, just pretending to be Katherine Corbin, steadfast defender of women's rights?"

A fetching blush bloomed in Katherine's cheeks, and she averted her eyes for a moment. "I have created a monster," she said with a little sigh.

Melissa smiled. "I know, but we weren't talking about Jeff, were we?"

Katherine gave a reluctant burst of laughter and then scolded, "Scamp. You know very well what I'm trying to say. It isn't wrong to attempt to please the man you love, Melissa, unless you're suffering because of the effort."

Melissa buttered a biscuit. "Did you work at pleasing Papa?" she asked.

A look of mingled joy and sadness flickered in Katherine's eyes. "I tried."

Uneasiness nibbled at the pit of Melissa's stomach. "Did you succeed?" she asked.

Katherine's smile was sudden and dazzling. "I gave Daniel four beautiful, healthy children," she answered, and it was tacitly understood that the subject of Melissa's father was closed.

"You've changed recently, Mama," Melissa observed in a thoughtful tone. "Something is different. What is it?"

Katherine hesitated only briefly before announcing, "I've fallen in love."

For the second time that morning Melissa was rendered speechless.

Her mother laughed happily at the astonishment on her face. "His name is Harlan Sommers, and he owns a ranch in California," she went on. "I met him two years ago, and he's been proposing marriage ever since."

Melissa was finally mobile. She flew out of her chair and raced around the table to hug her mother. "That's wonderful! Oh, Mama, you're going to say yes, aren't you?"

Something seemed to deflate within Katherine. She looked smaller, and the sparkle in her eyes dulled. "I want to," she confessed, "but it means living in California. I would be so far from the family—"

Melissa's eyes filled with tears, and she hugged her mother again. "You've been alone so long," she whispered. "Don't waste any more time, Mama—go and be happy!"

Katherine laid her hand on her daughter's. "Before I decide anything, Melissa, I need a promise from you. If whatever you're trying to do here—and I haven't the vaguest idea what that is—doesn't work out, you mustn't let your pride stop you from going home to your brothers."

Melissa had no intention of failing, so she agreed readily. "I promise, Mama."

"Good," Katherine said quietly.

An hour later Melissa's mother and brother boarded the train for Port Hastings.

Mrs. Quinn Rafferty cried just a little when they left, though she tried to hide it.

Quinn, keeping one arm around Melissa's waist, gave her a slight squeeze of reassurance and pretended not to notice her tears.

She turned her attention to the private railroad car where

this strange new life of hers had begun and started purposefully toward it. "Could you please unlock the door for me? There's something inside that I need."

Quinn brought a ring of keys from his pocket just as someone called out to him from across the street. He gave the keys to Melissa and walked away to answer the summons.

In the privacy of the railroad car Melissa reclaimed the money she'd hidden away. She would repay Mitch Williams before pursuing her plans for the day.

It was impulse, pure and simple, that made her stop on the threshold, take the key to the railroad car from the ring, and drop it into the pocket of her dress. If she had an explanation, even for herself, it was that she wanted a place to go to when she needed to be alone and think.

Asking Quinn to let her keep the key did not even cross her mind.

Her husband was talking to a man Melissa didn't know when she rejoined him on the other side of the street.

Quinn's jawline tightened as though he wished Melissa would go away or, better yet, that she'd never approached him at all.

"This the little wife?" his companion asked delightedly. The man had luxuriant white hair and wore an expensive suit of clothes that did much to conceal his girth.

Quinn gave Melissa a wilting look and confessed to the misdeed. "Yes, Roy, this is the—er—lady I married. Melissa—my dearest darling—this is Roy Bennington. He owns the First Union Bank."

Melissa beamed and offered one of her hands in greeting. "Hello, Mr. Bennington," she sang out warmly. "I'll be happy to sign papers transferring my funds to your bank."

Quinn nudged her in the ribs and favored her with another deadly glance. "Your money will remain where it is," he said. Though he was smiling, his teeth were clamped down tight.

Melissa laughed merrily. "But, darling," she chimed, "you did marry me for my money, didn't you?"

Mr. Bennington looked mortified. He muttered some excuse and hurried away, and the moment he was gone Quinn turned to Melissa, took her elbow in one hand, and started propelling her down the wooden sidewalk.

"Why the hell did you say that?"

Melissa wrenched her arm free of his hand before replying. "It's true, isn't it?"

"No!"

She gave him a sidelong look that was full of mischief and meaning. "You're in love with me, then?"

Quinn pushed back the sides of his suit coat to shove both hands into his trouser pockets. "Are you in love with me?" he countered.

Melissa felt her cheeks redden as the memory of his mouth on her breasts came out of nowhere and caused her nipples to tighten and throb beneath her dress and camisole. "Of course not!" her pride forced her to say.

"Then what makes you think I harbor any special affection for you, Mrs. Rafferty?"

Melissa felt as though he'd backhanded her. Still, she kept pace with his long, angry strides. "Exactly where are we going?" she asked as the main part of town began to fall away behind them.

There were saltbox houses on both sides of the road now, and the waters of the Strait of Juan de Fuca came into view. The road was rutted and still hard with the frost that had come in the night.

"I want you to see some of what I've accomplished on my own—without your money."

Melissa was quiet. She regretted taunting him in front of the banker, and if it were possible, she would have liked to go back in time and erase her behavior.

Hesitantly, Quinn took her hand in his. His grasp was strong and dry, and Melissa felt an overwhelming desire for him.

They passed the neatly painted houses and walked on. Melissa supposed that Quinn wanted to show her his mill, but she didn't hear the screaming whine of saws or the sound of lumber being stacked.

When they rounded a bend in the tree-lined road Melissa

drew in her breath. A few hundred feet ahead, facing the water, stood an enormous, truly elegant building of white brick, its windows gleaming in the sunlight. A broad veranda curved around the side in the style of a riverboat.

In the yard two men were busy hoeing out places for flower beds. From inside came the sounds of laughter and preparation.

"Are you going to live here?" Melissa asked, gazing up at Quinn. There was no hiding that she was impressed.

Quinn laughed and held her close for a moment, letting her go too soon. "No, m'lady. This is a hotel. The Seaside."

Melissa had seen many a hotel in her travels with her mother, but this one had a special magic about it: It was Quinn's. "I want a tour!"

Grinning, he took her hand and led her along a walkway sparkling with quartz. They climbed the steps, crossed the wide porch, and entered through doors carved even more ornately than the one at Quinn's house.

The lobby was enormous, with an ivory fireplace so big that Melissa could have stood inside it and stretched her arms full length above her head. There were leather settees and chairs set about, and the floor was covered by the largest Persian rug Melissa had ever seen.

On the second and third floors railed mezzanines overlooked the spectacular fountain that stood in the middle of the lobby.

Quinn showed Melissa an enormous ballroom with a stage and mirrored walls. He introduced her to the chef in the kitchen and took her through the elegant suite on the top floor. This had a terrace looking out over the sea and a gigantic round bed buried in silken cushions.

Melissa's heart rushed into her throat when Quinn drew her close and kissed her with a thoroughness that left her dazed.

With some reluctance he withdrew from her, took her hand in a resolute grasp, and led her out of the suite and down the grand stairs to the lobby. Instead of going out the way they'd come in, however, Quinn led Melissa toward the back.

"This is the best part of all," he said, pulling her along

behind him. They passed along a covered walkway into a round building reminiscent of a gazebo.

Inside was a natural pool lined with small white pebbles. The water bubbled and steamed, and with a gasp Melissa crouched to test it with her hand. It was deliciously warm.

"You'll have more guests than you can possibly accommodate," she said, looking up at Quinn with round, delighted eyes.

He drew her gently back to her feet, and for a moment Melissa thought he was going to kiss her again. She would have welcomed that, but alas, he only gave her a little swat on the bottom and answered, "You're right. The place is booked up from opening day until Christmas."

Melissa longed to bathe in that lovely pool. "When is opening day?" she asked innocently.

Quinn smiled, pleased at her interest, and led her outside. "A week from Saturday. There'll be several hundred people here—besides the registered guests—for the party my partner and I are giving."

Melissa was wounded. Not only had Quinn failed to invite her to this party, he'd kept the hotel itself a secret. "Y-your partner?" she echoed as they reentered the building through the kitchen.

Both of them stopped cold when they saw Gillian standing there chatting with the chef. She gave Quinn a sizzling smile that said all was forgiven and ignored Melissa completely.

"Did somebody mention little ol' me?" Gillian crooned. And then she walked right up to Quinn and straightened his collar with a practiced and very graceful motion of her hands.

"She's your partner?" Melissa asked in a thin voice.

Quinn didn't look away from Gillian's face; it struck Melissa that he was mesmerized, like a rabbit staring into the eyes of a cobra. "Yes," he answered, slowly removing the lady's hands from his chest.

Melissa wanted to die, but no one would ever have guessed that from her manner. "Oh," she said cheerfully. "That's nice."

Quinn gave her a quizzical glance, as though he didn't quite recall who she was. He started to say something but gave up before a sound had passed his throat.

Gillian, meanwhile, linked her arm through his. She looked radiant in a light blue woolen suit trimmed in ribbon a shade darker. "We need to talk," she purred.

To his credit, Quinn had not forgotten his wife—not entirely. He looked at her questioningly.

Melissa was damned if she'd let either of them know how threatened she felt. "Go ahead and have your meeting," she said brightly. "I've got things to do anyway."

She hurried out the nearest door before anyone could respond and didn't slow down until she'd rounded the bend in the road. Then, certain that no one could see her, Melissa gave way to the tears that had been burning behind her eyes.

By the time she'd reached Port Riley proper, however, she'd regained control. She sought out Mr. Mitch Williams's office, which turned out to be above the general store, and held out sixty-five dollars the moment they were face to face.

"Here is the money I owe you, Mr. Williams," she said with dignity. "Thank you very much for the loan."

Mitch looked at the currency and shook his head. "Can't take it, Mrs. Rafferty. Your husband already paid me back."

Melissa sank into a chair, even though she hadn't been invited to sit. "You told Quinn?"

The blond man smiled apologetically and spread his hands as he leaned against the edge of his desk. "We're old friends, Quinn and I. I was worried that he might be in some kind of financial trouble."

Melissa felt small. Her mother's implied warning about causing Quinn humiliation came back to her. "Why didn't he say anything?" she wondered aloud.

Mitch reached down and took one of Melissa's hands into both of his. "There's no harm done, now is there?"

Although Melissa wouldn't have admitted it to anyone, Mr. Williams's sympathy felt rather good. In some ways she missed being fussed over.

The lawyer was looking at the small gouges on her hand.

"I'm sorry about this, love. I'd never have recommended work at the cannery if I'd thought you really meant to follow through with it."

Despite the ache that had formed inside her the moment Gillian had made Quinn forget that he even had a wife, Melissa smiled. "I told you that I wanted to work," she reminded him.

He grinned ingenuously. "I know, Mrs. Rafferty, but I didn't believe you." He paused. "What are you going to do now?"

Melissa smoothed her calico skirts and sat up very straight. "I'm going to start a newspaper," she answered.

Mr. Williams let her hand drop. "What?"

"Port Riley needs its own paper," Melissa explained patiently.

"Just how do you mean to go about this?" Mitch challenged, and he sounded almost angry.

"I have no earthly idea," Melissa said, rising from her chair. "I only know that I'm going to do it."

With that she left Mr. Williams's office and walked down the outside stairs, her mind diverted, mercifully, from Quinn and his obvious fascination with Gillian.

Melissa didn't feel quite so resolute when, after five minutes, she was still standing on the rough plank sidewalk,
having no idea how to go after her shining dream of starting
a newspaper.

She would need presses and a building. Such items would
surely require vast sums to purchase.

Melissa stood gazing into the window of the general
store, seeing none of the merchandise displayed there. She
gnawed at her lower lip as her thoughts whirled.

It wasn't as though she didn't have money at her disposal.
There was probably enough in her trust fund to buy ten
newspapers, but Melissa's desire to make a success of herself on her own wits and merit had not abated. If she used
her inheritance to get her start, then the credit would not belong to her, but to her late father, who had built an enormous
fortune in timber and shipping, and to her brothers, who had
overseen the investments since his death.

The door of Kruger's Mercantile opened unexpectedly,
startling Melissa out of her quandary.

"It's lovely, isn't it?" chimed a happy female voice. "I think you'd look splendid in that shade of lavender."

Melissa turned to see a pretty young woman with thick brown hair and dancing hazel eyes watching her from the doorway of the mercantile. Reminded of Tess, her sister-in-law, she felt a pang of homesickness, but she covered that with a nervous chuckle. "I'm afraid I have no idea what you're talking about," she confessed.

"The dress!" the young lady cried good-naturedly, gesturing toward the window Melissa was standing before.

There was nothing to do but look at the dress, and when she did Melissa drew in her breath. The gown was made of pale orchid silk with a low neckline and puffed sleeves, and its very simplicity gave it a splendor all its own.

The woman was now standing beside the window, admiring the gown along with Melissa. She looked as proud and pleased as if she'd made the lovely garment herself.

"It's you," she said decisively. "It's really you."

Melissa was inclined to agree. In her mind's eye she could see herself wearing that wonderful gown, whirling around and around the ballroom of the new hotel—in Quinn's arms.

Melissa's sweet revelry was interrupted by another announcement. "I'm Dana Morgan—Mr. Kruger's niece."

Remembering her manners at last, Melissa turned, offering her hand in greeting. "Melissa Cor—Rafferty," she replied with a smile.

Dana's eyes were twinkling with merriment. "I confess that I already knew who you were. Do come in for a few minutes," she pleaded. "We'll have some soda water and talk."

Melissa's eyes strayed back to the dress in the window. To buy it would be an extravagance, but she couldn't go to the grand opening of the hotel in tattered calico. . . .

Maybe, she thought miserably, Quinn didn't mean to invite her to the party anyway. Maybe he and Gillian were planning to share the evening.

While Dana went to the fountain and drew flavored seltzer water from the taps Melissa stood admiring the dress. "Do you think it would fit?" she asked.

"Try it on," Dana responded practically. "Here, I'll get it out of the window."

Melissa slipped into the back room to change out of her calico and into the wondrous frock of silk.

The fit was perfect, and it was a delight to enjoy the familiar sensation of silk brushing against her skin again.

Mentally Melissa counted what remained of the sixty-odd dollars she had to spend. If she purchased the dress, she would need slippers, an ornament for her hair, and a petticoat. Fully a third of her funds would be gone.

She ought to have her head examined for thinking she could start a business without tapping her trust fund, but she still persisted in thinking exactly that.

She sighed as she came out of the back room wearing her calico again and feeling as Cinderella must have the day after the ball. Dana was waiting on a customer, but she approached Melissa as soon as she could.

"Well? What do you think?"

"It's very expensive," Melissa replied. It was so strange to worry about money.

Dana seemed to notice the disreputable dress Melissa wore for the first time. "But your husband is rich," she marveled. "Besides," she went on after a brief pause, "he has an account here. I'll just write down what you spend, and that will be all there is to it."

The mention of Quinn had swayed Melissa in one way: She would have the gown because she wanted him to see her in it. But she would never charge so much as a postage stamp to his account. "I can pay for the dress myself," she said.

Dana gave her no further argument. "Come and drink your soda," she said, setting the dress aside on the counter. "I haven't made a single friend since I arrived in this town, and I'm absolutely perishing for a nice, sociable chat."

Melissa joined Dana at the soda fountain counter and took a sip of the orange drink that had been drawn for her. She was realizing that her own chums were all either terminally married or off traveling somewhere. Like Dana, she'd missed the company of women her own age.

Dana related that she had come to Port Riley to teach, having just completed normal school in Seattle, but the position had fallen through at the last minute. She'd been forced to depend upon the kindness of her aunt and uncle, who had given her a place to stay and work to do.

"What happened to the job?" Melissa asked.

With a sigh, Dana answered bleakly, "They found a man and hired him instead. The school board felt that he'd be better able to control the children than I would."

Melissa's strong sense of justice was outraged. She muttered a word that widened Dana's eyes and then made her giggle.

"What about you, Melissa?" she asked after a few moments. "What brought you to Port Riley?"

Melissa didn't feel up to relating the whole grisly story, so she simply said, with a shrug, "I married Mr. Rafferty."

Once again Dana's eyes took in Melissa's old dress. "I surely never took him for a cheapskate," she said.

Melissa flushed and averted her eyes. Even though Quinn had hurt her, and badly, she couldn't let Dana's misconception stand. "I want to provide for myself," she told her friend.

Dana looked at her as though she'd gone mad, but she kept her opinion to herself. She helped Melissa choose a petticoat and slippers to go with the dress and was ringing up the sale when inspiration struck her customer.

Seeing a stack of paper tablets nearby, Melissa grabbed up ten, along with a pen and a bottle of ink. She would start writing another book that very day, and if her publishers bought it, there would soon be a small sum of money due her. In her spare time she would look for a building to house her newspaper and try to find a secondhand printing press.

Melissa stopped off at Quinn's railroad car to leave all but one of the notebooks, then hurried home with the rest of her purchases.

She hung the dress in the armoire and was about to settle herself at the desk and make notes of the story ideas that were brewing in her mind when Quinn suddenly walked in and spoiled everything.

To Melissa's utter and complete surprise, he was furious. "Don't you ever do anything like that again!" he shouted.

Melissa was taken aback, but only for a moment. "Anything like what?" she asked haughtily, raising her chin.

Quinn flung his arms wide of his body in a gesture of the purest agitation. "Anything like leaving!"

The memory of Gillian draping herself all over Quinn stung like venom, but she spoke in an even tone. "It seemed to me that my presence was quite superfluous, Mr. Rafferty."

A muscle in Quinn's jawline bunched. He muttered a swear word and strode across the room to the liquor cabinet. This time he did not resist temptation but poured himself a generous portion of brandy. It was when he turned to face Melissa, his mouth open to speak, that he saw the lavender dress through the half-closed door of the armoire.

He closed his mouth and crossed the room to touch the silken gown. "What's this?"

"It's a dress, Mr. Rafferty," Melissa said with disdainful patience. She hoped he wouldn't notice the writing materials she'd placed on the desk.

"Damn it, I know what it is," he snapped, and he was near again; Melissa could feel him directly behind her, and she grew flushed at the heat of his body so near.

She wouldn't have faced him, but he came around, looking at her quizzically, the brandy forgotten in his hand.

"You bought a dress," he mused, as though some great mystery was afoot. "Could it be, Mrs. Rafferty, that you want to go to the party at the hotel next week?"

Melissa blushed. "I certainly wouldn't intrude. I wasn't invited, you know."

The expression in Quinn's dark eyes was one of gentle amusement. "Of course you're invited. You're my wife."

She stepped back because Quinn was standing so close, and she knew what could happen when he did that. "I had no way of knowing that I was to be included, since ours is not a proper marriage."

Quinn remembered the brandy and set it aside. "We could make it proper," he suggested huskily.

Melissa retreated another step and nervously thrust her

hand into the pocket of her skirt. When she did, she found the money that Mitch Williams had refused to take from her that morning.

She reached underneath the mattress and brought out enough cash to make up for what she'd spent at the mercantile, then held it out to Quinn. "Here," she said.

Quinn was clearly baffled. "What—?"

"This is yours," she told him calmly. "When I tried to repay Mr. Williams this morning he told me that you had already taken care of the matter."

Quinn scowled at the money, making no move to accept it. His whim to make their marriage "proper" had evidently passed, for he looked furious again rather than amorous. "When and if you need money in the future, my dearest darling, I'll thank you to approach me and not my friends!"

Melissa stared at him. "Is that what Mr. Williams told you? That I walked up to him and asked for money?"

When Quinn ignored the bills she was holding out, Melissa flung the money into the air.

"He's a liar!" she cried.

Quinn gave her a scalding look that said it wasn't Mitch Williams he suspected of dishonesty and walked out.

"Oh, no, you don't!" Melissa cried, following after him at such a quick pace that she had to hold her skirts in her hands. "You're not going to walk out of here before this fight is over, Quinn Rafferty!"

Quinn wouldn't so much as look at her. He was placidly adjusting his collar as he went down the stairway, behaving just as though Melissa were invisible and mute. The maid, Helga, was standing at the bottom of the steps, all ears and eyes.

"I'll be right behind you no matter where you go!" Melissa insisted as Helga pressed herself against the wall like someone faced with a lighted stick of dynamite. "So you might as well stay here!"

Quinn had reached the entryway and was just about to open the door when Melissa darted around in front of him and barred his way, her arms outspread.

"I won't be called a liar," she said, "Not by you or anyone else."

Quinn sighed. "Melissa . . ."

Melissa stood her ground.

There was a gentling in Quinn's manner, and he slowly lifted his hands to brush Melissa's cheeks with the sides of his thumbs. "All right, I believe you. Now will you let me pass? I have some things to look into at the mill."

His touch had affected Melissa sorely, but she wasn't about to let Quinn know that. It would only make him more arrogant and cocksure. "Will you be home for supper?" she asked, as any wife would have done.

He shrugged. "I don't know. Things haven't been going well in the lumber camp lately. I might have to go back up the mountain."

The idea made Melissa feel strangely bereft. "You'd be gone all night?" she asked.

"Maybe for several days." Quinn grinned wickedly. "If I'm away that long, Mrs. Rafferty, will you miss me?"

Melissa opened the door and held out one arm in a sweeping gesture of dismissal. The man had such brass!

"Not for a moment, Mr. Rafferty," she replied.

Quinn laughed, shook his head, and left the house, his doting wife briskly shutting the door behind him.

Melissa watched from a window until Quinn was out of sight and then went back upstairs.

Although her mind was full of ideas for the new novel she meant to write, she felt too restive to sit down to her notes. Realizing that she had seen only one room on the entire second floor—Quinn's—she decided to do a bit of exploring.

There were three other bedrooms, Melissa discovered. One still held the scent of her mother's perfume, though there was no other sign that anyone had slept there the night before, and Helga was putting fresh sheets on the bed in the next.

The plain little maid gave Melissa a cautious look, as though she expected her to do something outrageous.

Melissa smiled and let herself out.

The next room brought her up short, for it was so obviously fitted out for a woman. The comforter on the bed was of pink satin, and there was a vanity table with a skirt that matched the bedspread.

Chairs covered in rose chintz faced a small ivory fireplace, and a delicate pair of slippers rested on the hearth.

Melissa knew that both Helga and Mrs. Wright slept downstairs in rooms behind the kitchen, and they were the only other people living in the house.

An uneasy sensation stirred in the pit of Melissa's stomach, but she was determined not to jump to conclusions. It seemed unlikely that the room had been Gillian's; she would have shared Quinn's quarters.

Practically on tiptoe, Melissa crossed the room and opened a lovely, wide armoire of honey-colored oak. It was filled with luscious evening gowns, day dresses, and wrappers.

Melissa stepped back, feeling as though she'd intruded on something very private. She carefully closed the doors of the armoire and crept out of the room. In the hallway her natural valor returned, and she went immediately in search of the housekeeper.

Mrs. Wright was in the kitchen, paring turnips for a stew. She looked up with her usual expression of polite alarm when Melissa entered her territory.

"That pink wrapper you lent me the other day—where did it come from?"

The woman sighed. "I think you know where it came from, Mrs. Rafferty," she hedged in a weary tone.

Melissa nodded. "I'd like you to tell me who uses that room, please," she said.

Mrs. Wright finished paring the turnip and reached for another. "You'd best ask your husband, missus," she replied, not unkindly.

If she was going to succeed as a reporter and the editor and publisher of a bold, innovative newspaper, Melissa reasoned, she would have to learn to be dogged in pursuing a point. She'd need the instincts, persistence, and initiative of a Nellie Bly.

She clasped her hands together behind her back and began to pace. Her gaze was intense, and it did seem to intimidate the housekeeper just a little.

"My husband," Melissa said, after this tense little interval had passed, "is away, possibly for several days. Who sleeps in that room, if you please?"

Mrs. Wright sighed again, sounding forlorn. "Very well," she answered, at length. "Mr. Rafferty's sister Mary stays there when she's home from school."

Melissa was intrigued. "I don't see why I should have had to drag that out of you that way. It's not as if he were keeping a mistress!"

The older woman flushed with indignation, probably offended by the suggestion that the saintly Mr. Rafferty might stoop to keeping a paramour. "Miss Mary is real special, and her brother is choosy about how she's treated."

"It's odd that he didn't mention her," Melissa said speculatively. "Especially when you consider that I've told him more than he wanted to know about my brothers."

Mrs. Wright broke down and smiled at that. "It takes time, Mrs. Rafferty, for a man and woman to get to know each other well," she said gently. "There's a lot your husband hasn't told you, and a lot you still need to say to him. You might be a lifetime getting around to all of it."

Melissa hoped that she would grow old with Quinn, but she had her doubts. If he kept on being as cussed as he had been, he probably wouldn't live to see forty.

She glanced at the pile of carrots that still needed scraping and felt yet another twinge of nostalgia. At home she'd often helped Maggie fix meals; she enjoyed cooking and was good at it.

"Would you like some help?" she ventured to inquire.

Mrs. Wright must have been a perceptive person. "Yes," she said quite formally, "if you must know, my feet hurt, and I'd like to lie down for fifteen or twenty minutes."

Melissa was thrilled to step into the culinary breach. She waved the housekeeper aside and began scraping and chopping carrots.

She wasn't conscious of Quinn's presence until he spoke

to her from just the other side of the cutting board, startling her so badly that she nearly stabbed herself.

"Do you do everything with the same fevered energy, Mrs. Rafferty?"

Melissa smiled, wildly glad that her husband was home. "Why didn't you tell me that you have a sister?" she inquired, ignoring his question because she knew he hadn't expected an answer.

"You didn't ask," Quinn said, helping himself to a slice of the peach pie Mrs. Wright had been saving for dessert. He sat down at the kitchen table and began to eat.

Melissa was determined to be the docile wife, at least for the next few minutes. If she could manage brief intervals of conventional behavior, she might get better at it over a period of time. She found a mug in the china cupboard and went to the stove to fill it with coffee.

Quinn looked at her in surprise when she set the cup down in front of him, smiling pleasantly.

"Would you like sugar or cream?"

He shook his head. "Sit down." The words were delivered as an order, but there was no unkindness in them, so Melissa complied, folding her hands in her lap.

"Tell me about Mary," she said.

Quinn's gaze dropped to what remained of his pie, but he didn't lift his fork again. "Mary is seventeen," he told Melissa quietly, "and she attends a special school in Seattle."

"What kind of school?"

A ragged sigh escaped Quinn. He was silent for a long time before he answered, "My sister is blind."

Melissa was stunned for a moment, but then she realized that Mary Rafferty must have adjusted rather well to her handicap if she possessed an armoire full of ball gowns. "When did she lose her sight?"

Quinn's answer was sobering. "Last year."

Melissa reached out tentatively to touch her husband's hand. "I'm sorry," she told him softly.

He drew back. "I don't need your pity, Melissa, and neither does Mary."

Melissa could scarcely have been more taken aback if he'd thrown his coffee in her face. "I didn't mean—"

Quinn pushed back his chair and stood up, and anything he might have said was forestalled by Mrs. Wright's inopportune return from her nap.

Mr. Rafferty left the room, and this time Melissa didn't have the heart to go after him.

She waited until she knew he was out of the house, then went upstairs to work on her notes.

Instead of planning her new project, however, she ended up writing a long, heartfelt statement of her situation to her sister-in-law, Fancy. All three of her brothers' wives were dear to her, but Jeff's wife Fancy had an especially gentle nature, and Melissa found it easy to confide in her.

When the dispatch was finished Melissa found an envelope, addressed it, and hurried off to locate the post office. If she was quick, she could mail the letter before closing time.

Twilight was falling as she started home again. Spring was on its way, though, and the days were getting longer. She waved at Dana when she passed the mercantile and exchanged a pleasant greeting with the lamplighter.

By the time she reached the train depot Melissa was in high spirits. Her energy was renewed, and she planned to scour the want ads in the *Seattle Times* for a used printing press as soon as supper was over.

She glanced toward the railroad car, thinking of the happy days she would spend there writing her book. Even as she watched an ancient engine backed onto the spur and attached itself to Quinn's car with a jarring clank.

Quinn himself appeared on the platform, smoking a cheroot and looking worried, and although Melissa called out to him and waved, he either didn't hear her or chose not to notice.

She was unaccountably injured by this and stood watching in bewilderment and frustration as the two-car train steamed its way out of the depot. Melissa could hear the boiler, and occasionally the whistle, long after Quinn's coach had disappeared from sight.

Slowly she started toward the house she had come to regard as home, her lower lip caught between her teeth, her shoulders stooped.

Darkness had fallen by the time Melissa let herself into the house by the kitchen door, and Mrs. Wright laid one hand to her elderly heart and drew her breath sharply at her appearance. It seemed Melissa was forever startling the poor woman.

Mrs. Wright's surprise at her entrance soon turned to gentle concern. "Why, what is it, child? You look downright sorrowful."

Melissa sighed. "I guess I'm just feeling lonesome," she said.

Mrs. Wright smiled, spooning fragrant stew into a china tureen. "He'll be back, Mrs. Rafferty," she said. "He'll be back."

It was true, of course, but Melissa couldn't seem to pull herself up by her bootstraps and get on with the evening. She missed Quinn with a keenness that intensified with every passing moment.

"I don't think I want any supper," she announced, and then she went up the rear stairway to the second floor and made her way along the hall to the master bedroom.

There was a fire burning on the hearth, and the lamps were lit, but the warmth and light couldn't reach into Melissa's heart.

She went to the window, drew back a curtain, and stood staring down at the sidewalk, willing Quinn to walk through the front gate, whistling.

A knock sounded at the door, and when Melissa turned around Helga was just entering, a tray in her hands. "Mrs. Wright says you've got to eat," the maid said, bracing herself for an argument.

Melissa only gestured for her to set down the tray and turned back to the window. Even though she knew that Quinn was far away, she still tried to conjure him up.

Nine

Frost made intricate curlicues on the windows of the railroad car, and the March air was so cold that Quinn stretched to reach the clothes he'd laid out the night before and pulled them on before getting out of bed.

Even then he was shivering as he dashed across the car to throw more coal into the little potbellied stove in the corner.

There was a rap at the door, and, never having been fond of mornings, he yelled, "Come in, damn it."

Since he'd expected the foreman of his timber crew, he was chagrined to be greeted by a good-looking and vaguely familiar blond woman carrying a steaming pot of fresh coffee. The scent of it restored Quinn's faith in civilization.

"Mornin'," the woman chimed. "My name's Becky Sever, and I'm here to help out the cook for a few days."

Quinn nodded and gratefully accepted the cup of coffee she poured for him before setting the blue enamel pot on the small stove to stay warm. Now that he'd had a chance to think about it, he recalled that Becky lived in a shack just a few miles away with a small child and a no-account husband. She came to help out in the cookhouse whenever

Wong, the regular cook, wanted a day off or fell behind in his work.

Quinn's thoughts turned to the past and the hardships his mother had known, living on this same mountain, tied to a man who'd seemed to delight in making her life miserable. He wondered if things were the same for Becky.

Becky answered the unspoken question by saying somewhat harriedly, at the door of the car, "I'm grateful for a chance to work, Mr. Rafferty. Jake can't seem to find a job that suits him, and my little girl needs so many things." She paused, looking shy as she drew her ragged woolen shawl more tightly around her shoulders. "The men'll be comin' in for breakfast in the next few minutes if you want to eat with them."

Quinn nodded and thanked Becky, and then she went out.

He drank two more cups of coffee before pulling on his cork boots, gloves, and heavy woolen coat. Remembering that Becky had been wearing nothing more than a shawl over her skimpy dress, he shivered as he stepped out of the car into the biting chill of dawn.

The scents of woodsmoke and fried pork filled the air as Quinn crossed the distance between the spur of track and the cookhouse. Here and there shreds of dirty snow lay on the ground, but the earth was reawakening, and spring was imminent.

Despite rumors that all was not well on his timber crews, the men seemed happy to see Quinn, and they included him in their boisterous conversations as they consumed heaping platefuls of meat, eggs, and toasted bread.

Becky Sever hurried between the tables, refilling coffee cups. She smiled a great deal and endured the men's good-natured teasing without taking offense. Her little girl, who looked to be about five, sat contentedly on the hearth, playing with a one-eyed rag doll.

Quinn was once again reminded of the old days, and he longed for Melissa. When she was around she kept him so distracted that there was no time for looking back into the past.

When breakfast was over the foreman lingered, as did a

couple of representatives from the labor union. The men had voted in favor of the alliance months before, and there had been grumbling and threats of trouble ever since.

Quinn sat watching them over the rim of his coffee cup, waiting. They'd demanded this meeting; they could make the first move.

"The men ain't makin' enough money," one of the strangers finally said. He was nothing more than a lad wearing a cheap suit and depending on bravado to see him through.

Quinn sighed. "They're making as much as any other crew in the state," he replied truthfully. Before Melissa had entered his life, when he'd still been able to think straight, he'd made a thorough investigation of the matter.

The foreman, a seasoned old bull of the woods named Eric Jergensen, gave Quinn a beleaguered look. "I try to tell them, Mr. Rafferty, but they don't listen—"

The union men broke in, both jawing at once, and so the parley went. No one paid any attention to anyone, and nothing was accomplished.

After an hour had passed Quinn was so disgusted that he ordered everybody but Becky, her child, and Wong out of the cookhouse.

"Do you think they'll strike?" Becky asked as she gathered the enamel mugs that had been left on the rough-hewn trestle table.

Quinn shrugged tiredly. He'd traveled all the way up that damned mountain and nearly frozen his backside off during the night, and for what? Things were worse than they had been before.

Becky was walking away when he stopped her by asking, "Does it bother you—being the only woman in camp, I mean?"

She smiled trustingly, her brown eyes alight. "I believe I have a few protectors among the loggers," she answered evenly. "Besides, I reckon it's safer here than it is over to our cabin right now."

Quinn realized that he was keeping her from her work and said nothing more. He did wish, suddenly and sorely, that he could go home.

He left the cookhouse and spent the morning felling timber, working as hard as any of his men did. Whatever labor problems the company might have, he knew he was respected and liked for his ability to not only keep the pace, but set it.

During the midday meal he hardly noticed Becky, because the workers were giving him an earful—what they wanted and didn't want, what they needed. Quinn listened with his good right ear—he was stone deaf in his left, thanks to the old man's temper—and when the food was gone he went back to the timber and manned his end of a crosscut saw until the day was over.

Quinn had been brought up tough, and he was no stranger to hard work, physical or otherwise. Even so, he was so tired that night that he could barely eat, and he fell asleep sprawled out on the fur bedspread, still wearing his clothes.

By the time Becky arrived first thing the next morning, with another pot of coffee, he missed Melissa so badly that he was on the point of walking down the mountain.

"It's nice and warm in here," she said cheerfully, and Quinn shivered.

"If you say so. Your husband—his name is Jake, isn't it?"

Becky nodded, her eyes wide and worried. "Yes."

"How does he feel about your working over here?"

She averted her gaze for a moment, looking shamefaced. "I told him I was lookin' after a sick neighbor woman, old Mrs. Higgins." She stopped and shook her head. "My man'd be real mad if he knew we were here."

Quinn sighed. He didn't like interfering in a marriage, and by keeping Becky on the payroll he was doing just that. "He's bound to find out the truth sooner or later," he reasoned. "What will you do then?"

Becky stuck out her chin. "No matter what, I won't let him stop me 'fore Margaret's got her shoes and her reader for first grade," she said. "I'll be here every day, as long as there's work, Mr. Rafferty, unless you send me away."

Quinn had already discerned that Becky was a hard worker, but it was the echoes in his mind, the memories of another woman's suffering, that made him say, "If you ever need permanent work, come and see me. There might be a place for you at the new hotel."

Delight brightened Becky's tired eyes. She nodded and left the railroad car to go on about her business.

The building where the newspaper had been located was three streets back from Center Avenue, and it was as depressing a sight as Melissa had ever seen. The walls were charred and jagged, resembling rotted teeth. Peering inside, she saw that the twisted corpses of desks and bookshelves and presses still lay on the floor where they'd died their writhing deaths.

She shivered, chilled by both the destruction before her and the insipid rain that had been drizzling down all morning.

"It's hopeless," said Dana Morgan, shaking her head so that her bonnet ribbons wiggled under her chin. "I think Uncle George is right, Melissa. You're going to have to put up a building, since there isn't a single one to rent in the whole of Port Riley."

Melissa hadn't expected to be able to resurrect the old newspaper, she'd come to investigate, to get a sense of what had happened there. She felt total desolation.

Her courage flagging a little, she turned away from the ruin with a sigh. "Somehow," she said, "I'll find a place. I know I will." She brightened a little as an idea struck her. "What about the people who published the newspaper—do they still live around here?"

Dana looked thoughtful, and when the realization struck it was visible in her hazel eyes. "Glory be!" she cried out, startling Melissa so much that she flinched. She started striding down the sidewalk, and Melissa had to scramble after her.

"Well?" Melissa demanded, irate. She hated it when people acted in a mysterious fashion.

"I just remembered Miss Bradberry!"

"Miss who?" Melissa asked, grateful that Dana was sharing her umbrella, if not her revelation.

"Miss Bradberry is the daughter of the man who owned the Port Riley *Courier!*"

"And?"

"And if anybody could tell you about the newspaper business, it would be Emma Bradberry." Dana drew in a breath and let it out in a huff. "Goodness mercy, Melissa—for a person with a university education, you can be very slow."

Melissa considered being insulted and decided against it. She needed all the help she could get, even if that meant intruding upon Miss Emma Bradberry and putting up with disparaging remarks from Dana.

Miss Bradberry lived in one of the pretty little saltbox houses facing the water, just around the bend from the new hotel. Melissa tried not to think about that place or its owner; she missed Quinn desperately, even though he'd been gone only a day and a half.

At their knock the plump spinster appeared not at the door, but in the side yard. "Come this way," she called, beckoning with one hand. "I cannot let you in by the front door because Sir Lancelot is lying on the rug in front of it."

Melissa gave Dana a look. "Sir Lancelot is lying on the rug?" she whispered.

"He's a cat, silly," Dana confided as they walked toward the place where Miss Bradberry was waiting.

She was standing on the steps of a screened sun porch, wearing a gray serge dress and a floppy straw hat like the one Katherine wore when she worked in her rose garden. Hurriedly Miss Bradberry shuffled Melissa and Dana inside the house, much as a hen would gather stray chicks under its wings.

"Imagine going calling on such a day!" she sputtered, shaking rainwater from her patched skirt.

Melissa and Dana glanced at each other and then away. "Miss Bradberry," Dana began, "I do hope we haven't inconvenienced you by dropping in unexpectedly. It's just that Melissa here means to start a newspaper—"

"Start a newspaper?" echoed Miss Bradberry in a shrill voice as she hurried through a small, beautifully kept parlor to stand beside a stove glistening with chrome. She continued to shake out her skirts. "Nonsense. No woman ever started a newspaper."

"I'm sure some woman has done it somewhere," said

Melissa firmly, Katherine Corbin's daughter through and through.

"Quite so," agreed Emma unexpectedly. "Did you know that I'm a twin?"

Dana cleared her throat. "Don't you think I should introduce my friend to you in the proper fashion, Miss Bradberry? This is Melissa Rafferty—"

"Rafferty?" interrupted the spinster. "Any relation to the rascal who burned down Papa's newspaper building?"

Melissa felt the starch flow out of her knees. She dropped into a rocking chair only to be terrified by the leaping, hissing indignation of the huge gray and white tabby cat she'd displaced.

One hand to her heart, her breath coming in ragged gasps, Melissa calmed herself enough to ask, "Are you saying that my husband was responsible for the fire?"

Miss Bradberry bent forward, squinting as she peered at Melissa through obviously myopic eyes. "Husband? Goodness, no—you're not old enough to have a husband!"

Melissa threw up her hands in defeat while Dana chuckled and laid a reassuring palm on her friend's shoulder. "We've all heard rumors about the fire, but nothing was ever proven, was it?"

"My papa knows, all right. It was that no-good Eustice Rafferty. Terrible, drunken man—beat his children, you know. And it's generally known that he murdered his own wife."

Melissa was on the edge of her chair by that point, but pressure from Dana's hand and some unnamed instinct kept her from asking any more questions. "I want to buy a printing press," she said instead.

"Papa lost the new ones in the fire," Miss Bradberry said. "Did I tell you that I'm a twin?"

Melissa let out a sigh, and Dana found her way to a chair, making sure there was no cat there before she sat down.

"My sister Doris, God rest her soul, was three minutes older than I," Miss Emma imparted. "They called her Doris—for Papa's only sister—right off, but you can't possibly imagine what a hard time they had thinking up a name for me. I went without one until I was five, you know, and then I just got tired of waiting and named myself."

Melissa's head was practically spinning. Was Eustice Rafferty Quinn's father? Had he really beaten his children and killed his wife? And why on earth would anyone make a little girl go without a name until she was five years old?

"Of course!" Emma blurted out, startling everyone except Sir Lancelot, a long-haired white cat who had remained placidly on the rag rug in front of the door throughout the interview. "Papa's old press wasn't burned up in the fire. It's right outside, in the woodshed."

Melissa sat up finishing-school straight. "Is it for sale?"

"I suppose. I certainly have no use for it, and Papa says if he never sees another bottle of printer's ink it will be too soon."

Moments later Melissa was inspecting the press. It was covered with dust and cobwebs, and looked as though it dated back to the revolution, but her heart leapt with the hope that she could have it for her own. Later, when her paper was a resounding success, she could buy a better one.

"How much?" she asked, seeing no point in beating around the bush.

Miss Bradberry didn't bat an eyelash. "Forty dollars. Have I mentioned that I'm a twin?"

"Sold!" cried Melissa.

"I believe you did bring it up," said Dana.

Melissa pulled two twenty-dollar bills from the pocket of her dress and handed them over, and Miss Bradberry gave her a receipt written in a flourishing hand. It was agreed that Dana's uncle would come for the press with a wagon as soon as possible.

"I'm in business!" Melissa crowed the moment she and Dana were out of Miss Bradberry's yard and hurrying down the road toward the main part of town.

It was late afternoon, and the rain had abated, although the sun was still behind the clouds. Dana glanced up at the sky and replied, "I'm so hungry!"

Melissa laughed. "I swear you're as flighty as Miss Emma Bradberry!"

Dana smiled. "Have I told you that I'm a twin?" she asked mischievously.

Melissa shook her head, but anything she might have said was drowned out by the shrill whistle of an arriving train. She squared her shoulders and lifted her chin, but from Dana's knowing look, it was obvious Melissa hadn't fooled her. Melissa was hoping against hope that Quinn was home.

Sure enough, the same noisy steam engine that had hauled him away was now bringing him back again. Melissa's heart leapt into her throat, and she forgot her friend and her printing press as she ran toward the railroad spur and waited shamelessly beside the tracks.

Quinn came out presently, and when he looked at Melissa she saw surprise and weary pleasure in his eyes. He was dressed like a lumberjack, he smelled of grease and sweat, and his chin was covered in prickly stubble.

He had never looked better to her.

His brash brown eyes swept over her dusty dress, and his mouth quirked at one corner. "Hello, ragamuffin," he said gruffly.

Melissa might have flung herself into his arms if she hadn't sensed that the whole town was looking on. She and Quinn were the subject of much gossip as it was.

"I've missed you," she confessed, averting her eyes. She was afraid to look at him, because then she might blurt out that she loved him. He'd apologize for not feeling the same way, and she would feel wretched.

Quinn offered his arm, for all the world as though he were wearing a top hat and tails, and Melissa shyly took it.

Together, oblivious to the stir they created, the Raffertys walked home.

Once they reached the house Melissa went to the kitchen to discuss dinner with Mrs. Wright while Quinn climbed the stairs to the master bedroom. He was in the bathroom, singing over the sound of running water, when Melissa arrived.

There was a mirror over the bureau, and she looked at herself in despair. Her dress was precisely as her mother had described it: horrid. Her hair was stringy from the combination of dust from Miss Bradberry's shed and the afternoon rainstorm, and there was a smudge of dirt on her face.

And yet, for all this, some deep, driving instinct told Melissa that she mustn't wait any longer for Quinn's declaration of love. After all, it might never come.

Quietly, while her husband engaged in a noisy bath, Melissa unwound her hair from its heavy plait, brushed it until it gleamed, and then braided it again. She washed her face and her hands and then, trembling, she stripped to her camisole and bloomers.

She found, to her mortification, that she could go no further, but that mysterious impulse to go to Quinn as a wife had not abated. Indeed, it had grown keener with every passing moment.

Despairing because she had no perfume, no allurements other than her own untried, quivering body, Melissa crept into the bathroom, moving as silently as a geisha. Her eyes were downcast.

"My God," she heard Quinn breathe.

She lifted her gaze to his face. He looked like a shameless hedonist, lying sprawled in that mammoth tub, a glass of brandy in one hand and a cigar jutting from his strong white teeth.

Uncharacteristic shyness overwhelmed her, and she would have fled except for Quinn's raspy command, "Don't go, Melissa. Please."

She stood still where she was, too stricken to speak.

Finally Quinn held his hand out to her. She went to him but took the cigar instead of his hand, making a face that drew a raucous burst of amusement from him. She tossed the offending thing into the commode, grimacing, and Quinn laughed again.

Melissa knelt beside the high edge of that great marble tub, and Quinn reached out and grasped her shoulder in one hand, as if to stop her from rising.

She heard his hoarse plea for her to stay again, but she was never sure whether he had actually repeated the words or she had just imagined them. In any case, she was trapped. She could not leave him.

He took her hand and laid it gently on his chest, which was matted with twists and sworls of glistening golden brown hair. She had never touched a man in so intimate a way, and the freedom, the glorious daring, nearly took her breath away.

Quinn groaned and closed his eyes as she touched nipples like brown buttons; he bore her explorations as long as he could before wrenching her into the tub. She landed astride him and felt his hardness touching her, but his hands created other distractions.

He made no move to open her camisole or lower it, as he had done before, but instead cupped water in his palms and made her wet. Her nipples leapt against the transparent fabric, aching to be free, to be Quinn's.

He chuckled low in his throat at their obedience, then leaned forward to tease one with the gentle scraping of his teeth.

Melissa moaned, so ferocious was her need, and tried to bare herself, but Quinn stopped her by grasping her wrists and holding them at her sides. And then he went back to taunting her with exquisite skill, making her certain that she would go mad if he didn't have her.

She was half blinded by need when he finally unfastened the buttons of her camisole and peeled it away from her breasts. Now he took her full into his mouth, and Melissa cried out with delight, but it was only the beginning of the joys he meant to teach her.

Now his hands were slowly lowering her drawers. She was whimpering as he caressed her fleshy, tingling bottom, but when he brought one hand around and began to stroke her she threw back her head and waited to die of the pleasure.

"Have me!" she pleaded when the joy became so exquisite, so delicious that she was sure she could not bear it.

"Not like this," he said, his mouth lazy at her nipple, "not the first time."

The rhythmic motion of his hand increased in pace, and Melissa stiffened violently as the first crushing wave crashed over her, nearly crushing her beneath it. "Oh!" she cried out. "Oh—my—"

"That should remove any doubt that we're really married," Quinn remarked with maddening calm as Melissa's body buckled in another primal response to his touch.

She gave a long, low wail and then fell against him, exhausted. After a time he rose from the water, drawing her with him, supporting her by both arms. He dried her with a towel and carried her to the bed, and his own powerful body was still covered in tiny droplets of cool water as he stretched out over her.

Melissa felt as though she'd had too much to drink.

"You've never done this before?" Quinn asked softly. His breath was cool against her temple.

She shook her head. "Never," she managed to say.

He nudged her legs apart ever so gently with one of his knees. "It hurts a little the first time," he warned.

Melissa didn't care. Everything within her craved union with this man. She ran her hands up and down his broad back in desperate caresses, urging him closer, and then she felt him pressing at her, tremendously hard. "I love you," she whispered into his left ear, but he made no response.

He eased into her, and every bit of progress he made increased the strange mingling of pain and pleasure Melissa felt. She finally arched her hips in a powerful thrust, and there was a stinging hurt as the barrier was irrevocably crossed.

Quinn cried out at this, muttering her name like a man tossing in a fever, moving at an ever-increasing pace as he linked himself with her and then withdrew. Over and over again he repeated this process until Melissa was as fevered as he was, until she was flinging herself at him. Her body was demanding something from his; she didn't know what it wanted, and she didn't care.

Their bodies were moving frantically, damp with exertion, before that shattering moment of reward came. Melissa knew then what the French meant when they spoke of the "little death."

Quinn's climax was evidently just as cataclysmic in force, for he made some senseless plea of heaven and delved so deeply into Melissa that another series of sweet ripplings were set off inside her. She was weeping softly when her husband gathered enough breath to ask, "Did I hurt you?"

The concern in his voice touched Melissa almost as profoundly as his lovemaking had. She entangled both her hands in Quinn's hair and tried to say again that she loved him, but she could not. She simply didn't have the strength to speak.

Finally she shook her head from side to side to assure him that she was all right.

He slid down over her presently, kissing her collarbone, the rounded upper parts of her breasts, teasing and tasting her nipples. Melissa was conscious not only of his tender attendance, but of the softness of the fur bedspread beneath them. A sense of sweet wickedness swept over her, and again she whispered to Quinn that she loved him.

He made no verbal response, but Melissa determined to think about that later, when the fog was cleared from her mind.

Their joining was easier the second time; there was almost no pain, and Melissa gave herself up to her husband as a willing sacrifice.

When it was over Quinn carried her back to the bathroom. He filled the tub with hot, clean water, and they bathed each other. That enterprise sent them back to the bed, although this time they took refuge under the covers because darkness had fallen and the room had turned cold.

The night was long and sweet, and when Melissa awakened in the morning she mourned it.

It might have been a dream, what had taken place between her and Quinn, for the bed and the room were empty.

In the distance the solemn *thom-thom-thom* of church bells rang out.

Ten

Melissa could not face the prospect of wearing either of her charity dresses again. Although her determination to succeed on her own terms was still with her, she was not the same person she had been even the day before. She had some new concerns now, and pleasing Quinn was one of them.

With a sigh Melissa got out of bed and attended to her morning ablutions. When the ritual was complete she went across the hall, wearing the pink wrapper, to Mary's room. There, after gently riffling through the armoire, she appropriated a crisp black sateen skirt and a royal blue blouse. It bothered her that she couldn't ask permission, but there was no helping that.

When she got downstairs Melissa learned that Quinn had already eaten and left the house, and she was a little injured by this, although she'd never have said so outright.

"You look real pretty today, Mrs. Rafferty," Mrs. Wright ventured to say as she served Melissa her breakfast at the kitchen table. Eating alone in the imposing dining room had held no appeal.

"Thank you," Melissa responded, beaming. There had been a marked deficiency of compliments since she'd taken to wearing calico, and it felt very good to be admired again. "Do you know where my husband has gotten himself off to?"

There was an expression of discreet wisdom in Mrs. Wright's eyes indicating that she was aware of the turning point Quinn and Melissa had reached.

Melissa dropped her gaze, embarrassed, while Mrs. Wright poured coffee for her and answered graciously, "Mr. Rafferty normally goes to the mill on Sunday mornings, not being a churchgoing man."

Melissa smiled to herself. She'd just pay Quinn a call; it was time she had a firsthand look at the enterprise anyway. "What does he do while he's there? Saw boards?"

Mrs. Wright chuckled and shook her head. "I believe he goes over the books. The millhands get paid on Monday, you see."

In Port Hastings the millhands and shipyard workers got their wages on Saturday, at the end of their shift, and Melissa said as much.

Mrs. Wright was at the sink, washing dishes. "Mr. Rafferty doesn't believe in doing that," she responded firmly. "Too many of the men would spend all their money on whiskey and women. Their families would suffer."

The point was a sensible one, and Melissa conceded it. After finishing her breakfast she carried her plate and silverware to the sink and then hurried out. The day was sunny, though still a little cold, and Melissa wore a pretty woolen cloak of blue plaid that she'd found in the closet off the entryway.

When Melissa had located the mill, which was at the opposite end of town from the hotel, she sought out the small building that probably housed the office.

Sure enough, Quinn was there, and the smile in his eyes when he looked up at her from his work belied his solemn expression. "Good morning, Mrs. Rafferty," he said in a low voice that stirred echoes of last night's responses within Melissa.

She executed a mocking little curtsy. "Mr. Rafferty," she responded with teasing formality.

Quinn rose from his desk and rounded it to approach her. He slid his hands under her cloak to rest on the curves of her waist and took in her clothes with a look of puzzled amusement. "Is this what you looked like before the calico crusade began?" he teased.

Melissa made a face, albeit a pretty one, and stood closer to him. "I'm willing to make a few concessions," she admitted somewhat grudgingly.

Quinn laughed and tightened his embrace, and Melissa felt like a fool because her cheeks were hot and all the starch had gone out of her knees. Despite her education and all the traveling she'd done, she was, where this man was concerned, as witless as a bumpkin. When he bent his head and kissed her without a word of warning, Melissa was left feeling as though she'd had the wind knocked out of her.

Quinn was breathing rather heavily himself when he set Melissa away from him and stepped back. He shoved one hand through his hair and avoided her eyes as he said raggedly, "You'd better go home."

Melissa delighted in having the smallest power over him, and she smiled as she came close to straighten his collar. "Why?"

He sounded almost as though he had something caught in his throat. "Because I'm about to take you right here, that's why."

The mill office was small, and three of its four walls had windows. Melissa retreated a step. She blushed a little as she asked, "You're not going to spend the whole day working, are you?"

Quinn smiled wickedly. "Have patience, Mrs. Rafferty. I'll take very good care of you when I get home."

Even though a warm tremor moved through her at the prospect, Melissa was outraged at his assumption that she would be willing to toddle home and twiddle her thumbs until he was ready to favor her with his affections. "Of all the—"

"Now, now," Quinn warned, grinning. "We've made some advances. Let's not spoil everything by bickering."

Melissa was calmer, but no less determined. She looked around until she spotted a single high-backed chair beside a glass-fronted bookcase. "If you're staying here," she said, sitting, "so am I."

Quinn sighed in apparent defeat and snatched his suit coat from a peg on the wall. "You win, Calico. I'll come back and do the payroll tonight."

Melissa had second thoughts. She'd made plans for Quinn's evening, and they didn't include writing out pay vouchers. She stood slowly, forced to make yet another concession. "I'll go for a walk or something," she said. "I'd like another look at the hotel."

Quinn shook his head. "Don't," he said. "The place is isolated, and there won't be anyone around, since it's Sunday."

Melissa had opened the door, and she stood looking back at him. The sunlight pouring in through the windows gave his brown hair a glistening richness that made her long to plunge her fingers into it. "All right, dear," she said sweetly.

He was already seated at his desk again, bent over the paperwork before him. "Umm-hmm," he replied.

Melissa ignored the hotel, although it pulled at her like the proverbial magnet, and concentrated on exploring Port Riley to its boundaries. It was a small but industrious place, very friendly, and boasted a library, among other amenities. Melissa made plans to return the next day and establish herself as a patron.

She was walking along one of the rutted roads behind Quinn's sawmill when Rowina Brown came out of a house with a sagging stoop, wiping her hands on a checked gingham apron, and called out a greeting.

Melissa stopped at the gate, pleased to see her friend from the cannery again and hopeful that she'd been forgiven for working at a job when she was in no danger of starvation. She was beaming as Rowina came down the walk.

"Come in, come in," Rowina said, gesturing wildly, and Melissa laughed as she worked the latch on the gate and stepped through.

The yard was neat and small, and though Rowina's house was weathered there was an air of pride about the place, and of dignity.

Inside, two other women, Indians like Rowina, were seated at a table. They both looked up when Melissa was brought in and introduced, but only the older woman smiled. The younger one gave the caller a defiant look and dropped her gaze back to her beadwork.

Rowina introduced Starflower as her mother. The beautiful young girl, with her flowing, raven-black hair, was Charlotte, Rowina's daughter.

Melissa had been walking for several hours, and she was tired. She gratefully accepted Rowina's offer of a chair and a cup of tea. "What's that you're making?" she asked of Charlotte. Although her interest was genuine, Melissa was also trying to reach some kind of pleasant accord with Rowina's daughter.

Enormous brown eyes met Melissa's, snapping with challenge. "We're making belts," she answered, speaking slowly and carefully, as though to an idiot.

"Charlotte!" Rowina protested.

There was no remorse in Charlotte—that was perfectly apparent, even though she smiled. Melissa wondered what she could possibly have done to make a total stranger hate her with such immediacy and force.

She took a steadying sip of her tea and turned to Rowina, who was seated again, her brown, scarred fingers moving nimbly as she plied her beadwork. "Are you still shucking oysters at the cannery?" she asked, because she could think of absolutely no other beginning to a conversation.

Rowina nodded. "I'll be doing that as long as I'm able," she answered. She paused to assess what she could see of Melissa's borrowed clothes. "Looks like you've come up in the world."

"She was never down," Charlotte put in without raising her eyes from her beadwork.

Melissa was hungry, as it was early afternoon and she'd had nothing to eat since breakfast. "It's time I was getting home," she said by way of excusing herself, and she stood.

"Thank you for the tea."

Rowina looked completely satisfied by their brief exchange. She nodded placidly and went right on with her beadwork.

Melissa was just opening the gate when Charlotte caught up to her and, with a malicious glint in her eyes, announced, "Mr. Rafferty won't turn his back on Miss Gillian just because you're here. The need of her, it's in his blood."

The words made Melissa feel as though a crosscut saw were tearing at her middle, but she hid that reaction behind a saucy smile. She'd had enough of Charlotte's unfounded hostility. "Are you jealous of his affections?" she asked.

Charlotte had apparently expected her ploy to reduce Melissa to fits of tears and handkerchief fluttering. Now that it had failed, she was at a loss.

Melissa turned and walked away, leaving Charlotte to stand in the yard looking after her.

Passing the mill on her way back to the main part of town, Melissa heard shouts and laughter, and for an instant she was very homesick. She rounded the office and the mill itself to investigate, and there, in an open lot beyond, a baseball game was going on.

Melissa looked on enviously as the batter stepped up to home plate and got ready to swing. Her own family played baseball, since there was such a horde of them, and she'd hit many a home run in her time.

The batter swung hard, and there was a satisfying crack as the hard wood and the ball met. The sphere soared into the blue sky, and Melissa paced on the sidelines, silently cheering the player as he ran around the bases and returned home in a glorious slide just as the catcher bent to put him out.

"Safe!" cried a familiar masculine voice.

Cheers erupted all around, but Melissa's attention had shifted from the game to the man who was serving as umpire. Quinn was standing directly behind the catcher, his tie undone, his sleeves rolled up to his elbows.

Melissa glared at him until he sensed her presence and looked in her direction, a process that took several minutes.

When Quinn noticed his wife he summoned someone in from the sidelines to take his place.

"I thought you had to work all day," she said accusingly. Melissa's ire was based on the fact that she loved baseball and all the players on both teams were men. She knew that if she asked to play, she would be refused, and that rankled.

Quinn frowned, more in bewilderment than displeasure, and rested his hands on her arms. "I'm finished," he said reasonably.

Melissa looked at the field, her eyes bright with blue fire, and then back at Quinn. "I want to play."

His frown deepened. "Why?"

"Because it's fun," Melissa replied, folding her arms. Braced for injustice.

Quinn sighed and shoved a hand through his hair. "It's not my game, Melissa," he explained. "It's theirs—the mill-hands'. And they don't allow women on the teams."

Melissa turned on her heel and stormed away toward home. She was most disappointed that Quinn didn't follow her.

Neither Mrs. Wright nor Helga was anywhere about, it being Sunday, so Melissa made a sandwich for herself and sat down to eat. She barely tasted the food, but when she'd finished she felt a little better. Since there was still something left of the day, she decided to make use of it and set out for the new hotel, as she'd wanted to all day. Her desire to explore the place again was simply too strong to be resisted.

Just as Quinn had said it would be, the hotel was quiet, since no one was there working, but Melissa found the solitude a comfort instead of a threat. Her mind and heart were still in an uproar, and she was so full of questions and energy and hurt that she was sure to burst.

The natural pool sheltered by the large gazebo drew her almost immediately. Inside the air was placid and steamy. Although some sunlight came in through the roof, it was strained and muted.

On a whim Melissa took off the borrowed skirt and blouse and the muslin underthings. Gooseflesh rose all over her as the cool March air struck her bare skin, but slipping into the spring cured that problem. The water was deliciously warm and very soothing.

Melissa luxuriated, so caught up in sweet languor that she nearly had heart failure when two strong hands caught her by the waist and thrust her up against a hair-roughened, rock-hard chest.

Eyes wide, heart pounding in her throat, Melissa gasped, "Quinn! Dear God, you scared me!"

He was glaring down at her. "Didn't I tell you not to come here by yourself?" he demanded in a furious rasp.

Melissa bit her lower lip. She wanted things to be right between her and Quinn, and they were so wrong. She swallowed her despair with all the excuses that came to her mind and countered, "How did you know I was here?"

"It was a wild guess," Quinn snapped, but there was an easing of the dark fury in his eyes, and his grasp on her waist, although as inescapable as before, had grown gentler. "Melissa, if anything happened to you—"

She let her forehead rest against his chest and wrapped her arms around him, hiding the pleasure his concern gave her. "What could possibly happen to me, Mr. Rafferty?" she asked, and in that moment all her worries and questions were wandering far from her mind.

His hand caught her chin and raised it. His lips were moist with springwater as they touched hers, tentatively at first, and then with an unwilling, protesting hunger.

Melissa gloried in her power as she pressed her bare, full breasts to his chest and returned the kiss with an abandon he alone had taught her.

Presently Quinn withdrew from the kiss and gently lifted Melissa off her feet so that she was floating atop the warm, bubbling water. Her nipples reacted to the cold air by growing taut.

When Quinn bent to take suckle, one of his hands supporting Melissa at the small of her back, she groaned. Her legs, weightless on the surface, parted at no conscious bidding from Melissa, issuing an instinctive invitation.

Quinn caressed her for a time, but then he left off to shift

Melissa to another position, and she was so drunk with wanting that she thought she could have drowned without caring.

She jumped with startled pleasure when she realized that her legs were now resting over Quinn's shoulders and felt him nuzzle her in a prelude of sweet agonies to come. His strong hands supported her back, and Melissa arched with delight, holding her breath against the water that splashed over her face, when he sampled her.

The joy grew keener with every passing moment, and Melissa held on tight with her thighs, her arms moving with gracious fever in the water. And then her body was caught once again in ferocious, buckling spasms of surrender that seemed to ripple on and on, far into forever.

When Melissa came back to herself she had no memory of those lost moments. She was standing, but Quinn was supporting her, his lips making warm mutterings against her temple. Some primitive instinct made her nip at his earlobe, and he moaned.

"Tell me you love me, Quinn Rafferty," she whispered, "and you'll own my soul."

He made no response, but Melissa didn't care at the moment. The evidence of his desire was plain, pressing its length against her abdomen, and she knew that words might already be beyond his reach.

He virtually dragged her to the side of the spring and laid her on the cold tiles before climbing out of the pool. Melissa whimpered, but not because of any discomfort; the chill seemed to heighten every sensation.

Quinn knelt astride her for a long, sweet time, his hands learning and relearning the contours of her breasts. His eyes never left her face; he relished her every response to his touch and to the tender, wicked words with which he tempted her.

Finally, when she could bear no more and neither could he, he fell to her, finding the shelter she offered and lunging into its heated solace with a cry of need and a powerful thrust of his hips.

"Oh, God, Melissa," he raved, "I've never wanted—never needed anyone—the way I need you—"

Melissa's release was a quick and merciful one, perhaps because he'd loved her senseless such a short time before. Still, she found a new pleasure in watching the emotions that played in Quinn's face as she loved him, her body putting his through its elemental, reflexive paces.

He gave a hoarse shout, part triumph, part despair, when she drained him of that essence that is man's to give and woman's to take and fell trembling to her side.

She comforted him, for there was a kind of despondency in his satisfaction, entangling one hand in his hair and stroking his muscular back with the other. When he sought her breast she brought it to his lips without hesitation and reveled in his greed.

"I still don't see why I couldn't play baseball," she fussed much later, when they'd both gotten back into their clothes. The sun was setting, and it was cold.

Quinn gave a cry of mock frustration and swept her up into his arms, pretending to be on the verge of throwing her back into the spring. He buried his face in her neck and growled, and Melissa squealed with laughter.

The warmth they'd shared beside the spring insulated them both until they were home, and they ate hungrily the roast pork Mrs. Wright had put on to cook before leaving for her daughter's house that morning. Following the meal a belated chill struck them both, and they went upstairs to the master suite, where Quinn built a roaring fire on the hearth.

Instead of getting into bed, however, he sat down in one of the chairs facing the fireplace and stretched out his long legs, making a sound of such blatant contentment that Melissa laughed at him.

She poured him a glass of brandy and stood beside his chair to offer it.

He accepted the drink, only to set it aside immediately and catch Melissa by the wrist. He hauled her onto his lap and kissed her soundly.

After that Melissa had no need for brandy; she was intoxicated by something else entirely. When Quinn had had his fill of kissing her—and he was a long time at that—he turned her toward him and began unbuttoning her rumpled blouse. When he'd laid the fabric aside and drawn down her camisole, so that she sprang up for him in plump, pink-tipped wealth, he groaned.

Acting on sheer mischief and spontaneity, Melissa plunged her fingers into his brandy glass, which had stood forgotten on the table until that instant, and then touched her nipples.

A grinding moan came from the depths of Quinn's chest, and he touched his tongue to her, first on one side, then on the other. The firelight flickered around them, giving the moment a primitive flavor.

Quinn finally stood Melissa on her feet, watching her in bemusement and hunger as she stripped away her clothes and then began removing his. She wanted to repay him for the mysterious pleasure he'd given her in the spring. She slipped gracefully to her knees.

He tensed as she touched him, and she feared for a moment that he would stop her, but in the end he gave himself up to her in quiet, magnificent submission. His hands were frantic in her hair as she pleasured him, and like a man lost in the darkness he cried out to be found.

When a shudder seized him Quinn drew Melissa back to her feet and took her to the bed, where the mink spread waited to receive her. Every element other than Quinn and the fire and the fur beneath her seemed to fall away, and she was carried into a dream world as he loved her. She became a cave woman, and Quinn was a hunter, and beyond the dancing firelight there were wolves howling. . . .

The fantasy ended in an explosive fusion of the real world and the one Melissa had created in her mind, and Quinn was kissing the length of her neck when she returned from that other time and place.

Melissa slept soundly that night, and when she awakened in the morning, Quinn was up and dressed, drinking coffee and scowling at some article in the *Seattle Times*.

Melissa stretched, full of delicious well-being, and said,

"It's a wonder that paper doesn't catch fire in your hands."

He smiled and sat down on the edge of the bed. "Like you did?" he teased.

Melissa blushed, but she wasn't ashamed of her responses to Quinn. They just seemed to come naturally to her, and she didn't see how she could be taken to task for something so instinctive. "Where's my coffee?" she countered, ignoring his question.

Quinn left the bed, returning a few moments later with a cup from the tray sitting on his desk. It was steaming and fragrant, but when Melissa reached out Quinn withheld it.

"I want something first," he said, and his voice was low and throaty.

"What?" Melissa inquired.

He put the coffee on the table and drew down the sheets so that her breasts swelled, proud and naked, in full view.

"Lordy," he said, with a shake of his head, and then he covered her again and gave her her coffee.

Melissa laughed as he stood and strode resolutely away, grabbing his suit coat from the bedpost as he passed it and pausing at the door.

"Whatever else you do today, buy some new clothes," he told her blithely. And then he was gone, off on his husbandly business, leaving the little woman behind to do his bidding.

Melissa finished her coffee and then flung back the covers and got out of bed. She was about to purloin another of Mary's dresses from the room across the hall when Quinn returned carrying a huge box.

He set it on the upholstered bench at the foot of the bed and said, "Your mother has evidently taken pity on you. There are five more of these downstairs."

Melissa opened the package to find some of her own clothes packed inside. She was wildly glad to see them, and so, evidently, was Quinn, for he was grinning as he watched her pull one favorite after another out of the box.

"God bless my mother," she said in a delightedly devout whisper.

"Amen," said Quinn. And then he kissed Melissa's forehead. "Guess you won't have to spend the day shopping after all."

Melissa tilted her head to one side. "I wasn't planning to, sweetheart," she chimed in her sunniest voice.

Quinn laughed and left the room for the second time. He hadn't been gone more than two minutes when a furious bellow swelled up the stairs.

"Melissa!"

She took the time to put on a simple cambric dress before answering the summons, and she was still braiding her hair as she came down the stairs.

Mr. Kruger had delivered the printing press; there it sat in the entryway, big as life and dusty as a bachelor's parlor. Quinn stood beside it, his arms folded across his chest, looking as though Melissa had just introduced him to six children from a previous marriage.

"Isn't it wonderful?!" she cried, circling the press. It seemed much more impressive in this good light than it had in Miss Bradberry's shed.

"I shouldn't ask," Quinn reflected after a few moments of strained silence. "But I will. Melissa, what is this dilapidated press doing in the middle of my entryway?"

Melissa drew a deep breath and let it out again. "You're right," she said with a bright smile. "You shouldn't have asked."

Eleven

"I'm going to start a newspaper," Melissa told Quinn staunchly, her chin out.

He looked appalled for a moment, but then a smug expression appeared in his eyes, and he smiled and spread his hands. Melissa knew without being told that he thought she hadn't a prayer of succeeding and had therefore decided not to provoke domestic tumult. "Enjoy yourself, sweetheart," he said expansively, and he kissed her forehead. "I'll see you later."

Melissa said nothing at all, but her arms were folded stubbornly across her bosom, and her determination to win out over all the obstacles that faced her was redoubled.

With the help of Helga and Mrs. Wright Melissa dragged the small but cumbersome printing press into a corner of Quinn's study. She spent the next hour thoroughly cleaning the mechanism, except for the typeface; then she covered it with an old sheet.

She was dusting her hands together, filled with satisfaction and hope, when a knock at the front door signaled the arrival of a visitor.

Melissa, rendered breathless by surprise, dodged back into the study when she realized that the caller was Ajax.

"I am seeking Miss Melissa Corbin," he said in his precise British way.

Helga had apparently taken an immediate, if polite, dislike to Ajax. "It's Mrs. Rafferty now, sir, and I'll have to ask if she wishes to see you. Wait, please."

Melissa wanted to flee along the hallway to the kitchen and the back door, but she couldn't keep running away from Ajax forever. A confrontation was inevitable. When Helga came to her with a questioning look on her broad, plain face, Melissa nodded nervously and smoothed her hair.

She was standing in front of the hearth when Ajax entered the room, doing her very best to look nonchalant.

"Melissa," he said, and the word contained a gentle reprimand.

Melissa had loved this man, or thought she had, but in the short space of their separation he'd become a stranger. He was still as handsome as a Greek statue, of course, but his blond, blue-eyed good looks left his runaway bride unmoved. "Ajax," she responded, moderately and at length.

He started toward her but stopped cold at the expression on her face.

"You are afraid of me?" he asked, sounding stricken. The look in his royal blue eyes was one of wounded disbelief.

In that moment Melissa realized that Ajax had bargained for a certain response, and she could see, in looking back, how he had long made a practice of manipulating her into saying and doing what he wanted. She felt stupid and gullible, and those emotions intensified her aversion to the man.

"Of course I'm not afraid of you," she answered presently, with a straightening of her shoulders. She decided to go directly to the heart of the matter. "What brings you here?"

Ajax spread his hands; they were smooth and white and lithe. So unlike Quinn's. "You have made a terrible mistake, Melissa, marrying this stranger—this lumberjack."

Melissa smiled. "Oh? And how do you suggest that I correct this dreadful error?"

An air of strange desperation came over Ajax, although his manner was as polished as ever. "You must come to your senses, my darling, and let me take you away from here. Now, today."

Melissa was already shaking her head. "I'm married to the man, Ajax." she replied. "I love him."

Ajax looked as apoplectic as his well-schooled features could. "That is madness! You could not possibly love a stranger!"

Standing behind Quinn's favorite chair, Melissa curved her hands around its leather-upholstered back and smiled. "Nevertheless, I do. But even if I despised my husband, even if I regretted this marriage with all my heart, Ajax, I wouldn't so much as cross the street with you."

He was pacing now, the princely Briton, radiating frustration and annoyance. "We can have you divorced from this fortune hunter, and after a decent interval you and I will marry." He paused to wave an index finger at her. "You really have made a jumble of things by behaving so impetuously!"

Melissa folded her arms. "You weren't listening, Ajax," she said in a pleasant but inflexible tone. "I want nothing to do with you now or ever. Go back to your mistress—back to England, for all I care—and leave me alone."

Ajax stopped pacing and stared at her. "I will be ruined without you," he said.

"You should have thought of that sooner," Melissa replied, immovable.

The Englishman looked as though he would relish tearing her limb from limb, but in the end he simply sputtered, "You have not heard the last of me, Mrs. Rafferty," and he stormed out of the house.

Melissa rounded Quinn's chair and sagged into it, letting out a long breath. Although she had stood fast during the interview itself, she now felt drained.

"Are you all right, ma'am?" Helga asked shyly from a little distance away.

Melissa looked up to see that the maid was carrying a tea tray. She nodded, smiling when she noticed that there was only one cup. Apparently Helga had had no confidence in Ajax's courting.

Helga poured the tea and then left, looking back over her shoulder at Melissa two or three times before she disappeared through the doorway.

As Melissa sipped her tea the shaken, defensive feeling Ajax's unexpected visit had inspired in her began to abate. She would never have gone back to him, of course, but she did wonder if he hadn't been right in thinking that her marriage was a lost cause. Love Quinn though she did, there were many problems that might well bring ruin upon the union.

Serious questions had been raised, after all—things Melissa needed to discuss with her husband. Miss Bradberry was convinced that someone named Eustice Rafferty had burned down the newspaper building. Melissa had not questioned Quinn about this allegation yet, but she knew she would have to, and soon.

She finished her tea and resolutely stood, giving the shrouded printing press an affectionate look before starting for the door.

The day was cold and somewhat gloomy, the sky heavy with either rain or snow, but Melissa was determined not to allow either the weather or the confrontation with Ajax to dash her spirits. She had a goal to work toward, and she meant to concentrate on that.

It was very chilly inside Quinn's railroad car, so Melissa built a fire in the stove as soon as she'd finished lighting all the lamps. When the place was cozy she settled herself at Quinn's desk with ink and a pen and one of the tablets she'd bought and began to write.

The story she'd been framing in her mind flowed fluidly onto the paper, and Melissa worked rapidly, her cheeks glowing with concentration and commitment. Before long the pages were piling up beside her while others, crumpled, billowed around her feet. Still Melissa wrote.

Several hours had passed when she was jarred out of her imaginary world by a loud clank and a lurch that nearly upset her ink bottle. She gave a little cry of surprised alarm when she realized that the railroad car was moving.

Hastily she put the lid back on the ink and got to her feet. "Wait, stop!" she cried, knowing even as she spoke that the words were futile.

Melissa hurried to the rear door and wrenched it open, but even though the train was still moving at a fairly slow rate of speed she could not bring herself to jump. The ground looked entirely too unaccommodating for that.

She went back inside the train and closed the door, her thoughts tumbling wildly as she tried to think what to do. She decided that a word with a conductor or even the engineer himself was in order.

Traveling between cars was not as easy as Melissa had remembered. When she opened the inner door she saw that there was an unnerving gap between Quinn's car and the next one. She put one hand to her heart, thinking that she must have been delirious with fever not to have noticed how easily one could make a misstep and tumble onto the tracks to be run over.

While Melissa deliberated the train's pace increased until the tracks were a blur beneath her, and she grasped the door frame, feeling dizzy. In the end she had to go back inside and sit with her head between her knees until she'd regained control.

She was startled when there was a knock at the door, but she called out shakily, "Come in." Only later would she reflect that being so cordial on a train full of strangers could have been a disastrous mistake.

A smiling black man wearing a conductor's impressive suit of clothes entered the car. He looked surprised when he realized that Melissa was alone.

"You must stop the train immediately," Melissa said firmly. "You see, I hadn't planned to go anywhere—"

The conductor's grin faded. "I'm sorry, miss, but this train don't stop till it gets to Port Hastings."

Melissa was aghast. "You don't understand—I don't want to go to Port Hastings!"

"I'm sorry, miss," the man repeated.

Tears of frustration burned behind Melissa's eyes, but she would not shed them. She tried to speak calmly and with dignity. "Who gave the order to attach this car to a departing train?" she demanded.

"Mr. Rafferty himself, ma'am" was the polite response. "I expect there's somebody going to get aboard at the other end of the line for the ride back."

Melissa faced defeat. She was going to pay her family an unexpected visit, and that was that. But she'd missed the midday meal, so completely absorbed had she been in her work, and it was now, judging by the light at the windows, time for dinner. She asked for a tray and went dismally back to the desk to assess the situation.

Within two hours Melissa was standing beside the tracks in Port Hastings with no money and no baggage. The Western Union office had already closed, so there was no way that she could let Quinn know where she was.

Since Jeff and Fancy lived close by, Melissa set out for their house. When she reached the corner and saw the familiar bright windows glowing in the night, unexpected tears brimmed in her eyes. It seemed a hundred years had passed since she'd been home, when in reality it had only been a little over a week.

She worked the gate latch and went through, drying her eyes with the back of one hand, and by the time she rang the bell she was smiling.

Fancy answered the door herself, and for a moment she just stood there staring at Melissa as though she couldn't believe her eyes. In that interval Melissa noticed something in her sister-in-law's face that had eluded her before, when she was busy preparing for her ill-fated wedding—Fancy was unhappy.

"Aren't you going to ask me in?" Melissa said finally, in a soft voice.

Fancy laughed and drew Melissa into her house and her arms in one and the same motion. "What are you doing here? My heaven, what stories we've been hearing about you!"

Melissa laughed. "I'm here because I was unintentionally shanghaied, and as for the stories, I admit nothing!"

Jeff was coming down the stairs as they spoke, and Melissa noted that he looked as dismal as Fancy did. There was a hollow expression in the depths of those intense indigo eyes.

"Hello, brat," he said, lifting Melissa into his arms and swinging her around once. It was the way he had always greeted her, and if he still had the strength, he'd probably do the same thing when she was ninety and he a hundred and four.

The house, once so full of happiness, mischief, and laughter, was strangely quiet. "Where are the children?" Melissa asked as Jeff set her back on her feet. Fancy took her cloak, and she was being led into the parlor before her sister-in-law answered.

"They're all in bed."

"We hope," Jeff added with quiet skepticism.

Melissa looked from one beloved face to the other and asked forthrightly, "What's the matter?"

Jeff thrust a hand through his fair hair and averted his eyes while Fancy briskly changed the subject.

"Melissa was shanghaied," she said, and the tone of her voice was the same warm, gentle one that she had always used with Jeff. "An experience like that must be exhausting. Come and sit down, dear, and I'll get our Mary to make up a pot of tea."

Melissa accepted a chair but declined the tea. She'd had more than enough on the train while she'd fretted over how worried Quinn must be at her strange disappearance.

She explained how she'd come to be in Port Hastings, and when the brief story ended Jeff frowned and asked, "But what were you doing in the railroad car in the first place?"

Melissa swallowed. No one in the family knew about her writing career except Adam's wife, Banner. She wasn't sure she was ready to reveal a secret she'd kept for so long.

"Well?" Jeff prompted when she hesitated.

"I was writing—a journal," Melissa lied, hoping that her brother wouldn't press the point. She yawned, and that inspired Jeff to suggest walking her home.

Minutes later Jeff and Melissa were making their way

up the steep hill that led to the big house where Katherine lived, along with Adam and Banner and their children.

Melissa dared to broach the touchy subject again. "Something's happened between you and Fancy. What is it, Jeff?"

He gave a ragged sigh. "Don't worry about it, brat," he said. "It'll pass." He didn't sound at all certain of that, however, and Melissa had her doubts as well.

When they reached the main house Jeff refused to come any further than the front gate, no matter how Melissa tried to persuade him, so she finally gave him a kiss on the cheek and set off up the walk.

Katherine swept from the parlor to the front hall to kiss her daughter and demand, "What on earth are you doing here?"

Melissa told her the same story she'd told Jeff and Fancy and the conductor. It was getting wearisome.

"Quinn must be frantic," Katherine said as a tall, powerfully built man with silver hair and kindly brown eyes appeared behind her.

Melissa was distracted, wondering if this was the man her mother loved.

"I don't believe we've been introduced," he said, taking Melissa's hand in the continental fashion and kissing it delicately. "I'm Harlan Sommers."

Mr. Sommers didn't look like any rancher Melissa had ever seen; his clothes were impeccably tailored, and his boots were of the finest Italian leather. His hands were scarred by hard work but no longer callused.

Katherine had taken her arm. "Of course, this is our Melissa," she was saying. Her dark blue eyes turned to Harlan. "Have you seen Adam tonight, dear? I really think he should wake someone up at the Western Union office and send a message to Port Riley."

Harlan told her Adam was off delivering a baby and hadn't returned yet, and he said he'd send the wire himself. Melissa wrote out Quinn's name and felt gratitude as well as liking for the elegant rancher as he left to saddle a horse.

"He's wonderful, Mama!" Melissa crowed the moment she and Katherine were alone.

Katherine smiled softly. "I know."

"When are you going to marry him?"

"Some of us are not so impetuous as to marry on a whim," Katherine replied dryly. "We like to wait until we know a man."

Exasperated, Melissa sank into a chair and sighed. "Honestly, Mama— how long do you want? You told me in Port Riley that you met Mr. Sommers two years ago." She waved her index finger at Katherine. "And don't think I've forgotten that you married Papa two weeks after you met him."

Katherine shook her head. "Your brothers are right," she said with a twinkle in her eyes. "You've gotten completely out of hand."

Melissa smiled sadly, thinking of one particular brother. "I'm worried about Jeff and Fancy," she admitted, feeling rueful. She had been so caught up in her own life and her planned marriage to Ajax that she hadn't even noticed that two of the people dearest to her were hurting.

Her mother sighed. "The problem is rooted, I think, in Fancy's newfound devotion to the suffrage cause," she said.

"Have you talked to either of them?"

Katherine smoothed her skirts. "No, and I don't intend to," she said firmly. She assessed Melissa with tenderness in her eyes. "You look different somehow," she observed.

Melissa blushed and lowered her eyes, never knowing what she'd revealed.

Katherine was smiling when their gazes met. "You're tired, darling," she said. "Why don't you go upstairs? I'll have your bed done up while you're bathing."

Melissa nodded and excused herself, so weary she could barely climb the steps, but when she'd had her bath and crawled into her own bed, in her own room, she could not sleep.

She was too busy wondering about Quinn. Was he worried about her? Did he even know she was gone?

Quinn had been from one end of Port Riley to the other looking for his wife. He'd tried the mercantile, the cannery, the library, and even Miss Bradberry's house, and he hadn't turned up a trace of Melissa or the man who had visited her that morning.

Mrs. Wright and Helga were both blubbering away in the kitchen, convinced that their mistress had run away with her erstwhile bridegroom, and Quinn was doing his best not to believe the same thing.

After refilling his glass with brandy Quinn continued what he'd been doing for the past twenty minutes—he paced the length of his study, searching his mind and his memory for any clue to Melissa's whereabouts. There was a knock at the front door, and he answered it himself, hoping against hope.

It was only Mitch. "Any word?" his friend asked quietly, stepping inside the house at a curt gesture from Quinn.

Quinn shook his head.

Mitch hung up his hat in the study and then went to pour himself a drink. Hesitantly, his back still turned to his host, he ventured, "Do you think she's left you?"

Quinn ran splayed fingers through his hair. Once before, when faced with a situation she couldn't handle, Melissa had fled without a word of explanation to anyone. It was possible that she'd had some dramatic change of heart after sending Ajax away from the house that morning and had gone after him. But some instinct told Quinn that Melissa would have told him good-bye face to face, or at least left a note, because of the new closeness between them.

"I don't know," he answered at last.

"Was there an argument?"

Quinn bit his lower lip, remembering how it was to make love to Melissa, how it was to hold her. There had been a few minutes of upheaval over the delivery of that damned printing press, but nothing that should have caused her to leave without saying good-bye.

"No," he rasped finally. "Things were good between us. Better than they've ever been."

Mitch sighed and then froze, his glass halfway to his mouth. He muttered a swear word.

"What?" Quinn demanded instantly.

"It's a crazy idea, but—"

"Tell me, damn it!"

"When I left my office tonight I noticed that the railroad car wasn't on the spur. Did you send it up the mountain or something?"

A light glowed in Quinn's mind. He'd given Melissa the spare key to the car, and she'd never returned it. . . .

He began to laugh.

"What's so funny?" Mitch frowned.

Quinn's amusement had subsided slightly. "I think I know what happened to my bride," he said, setting aside his drink and snatching his coat from the peg. He started toward the door, and Mitch had no real choice but to follow him.

"You think she was in the car when the train pulled out?"

Quinn nodded, grinning as he pictured the expression that would have come over Melissa's face when the wheels started turning. "That's what I think, all right," he confirmed, "but I intend to find out for sure."

They'd walked no more than a block when they were met by the telegraph operator's little girl, bearing a yellow envelope in one hand. She held it out to Quinn with a solemn expression on her face. "This here's for you, Mr. Rafferty."

Quinn gave the child a coin and ripped open the message. It was all very well to imagine that Melissa had been accidentally carried off in his railroad car, but there were other possibilities that weren't so appealing.

MELISSA HERE IN PORT HASTINGS, SAFE AND SOUND, the missive read. It was signed with the initials H.S., and Quinn wondered who the devil that was even as he silently thanked God that his wife was all right.

The child lingered. "My papa said to find out if you wanted to send an answer," she told Quinn. "If you do, you better get there quick, 'cause this is his poker night."

Five minutes later, inside the telegraph office, Quinn wrote out his response with an amused Mitch looking over his shoulder.

They were halfway to the saloon, where they planned to celebrate his recovery of Melissa, when it occurred to Quinn to wonder what the hell she'd been doing in that railroad car in the first place. There was still the possibility that Melissa had reconsidered after sending Ajax away. Maybe she'd found him again, and their passion had been too great to resist, and she'd taken him by the hand and led him into the luxurious privacy of the car. . . .

Quinn whirled on one heel without a word to Mitch and started toward home, his strides long and purposeful.

"What the devil—?" Mitch complained, hurrying along beside him.

"I'm going to Port Hastings," came the abrupt answer.

"Tonight?"

Quinn nodded, his jawline tight.

"On horseback? Good Lord, man, you'll be riding all night!"

The prospect didn't daunt Quinn in the least.

Melissa had slept very well, and she was lounging in bed when a smiling Katherine brought her a breakfast tray. Beside the plate was a telegram.

"It arrived late last night, after you were asleep," her mother informed her.

Melissa's heartbeat quickened. She ripped the envelope open and unfolded the paper inside, her fingers trembling.

LIFE IS MUCH TOO PEACEFUL WITHOUT YOU. COME
HOME SOON. QUINN.

Melissa read the message again carefully, looking for a word that wasn't there. Her disappointment must have shown clearly in her face, for Katherine smiled and said, "Don't worry, darling. The man adores you."

"What makes you so sure?" Melissa retorted, setting the telegram aside and taking up a piece of toast.

Before Katherine could answer, some kind of disagreement broke out downstairs, and Maggie, the housekeeper, could be heard yelling, "You'd better stop right where you are, mister, or I'll shoot!"

Melissa upset her tray scrambling out of bed, but Katherine got to the door first.

"In the name of God, Maggie," she cried, "hold your fire! That man is my son-in-law!"

Melissa put one hand to her mouth. Sure enough, Quinn was midway up the stairs, looking as though he hadn't slept in a month. When he caught sight of his wife he smiled.

"It's good to know you're so well guarded, Calico," he said.

She ran to put her arms around him, heedless of her tangled hair and the splotches of spilled tea on her nightgown. Maggie was still standing at the bottom of the stairs with her shotgun in hand, and wild images of Quinn lying bloody and broken filled Melissa's mind. She held her husband all the more tightly.

He kissed her forehead. "Aren't you going to ask me why I'm here?" he asked gruffly.

She drew back far enough to look into his eyes, her head tilted to one side, her gaze questioning.

Quinn let out a ragged sigh. "I'm a jealous fool, that's why," he confessed. "Melissa, I have to know—are you still in love with Ajax?"

It dawned on Melissa that Helga or Mrs. Wright must have told him about Ajax's visit the morning before, and she was quick to shake her head. "No," she answered with a smile. "I'm not in love with him."

Dark eyes searched Melissa's face, but she said no more. She'd already declared her feelings for him on two occasions and been ignored both times. If anyone said "I love you," it would have to be Quinn.

Twelve

Quinn said nothing, but the weary relief in his eyes touched Melissa so deeply that she reached out and took his hand in hers. "You must be exhausted," she said, and she led him down the hallway to her room. There she closed the door, entirely forgetting the world that lay beyond it, and began loosening Quinn's string tie.

He caught her hands in his and held them still. His voice sounded gravelly when he asked, "What were you doing in that railroad car?"

Melissa was hurt. "You think I was with Ajax, don't you?" She tried to pull her hands free, but Quinn wouldn't let them go. Tears brimmed in her eyes, and she blinked them away before bursting out in a ragged whisper, "I was writing, if you must know!"

Quinn's expression was a mixture of skepticism and wariness. "Writing what?"

"My new novel." Melissa made the confession defiantly, with her chin high and her gaze direct.

His weariness appeared to be surpassed only by his annoyance. "Not another towering epic about a woman 'bound for destruction,' I hope."

Melissa felt her cheeks turn hot. "Your opinion of the quality of my work is not important to me, Mr. Rafferty," she lied stalwartly.

Quinn had released her hands, but only to take her waist in a gentle grasp. "Good," he said, and warmth caressed her lips as his mouth drew near. "I've missed you very much."

She longed for the strength to resist him, even to box his ears, but it was not forthcoming. It was as though she'd been away from Quinn for years, and as he held her close to him, as he kissed her, every nerve ending in her body leapt in response. Melissa stood trembling, barely breathing, when he drew her nightgown up over her head and tossed it aside.

She was naked before him and could make no move to cover herself, for he had already defeated her. She was his, without question or quarter, and as he removed his clothes, she felt as though he was already touching her. By the time Quinn lowered Melissa gently to the bed she was throbbing with need.

She whimpered, longing to be taken, as he caressed her and availed himself of her breasts. Only when she was tossing wildly and muttering incoherent pleas did Quinn make her his own, and even as he thrust himself within her he covered her mouth with his to quiet the welcoming cry she gave.

Her body flailed beneath his, and as satisfaction came Melissa flung her arms over her head and raised her hips high in order to receive him as completely as she could. Moments later, laughing breathlessly, she kissed the fingers that had clamped themselves over her mouth to silence her.

By this time Quinn was caught in the throes of his own pleasure. Melissa kept pace with him, both taunting and encouraging him with her body and her words until rapture seized him and he stiffened upon her in a violence of joyous despair. The flesh along her neck muffled his groans, and her hands moved wildly over his back and buttocks as she held him prisoner.

They talked a while when they'd regained the breath for it, but it was plain to Melissa that Quinn could barely keep his eyes open. Finally, her head resting on his shoulder, one hand making a slow, soothing circle on his belly, Melissa let the conversation die. Moments later Quinn was asleep.

She got out of bed, took a bath, and assessed the contents of her wardrobe. Even though Katherine had sent many of her things to Port Riley, there were still enough clothes to accommodate three or four women.

She selected a green corduroy skirt and high-necked, frilly blouse and put them on over taffeta underthings and silk stockings. She groomed her hair with the sterling comb and brush set her father had given her the Christmas before his death and went downstairs.

The place was a happy bedlam, with children running in every direction. Melissa was smiling as she knocked at the door of her mother's study and slipped inside.

"How on earth do you manage to concentrate in this place?" she asked, seeing that her mother was sitting pensively at her desk, frowning at her typewriting machine.

Katherine sighed. "I do believe I've lost the knack of it," she admitted. "Sit down, darling, please."

Melissa took a chair facing her mother's desk. "What are you writing?"

Again Katherine sighed. "Still another argument to read before still another gathering of the state legislature." She rolled the sheet of yellow paper out of the machine and glared at it as though it had somehow offended her. "We absolutely must win the vote, Melissa."

Melissa agreed, of course, and she meant to work for suffrage through her newspaper, once she got it started. Still, she changed the subject because she had more immediate matters on her mind. "Have you told the boys that you're going to marry Harlan?"

Katherine bit her lower lip and then shook her head. "No, and I'm going to lose him if I don't. Last night he told me that he'd be going back to California, with or without me, at the end of the week."

Although she had met Harlan Sommers only briefly the

night before, Melissa had sensed the powerful attraction between the handsome rancher and her mother. "You mustn't let him go," she warned.

Rising from her chair, Katherine left the desk to go and look out a nearby window. The morning sunlight glowed around her, illuminating her lovely fair hair and accentuating her still-youthful figure. "I've fought so long and so hard for the cause," she said quietly, "but now I'm tired. Harlan wants to love me, to pamper me—and I want to let him."

Melissa sat in silence, knowing there was more, waiting for Katherine to go on.

Her mother turned to face her, her indigo eyes bright with tears. "Harlan is a good man, and I adore him, and I know I can be happy in California. But once I say my vows, Melissa, I'll have to let go of far more than my grandbabies and my work in the suffrage movement. I'll have to let go of your father, and I still have feelings for him. Strong feelings."

With that Katherine covered her face with her hands and sobbed softly, and Melissa hurried over to her, longing to comfort. Just as she would have put her arms around her mother Harlan entered the room, his expression full of quiet love.

"This is it, then?" he asked. "It is the memory of Daniel that has been standing between us all this time?"

Katherine sniffled and raised her chin. Melissa would have made a hasty exit, but her mother held onto her arm as if for dear life. "I helped Daniel Corbin build an empire," Katherine said. "I bore him four strong children. And even though I love you, Harlan, I can't put Daniel out of my mind and heart as though he never existed. He was a part of me."

Harlan's eyes held such gentle understanding that Melissa was moved almost to tears. He approached Katherine and took her hands in his, and only then did she release her daughter.

"I would never ask you to forget the father of your children," Melissa heard Harlan say as she hurried toward the doorway. "Oh, Katie, why didn't you tell me that you were thinking such a thing?"

Melissa had never heard anyone call her mother "Katie," not even her papa. She was smiling as she crossed the entry hall and then the dining room. She hurried along the walkway that led to the small hospital and clinic that Banner and Adam ran together.

Adam and his wife were both out making rounds. While Melissa was disappointed at not seeing them, she had long since resigned herself to their hectic schedules. She found a cloak and set out for Keith and Tess's house, which was nearly a mile away.

When she arrived Tess was on her hands and knees spading out a flower bed. She leapt to her feet with a cry of delight and threw her arms around Melissa. When a hearty hug had been exchanged Tess led her sister-in-law toward the house. "Tell me everything! Is it true that you ran away with a man who has a private railroad car?"

Melissa laughed. "Not exactly," she answered, feeling warm and achy at the thought of that man, now sleeping soundly in her bed.

As she and Tess walked toward the large but otherwise modest frame house Keith had built for his family Melissa turned her mind to her brothers. All of them were wealthy, but they had more to distinguish them from other men than money. Adam was a doctor, and although his was essentially a country practice, he was known and respected throughout the medical profession. Jeff had been a virtual legend as a sea captain, and now he was a shipbuilder employing dozens of people. Keith was a Methodist minister, and though his accomplishments weren't as visible as those of his brothers, he was in many ways the most successful of all.

He came out of the house to greet Melissa, whirling her around exactly as Jeff had done, then giving her a sound kiss on the forehead. There was a special bond between Keith and Melissa because they were the youngest of the four, and they had often been in league against Adam and Jeff.

Once again Melissa told her story of being hauled away in the railroad car. This time she embellished the tale with an account of Quinn's being menaced on the stairs by Maggie and her shotgun.

Keith laughed at the picture his sister painted, and Tess commiserated. "Poor Quinn! He must be wondering what kind of family he's married into."

"By now," Keith said dryly, "there can be no question."

Tess gave Keith a look and turned back to Melissa. "How long will you be staying? I'm dying to meet this husband of yours!"

Melissa sighed. "I doubt we'll be staying long. Quinn has his hotel, among other interests, and of course, there's my newspaper."

Keith, sitting astraddle of a kitchen chair with his arms draped across the back, watched her with gentle amusement in his eyes. "What newspaper is that?" he wanted to know.

"I mean to publish one," Melissa said forcefully. "And don't try to discourage me, Keith Corbin, because I'm going to succeed at it."

"What do you know about publishing a newspaper?" Keith persisted. There was no disapproval in his voice, only curiosity and a certain brotherly concern.

Tess patted Melissa's hand. "She can learn," she said.

Keith sighed. "Right," he replied.

After that the conversation turned to other matters. An hour had passed when Melissa set out for the railroad station. She knew that Quinn kept spare clothes in the car, and that when he awakened he would want them.

She was very careful to ascertain that no engine was about to hook up to the car and pull it away before she went inside. When she rounded the familiar partition Melissa was greeted by a scream so startling that she let out a shriek of her own.

Gillian Aires sat bolt upright in the huge bed, her blond hair rumpled, her violet eyes wide. She held the chinchilla spread to her chin and demanded, "What are you doing here?"

Melissa folded her arms across her chest. "I might ask you the same thing," she said.

Quinn's former mistress—at least, Melissa *hoped* she was a former mistress—yawned delicately, taking her time. "Quinn sent the car to fetch me," she finally said, in dulcet tones that made Melissa want to box her ears. She gestured toward a stack of fancy dress boxes. "I've been shopping in Seattle, you see. I want to look my very best on Saturday night when the hotel opens."

A hard lump formed in Melissa's throat, and she had to swallow it before she could speak. Even then all she managed was a rather lame "Oh." Trembling a little, not knowing how to deal with the situation, she went to the wardrobe and took out the fresh clothes Quinn would need.

"What are you going to wear to the party?" Gillian asked, settling back onto the pillows in a way that said she was used to sleeping in that particular place and saw no reason to change.

Melissa was in no mood to make conversation with a woman lounging in her husband's bed. "I don't know," she said, thinking of the lavender gown she'd bought at Kruger's Mercantile. All of a sudden it seemed drab and spinsterish, that dress.

She turned, holding Quinn's shirt and trousers and jacket over one arm, and made herself smile. "I'll be leaving now. I-I'm truly sorry that I startled you." She took a few more items from the bureau and was about to depart when Gillian stopped her.

"Wait," she said. "Please."

Melissa stood still on the other side of the partition, her heart beating hard against the base of her throat. She thought she knew what Gillian was going to say, and she closed her eyes against the knowledge.

"I lost a great deal when you stole Quinn from me," Gillian said. "Why did you do it?"

Melissa turned and saw that Gillian had put on a wrapper and stepped from behind the partition. Melissa couldn't explain to the woman what she'd done because she didn't entirely understand it herself, but there was one thing she was very certain of indeed. "I love Quinn."

Gillian tilted her beautiful head to one side. "Enough to fight for him?"

Melissa spoke without hesitation or doubt. "Absolutely."

Eyes so blue that they were nearly purple slid over Melissa's corduroy skirt and braided hair. A dismissive expression crossed Gillian's face, one that discounted her rival as an unsophisticated country cousin. "You'll pardon me if I'm not terribly worried," she reflected idly. "There have been many, many women in Quinn's life, and he's always gotten bored and sent them packing."

Keeping her composure required every ounce of self-control Melissa had. She sighed. "Has he married any of them?" she inquired. "Besides me, that is?"

Gillian's aplomb faltered, but only for the briefest moment. "No," she admitted presently, in a cheerful voice, "but if he felt that marrying you would get him what he wanted, he'd do it."

Melissa knew that Quinn had wanted an alliance with her family—he'd admitted that much—and he'd certainly never said that he loved her. For all that, she knew he cared; he'd revealed that by the tenderness of his lovemaking and by riding all night to find her. "I have to go," she said, feeling stronger. "My husband is waiting for me."

With that she left.

Quinn was sitting up in bed when she arrived at the house, drinking coffee and scowling at the morning newspaper. "Where have you been?" he asked.

Melissa flung the clothes she'd brought him in his face. "You sent that car here to fetch Gillian!" she accused, pacing, her arms folded, her cheeks hot. She'd been stewing all the way home from the railroad yard.

"Yes," Quinn admitted, setting aside his coffee and laying his clothes out of harm's way. He didn't sound one bit repentant, she thought. The rake!

"I'm sure she appreciates the courtesy," Melissa said.

An insolent grin spread across Quinn's face, and he rubbed his beard-stubbled chin with one hand. "You're jealous," he observed.

Melissa stomped one foot. "I'm merely concerned with the—the proprieties. You're a married man, and you have no business letting other women ride in your railroad car and sleep in your bed!"

Quinn struggled for a circumspect expression and failed

roundly. "You're overlooking an important point, Calico: I'm not sharing the bed or the car with 'other women.'"

With a little sigh Melissa sank into a chintz-covered chair a good distance from Quinn. "I can tolerate swearing and cigar smoking and even poker playing," she said seriously, "but I will not look the other way when it comes to philandering."

He chuckled, raising one hand like an Indian making a pact. "Fair enough," he said.

"You still haven't explained why your railroad car is at Gillian's beck and call," Melissa pointed out.

Quinn sighed. "Gillian is my partner." He paused and took a steadying sip of his coffee. "Now, if she weren't a woman, it wouldn't bother you that she and I are in business together, nor would you care if I sent the car for her when she needed it."

"But she *is* a woman," Melissa reminded him, sounding a little desperate.

Quinn arched one eyebrow. "And therefore I shouldn't extend the same courtesies to her that I would to Mitch, for example, or one of your brothers?"

Melissa shot out of her chair. "Damn you, Quinn Rafferty, you're deliberately confusing the issue!"

"No," Quinn responded, with infuriating calmness, "you are. It isn't your place to dictate whom I do business with, Melissa. I'm faithful to you, and that's damned well all you need to know."

Fury simmered in Melissa's veins. "Coming from a man who just rode all night to make sure that I hadn't run away with someone else, those are remarkable words!"

Quinn glared at her as he tossed back the covers and got out of bed, gloriously naked. "That was different," he had the audacity to say. "You're a woman, and women need protecting."

Melissa gave a little cry of frustration.

Someone, probably Maggie, had brought Quinn a robe, and he put it on and went down the hall to the bathroom. The next time Melissa saw her husband he was bathed, dressed, and freshly shaven.

"I want to meet your brothers," he announced. "Where do we start?"

Melissa sighed. "With Jeff, I suppose," she said, and when Quinn offered his arm she took it, even though she longed to rebel.

The walk to Jeff and Fancy's house was relatively short, and when they arrived they were greeted by a tremendous clatter. They stood frozen at the gate, amazed, when Jeff thrust a narrow bed through the gaping front door and then kicked it down the porch steps.

"What the—?" Quinn muttered.

"They're having marital problems," Melissa confided in a whisper.

"By God, Frances," Jeff bellowed, "you're my wife, and you'll share my bed, do you understand me? I'll be damned if I'm going to sleep on some puny army cot with you lying six feet away on one just like it!"

Just as he was finishing this diatribe Jeff spotted Melissa and her new husband and strode toward them, looking as though he'd like to do to Quinn what he'd just done to the bed.

"This is him?" he demanded, stopping just short of the fence.

Before Melissa could say anything at all Fancy came bursting out of the house in a storm of angry tears. It was clear that she hadn't noticed the visitors, for she shouted, "You can sleep right here on the front lawn for all I care, Jeff Corbin, but you're not sleeping with me!"

Quinn chuckled at this, an indulgence that won him a sweltering look from Jeff.

"Maybe we should come back another time," his sister's husband said moderately. One corner of his mouth was twitching almost imperceptibly, and Melissa knew he wanted to laugh.

By then Fancy had noticed the company and was looking embarrassed. Still, she smiled and offered her hand as she approached. "Hello," she said with warm dignity, obviously pretending that her husband had not just thrown a bed into the front yard.

Melissa was quick to make introductions, during which Jeff never took his eyes from Quinn. He was regarding him as an archangel might regard a demon.

Quinn, for his part, seemed unruffled. He was affable, even to the point of pretending not to see the twin bed that lay broken and mangled at the base of the porch steps. After a very strained interview of about an hour's duration the newlyweds took their leave.

Melissa was worried, and she said as much to Quinn, who surprised her by squeezing her hand and saying, "Don't fret, Calico—if there's one thing greater than the fury those two are feeling toward each other right now, it's the passion. They'll be okay."

She let her forehead rest against his shoulder for a moment, loving him for the attempt to reassure her and hoping to high heaven that he was right. She was embarrassed to realize that there were tears in her eyes; her emotions had been close to the surface lately. "I think I need to go home," she confessed in a small voice.

Quinn stopped and turned to face her, there on that wooden sidewalk, his hand cupped under her chin. "To that big house back there on the hill?" he asked gravely.

Melissa shook her head. "To Port Riley. If coming back here has taught me one thing, Quinn, it's that home is wherever you are."

He kissed her then and there, with nary a thought for the opinions of passersby or matrons who might be peering out their windows. He had just drawn back and was searching her face with those audacious brown eyes of his, about to say something, when a buggy drew to a stop on the road beside them.

"There you are!" chimed a familiar female voice.

Melissa and Quinn both turned, a bit woodenly, to see Banner smiling down at them from her perch on the seat of the rig. Cinnamon curls framed her face, and her green eyes were dancing with mischievous suppositions. "Kissing on the street. For shame!"

Melissa laughed and introduced her husband to Adam's wife, adding, "You remember my mentioning that Banner is a doctor. I believe you said she probably had a face ugly enough to stop a grizzly bear's heart."

Quinn gave Melissa a nudge in the ribs but tipped his hat to Banner. "I'll be the first to admit to a grievous wrong," he said suavely.

Banner smiled and applied herself to the subject at hand. "Katherine has called a meeting, and I'm out trying to round up the family." She paused and drew a deep breath. "Did you know that Jeff and Fancy have a bed in their front yard? I'm not sure I'm up to asking why." Quickly she lifted the reins. "I'll see you at home in a little while," she said, and then she was gone.

Melissa had intended to introduce Quinn to Keith and Tess, but the task had become unnecessary now because of the meeting, so they turned around and set out for the main house.

Luncheon was being served when they arrived, and they joined Katherine and Harlan, Adam, Fancy, and a very subdued Jeff in the dining room. The children were eating in the kitchen.

Presently Banner and Tess arrived, but Keith didn't show up until the meal was nearly over. He greeted Quinn with a grin and a handshake and took his place at the table beside Tess, favoring her with a quick kiss before turning his attention to his mother.

Katherine stood up, cleared her throat, and said, "Harlan has asked me to be his wife, and I've accepted."

There was a deep silence, then Melissa, Fancy, Tess, and Banner all burst out with simultaneous congratulations. Several minutes had passed before any of them realized that Katherine's sons weren't showing the same kind of enthusiasm, even though none of them seemed surprised.

Adam looked pensive, as though he might be thinking about a medical problem instead of the subject at hand, but Melissa knew better. Keith, perhaps the most tractable of Katherine's sons, was gazing off into space, while Jeff, it appeared, would explode shortly.

He broke the uncomfortable silence. "What do we know about this man?" he demanded, glaring at Harlan. Fancy laid a restraining hand on her husband's arm, but Jeff shook it away.

Harlan did not flinch, and his gaze was steady as he regarded Katherine's middle son. "I love your mother more than my life," the rancher told Jeff evenly, "and that knowledge will have to suffice for now."

Melissa saw respect in Quinn's eyes as he looked at Harlan, and Keith and Adam were clearly beginning to assimilate the news, but Jeff's attitude was still coldly relentless.

For a long time no one spoke, and then Banner jumped determinedly into the conversational breach and said, "Two weddings in two weeks! Isn't that wonderful?"

"I happen to think so," Fancy said, ignoring her husband as she spoke. A blush of conviction climbed her cheeks; she was prepared to stand her ground and defend the institution of marriage despite her own problems with Jeff.

"Thank you," Harlan said quietly.

At that Adam unbent a little and offered his hand to his mother's future husband, and Keith followed his lead with a mumbled "Congratulations."

Much later, when they were alone in her room, Quinn stretched out on the bed, fully dressed except for his boots, and pulled Melissa down to lie beside him. He unbuttoned her blouse and trailed his tongue along the lacy edge of her camisole.

Although they hadn't discussed the fact, they knew that a parting was inevitable, since Melissa would want to stay for Katherine's wedding and Quinn needed to get back to Port Riley and his work.

Melissa made a crooning sound and squirmed in shameless delight as Quinn bared one of her breasts and began a sweet farewell.

Thirteen

The stars had barely faded from the sky when Quinn kissed Melissa, crawled reluctantly out of bed, and began getting into his clothes.

It took a moment for Melissa to remember that they were in Port Hastings, rather than at home in Port Riley, and that she would be staying for her mother's wedding while Quinn would not. "It can't be time for you to leave," she protested, stretching beneath the warm covers and yawning.

He smiled, but even with the early morning shadows Melissa didn't miss the touch of sadness in his manner. "Go back to sleep," he said gruffly. "You're going to need your rest."

"Are you taking the train?" Melissa hoped the question sounded cheerful rather than suspicious, but what she really wanted to know was whether or not Quinn would be riding back to Port Riley with Gillian and a fur bedspread, and both of them knew it.

Quinn chuckled. "Yes, Mrs. Rafferty," he answered, "I am. But the car and Gillian are both gone, so I'll have to ride in the passenger section like everybody else."

Melissa was wildly relieved, although she gave no sign of it. "What about your horse?" she asked, to show that she was a modern woman and that she could dispense with the question of Gillian and the railroad car without harping on it.

"He's not riding with the passengers," Quinn replied with a straight face.

Melissa laughed and held out her arms, and Quinn came to her, if only to bend over the bed and favor her with a brief but very potent kiss. "Don't go," she said when he withdrew.

Quinn pretended he hadn't heard Melissa's plea, and she was grateful. For a moment there she'd behaved like a clinging vine, and she wanted to forget that. "When shall I send the car for you?" he asked, lingering at the door, his hand on the knob.

Melissa shook her head. "There's no need for that. I'll be on the first train Saturday morning."

With a nod Quinn opened the door and went out, and Melissa felt total desolation at the prospect of being separated from him even for so short a time.

As it happened, she was so busy helping Katherine with packing and arrangements that the days flew by. Soon it was Friday evening, and the Corbin house was brimming with friends and family.

Melissa was happy for her mother, but now that it was nearly time to say good-bye—perhaps years would pass before they saw each other again—she was tearful. When she joined Katherine in the large master bedroom that would now belong to Adam and Banner she had to work at smiling.

Fancy, who had just finished buttoning Katherine's wedding dress—a wispy creation of ice-blue silk—kissed her mother-in-law's cheek, nodded to Melissa, and left the room.

Katherine's eyes were suspiciously bright as she took Melissa's hands in hers. "I'll miss you very much, my darling," she said quietly.

Melissa embraced her. "And I'll miss you. But I know you're going to be happy, Mama—Harlan is a wonderful man."

"I'm of the same opinion about Quinn," Katherine said, and now there was an expression of stern affection in her eyes. "But you are as bullheaded as any of your brothers," she warned, going to her now-empty bureau and taking a worn velvet box from its top. "And you could spoil your chance for a happy life if you forget that there are many, many facets to womanhood. You may want to be a businesswoman, but you are also a wife, and at some point I hope you will be a mother. You must strike a balance among these roles, Melissa, and not focus yourself completely on any single one."

Melissa nodded, thinking that she had a remarkable mother, and was surprised when Katherine handed her the velvet box.

"Your father gave me this the day after I gave birth to you. Now I'd like you to have it."

Melissa's throat was thick with emotion as she lifted the battered, scuffed lid. Inside was a delicate choker of diamonds and amethysts set in filigreed gold. She swallowed, too moved to speak.

Katherine kissed her forehead. "You came as quite a surprise, you know—we'd thought our family was complete. Oh, but Daniel was thrilled to have a daughter!" She paused, recollecting, and her voice was soft when she went on. "Your papa believed that you were my gift to him, and he said this necklace was a poor present by comparison, but I treasured it. As I've always treasured you, Melissa."

At that Melissa wept in earnest, and so did Katherine, and it was thus that Keith found his mother and sister when he rapped briefly at the door and then let himself in.

"What's this?" he asked with a gentle smile. He put one arm around Melissa and one around Katherine. "Shall I go down there and tell Harlan that you've changed your mind, Mama?"

"Don't you dare!" Katherine cried through her tears.

"In that case, I think you'd better pull yourself together. In another moment or so you're going to be hearing the first strains of the wedding march."

As if on cue, the little-used pipe organ sounded ponderously in the distance.

159

Melissa sniffled and dried her eyes with a hankerchief, then tucked the necklace, still in its velvet box, into her brother's coat pocket for safekeeping. The two women embraced once more, and then Melissa went out into the hallway to stand at the top of the stairs.

Being the matron of honor, Melissa led the way, followed by the bride, who would be given away by Keith. The ceremony would be performed by Father McConnell, the local priest, since everyone in the family except Keith was Catholic.

The parlor was filled with people and with love and lit only by candlelight. Harlan stood, tall and spectacularly handsome, beside the fireplace, his eyes caressing Katherine as she approached him.

The wedding itself was a blur for Melissa, and when it was over she was filled with contradictory emotions. Something grand had begun for her mother that night, but something had ended, too. As soon as she could leave without attracting undue attention Melissa fled to the kitchen.

Her efforts to escape unnoticed had not been successful, she soon found, for Adam and Jeff both soon joined her. She was sitting at the table with her chin propped despondently in her hands, and they took seats on either side of her.

"Things change, brat," Jeff said gently, reaching out to take her hand.

"This is stupid," Melissa lamented through her tears. "Mama's had this wonderful thing happen to her, and I'm sitting out here blubbering away like a fool! Anyone would think that I wasn't happy for her."

Adam slid back his chair to go to the stove. "Anybody want a cup of coffee?" he asked.

Jeff made a face. "Good God, no," he boomed. "That stuff is probably strong enough to raise the dead!"

Melissa laughed, feeling better. The world hadn't changed so very much if Jeff was still Jeff and Adam still liked his coffee pungent as kerosene.

Jeff's hand lingered on hers, and he grinned at his sister as Adam sat down at the table again, this time with a mug of day-old coffee in front of him. "The man must have paralysis of the tastebuds," he remarked.

That made Melissa laugh again, and her eldest brother swept both her and Jeff up in a look he usually reserved for raving hypochondriacs. But Adam's words were gentle.

"He's not a bad sort, that husband of yours," he conceded.

Melissa glanced at Jeff and saw that he was looking sheepish. He squeezed her hand and said, "I guess I probably didn't make too good an impression. I'm sorry, brat."

"I may or may not forgive you," Melissa teased in a haughty voice.

Jeff's tone and expression were still serious. "What kind of husband is he going to make, this Rafferty?"

"The same kind Papa was to Mama, I hope," Melissa said dreamily, thinking of the beautiful necklace and the love that had inspired its presentation nearly twenty-three years before.

A look passed between Jeff and Adam at these words, one that stirred a vast unsettling within Melissa, but before she could ask what had prompted it, Keith came in. He took the velvet box from his pocket and extended it to his sister. "There's somebody here to see you," he told her.

Melissa set the box on the table and rose to her feet. "Who?"

Keith turned and pushed the kitchen door slightly, and Melissa watched Ajax come in. She was amazed at the change in his appearance since she'd seen him in Port Riley just a few days before. He looked as though he'd been falling-down drunk every moment of that time; his eyes were red-rimmed, his skin was sallow, and his clothes were rumpled.

"Melissa," he said hoarsely.

"Do you want us to stay?" Adam asked his sister. He must have known what the answer would be because he had already risen from his chair at the kitchen table.

Melissa shook her head, feeling pity for Ajax, but certainly not love. She knew now that she'd never really loved him at all. "I'll be fine," she said.

Jeff looked reluctant, but he left the kitchen with Adam

and Keith, and Melissa once again found herself alone with the man she'd almost married. She was fully prepared to hear him say that he was returning to Europe with his mistress.

Instead he grasped one of her hands in his and blurted out, "I cannot bear to lose you!"

Melissa was stunned. After all, she'd made her feelings clear on two separate occasions, and Ajax had never struck her as being prone to emotional displays. She retreated a step, almost wishing that she had not sent her brothers away. "Ajax, it's too late. I'm married to someone else."

He let her go and grasped the back of a kitchen chair so hard that his knuckles showed white through his skin. "You were rash," he spat out furiously. "You were very rash!"

A chill swept over Melissa, even though the kitchen was warm. She hugged herself and said, "It would have been a terrible mistake for us to marry."

"No!" Ajax protested. "We could have had a fine marriage!"

Melissa was beginning to think that she was dealing with a madman, but she wasn't afraid because she knew that even the most halfhearted cry would bring more help than she needed. "You have a mistress," she reminded him.

Ajax was a study in frustration. "Why does that bother you so much? Half the men I know keep mistresses—"

"I don't care how many statistics you quote," Melissa interrupted, shaking her head. "I won't have a man who doesn't love me enough to be faithful."

The jilted bridegroom thrust splayed fingers through his hair. Melissa marveled that she'd never seen the weakness in him, the self-indulgence. "Your own brothers probably keep mistresses," he said.

Melissa folded her arms and shook her head. "Port Hastings is a small town," she told him. "If that were true, it would be common knowledge. I would have heard about it."

Ajax arched one pale-gold eyebrow. "Oh? The way you heard about your father, you mean?" He spread his hands in a resigned fashion. "He was a notorious philanderer, you know."

Melissa felt a stinging fury. "That's a lie!"

"Is it?" taunted Ajax. "Ask your mother—or one of your noble brothers."

"Get out!"

Again Ajax spread his hands. "You are a fool, Melissa. A spoiled, naïve little fool. And one of these days you're going to learn that there are no fairy-tale princes in that big world out there—just ordinary, mortal men."

Melissa started toward the inner door, but Ajax stopped her by grasping her arm in a bruising hold and wrenching her against his chest. She squirmed and struggled, too furious to cry out, but he was strong, and she could not escape him. He caught his hand in her hair and pulled her head back, subjecting her to a cruel, hurtful kiss. He smelled and tasted of liquor and of hatred.

She twisted and fought, but it wasn't her own efforts that freed her. No, a hand closed over the front of Ajax's neck, and he was thrust backward, striking the brick wall beside the fireplace with a force that made Melissa wince.

"I think you'd better leave now," Keith said in a low drawl before he released his sister's persistent suitor.

Ajax was dusting off his rumpled clothes as though he'd taken a fall, and he looked at Keith's clerical collar with amused contempt. "I'll hurry off to vespers," he said.

"Good," Keith replied. "While you're saying your prayers, make a point of thanking the good Lord that I was the one who walked in here just now. If it had been Jeff or Adam, they'd still be working on you."

Ajax was full of cocky bravado, but he was also pale. He nodded curtly at Melissa and strode out through the back door.

"Are you all right?" Keith asked, taking Melissa's shoulders in his hands and bending his head to look into her eyes.

Melissa was gnawing at her lower lip. She'd been barely thirteen when Daniel Corbin drowned, and the news had shattered her. She'd loved and respected her father and had never completely stopped mourning him. Now Ajax's implications stuck like burrs. "Y-yes," she said.

Her brother cupped her chin in one hand. "The truth, brat," he said gently.

"He said something awful about Papa," she confessed. "Something really awful."

Keith was silent, waiting.

"He said Papa was like—like him. He said he kept a mistress."

Keith looked away for a moment, then said, "Suppose he did, Melissa? Would his memory mean any less to you than it does now?"

Melissa swallowed. It was all she could do not to put her hands over her ears like a child. "I don't want to hear this," she fretted. "Keith, I don't want to know!"

He kissed her forehead. "Papa was a good man, sweetheart. He loved Mama and he loved us. Isn't that what matters?"

Melissa's eyes were burning with tears. She ached with disillusionment and a fury she had no way to vent. "I suppose Ajax was right about you and Adam and Jeff, too!" she cried in a stricken whisper. "You've all got mistresses, and you think it's all right because you 'love' your wives and you 'love' your children—"

Keith gave her a gentle shake. "Listen to me. I can't answer for Jeff and Adam, but I can tell you that what I have with Tess is too good to risk losing."

Melissa let her forehead rest against her brother's strong shoulder. "I wanted to believe that Papa was perfect," she said sadly.

"Then you did him an injustice," Keith replied quietly. "Now, Mama is about to drive away in a carriage with her brand-new husband. Shouldn't we go out there and wish them well?"

Melissa nodded, dried her eyes on one of Maggie's checkered table napkins, and followed her brother out of the kitchen.

An hour later Katherine and Harlan were off to catch the last steamer to Seattle, and Melissa was so homesick for Quinn that she wished she hadn't refused his offer to send the railroad car for her.

Settled in her own bed, a lamp burning on her nightstand, she held the diamond and amethyst choker in her hands and remembered Daniel Corbin. He'd been a big man, like his sons, and so handsome that Melissa had been proud to point him out to her friends. He'd called her his little princess and read her stories and taken her with him when he traveled to Seattle on business, and Melissa had adored him.

To find out that he'd been a stranger, at least in part, was painful, especially now, in this topsy-turvy time in her life. She was married to a man she hadn't even known two weeks before, and wildly in love with him in the bargain. Her mother, the center and core of the family, had a new name and a future that lay in a far-off place. And then there was the situation with Jeff and Fancy.

The unchangeable was changing, and Melissa was frightened and confused. Only when the fire had burned down to embers did she sleep, and then it was to dream that Fancy had run away with a traveling salesman and taken all four of her children along.

Melissa was waiting at the depot long before the morning train was due to pull out, and her heart was already in Port Riley, with Quinn. She could barely wait to catch up with it.

Since she'd said good-bye to the family the night before, only Fancy was there to see her off, and she wasn't very good company. Her eyes were red-rimmed from crying, and there was no color at all in her cheeks.

"Last night I dreamed that you ran away with a peddler," Melissa said, giving the words a light tone.

In the distance the train whistle gave a mournful cry.

Fancy shook her head. "I could never leave Jeff," she said miserably. "But I'm very afraid that he's going to leave me."

Melissa drew a step closer, wanting to put her arms around her sister-in-law but not quite daring to do that. "Oh, Fancy, are things really that bad?"

Fancy nodded. "He's so strong-willed, so domineering. Melissa, the very things I love about Jeff are the things that are destroying me."

"What is it you want to do?"

Small, trim shoulders moved in a despondent shrug. "I

want to be important in some way, like Katherine—and Banner and Tess—and you."

"Me?" Melissa put her hand to her chest.

"Katherine and Banner have their cause, and Tess has her photography, and you—you have your wonderful education. You've traveled all over the world. All I ever did was pull a rabbit out of a hat in a carnival sideshow and have babies!"

Melissa would have laughed if she hadn't known that Fancy was serious. "Having babies is no small matter," she said gently, touching Fancy's arm. "After all, half the population can't do it!"

Fancy smiled tentatively at that, but her expression was soon sober again. She looked down at her feet. "Jeff is already talking about wanting another daughter," she said in a small voice. "But there aren't going to be any more babies. There was damage when Caroline was born."

Melissa was beginning to understand. "Doesn't Jeff know that?"

Fancy's eyes were wide and full of disquiet when she looked at Melissa and shook her head. "No, and I can't bear for him to find out. He'll be so disappointed in me."

"Only if that was all he wanted you for," Melissa replied, annoyed. "And I know you mean far more to Jeff than some kind of baby machine!"

The conversation had to end then, for the train had arrived, and the noise was horrific. Melissa and Fancy exchanged a hug and parted.

The passenger section of the train was crowded with people on their way to Port Riley for the grand opening of Quinn's hotel—Melissa rarely allowed herself to dwell on the fact that the enterprise also belonged to Gillian—and she was lucky to find a seat.

The car was cramped and poorly ventilated, and the first thing Melissa did when she got off the train was hurry around to one side of the building and throw up in the tall grass.

A friendly woman in a calico dress had spotted her, although Melissa had prayed that no one would witness her humiliation. The stranger brought a dipperful of cold, clean water from inside the depot, and she held it out with a warm smile.

"Is this your first?" she asked as Melissa rinsed her mouth and spat unceremoniously.

"My first what?" she wanted to know.

"Baby, of course," the Samaritan answered.

"No!" Melissa cried, shaken. "I mean, yes!" She paused, drew a deep breath, let it out again. "I mean, I'm not—not in the family way."

The woman only smiled smugly, shrugged, and moved away, taking the dipper with her.

Melissa walked home in a daze, leaving her baggage to be picked up later. She couldn't be pregnant, she thought. She just couldn't. It would spoil all her plans for starting up the newspaper, and besides, she and Quinn didn't know each other well enough to have a child together.

By the time she'd arrived at the house she now thought of as home, Melissa had a pounding headache. She greeted Helga and Mrs. Wright in a disconcerted manner, climbed the stairs, entered the master suite, and collapsed face down on the bed.

To her amazement, she slept, and very soundly. It must have been nearly suppertime, judging by the thinning light at the windows, when she was awakened by a gentle but insistent hand on her shoulder.

"Mrs. Rafferty? Mrs. Rafferty!"

Melissa rolled over and sat up, staring sightlessly at the intruder until Helga's face came into focus. "Where is my husband?"

"He sent word that he wants you to join him at the new hotel for dinner," Helga announced, apparently seeing some romance in the situation that eluded her mistress.

Melissa wanted to cry. She hadn't seen that man in three days, and he couldn't even be bothered to come home and greet her. It only went to show how little he cared.

Helga had brought a service cart along with her, and its delicate contents rattled expensively as she wheeled it closer and poured Melissa a cup of tea. "There now, that'll make you feel better. You can't go to the party looking peaky!"

Melissa sighed. She felt like staying home and hiding under the covers, but she wasn't going to miss that party. It was too important to her, and to Quinn. She took a cautious sip of the tea and waited to see if it would stay down.

"Are you all right, Mrs. Rafferty?" Helga persisted, peering at Melissa and frowning.

"I'm perfectly fine," Melissa insisted. "It's just that the past few days have been—well, rigorous, that's all."

Helga was beaming. "Mr. Rafferty told us that your mother was being married. She's a beautiful woman, if you don't mind my saying so, and I loved laying out her clothes for her."

Melissa smiled. "Mama was a lovely bride," she said, and Helga looked so eager that she felt honor bound to describe the entire wedding, right down to the cake and the candlelight and Katherine's ice-blue gown of whispering silk.

Helga's eyes got wider and wider as Melissa talked, and she couldn't contain an occasional "You don't say!" When the story was over she walked into the bathroom and started Melissa's bath, and when she came out again she still looked like a happy sleepwalker.

"I just love weddings," she said as she wheeled the cart out of the room.

Melissa was feeling better by the time she'd finished her bath and used some of the talcum and perfume she'd brought from home. Wearing a lemon-yellow wrapper of lace-trimmed taffeta, she brushed her hair until it glimmered and then pinned it atop her head in a simple but elegant arrangement.

She put on her lavender silk and even managed to button it herself, but the exercise left her in a testy mood, and when Quinn appeared just as she was clasping her diamond and amethyst necklace she spurned his offer of help with an impatient "I can do it myself!"

Although his eyes darkened with annoyance, he bent his head and kissed the alabaster smoothness of her shoulder by way of a greeting. "You're tired," he said. "I'll understand if you don't want to go to the party."

Melissa turned into his arms, wanting peace with him but

unsure how to get past her formidable pride to reach out to him. "Do you love me, Quinn?" she asked.

This time there was no doubting that he'd heard her. His hands slid from her waist, and he gave her a bewildered look. "Do I what?" he countered.

"Do you love me?" Melissa repeated.

Quinn sighed and reached for her, then let his hands fall back to his sides. "I don't know," he admitted. "I feel something, but whether it's love or not . . ."

Melissa thought of the lady who'd brought her water when she was sick behind the railroad depot that day. The woman had assumed that she was pregnant, and maybe she'd been right. The future looked bleak, for her and for her baby, if she was carrying one, without her husband's love. She dropped her eyes to hide the tears that came too readily these days. "I understand," she said at last.

"I don't think you do," Quinn said thickly. "But we can talk about this later." For the first time Melissa noticed what he was wearing—a very formal and beautifully tailored suit. "Right now we're late for dinner."

Fury restored Melissa as nothing else could have done. Now she knew what was really important to Quinn—his hotel—and she could plan her life accordingly.

The first thing she would do was learn to live without love.

Fourteen

The dining room of Quinn's new Seaside Hotel was huge, and it was filled to capacity with guests and well-wishers. Melissa smiled broadly, waving to her friend Dana, who sat at a distant table with her aunt and uncle. She pretended that all was well as Quinn escorted her to the head table and seated her before taking the chair beside hers. Gillian, who sat to his immediate right, gave Melissa a brief nod and then devoured Quinn with her luminous violet eyes.

Under other circumstances Melissa would have shown the poise she'd been schooled in since childhood, but she was tired, she feared that she might be pregnant, and she felt very much alone in the world. These elements combined to shake her considerable self-confidence.

Quinn tried several times to engage her in conversation, but she only stared dully at her plate and continually re-arranged its contents with the tines of her fork. While her earlier nausea had passed, she certainly didn't possess an appetite.

Quinn eventually turned to Gillian, who was more than willing to chat, and each of her trilling, melodic little giggles increased Melissa's ire until her lethargy was burned away. She was simmering inside when the interminable meal finally ended and the orchestra began to tune up in the ballroom.

Catching her hand in his, Quinn pulled his wife into one of the offices and rested his hands on her bare, silken shoulders. "Melissa, do you want me to take you home?" he asked indulgently. "It's obvious that you're not up to all this."

So, Melissa deduced, he wanted to get rid of her. Probably so that he could have a high old time with his "partner," Gillian Aires. Without warning she drew back her hand and slapped Quinn across the face.

For a moment he looked stunned, but then his brown eyes took on a veiled expression. His fingers came back to Melissa's shoulders, and he gave her a slight shake. "What was that for?" he demanded in a raspy voice.

When Melissa remained stubbornly silent, Quinn released her and walked out, leaving her to stand in that small, shadowy office, gnawing at her lower lip and wondering what on earth was the matter with her. Tears came to the surface— dear God, how she hated them—and she lingered in her hiding place until she was sure that all traces of them were gone. Music had been swelling from the ballroom for a long time before she dared walk into that room.

She held her head high and her shoulders straight. Only Quinn was close enough to Melissa to know that she was falling apart inside. But he was dancing with Gillian in the center of the ballroom, and the two of them made a spectacular couple.

Melissa realized that everyone who knew she was Quinn's wife was watching her, waiting to gauge her reaction. She smiled and lingered in the doorway for a moment, as she'd been taught, and then strolled in as though she were Queen Victoria herself and all the guests were her subjects.

Mitch Williams approached her almost immediately, looking handsomer than ever in his fancy evening clothes. His blue eyes glittered as they swept over her low-cut lavender gown, and he gave a slight bow before offering one hand. "May I have this dance?" he asked.

At least, Melissa reflected sourly behind her fixed smile, there was one gentleman in this place. She swept into Mitch's arms for the waltz that was just beginning and decided to forgive him for telling Quinn she'd asked him for money when she hadn't.

Quinn gave her a look of glaring disapproval as she and Mitch whirled past him and Gillian, and from that moment on Melissa flirted outrageously. She smiled up at Mr. Williams as though he'd just been elected president, drinking in whatever he said, batting her eyelashes at him, allowing him to bring her punch, and dancing every dance with him.

Finally Quinn could bear it no longer—that was exactly the end that Melissa had had in mind—and he walked up to her, took her hand, and pulled her out of the ballroom. He dragged her across the lobby and up the stairs, and on the first landing Melissa realized that she had pushed him too far. She tried to pull free of his grasp, but that effort proved hopeless, for Quinn only lifted her into his arms and continued on his way. His jawline looked hard as tamarack, and his brash eyes were snapping with fury as he strode along the upper hallway and pushed open the door to the exquisite suite he had shown Melissa before. To her utter amazement, he hurled her onto the bed and snarled, "There are a great many things I will tolerate, Calico, but being taunted in public is not one of them."

Melissa had recovered some of her aplomb; she sat up on the silken coverlet and fanned herself with one hand. "Well, then," she said with grudging primness, "I'm sorry."

"Not good enough," Quinn replied coldly.

Melissa felt her eyes go wide. "What do you want, then?"

He drew her up so that she was kneeling on the bed and bent his head to touch his mouth to hers. It was not a loving kiss, but one meant to demonstrate mastery, and, to Melissa's eternal mortification, it succeeded.

She was breathless when Quinn finally let her go, and she would have agreed to anything.

But he was not ready to discuss terms; he clearly meant to conquer her fully. He unfastened the top few buttons at the back of her gown and then lowered the bodice, bearing her breasts to his view.

Melissa trembled, waiting for him to touch her with either his mouth or his hands, but he did nothing—not then. He simply looked at her, and under his smoldering eyes her nipples grew taut and her breasts took on a fullness that only he could relieve.

"I don't like to be teased, Melissa," he said evenly, and at last he encircled one straining nipple with the tip of his finger. "Do you?"

No one else had ever had the power, or the opportunity, to tease Melissa. Now, as she yearned to give herself to a man who would not take her, she knew a grinding regret. "Please," she whispered, "I'm sorry."

Quinn strode across the room, and for a moment Melissa believed that he was going to leave her. Relief and wild disappointment battled within her, and she didn't know whether she'd achieved victory or suffered defeat when he locked the door and turned down the gaslights until the room was shadowy.

She was still kneeling on the bed, but Quinn brought her to sit in his lap, and when he bent to taste one aching nipple she let her head fall back and moaned in sheer, shameless pleasure.

Quinn took his time at her breasts, stopping every now and then to madden her with another rebuke. Presently, when Melissa was almost crazed with the need of him, he laid her down gently and lifted her skirts and petticoat, then brought down her smooth taffeta drawers.

Melissa trembled as he stroked the bare flesh of her inner thighs, parting them so subtly that she never felt the motion. He nuzzled the warm, silken mound where her womanhood was hidden, and she gave a little cry, catching her hands in his hair.

He lapped at her, and her hips ground against the mattress as ferocious pleasure fanned out from his tongue to scald her blood. For a seeming eternity Quinn pleasured her, driving her to the edge of madness again and again, only to draw back each time.

Finally, when Melissa could bear no more, she pleaded aloud, "Oh, God, Quinn, please—"

It was then that he withdrew and rose back to his feet. Even in the dim light of the gas lamps she saw the cold glitter in his eyes. Unbelievably, he turned away.

Melissa found the strength to right her skirt and sit partway up to stare at him. "Quinn," she whispered brokenly, unable to grasp what he'd done to her.

In the light from the hallway she saw him shrug. "As you're so fond of telling me," he said in a hoarse drawl, "you can take care of yourself. I guess you'll have to do that now, won't you?"

It was impossible to discern which was worse: the ache of humiliation in her soul or the physical disappointment her body had endured. Melissa held back her tears until Quinn had closed the door, and then she wept in earnest.

Her regret was bitter, and considerable time passed before she rose from the bed and went into the washroom to splash cold water over her face. She hurried now, remembering how Quinn had told her that all the rooms in the hotel were rented. She wouldn't be able to stand it if someone came in and found her in such a state.

When she was again presentable, her hair tidy and the worst of the wrinkles smoothed out of her gown, Melissa found a smile to wear and walked regally down the stairs, her head held high. She had reviewed her options and decided to stay, as much to vex Quinn as to prove to herself that she was no scared rabbit. Every inch the woman of the world, Melissa walked into the ballroom and straight up to her husband. He was standing near one of the tall windows on the opposite side, looking murderous, and his expression did not soften when he found his wife standing before him.

"I will despise you all my life for what you just did to me," she said, smiling up at him warmly, her cheeks flushed, her eyes adoring.

A flamboyant Strauss waltz began, and Quinn pulled Melissa into his arms without warning and thrust her against him, hard, before swirling her into the sweeping richness of the music.

"And I thought you'd come to apologize for your infantile behavior," he said belatedly.

Melissa beamed at him, not wanting anyone to read her real feelings and perhaps guess at the mortification she had undergone earlier. If that ever became public knowledge, she would be ruined. "Apologize?" she chimed. "I'll see you sizzle in hell before I apologize to you, my dearest darling."

Quinn scowled down at her for a beat or two, then gave a grudging laugh. "My God, but you've got brass enough for ten women, you little hellcat. I ought to take you over my knee."

"You try that, Quinn Rafferty, and you won't live long enough to pass on the story."

He arched one eyebrow. "First teasing, now threats. You've got a lot to learn about wifely obedience, precious."

"Wifely obedience, hell," she spat back, batting her eyelashes in a convincing display of worship. "As far as I'm concerned, Mr. Rafferty, you and I are at war."

"So be it," Quinn sighed. "Have you considered the possibility that you might lose, my dear? If not, be advised that I'm taking no prisoners."

A thrill, made up partly of sweet challenge and partly of something else that she didn't care to examine too closely, raced through Melissa. She reached up and touched Quinn's face very gently just where she'd slapped him before. "Neither am I," she replied with a dazzling smile. The music came to a graceful halt, and Melissa lingered in Quinn's wooden embrace, waiting for the orchestra to begin playing again. She deliberately brushed her breasts against his chest as, with an almost inaudible groan, he drew her into another dance.

They spent the rest of the evening that way, whirling around the crowded ballroom, beaming at each other and exchanging veiled insults, until the party finally ended at one o'clock.

Melissa collected her cloak and was about to join the others waiting outside for their carriages and buggies when Quinn caught her by the elbow and steered her toward the stairs again. This time she balked, wrenching free and glaring at him.

"Just what do you think you're doing?" she demanded, flushed and overwhelmed.

"We're going upstairs to our suite," Quinn said cheerfully, again playing the part of the adoring husband.

"You said it was taken!"

"It was—by me."

Quinn had to have reserved those luxurious rooms weeks before, since the hotel was full to the rafters. And he hadn't even known Melissa when he'd made romantic plans; obviously, he'd meant to share the suite with Gillian.

Melissa whirled, now beyond caring what anyone else thought, and started back down the stairs. Quinn brought her up short by stepping in front of her and barring her way.

"Not so fast, Mrs. Rafferty," he said, taking one of her hands in his and kissing the heel of her palm and then the more sensitive underside of her wrist. "You're not going anywhere."

With a toss of her head Melissa started around her husband, but he proved impassable, like a rockslide on a narrow mountain road. "I want to go home," she hissed through her teeth. "You will let me by, Mr. Rafferty, without further delay!"

He merely laughed. "My God, where do you get that boneheaded confidence of yours? It must be bred into you Corbins, like quick tempers and blue eyes."

Melissa would have spat on him if it weren't for the fact that that was definitely an unladylike thing to do, and she didn't want anyone saying that the editor and publisher of the town newspaper was no lady. She lifted her chin. "For the last time, Mr. Rafferty, let me pass. If you don't, I will make a pure hell of your entire life."

"You've already done that," he crooned as a group of couples moved by them on the stairs, on their way to rooms and suites of their own. "Now come with me, sweetheart, and I'll finish what I started earlier."

Melissa felt a heated jolt go through her at the suggestion, and she was furious, not only with Quinn, but with herself for responding so readily to every innuendo and scurrilous promise the man uttered. She was angry with him, and she had to remember that.

His brown eyes were caressing her now, and one of his fingers traced the delicate choker of amethysts and diamonds that graced her neck. "Surrender, little soldier. You're already beaten."

"I'm leaving," she insisted, and she moved around him and started down the stairs. She was just congratulating herself on her fortitude and daring when Quinn, apparently lacking her desire to avoid a scene, hoisted her awkwardly over one shoulder and started back upstairs.

"I never got to carry her over the threshold," he explained to the staring onlookers.

Having seen their expressions, Melissa buried her face in Quinn's back, not wanting to look again. When he set her down in the privacy of their room, however, she hurled herself at him, wild in her outrage, and would have bitten and clawed him to pieces if he hadn't imprisoned her hands at her sides and thus subdued her.

She was still breathing heavily, her hair falling from its pins, when he finally released her. The moment he did she was a mountain cat again, scratching, kicking, and doing her best to bite him.

With a rumbled swear word he wrenched her around so that her back was to his chest and held her fast with one steel-like arm. With his free hand he tugged downward on her bodice so that her breasts spilled out, warm and lush, eager to become his playthings.

He began to caress her very gently, all the while holding her against him, and Melissa gave a little cry of mingled rage and submission. She closed her eyes and let her head fall back against Quinn's shoulder, murmuring, "I hate you—oh, God—how I hate you."

Quinn was kissing the ivory length of her neck, occasionally flicking her earlobe with the tip of his tongue, and Melissa was dizzy with wanting him. She could only hope now that he would not make her need him terribly and then desert her, as he had before.

His hand left her swollen breasts to begin lifting her skirts, then dispensing with the ribbon ties on her drawers. Thus loosened, the slippery taffeta bloomers slid down over Melissa's trembling legs of their own accord.

She shivered as he began to stroke and tease her, bringing her back to the same fever pitch of desire that she had known before. The word "please" swelled in her throat, but she would have died rather than say it.

Presently the caresses stopped, but only briefly. Quinn had unfastened his trousers, and he sat down in a chair, drawing Melissa with him. Now, however, as she descended she sheathed him in her femininity, and Quinn let out a lusty groan.

Melissa was by this time so aroused that the first thrust of Quinn's hips set her body to buckling with sweet spasms of release. The whole while he spoke softly to her and caressed her full breasts.

The realization that she had taken command of the situation was heady as wine to Melissa. Drunk with power, she began moving upon Quinn in a way she knew would render him mindless. She gloried in every moan he uttered, and in the senseless words he gasped as his own fulfillment was reached.

His breath was ragged as he kissed the nape of Melissa's neck. Deep inside he was still stroking her, however slowly, and her body betrayed her with a suddenness and power that left her breathless. With a cry, her eyes wide with surprise, she convulsed in incredulous pleasure.

Melissa was hardly aware of being carried to the bed, so sated was she, though she knew when Quinn stripped off his clothes and crawled in beside her, taking her into his arms and tucking her against his torso. She yawned and slipped into a fathomless sleep.

When she awakened Quinn was poised above her, looking down at her with a wicked grin. She started to protest, but her body was instantly ready for him. With a soft laugh he eased into her, and she could not help welcoming him.

They moved together in ferocious unison, clothed only in night shadows, until passion seized them both and wrung hoarse cries of surrender from their throats.

Quinn realized that he was alone even before he opened his eyes, and the knowledge produced a strange sense of vulnerability inside him. Sunlight pooled around him, making him blink and mutter a curse as he groped for his pocket watch on the bedside table. Eight-fifteen.

Laughter and cheers, punctuated by an occasional cracking sound, came to him through the windows, along with a springlike breeze. He sat up, grumbling, and rubbed his eyes with a thumb and forefinger until the room came into focus. A knock sounded at the door, and he prayed for coffee before calling out, "Come in!"

His father, grizzled and rough and smelling mightily of the whiskey he loved, loomed in the chasm. Quinn would not have been more surprised to see the devil himself.

"What the hell—?" he ground out, reaching for his pants.

Eustice Rafferty stepped into the suite and closed the door. His dark brown eyes, representing virtually the only resemblance he and Quinn bore to each other, scanned the sumptuous room. His face was seamed with dirt, and his bushy gray beard stood out from his face like bristles on a coarse brush. He smiled, showing rotten teeth. "You've done all right for yourself, son," he said, as though they'd been the best of friends. "It's a far cry from that shack up on the mountain, ain't it?"

"What do you want?" Quinn demanded. He scrambled out of bed and pulled on his trousers when Eustice looked away.

His father had gone to stand in the open doorway leading out to the stone terrace. "She's a pretty little thing, that wife of yours. For a while there I thought you was never going to marry up with anybody."

Quinn drew a deep breath and let it out again in an effort to gain control over his emotions. Surprise had put him at a disadvantage. "Never mind Melissa. I asked what you were doing here."

"That her name? Melissa?" There was another loud crack outside, followed by more cheers and whoops of delight.

Curiosity drew Quinn to the window, and he smiled at what he saw. There was a baseball game going on in the field just beyond the hotel, and Melissa, clad in a pair of checkered bloomers, was hopping back and forth between second and third bases, good-naturedly taunting the pitcher.

Finally the batter, who, like every other player on both teams, was female, got a base hit. Melissa streaked past third and made home in a glorious belly slide just before the catcher would have put her out.

It was Eustice's appreciative laughter that brought Quinn back to the reality of the situation. "You've got a hell of a nerve coming back here, old man," he said, "after what you did."

Eustice's voice took on the whiny note that had always nettled Quinn. "There's such a thing as forgivin' a man, ya know," he complained. "It'd mean a lot to your ma, our buryin' the hatchet and all."

Quinn moved out onto the terrace and grasped the stone railing in his hands. Melissa was still engaged in the baseball game, and he wondered idly where she'd gotten those God-awful bloomers.

His father was beside him immediately. "All I really need is a little grubstake, boy—then I'll be outta here for good."

"That's what you said last time," Quinn reminded him. He felt a tickle near his deaf ear and rubbed it with his fingers. "Just get out of my sight, will you? The temptation to throw you over this balcony is almost more than I can stand."

Eustice moved a step further away. "You wouldn't do that," he muttered, but he didn't sound entirely sure.

"Get out," Quinn repeated quietly.

"I need money," Eustice insisted, standing his ground.

Quinn turned from the balcony and went back into the suite. He'd felt Melissa's gaze on him for a moment there, and he hoped devoutly that she wouldn't decide to come back inside and investigate. Play your baseball game, Calico, he thought. But stay away.

He took his wallet from the inside pocket of the cutaway coat he'd worn the night before and counted out a respectable sum. Every time Eustice showed up it was the same; Quinn gave the old man money in return for a promise that he'd stay away.

But promises were never any better than the man who made them, and Eustice was, in Quinn's opinion, just barely human.

The old man snatched the money from his son's hand. "You got trouble up on the mountain," he mused, flipping through the currency with grubby, practiced fingers. "Old Jake Sever, he's of a mind that you been tossin' up his wife's skirts now and again. Means to kill you and her both, to hear him tell it."

Quinn sighed and ran a hand through his hair. "You have your money," he said wearily. "Now get out."

Eustice started toward the door, tucking the folded bills into the pocket of his dirty plaid shirt. "Wonder what that fancy little lady of yours would think if she knowed that you got me for a daddy. Bet it'd come as a shock to her delicate senserbilities."

Quinn closed his eyes for a moment, and in his mind he could hear his mother crying, see Mary crouching in a corner of that shack up on the mountain, scared to death.

Eustice left, finally, but he must have encountered Melissa in the hallway, because she came in smudged with dirt, hair all atangle, and asked, "Who was that strange old man?"

"Never mind," Quinn replied a bit too brusquely. He saw that he'd hurt her but didn't know how to make up for it. He grinned sadly. "Where the devil did you get those trousers?"

Melissa had already recovered from his rude answer to her question. "From home, of course. They were in one of the boxes Mama sent." She whirled. "Do you like them?"

Quinn laughed and held her close; she was like a cool and soothing breeze moving through his mind and heart, carrying away all the grief and insanity of the past.

"I thought you and I were at war," Melissa said, looking up at him with puzzlement in her beautiful azure eyes.

He kissed her forehead. "We were," he answered as a sweet, thundering pain filled his chest. "You win, Calico. You win."

✑ *Fifteen*

Melissa had washed her face and straightened her hair, but she was still wearing the bloomers and loose blouse that she'd rushed home to fetch before organizing the baseball game. Quinn commented on neither her clothing nor the game, and Melissa didn't push for an opinion. She simply allowed him to escort her down the stairs, past the sparkling, merry fountain, and into the dining room.

There her unconventional appearance did attract some notice, and defiant color rose in her cheeks as rich women from all over the state made whispered comments behind their fans. Quinn was still distracted and moved along the buffet table without noticing that his wife had caused a stir.

Melissa was ravenous, and she helped herself to sliced peaches, a flaky roll, a sausage patty, and some scrambled eggs. She and Quinn were both seated, Quinn staring bleakly into space as he chewed, when Gillian and Mitch entered the room arm in arm.

When Gillian nodded at her, Melissa realized that she'd been staring and looked away, embarrassed. She turned to Quinn after a moment of recovery and said brightly, "Tomorrow I'll begin gathering stories for the first issue of the Port Riley *Clarion*. The hotel opening will be front-page news."

At last Quinn came out of his reverie to smile at her. "I'm honored," he said.

Melissa didn't know whether he was being kind or contemptuous, and that nettled her. "You behave as though this newspaper were some childish game of mine," she protested. "You don't think I can do this."

Quinn raised one hand in a plea for peace. "I think," he began diplomatically, "that you don't have the first idea of what's involved. I'm also aware that you've probably never suffered a really notable failure in your life, and you therefore have no conception of the fact that not every idea that rises to the surface of that formidable mind of yours is going to work."

Melissa stopped eating and folded her arms, but before she could say anything Gillian and Mitch arrived, holding their plates.

"May we join you?" Mitch asked.

"Sure," Quinn replied in masculine fashion—thoughtless of Melissa's reaction.

Melissa and Gillian, equally uncomfortable, exchanged a look.

By the time Mitch had seated her, however, Gillian was in fine fettle. "Remarkable," she said, with a deprecating glance at Melissa's dusty blouse.

The men, involved in a conversation of their own, paid no attention to the small drama being played out at their table.

"Thank you," Melissa replied, as though Gillian had complimented her.

Gillian gave a little twittering laugh that was devoid of mirth and speared a strawberry with her fork, chewing it delicately before inquiring, "I must know, darling—were you part of that spectacle in the field this morning?"

Melissa smiled at Gillian's reference to the baseball game. "Oh, definitely—darling. My team won, in fact."

With a knowing glance at Quinn's profile Gillian replied, "I wouldn't be so sure of that, if I were you. Tell me, though. Wherever did you get enough harridans to make up two teams?"

Melissa longed to throw something at Gillian; instead, she smiled again. "Why, I advertised, of course," she answered sweetly. "I put up fliers that read 'Harridans Wanted for Baseball Game.' And I must say, we were all surprised when you didn't apply."

Gillian had the good grace to blush and look away, and Melissa turned to Quinn, hoping to make a place for herself in his conversation with Mitch. Instead, she watched in round-eyed horror as her husband's friend poked his fork into a slimy mess of raw oysters and swallowed one with relish.

Nausea erupted in Melissa's stomach like a geyser, she clapped one hand over her mouth and fled toward the nearest exit, the French doors leading out into the side garden.

Fifteen minutes later, when she let herself into the suite, Quinn was there, pacing, looking as colorless as Melissa felt.

"Sweetheart, where were you?" he asked, taking her shoulders in his hands. "I looked everywhere."

"I didn't want you to see me," Melissa confessed in a small voice, and when she started toward the bathroom Quinn let her go.

She scrubbed her teeth and splashed cold water over her face. When she looked into the mirror she saw that Quinn was standing behind her, leaning against the door jamb, his arms folded.

Although he didn't speak again, his stance and expression said that he would wait as long as he had to for an explanation, probably blocking the bathroom doorway the whole time.

Melissa sighed and faced him squarely. "I was throwing up in the shrubbery, if you must know," she announced. "I probably have the grippe or something."

Quinn was staring at her in much the same way she'd regarded Mitch's raw oysters at breakfast. "Or you could be pregnant," he said.

His feelings concerning fatherhood were perfectly apparent in the way he spoke—he wanted no part of it—and Melissa felt as though he'd run her through with a sword. She turned away to hide her reaction, only to realize that he could see her face clearly in the mirror above the sink.

"Melissa—"

She stiffened, sensing that he was reaching for her, not wanting to be touched. "Go away, Quinn," she whispered despondently, hunched over the sink. "Please. Just go away and leave me alone."

He lingered a while and then left, but Melissa didn't move until she heard the door of the suite close behind him. Then she went out onto the terrace, letting the fresh breeze revive her and dry her tears.

When she felt ready to pass through the lobby and bear the inspection of any guests who might be lingering there, she went downstairs. She was outside and well down the road that led toward town when she was nearly run over by a buggy rounding the curve.

Mitch Williams drew his horse and rig to a stop beside her, grinning at her and touching the brim of his hat. "Hello, sunshine," he said. "Like a ride home?"

Melissa's stubborn nature urged her to walk, but she was still feeling queasy and undone, and she wasn't sure she was up to covering the distance on foot. She nodded and had climbed into the buggy before Mitch could wrap the reins around the brake lever and assist her.

He chuckled, taking in her bloomers and soiled blouse with far more interest than Quinn had shown. "You are an independent little mite, aren't you?" The words were more of a comment than a question, and since he didn't seem to expect an answer, Melissa didn't offer one.

"Where's your friend?" she asked instead.

Mitch looked baffled for a moment, before a revelation struck him. "Gillian?" he said.

Impatient, Melissa nodded. She thought Mr. Williams was awfully thick at times, for a lawyer, but she didn't say that aloud. One had to be on fairly intimate terms with a person in order to insult him outright.

"Gillian's in a meeting with Quinn," he finally said, as

though there were no reason for anyone in the world to be upset by such news.

But Melissa was upset. In fact, it was all she could do not to jump out of the buggy, race back to the hotel, and burst in on their conference, demanding to be a part of it.

Mitch had noticed her troubled expression, and he tilted his head to look into her eyes. "It bothers you that Gillian and Quinn are alone together?"

Melissa swallowed. There was no sense in lying, for she knew her face betrayed her completely, but she hated having anyone know. "I realize that they're business partners," she began miserably, expecting Mitch to take that tack in comforting her. Her voice trailed away.

It soon became apparent that reassuring Melissa was not a duty Mitch cared to assume. "The sooner you accept the way things are between those two," he said seriously, "the better off you'll be. Quinn and Gillian go back a long, long way."

Melissa grasped the edges of the narrow buggy seat to steady herself. "What do you mean?" she asked, almost in a whisper.

"They grew up together," Mitch answered, sounding surprised that Melissa hadn't known. "You'd find their initials carved in the trunk of more than one tree, if you knew where to look. Quinn and Gillian must have been engaged half a dozen times—things just have a way of stopping and then starting up again, when it comes to those two."

A wild feeling possessed Melissa, a need to escape that rolling, pitching buggy and Mitch's kindly, hurtful words. "Why didn't they marry?" she ventured when she could trust herself to speak.

"Gillian's daddy founded this town," Mitch replied. "He'd already made his fortune in California back in 'forty-nine, and he was a rich man when he came here. In short, he never thought Quinn was good enough for his baby girl, the Raffertys being what they were, and he did everything he could to keep them apart." He paused and sighed heavily. "It's common knowledge that Quinn made his fortune just to show that old man he could do it."

Melissa was broken inside. It was such a romantic story, but she had no place in it. She lowered her head. "That still doesn't explain why they never married."

"They were planning to," Mitch responded affably. "But then Quinn up and married you."

Melissa lowered her head. She'd known that Quinn and Gillian were engaged when she and Quinn met, but somehow the significance of that had escaped her until now. Thinking of her husband's reaction to the possibility that she might be pregnant, she fought back tears of utter despair.

When they reached Quinn's house Melissa babbled something incoherent, jumped out of the buggy, and ran up the walk without looking back. Her vision was blurred and she was gasping for breath when she burst into the entryway.

A strange woman in very plain clothes was just about to start up the stairs with a tray, and Melissa's appearance apparently startled her so thoroughly that she nearly dropped her burden.

"Land sakes!" cried the woman, dragging horrified eyes from Melissa's head to her feet. "Mrs. Wright, come quickly! There's a vagrant here!"

At that Melissa began to laugh, despite her complete despondency. She laughed until weakness overcame her, until she was forced to grip the newel post at the base of the stairs in order to stand. Strangely, at the same time, tears were streaking down her face. Mrs. Wright, when she arrived, was so concerned that she put her arms around Melissa and said, "There, now, Mrs. Rafferty, everything will be all right."

With that the housekeeper started ushering Melissa up the stairs. She brought her to the master suite and seated her on the settee facing the empty fireplace.

"Shall I bring you tea, Mrs. Rafferty?" she asked.

Melissa had regained her composure by that time, except for periodic gasping hiccups, and she nodded. "Yes, please," she said, with as much dignity as she could muster. "But before you go—who was that woman downstairs?"

Mrs. Wright smiled. "That's Miss Alice. She was a sister to Mr. Rafferty's mother, and she looks after Mary."

"I thought Mary attended a private school," Melissa said.

The housekeeper was easing toward the door. "She did, but she didn't board there. She and Miss Alice had an apartment within walking distance."

"I see," Melissa replied, although she didn't see at all and, furthermore, didn't care. She was too full of misery to sort out the situation or even to ask what Miss Alice's presence in the house signified.

Quinn longed to escape the small office he'd set aside for himself at the hotel; between Gillian's perfume and her outrage, he was suffocating.

"How can you permit her to organize baseball games and run about dressed like a boy?!" His partner's shrill voice intensified Quinn's headache. "Do you know that she recruited those players from among our *guests?"*

Quinn allowed himself a wan grin at the memory of Melissa diving for home plate. "They seemed to be enjoying themselves," he said. "Maybe we should make baseball a regular part of our schedule."

"I was thinking more along the lines of croquet," Gillian said petulantly. "It's far more—dignified. A game a lady can play in good conscience."

Quinn left the window, from which he'd seriously considered jumping, and sank into the swivel chair behind his desk. "Spare me the dramatics, Gillian," he said. "I know you, remember? As far as I've ever been able to discern, you don't even have a conscience."

Gillian was facing the desk, grasping its edges in immaculately gloved hands, and she leaned forward to provide Quinn with a glimpse of her cleavage. "She's pregnant, isn't she?" she demanded in an acid whisper. "Damn you, Quinn, you've gone and gotten that little idiot pregnant!"

In his mind Quinn saw his mother giving birth to baby after baby, year after year, only to bury them, along with a part of her own dwindling spirit, a few months later. He hated himself in those moments for not shielding Melissa from the possibility of that ordeal. "Go away and leave me alone," he said with a dismissive gesture of one hand. "I've got problems enough without you adding to them."

But Gillian lingered, her words rife with bitter accusation. "You never loved me, did you? That's why you could marry a total stranger—someone you found running down a railroad track, for God's sake." She paused at the murderous expression on Quinn's face and then blurted out, "You're half-sick with worry over that little hoyden, aren't you? Tell me, Quinn Rafferty—where was all this concern seventeen years ago, when I had to go away and have your baby?"

Neither of them had raised that subject in a long time, and Quinn was incensed that Gillian would bring it up now. "I was sixteen when that happened," he said coldly. "Believe me, I was concerned—especially after my dear father found out and beat me senseless in a drunken rage—but there wasn't a hell of a lot I could do. Beyond asking you to marry me, of course. You declined, if you'll remember."

"I was only fifteen!" wailed Gillian.

Quinn got up and thrust open the window, dragging fresh air into his lungs. He felt besieged on every side, like a deer being torn apart by wolves, and he knew he was going to have to sacrifice a dream to survive. "I want out, Gillian," he said evenly.

"Out?" Her voice was soft, breathy, and full of delicate injury. "What do you mean?"

He turned to face her, bracing his hands behind him on the windowsill. "I'm offering to sell you my half of the hotel," he said flatly.

Gillian stared at him. "But that would sever our last tie, except for—"

"Except for Mary," Quinn finished for her, his voice ragged. "It has to be this way, Gillian."

Her violet eyes glimmered with desolation. "Why?" she whispered.

"Because I love my wife," Quinn answered, and the words surprised him as much as they did Gillian.

She swallowed visibly and then nodded, her eyes still swimming. "I-I'll consider your offer to sell," she said, and then she reached for her handbag and left.

* * *

Mary held onto the banister with both hands as she made her way carefully down the stairs, her beautiful face alight with pride. "See, Quinn? Are you watching? I can do this and a lot more!"

As Quinn looked upon this lovely child who had been raised believing herself to be his sister he felt a thickness in his throat. "Of course I'm watching, pumpkin," he said with an effort. "In fact, I can't take my eyes off you."

She reached the bottom of the stairs and waved both arms until Quinn moved into her embrace. Then, with a squeal of delight, she half choked him with the exuberance of her greeting. Her soft, fair hair, just the color of Gillian's, was like silk against his cheek.

He set her back from him and tried to sound stern. "I don't remember giving you permission to leave school," he said.

Mary laughed, her sightless brown eyes shining with the pure joy of rebellion. "I've learned everything those people can possibly teach me," she said. "I want to stay here in Port Riley from now on."

"We'll discuss that later." Quinn shoved a hand through his hair and started up the stairway, his arm around Mary's waist. He wanted to introduce her to his wife, or at least mention that he had one, but he was hesitant, having no idea what state of mind Melissa might be in.

It turned out that Helga had spared him the trouble of making an announcement. "The maid tells me that you've taken a bride," Mary said. She sounded hurt, though she jutted out her chin and added defiantly, "I'm glad you didn't marry that dreadful Gillian. I don't like her."

Quinn allowed himself a smile at the irony of that and spoke gently. Since the accident that had blinded her a year before, Mary had been prone to emotional outbursts, and he was always careful not to upset her. "Maybe you won't like Melissa either," he teased as they moved along the upper hallway. "Did you ever think of that?"

Mary shook her head purposefully. "I know I'll adore anyone with the nerve to wear bloomers and buy her own printing press," she insisted.

They reached the master suite, and Quinn was just about to knock when Helga came out of another room and said quickly, "Oh, please don't wake her, sir! Mrs. Rafferty's plumb done in!"

"I'll meet her later," Mary said considerately. "Right now it's time for Auntie to read aloud from Mr. Shakespeare's sonnets."

Quinn helped Mary across the hallway into her own room and was greeted by an ominous look from his aunt. She sat in a rocking chair near the cold fireplace, a thin woman with scraggly red hair that had once been a rich auburn, clad in a sensible serge dress of faded blue.

Quinn inclined his head to her and would have slipped out but for the fact that she made one of those imperious gestures of hers that invariably froze him in his tracks.

"Your brother and I will have a word, Mary," she said, rising from her chair, "and then we'll read."

In the relative privacy of the hallway Alice gripped both Quinn's hands in hers and looked up into his eyes. "I have wonderful news," she told him in a whisper.

Quinn was weak with relief. Given the way the day had been going, he'd expected more trouble.

"There is hope for Mary, Quinn. Real hope."

Quinn rested against the wall and gave an exasperated sigh. "You've been to another phrenologist? Another faith healer?"

"Dr. Koener is a physician," Alice said. "A surgeon. He's examined Mary's eyes, and he believes that a simple operation could restore her sight. However, there are risks."

Mary had visited virtually every doctor between Seattle and San Francisco, all to no avail. Quinn believed that it was time for her to accept her limitations as a blind person and make what she could of her life. He glared at his aunt and ground out, "You shouldn't have done it. You know what I think about—"

Alice met his gaze squarely and folded her arms. "I know what you think, all right. The truth is, Quinn Rafferty, that when it comes to that child you're just plain cowardly!"

"What's so special about this Dr. Koener?" he hissed, ignoring his aunt's last remark. "What makes him different from the nine thousand nine hundred and ninety-nine other doctors she's seen?"

"He has had special training in Austria, that's what. Quinn, he is a very fine doctor—I know he can help Mary!"

"He can disappoint her, you mean," Quinn retorted, furiously weary. "Not to mention putting her through hell and maybe even killing her!"

Alice gripped her nephew's arms firmly in her thin, strong hands. "At least go and talk to the man, Quinn."

He felt his face contort as he imagined what Mary could be forced to endure. "What if it doesn't work?" he demanded.

Alice was intrepid. "What if it does?" she countered, and when her words had had time to sink in she reached up and touched his cheek with one hand. "His name is Albert Koener, and his office is on Third Avenue."

Quinn turned away and, having nowhere else to go, slipped quietly into the rooms he shared with Melissa. She was not lying on the bed, as he'd expected, but stretched out on the settee, both feet propped on the arm. Her lashes lay thick and dark on her pale cheeks, and her hair was coming loose from the heavy braid trailing down over one shoulder.

Unable to resist, Quinn bent and kissed Melissa's forehead. If he'd gotten one thing out of this crazy day, it was the realization that he truly loved this woman, and that was something to hold onto.

Sound asleep, Melissa squirmed a little, fluttered one hand in front of her face, and said, "Stop it, Ajax!"

Quinn grinned and shook his head. "How brief is glory," he said, and then he carefully rearranged the blanket that covered her and left the room.

He made his way through Sunday-quiet, sunny streets to the little building that housed both the Western Union office and the operator himself, and he knocked on the door.

Charlie resented being made to send wires on Sundays or after hours, and he made his feelings clear, but he sent out the message Quinn dictated and waited patiently for the response.

A full forty-five minutes had passed when Adam Corbin wired back from Port Hastings:

> ALBERT KOENER IS A GOOD MAN. YOU CAN TRUST
> HIM. HOW IS MELISSA?

Quinn wasn't sure how to answer that question. To say that she was fine wouldn't be entirely honest, and he didn't want her family worrying unnecessarily, either. Finally he responded:

> YOUR SISTER IS AS ORNERY AS EVER. THANKS FOR
> EVERYTHING.

After that Quinn went back home, but instead of entering the house he walked around to the stables and saddled his horse, a temperamental gelding he'd never taken the trouble to name.

An hour's ride brought him to the falling-down cabin where he'd been raised. Smoke was curling from the chimney, and while Quinn was tying his horse to the hitching post Eustice came out, grinning.

"This a social call?" he crowed. The look in his eyes told Quinn he'd guessed what the visit was about, and that he was relishing his son's discomfort.

Even now, after so many years, Quinn hated to set foot inside that place. "Sure it is, old man," he said in a cold voice. "I can't think of anybody I'd rather pass the time of day with."

Eustice howled with laughter at that and stepped back inside the one-room cabin. Quinn followed, unable to keep from glancing up at the loft where he'd spent so many miserable nights as a boy.

"You knew Mary was coming back, didn't you?" he made himself ask, facing his father over the huge cable spool that served as a table. "That's why you're here."

The old man sighed and scratched his protruding belly through a layer of flannel. "She's my daughter," he reminded Quinn expansively. "I reckon it's my duty, so to speak, to know her whereabouts."

"She's not your daughter," Quinn bit out, "and that's exactly the point. And if you go near her, you poisonous old bastard, I'll boil your gizzard and feed it to the squirrels!"

Eustice chuckled and shook his head. "Still ain't told her the truth, have you? I'll bet that sweet little wife of yours don't know, neither. My, my, but that does sweeten the pot. It does indeed."

"Melissa would understand," Quinn said flatly. The fact was, however, that he wasn't all that sure of her reaction, and Eustice knew it. Still, something compelled him to try and bluff his way through. "As for Mary, she's no prouder of being yours than I am. I'll risk losing her and Melissa, too, before I'll let you blackmail me again."

Eustice's expression had turned solemn. "You know somethin', boy? You're an ungrateful whelp—I didn't take the strap to you near often enough!"

The cabin was suddenly filled with ghosts. His mother was there, weeping and pleading with Eustice to show mercy. Quinn could hear the shaving strap slicing through the air, could almost feel it making contact with his flesh.

He dashed outside to stand gasping for air, struggling against a hatred so deeply ingrained that it made him yearn to kill. With his father's laughter ringing in his ears— whether he was remembering that or hearing it then, he could not tell—Quinn untied his horse, mounted, and started back down the mountainside to Melissa.

Sixteen

Sunday dinner would have been a glum affair, as far as Melissa was concerned, if it hadn't been for Mary Rafferty's insistent good spirits. Quinn had just returned from a ride, and he was in a distracted, uncommunicative mood. After systematically dividing the food on his plate into heaps he muttered an excuse and left the table.

Melissa immediately rose and went after him, stopping him in the hallway with an urgently whispered "Quinn!"

He paused, and Melissa could see the muscles go tense beneath the white fabric of his shirt, but he did not turn to face her. "I'm tired," he said. "I'm going to bed."

It was barely seven-thirty. "Are you sick?" Melissa asked, remaining a few feet behind Quinn even though she longed to step around him and read the expression in his eyes.

He gave a ragged laugh then, and his hand curved briefly around the newel post as he started up the stairs. "You could say that," he replied curtly.

Melissa let him go without another word. She was grateful that he'd gone upstairs instead of to a saloon or a mistress, as another man might have done. When she returned to the dining room Mary heard her approach and asked anxiously, "Is Quinn all right? Why did he leave?"

Miss Alice nodded at Melissa's questioning glance, granting her permission to intercede. Melissa could not tell the truth, since she didn't know what it was, so she answered, "The last few days have been hectic for him, Mary, what with the hotel opening and everything. I'm sure he'll be fine with a little extra rest."

Mary seemed mollified by this explanation and launched into an entirely new subject. "I'm glad Quinn married you, Melissa," she said with conviction. "I did despise Gillian Aires with my whole heart!"

Melissa suspected that her young sister-in-law did everything with her whole heart, and she already loved her for it. "Why?" she asked before noticing that Miss Alice was glaring at her in warning and shaking her head.

Quinn's sister found her water glass and raised it carefully to her lips. "There's no love inside her," she replied after taking a sip from the goblet. "You can tell that about people, you know—just by how they make you feel."

Miss Alice brought the conversation skillfully back to weariness. "As Quinn is tired, Mary," she said, "so are you. It's been a long journey from Seattle, and you need to be in bed soon."

"I'm not a child," Mary protested, but there were shadows under her eyes, and her skin looked drawn and pale. She pushed back her chair in a dejected gesture of concession and blurted out, "Did you talk to Quinn about Dr. Koener, Auntie?"

Alice's thin lips tightened across her teeth for a moment. "Yes, and I got just the reaction we expected, but you mustn't be discouraged. Quinn will come to see reason once he's had time to think."

Melissa was left adrift when the two women excused themselves and quit the table, and her appetite was gone. Given what Mitch had told her in the buggy that afternoon, she had been full of questions about Quinn and Gillian, and now a new mystery had been added. She wondered who Dr. Koener was and why Quinn's opinion of him was so important, but she had no one to ask.

When Alice did not come back downstairs Melissa retired to the master bedroom. Quinn was not in bed asleep, as Melissa had expected him to be, but seated at his desk, working over a column of figures. His shoulders looked so painfully tense that she went to stand behind him and began massaging the muscles in his upper back.

He sighed and submitted to Melissa's ministrations, laying down his pencil. "My God, that feels good," he said.

"Who's Dr. Koener?" she asked after a long time, working at his neck now, her thumbs plying the nape.

Quinn groaned softly and let his head fall forward. "He's a surgeon practicing in Seattle. Alice wants him to operate on Mary's eyes."

Melissa tried to pose her question in a tone and manner that would encourage further confidence. "And you're opposed to that?"

"I don't know." Quinn caught Melissa's hand in his and drew her around, at the same time pushing back his chair so that he could set her on his lap. He looked so tired and forlorn that she was filled with love for him, and all the things that Mitch had said were far from her mind in those moments. "I wired Adam this afternoon," he went on. "He thinks Koener is all right."

Melissa traced the outline of Quinn's lips with the tip of her index finger. "When it comes to medicine, Adam's word is as good as gold. He even made Banner show credentials when they went into practice together."

Quinn kissed Melissa's finger lightly, then pulled it away. Misery lingered in his eyes, along with a forlorn sort of amusement. "Go to bed, Calico," he said. "I've got work to do, and you're distracting me."

Melissa happened to think that he needed distracting, so she began unbuttoning his shirt. He groaned when she slid the fabric aside and started teasing and caressing him in much the same way he liked to do with her.

"Melissa . . ." He ground out the name.

She bent to touch one taut masculine nipple with the tip of her tongue. "Hmmmm?"

Quinn moaned, and Melissa could see the muscles standing out in his neck as he tilted his head back. She continued to devil him, very sure of herself, until he suddenly grasped her by the waist and thrust her away with such force that she nearly landed on the floor.

He shot out of his chair and began pacing, and he fastened the buttons of his shirt as he moved. "My God, Melissa, give me room to breathe, will you?"

He might as well have slapped her as said that. Melissa retreated a step, smarting as though he had. "I-I'm sorry."

Quinn stopped in his tracks. *"What?"* he demanded. "What did you say?"

"I said I was sorry," Melissa answered miserably.

"Well, don't be!" came the furious retort. "I'm the one who's in the wrong here, and don't forget it!"

"Oh," said Melissa, her eyes going wide as Quinn began to pace again. The realization came to her that he was in a great deal of emotional pain, but she had no idea what was causing it or how to help. She longed to put her arms around him but was afraid of being rejected again, so she just stood there wringing her hands.

Presently Quinn stopped and faced her again. "I never meant to hurt you," he said, and then he started toward the door.

Melissa beat him to it, pressing herself to the paneling as she had done once before downstairs. "You're not leaving without me," she told him firmly. "I won't be left to agonize over where you are and what you're doing!"

A muscle bunched in his jawline, and the audacious eyes snapped with annoyance. "There is a simple solution to your dilemma, my darling," he said. "Don't think about me at all."

"I can't help thinking about you, and you know it!" Melissa cried, beyond patience. "Damn it, Quinn, if you leave this house tonight, I won't be here when you get back!"

He paused. "You're worried that I'm planning to spend the night with Gillian, aren't you?" he accused. His tone made Melissa out to be a poor sport.

"Yes," she answered, calmer now.

Quinn was reaching for the doorknob. "Then I guess it's about time you learned to trust me," he said, and then he stepped past Melissa and walked out into the hallway. When she heard the front door close loudly in the distance she stuffed some of her things into a valise and fled the house.

The idea of making a tumultuous entrance at a hotel with just her valise was more than Melissa could tolerate. She made her way to the train yard, where Quinn's railroad car sat sidetracked on a spur, and let herself in.

After lighting a lamp and building a fire in the stove Melissa willed herself to cry—the pressure building up inside her was nearly intolerable—but she found that she couldn't. She'd exhausted her store of tears since meeting Quinn, and now there were no more to shed.

Knowing that she wouldn't be able to sleep, she got out pen and ink and sat down at the desk to work on her story. She wrote feverishly, pouring all her emotions into the book, until well after midnight. Only when she was too spent to think at all did she crawl into the decadent bed with its covering of chinchilla and sleep.

Quinn watched the light fade from the windows of the car and longed to be inside it, and inside Melissa, with such savage intensity that he didn't trust himself to approach her. To make matters worse, he was roaring drunk, and he made it a point never to touch a woman when he'd had too much whiskey. Doing that would have reduced him to the same level as his father.

He was about to walk away when it occurred to him that Melissa was vulnerable, alone in that railroad car. There were men in town who wouldn't be above taking advantage of her.

Frustration seized Quinn, and the sheer force of the emotion sobered him somewhat. He was about to go into the car and insist that Melissa come home with him when, out of the corner of his eye, he noticed a familiar form leaning against a lamppost.

"Looks like you're havin' trouble keepin' the two of 'em under your wing," Eustice observed, and then he laughed.

Quinn wheeled on his father, sick with hatred. The old man was haunting him like a ghost, and he'd go right on doing it until he'd gotten what he wanted. Quinn's bearing must have conveyed some of what he felt, for Eustice immediately backed up a step.

"Now, I didn't mean no harm, boy," he hastened to say. "I was just funnin'."

Quinn cursed under his breath, willing his brain to clear. "What do you want?" he asked. "What will it take to get rid of you once and for all?"

Eustice sighed. "Thanks to that money you gave me this morning, I ain't in no particular hurry to move on. I reckon I'll hang around Port Riley for a time, and see what comes of this—marriage of yours."

Shoving a hand through his hair, Quinn sucked in a deep breath. It steadied him, driving more of the whiskey fog from his mind. "That wasn't the deal, old man. I paid you to leave."

Eustice pretended that he hadn't heard Quinn's words. "From what I hear, she's got rich folks, that wife of yours. You ain't good enough for her any more than you was for Miss Gillian Aires."

The streets were dark, and they were empty, and for one insane moment Quinn considered getting rid of his father for good. In the end, however, despite all he'd suffered from the man, he found it strangely difficult to lift his hand against him. "Where would I be, Pa," he drawled, "if I hadn't had you to encourage me all this time?"

The old man gave a hoot of disgusted amusement. "You're lucky I didn't just hand you back to that whore and spit on her as she walked away."

"What are you talking about?" Quinn demanded, striding over and grasping his father by his fetid lapels.

Eustice's aplomb had deserted him. "I didn't mean nothin', boy," he whined. "Let me go!"

Quinn's fingers tightened on Eustice's flannel shirt. "Tell me!"

"I didn't get you off your ma!" Eustice spat out. "Damn you, you're the son of a whore, and I wish she'd drowned you afore she brought you to me!"

Not knowing whether to believe his father or not, Quinn released him, more in shock than mercy, and rasped out, "You'd better tell me the rest, old man—right now."

"There ain't much to tell." Eustice was blustering, straightening his clothes with the affronted ceremony of an accosted gentleman. "Your ma—my wife, I mean—she never could carry a brat long enough to get it strong, and she'd just lost another one, so she wanted you. She said she'd run off if I didn't let you stay, and I gave in. A man needs a woman handy."

Quinn's stomach was roiling, but he wasn't about to let on that he was shaken. "What was her name? Where is she now?"

Eustice gave a guffaw of amusement. "Don't rightly remember her name, boy. As for where she is—how the hell could I know that? Tell you one thing, though—if I was you, I'd be careful who I laid down with."

At that Quinn's reason snapped. He lunged for his father's throat, closing his hands around it. He'd surely have killed the old man if Melissa hadn't come flying across the street in a flowing flannel nightgown, screaming, "Quinn! No!" Her small fingers pried at his hands, strong and frantic. "No!"

Slowly, reluctantly, Quinn gave in to her pleas and released his grasp on Eustice's neck. The old man turned and fled down the sidewalk, and Quinn stared after him, aching to finish what he'd started.

"Quinn?" Melissa grasped at his arm, and when that failed to draw his attention from the figure retreating into the darkness she came around and cupped his face in her hands. "Quinn!"

He dared not speak, so he simply stood there, regarding his wife with hot, angry eyes and needing her more than he had ever needed any woman.

Melissa's eyes were glistening with tears as she looked up at Quinn, seemingly unaware that she was standing on the street in a nightgown. "That man—he was your father?"

Quinn was still seething, and he had to drag in three or four breaths before he could answer. "Yes, God help me. Yes."

She took his arm and led him toward the railroad car. "What was he saying to you that made you go crazy like that?"

Quinn knew a sensation of sweeping relief. Melissa hadn't heard; she didn't know that the one claim to goodness and decency he'd ever had—his gentle mother—had been stripped away. He didn't answer because he couldn't speak.

When they were inside the car Quinn staggered to the bench where Melissa had sat not so long ago in her sodden wedding dress and collapsed.

"How did you know he was my father?" he asked when several minutes had passed.

Melissa was reheating coffee, and it smelled stout enough to strip paint. Her slender shoulders moved in a shrug. "I don't know—I guess it was just something about him."

"Probably the horns sprouting out of his head," Quinn muttered.

Melissa poured some of that turpentine she'd brewed into a mug and brought it to Quinn. She sat beside him on the bench. "You really hate him, don't you?" she said, marveling.

"Yes," Quinn breathed after taking a sobering sip of the coffee. "Oh, God, yes."

"Why?" Her small hand was making slow, comforting circles on his back, and her voice was gentle. Everything about her invited confidence, and Quinn needed desperately to talk to someone.

"Every memory I have of that man is brutal." He grated out the words. "He was always drunk, and always abusive, and my—my mother got the worst of it. He kept her pregnant from the day they were married until the day she died. She was—fragile. Pa made her life so miserable that she couldn't carry a child full-term, then he cursed her for failing him."

"Oh, Quinn," Melissa whispered, her hand resting on the

taut nape of his neck. "I'm so sorry." She stood, lithe in her nightgown. "Come to bed," she said, taking his hand. "Let me comfort you."

Quinn shook his head. The stench of whiskey, and of Eustice Rafferty, was all over him. To touch Melissa would be to foul her. "Not like this," he said brokenly. "In case you haven't noticed, I'm drunk."

She smiled, though her eyes still sparkled with sympathetic tears. "I'm your wife, Quinn. I promised to love you no matter what."

Quinn had to avert his eyes for a moment.

When he looked back Melissa was at the stove. She ladled water into a basin and set it on to heat, moving the coffee pot aside.

"So you really left me," Quinn observed, to make conversation.

She laughed. "I didn't go far, did I?" she confessed. "But I'd said I wouldn't be there when you got home, so I had to keep my word."

Quinn thought of what he might have done if Melissa hadn't been on hand to stop him, and how that act would have separated him from her forever, and said, "I'm glad you were around when I needed you."

Melissa came to him, drew him to his feet, and stripped him of the coat and then the shirt beneath it. Quinn was powerless to stop her until she began working at his belt buckle; he grasped her hands then and held them still.

"I meant what I said, Melissa. I won't make love to you."

Her eyes were round and full of innocence when she looked up at him. There were so many things she didn't know, things she'd been shielded from by her friends and family. Quinn wanted to be part of that conspiracy and keep Melissa the way she was forever, even though he knew the task was futile.

"I don't think you understand," she said reasonably. Heat was surging through the basin on the stove, and she went to set it aside, using handfuls of her nightgown as pot holders.

She went into the water closet and came out with a washcloth, which she dipped in the basin. Her blue eyes warmed

Quinn's bare chest and shoulders long before she began bathing him.

The sensation was one of such profound solace that Quinn could not bring himself to protest. He closed his eyes and allowed his wife to wash his back, his middle, his arms.

He had no memory of moving to the bed or taking off his trousers. He was just there all of the sudden, beneath the sheet and the chinchilla spread. Melissa's caresses warmed him long after the water in the basin had turned cool; when she'd prepared him, she drove him into a place of light and thunder and made him cry out in rapturous grief.

He slept deeply, and without dreams.

Melissa was up long before Quinn awakened; in fact, she'd written half a chapter before he even opened his eyes. When he stumbled into the water closet, grumbling under his breath, she smiled and put the lid back on her ink bottle.

Quinn came out presently, smelling of peppermint tooth powder and looking rumpled. He squinted at the neat pile of papers on the desk as he got into the clothes Melissa had laid out for him on the bench. "The book?" he asked in an ominous tone.

Melissa sat up very straight. "Yes," she answered firmly.

Quinn shook his head and busied himself with the pulling on of his boots, which seemed to be a major undertaking. All the while a mischievous grin lurked at the corner of his mouth.

Melissa pushed back her chair. "Don't you dare patronize me, Mr. Rafferty," she warned. "It's not easy making all those imaginary characters do what they're supposed to!"

Quinn laughed. "I don't imagine it is. Let's go have some breakfast, Calico. I'm starving."

"Breakfast?" Melissa retorted. "It's nearly time for lunch."

Quinn muttered a curse. "Why didn't you wake me?" Melissa went back to her desk and opened her ink bottle again, struck by fresh inspiration. "It's not my job to open your eyes for you," she said. "If you're going to drink yourself into a stupor, you're on your own."

He chuckled at that—he was good-natured for a man with a hangover, to Melissa's way of thinking—and finished dressing. In the middle of a paragraph she felt his hand under her chin as he lifted her mouth for his kiss.

"Thank you," he said.

"For what?" she asked, dazed as always by his touch.

"For last night," he answered, nibbling at her lips once more before withdrawing.

Melissa blushed. In all truth, she'd hoped he wouldn't remember. "I behaved like a shameless hussy!" she lamented.

Quinn laughed at her expression. "And I'll be eternally grateful," he replied.

She blinked, uncertain whether he was teasing or not. "Go on with you," she finally said, with a self-conscious wave of one hand.

He drew her to her feet and held her very close for a moment. "My bed is the one place where I don't want you to be a lady, Melissa." He sighed heavily and set her away. "If I didn't have a meeting, I'd take you there right now."

"I've got newspaper stories to gather anyway," Melissa was quick to point out. She reached for a notebook and a freshly sharpened pencil. "Come to think of it, I'd better sell some advertising as well."

Quinn kissed her again and left the railroad car, still shaking his head.

Melissa devoted the morning to selling advertising space in her newspaper, as she had told Quinn she would, and the effort was entirely fruitless. Even Mr. Kruger, her last and best hope, was lukewarm to the idea. He wanted to see at least one issue come out before he invested the fee.

It was midday when Melissa returned to the house to find Mary sitting at the bottom of the stairs, weeping.

Melissa immediately sat down and took her sister-in-law's hand. "Why, Mary, what is it?"

Mary sniffled. "It's Quinn. He isn't going to let me have my operation!"

"I'm sure he'll reconsider after he's had some time to think about it," Melissa told her, trying to sound reassuring.

Mary shook her head. "No," she sobbed. "He told me he'd made his decision, and that it's final!"

"Where is he?" Melissa asked gently.

"I don't know," Mary said, getting to her feet and groping for the banister. "And I don't care!"

Melissa glanced toward the study doors and saw that they were closed. "Shall I help you up to your room?" she asked quietly.

Alice appeared before Mary could answer and solicitously led her charge up the stairs.

After smoothing her hair and summoning a calm attitude Melissa knocked at one of the study doors. When there was no answering invitation she went in anyway.

Quinn was seated on the edge of his desk, talking earnestly with someone who was hidden from Melissa's view by the high back of a chair. At her entrance he glared at her, and it was clear that the gratitude he'd felt that morning was a thing of the past.

"I'm busy at the moment," he said in a clipped tone, as though Melissa were a troublesome child instead of his wife.

Gillian peeked around the back of the chair and waggled gloved fingers. "Hello," she sang out.

Melissa struggled to keep her temper. "Hello," she said sweetly, wanting to find one of those trees where Quinn's and Gillian's initials were carved and tie them both to its trunk.

Quinn's look was ominous. "Whatever it is, darling, can't it wait for a few minutes?" he said.

Gillian bounced out of her chair. "Now, Quinn," she chimed, "I've taken up enough of your time for one day. I'll just run along now—we can talk tomorrow."

With that Quinn's partner left the study, and he was alone with his wife.

"Mary tells me that you're not even going to talk with Dr. Koener," she began.

Quinn turned away. "There's no point in it."

"There is every point," Melissa insisted. "Mary's sight could be restored. Surely you can understand what hopes she must have pinned on this."

"I won't take the chance," Quinn said flatly.

Heat pulsed in Melissa's cheeks. "I thought we were talking about Mary, not you," she dared to say.

Quinn faced Melissa at last. "Do you have any idea of the pain she might have to suffer?" he demanded in a furious undertone. "Even Aunt Alice admits that the chances are seven out of ten that Mary will still be blind after the surgery. What kind of odds are those?"

Melissa stepped close to Quinn and put her arms around his neck. "Just talk to the doctor, darling—that's all we're asking. Go to Seattle and talk with him."

Quinn sighed and rather grudgingly embraced her. "If I do, will you go with me?"

Melissa thought of her vain efforts at interesting the local merchants in advertising and nodded. She was getting nowhere with her newspaper anyway.

Quinn kissed her thoroughly, then mumbled against her mouth, "Come upstairs, Mrs. Rafferty, and let me love you."

Melissa could have named ten thousand reasons why Quinn's idea wasn't a good one, but she missed supper all the same.

✑ *Seventeen*

There were a great many unanswered questions in Melissa's mind and heart when she set off for Seattle with her husband that rainy Tuesday morning aboard the steamer *Excelsior,* but the time wasn't right for asking them. Quinn was in an uneasy, pensive mood, and more than the upcoming conference with Dr. Koener was troubling him.

Their table in the ship's salon was beside a window, and even shrouded in rain the scenery along the northern part of the Olympic Peninsula was beautiful. Quinn didn't seem to notice that, even though he was staring through the water-beaded glass.

Mary came in, laughing, perfectly dry inside her hooded rain cloak. As always, Alice was hovering nearby, but today a new element had been added. A nice-looking young man with thick brown hair and blue eyes had given Mary his arm.

Melissa's smile brought Quinn out of his glum reflections, at least temporarily, and he turned to find what had inspired amusement in his wife. Seeing Mary openly flirting with the handsome boy, he made a grumbling sound and started to get up.

"Don't you dare interfere!" Melissa whispered, quickly catching hold of his arm. "No harm is being done—they've only been walking on the deck."

Quinn sighed and sank back into his chair. "You're right," he admitted raggedly. "Melissa, what's the matter with me?"

Melissa had given a lot of consideration to that question, and she had a ready answer. "I think you're overtired."

An ironic glint appeared in his eyes, and one corner of his mouth twitched slightly in an attempt at a smile. "It's hard to believe what can happen in the space of two weeks, isn't it?"

Melissa dropped her gaze, knowing he was referring to her abrupt intrusion into his life the day she'd run away from Ajax and quite unsure whether he thought those weeks had been bad ones or good. "Yes," she said, feeling miserable.

A waiter arrived, bringing a tray that contained a carafe of hot, fresh coffee, a pitcher of cream, a bowl of sugar, and two cups. He poured for both Melissa and Quinn, but Melissa, queasy again, ignored her coffee.

"It wouldn't be a bad idea for you to see a doctor yourself while we're in Seattle," Quinn ventured to say.

Melissa bit her lower lip before answering, "It's too early to tell whether I'm pregnant or not."

"When were—when would you have—"

Melissa knew he was trying to ask if her period was overdue, and she rather enjoyed his embarrassment, since her own was so acute. "A few days ago," she said.

"Oh," Quinn replied, and he dropped two lumps of sugar into his coffee. He turned his attention to the window again and looked as glum as ever.

Melissa couldn't stand it. "Would it really be so bad?" she whispered. "If you and I had a child, I mean."

When he looked at her, she saw torment in his eyes. "If the child survived, it would be wonderful," he replied. "But they often don't, you know, and a lot of times the mothers don't make it, either."

At last Melissa felt she was getting somewhere, and her spirits were greatly lifted to know that he would welcome the baby when it was born. She dared to reach out and take Quinn's hand. "I've got three brothers," she said softly, "and all of their wives have had children. Not only did my nieces and nephews survive, so did my sisters-in-law."

Quinn did not look reassured; instead, he seemed almost haunted. "My mother probably had a dozen pregnancies, Melissa, and she failed every time. The last one took her with it."

"Your mother couldn't have failed every time," Melissa pointed out. "She had you and Mary."

Quinn started to say something, then stopped himself. After nearly a full minute had passed he mumbled, "I wish we could just keep going from Seattle, Melissa, and never go back to Port Riley."

Melissa thought of all he'd built, notwithstanding the fact that he'd done much of it to spite Gillian's father, and she shook her head. "You don't mean that."

The expression in Quinn's eyes said otherwise, but Melissa didn't press the subject further. Mary brought the young man over to her brother's table and introduced him as Scott Murray. He was a student at the University of Washington, in Seattle, and he was obviously very taken with his new acquaintance.

"He probably thinks she'd be easy to take advantage of," Quinn grumbled when Mary and Scott had gone outside for a walk around the rainy deck.

By then Alice had joined them, and she looked up from her needlework with fire in her eyes. "Quinn Rafferty, if you make a remark like that in Mary's presence, I will personally box your ears. She is pretty and sweet, and it's quite natural for young men to like her."

"She's also blind," Quinn said, and then he pushed himself out of his chair. "I need some fresh air."

Melissa, who agreed with Alice on the matter of Mary's living as normal a life as possible, gave him a warning look and said, "Is it fresh air you want, or are you planning to spy on poor Mary?"

His guilty expression told all, but neither Melissa nor Alice tried to stop him when he left the salon. Melissa, for her part, was relieved to be spared his dour mood for a while.

"Tell me about Quinn's father," Melissa ventured to say after a few minutes, her arms folded in front of her on the table.

Alice lifted her gaze from the sampler she was embroidering and said, "I've always wondered what the good Lord could have been thinking of the day he made Eustice Rafferty. He's as close to a devil as any man I've ever met."

"Then the rumors I've heard are true—he did abuse his wife and children."

Alice sighed sadly and nodded. "Ellen—Quinn's and Mary's mother—was my sister, you know. She was always a gentle, delicate little thing. I never did understand what she saw in that brute of a man, but I think she must have loved him, because she stayed. Through it all, she stayed."

"Maybe she was afraid to leave," Melissa suggested tentatively.

But Alice shook her head. "We had family, Ellen and I, over in the wheat country. She could have gone to them at any time, and they'd have taken her in."

Melissa was frowning. "There's quite a gap between their ages—Quinn's and Mary's, I mean."

"Sixteen years," Alice said.

With a shrug Melissa replied, "I guess that's not so strange. The youngest of my brothers is thirteen years older than I am. I was a surprise to the whole family."

Alice nodded. "So was Mary. And she was the light of poor Ellen's life. She started her decline when Mary was five. Quinn had made some money by then, and when his mother got so weak he came back and took his sister away to board with a preacher and his wife in Port Riley. I didn't blame him, Eustice being what he was, but it was the beginning of the end for Ellen. She just gave up after that."

Melissa looked out at the rainy coast of the peninsula, wondering whether or not to trust this woman. She finally decided that she had to, or burst from trying to contain her curiosity and concern. "The night before last Quinn tried to choke his father."

Alice set her needlework aside on the table, her full attention fixed on Melissa. Her cheeks had been drained of their
color, and her eyes were wide. "Eustice is in Port Riley?"

Melissa nodded, more concerned than ever. Alice looked
as though she might faint.

"Dear Lord," she whispered.

Quickly Melissa poured Quinn's aunt a glass of ice water
from a pitcher the waiter had brought earlier.

Alice drank most of the contents of her glass and then
asked brokenly, "Why didn't Quinn tell me? I would have
insisted upon taking Mary away immediately."

Melissa could not answer that question, but she offered
some of her own. "Why are you so afraid of Eustice? And
why did Quinn want to kill him?"

Alice was still trembling. "He's a monster," she replied.
"He hates Quinn, and he'd use anything or anybody to hurt
him."

A shiver moved down Melissa's spine. Her father had
cherished his sons, although he'd been strict with them, and
she found it impossible to grasp Eustice's relationship with
Quinn. "Why?" she whispered, stricken. "Why would any
man hate his own son?"

"Quinn was always better than Eustice, better and
smarter, and that old man knew it. The jealousy made him
mean, like a rabid dog."

Melissa's eyes were wide. The realization of what Alice
was saying was finally dawning on her. Eustice wanted to
destroy his son, and he would go to any lengths to do it.
That meant that Mary was in danger, but so was she—and
so was the baby she was surely carrying.

Lost in troubled thoughts, Melissa got out of her chair,
mumbled something to Alice, and put on her cloak as she
walked away from the table.

The coolness of the rain calmed her a little, and when she
rounded the deck she found Quinn on the other side, gazing
out at the water. Mary and her friend Scott were nowhere in
sight.

Melissa went to stand beside her husband at the rail, slipping her arm through his. A mixture of rain and saltwater

misted around them, but they were both oblivious to the weather.

"I love you," Melissa said boldly.

Quinn didn't respond to her at all, and she couldn't overlook such a rejection. Not again.

She pulled at his arm. "Quinn!"

He looked at her in total surprise, and in the next instant Melissa realized that he hadn't even known she was there. "What are you doing out here? Go inside where it's warm and dry."

Melissa didn't move. She held onto his arm and looked up at him. "Didn't you hear me when I spoke to you just now?" she asked.

He shook his head.

"But I was right here beside you!"

Quinn looked bewildered and a little impatient. "I'm deaf in my left ear," he said. "You must know that."

"No—no, I didn't," Melissa said, remembering the other instances when she'd whispered "I love you" to Quinn. All this time she'd thought he was ignoring her, when in reality he most likely hadn't heard her. She began to laugh.

Quinn took her arm and shuffled her away from the railing and out of the rain. They stood under the dripping eaves of the wheelhouse. "What the hell—"

Melissa stopped laughing and reached up to touch her husband's troubled face. "Oh, darling—I'm sorry. It's just that I've bared my soul to you several times and thought you didn't care, when the truth was that you didn't hear me."

He drew her very close to him, heedless of the crew members and the occasional fresh-air seeker passing by on the deck. "You bared your soul, did you? And what did you say?"

Melissa drew on all her courage. "I said that I loved you, Quinn Rafferty."

"When?" he pressed, and for the first time since before the incident with Eustice there was a happy light in his eyes.

Melissa blushed. "Once when we were in the hot spring at the new hotel, and another time when we were in bed."

Now it was Quinn who laughed, with hoarse, ragged joy,

and he held Melissa tighter still. He bent his head and kissed her, and she was so overwhelmed by her feelings for this man that she knew she would have slipped to the deck like a formless jellyfish if he hadn't been supporting her.

Her very vulnerability to him made her pull back a little, when she'd caught her breath and restored the starch to her knees, and say, "You did tell me once that you weren't sure what you felt for me."

"I know what it is now," Quinn answered, his mouth very near hers again. Dangerously near.

"What?" Melissa croaked.

His chuckle was a warm vibration against her lips. "I love you, Mrs. Rafferty," he said, and then he swept her into another kiss.

Melissa's spirit soared within her. All the other problems facing her could be dealt with in good time; the important thing was that Quinn loved her. In that moment and that place nothing else mattered.

An hour later the steamboat docked in Port Hastings to take on passengers. Among them, to Melissa's delighted surprise, were Fancy and Banner, her sisters-in-law, who were on their way to a suffrage rally in Seattle. Fancy's new baby, Caroline, was with them, in the care of a nanny.

"How does Jeff feel about this?" Melissa inquired of Fancy when she and her brother's wife had a moment alone at the buffet table in the ship's salon.

Worry filled Fancy's bright eyes. "He said if I went, he was going to leave me," she confessed. "By now I imagine he's taken the boys and gone to live at the main house."

At this point Banner arrived, and it was clear that she'd heard part of the conversation and discerned the rest. "Stop fretting," she said, patting Fancy's shoulder. "Jeff will never be able to tolerate the noise and confusion in that house, with all my brood."

"He's used to noise and confusion!" Fancy wailed softly, in abject despair.

"Not in a double dose, he's not," Banner immediately replied.

Melissa smiled. "Banner's right, Fancy," she said. "By the

time you get back from the rally Jeff will not only be home again, he'll be prepared to negotiate."

"I hope so," Fancy said with a sad little shrug, "because I don't know what I'd ever do without that impossible man."

The afternoon passed quickly for Melissa, and it was with reluctance that she said good-bye to her sisters-in-law on the wharf that evening. They were off to a hotel quite some distance from the one where Melissa would be staying.

"Do you want to join Fancy and Banner in their fight for justice?" Quinn asked with a grin when they had reached their own hotel and he had arranged for a room. Mary and Alice had gone to their apartment near the school for the blind.

Melissa lowered her eyes. Ever since Quinn had told her that he loved her, beneath the wheelhouse eaves on that rainy deck, she'd been eager to be alone with him. She blushed and said, with the sincere shyness of a new bride, "I'd rather stay with you, Mr. Rafferty."

He lifted her chin with his hand but did not kiss her, since the lobby was crowded with people. "I'll do my best to see that you don't regret that decision, my love," he promised in a low voice that sent sweet tremors through Melissa.

In their room, which was spacious and afforded them a grand view of Elliott Bay, Quinn appeared to be in no hurry to enjoy husbandly privileges. He went to stand at the window, gazing out at a world curtained in rain. Since the big fire three years before, Seattle had become a modern city, with towering brick buildings and telephone lines and paved streets.

"What do you see out there that's so fascinating?" Melissa asked, putting her arms around Quinn and resting her forehead in the hollow between his shoulder blades.

Quinn sighed. "Lots of possibilities and lots of dangers," he answered at length.

Melissa smiled and kissed his back through the fine fabric of his white shirt. "It just so happens that there are a few possibilities right here in this room," she said brazenly.

She felt Quinn's chuckle against her cheek before he turned in her embrace and rested his hands on her waist.

"Not to mention a few dangers. I have an idea that my heart is in imminent peril, Mrs. Rafferty."

Tilting her head back, Melissa looked up at him and answered, "I'll capture it if I can, and I'll never give it back."

Quinn kissed her forehead. "I've been deluding myself. You've owned me, Melissa, since the moment I pulled you up onto the platform of my railroad car. Do you remember how we collided?"

Color blossomed in Melissa's cheeks, and she nodded mischievously. "I remember."

His hands were moving languorously up and down her back, but instead of soothing Melissa, relaxing her, they wound a tight coil of delicious tension inside her. "If I'd been willing to face facts," Quinn said, "I'd have had to admit that I was in love with you then. I do recall the devout conviction that if I didn't have you before nightfall, I was going to die."

Melissa laughed. "But you didn't."

Quinn's hands came around to caress her breasts, still safe beneath her prim white shirtwaist with its high collar and little pearl buttons. "I progressed from fearing death to longing for it," he said. "My God, Melissa, I wish I understood what it is that you do to me—if I did, I'd have some defense against you."

She looked up at him, hurt. "But you can't think that I'm your enemy."

"You have far more power over me than an enemy ever could" was his startling reply. "No one, not even that son of a bitch who calls himself my father, has ever made me crawl. But you, Melissa—you could do it."

"I wouldn't!" she cried in dismay. "I love you too much to ever hurt you!"

Quinn traced her mouth with the tip of a gentle index finger, then bent to sweep her into a consuming kiss. Melissa broke from it, gasping, and whispered, "Oh, Quinn, let me lie down—I can't stand on my own."

He laid her tenderly on the bed, as though she were made of the most precious and delicate stuff, and began unfastening the buttons of her blouse. When he'd reached the swell of her breasts he stopped temporarily to kiss that satiny flesh and taste it with his tongue.

Melissa whimpered as he drew up her skirts and petticoats to stroke a silk-covered thigh with his hand, and her head began to toss from side to side in the beginnings of ecstasy when he finally bared one of her breasts and took its aching peak in his lips.

In the meanwhile he eased her drawers down, sliding them over her legs and tossing them away. Melissa moaned fitfully when he began to stroke her; she had been wanting Quinn for hours, and she wasn't sure she could endure the preliminaries, no matter how delicious they were.

"Please," she whispered, her hands entangled in his hair, "take me, Quinn. Take me now."

The request was not one Quinn generally granted—the more excited Melissa was, the better it pleased him—but in this instance he accommodated her. He allowed her to open his trousers and push them down over his buttocks, and he trembled when she caressed him for a few moments.

He needed little help to find his way inside her, but still, in her eagerness, she guided him.

Quinn regarded Melissa with hot, hungry eyes as he poised himself above her at one point in their lovemaking, pausing to savor the intimate contact. "I love you," he said hoarsely.

Melissa's hands were moving slowly and softly over his back, which was damp with perspiration. "And I love you," she answered.

Then, with an upward thrust of her hips, she reestablished the friction that would soon ignite flames hot enough to consume them both, and Quinn cried out like a man suffering the most exquisite of agonies.

Melissa was drawn into his satisfaction, her body moving like a ribbon in a high wind, her hands frantic along the corded muscles of his back. Quinn, powerless in the throes of his own release, allowed her the shouts of triumph he usually muffled with a kiss.

When it was over he collapsed beside her, gasping, his head pressed to her heart. Melissa, beyond speech herself, buried her fingers in his hair, closing her eyes against tears of sheer happiness.

They went to the symphony that evening, but even Mozart's compositions contained no crescendoes as sweet or as sweeping as those they'd known in their lovemaking. Still, Melissa heartily enjoyed the concert, and she was reasonably certain that Quinn had, too.

Since the rain had let up, they walked back toward their hotel hand in hand. "I guess you could say this is our honeymoon," she said shyly.

Quinn favored her with a sidelong grin. "I guess you could."

A streetcar clanged past, and when it was quiet again Melissa asked, "What do you think of the suffrage movement?"

Quinn's grin broadened. "Considering joining those two rabble-rousing sisters-in-law of yours over at the rally?"

Melissa shook her head. "I believe in the cause, but I meant what I said about wanting to stay with you."

Quinn squeezed her hand. "I think women should be able to vote, Melissa, if it's any comfort to you."

It was, and the glow in Melissa's eyes must have told him so, even though she didn't. "Fancy says Jeff is really angry with her for coming to the rally. He threatened to leave her."

They were nearing the hotel now, but Quinn pulled Melissa into a small coffee shop instead of going on. He made no comment on what she'd said until they were seated at a table with huge slices of cherry pie in front of them.

"I've heard of people being blinded by love," he said, "and I think that's what's happened with Jeff. If he does leave, he won't be able to stay away."

The thought of Jeff and Fancy's trouble took a bit of the sparkle from Melissa's own happiness. "Then you wouldn't be angry if you'd been in his place and I came over here to participate in a rally for women's rights?"

A muscle tightened in Quinn's jaw, and Melissa thought again what very complex creatures men are.

"I didn't say that," he pointed out. "A woman belongs at her husband's side."

"Couldn't he get bored with her rather easily that way? Or she with him?"

Grudgingly, Quinn grinned. "I hate it when you're right," he said.

Melissa laughed. "I know."

"I want to stay in Seattle," Mary announced first thing the next morning, when she and Alice and Quinn and Melissa all met in front of Dr. Koener's office building on Third Avenue. "I'm going back to school."

Quinn looked pleased until he made the connection between Seattle and young Scott Murray, the university student Mary had met on the steamer. Alice and Melissa, of course, were way ahead of him. "We're going to have to talk about this," he said sternly.

Melissa reached up and laid a finger to his lips. "Another time, darling," she said gently.

With obvious effort Quinn put Mary's budding romance out of his mind. Soon they were all upstairs in Dr. Koener's outer office.

The doctor's receptionist, a pretty young girl, smiled broadly up at Quinn, who had wired ahead for an appointment before leaving Port Riley. "Come right in, Mr. Rafferty," she said, rising from her chair. "Doctor will want you, too, of course, Mary."

Alice and Melissa were left to wait in the reception area. There was an assortment of magazines to read, but neither of the women was able to work up any interest in world events or fashion. Their thoughts were with Mary.

When the young woman came out she was in tears, and Alice went to her immediately, taking her out into the hallway.

Melissa waited for Quinn. "Dr. Koener didn't change your mind," she said, careful to keep all emotion and all judgment from her voice.

Quinn took Melissa's arm and brought her into the inner office, where a man with bushy black hair and small glasses resting on the tip of his nose greeted her with a smile. "Hello, Mrs. Rafferty," he said. "Your husband has asked me to explain to you the risks involved in the operation Mary needs."

Melissa sank into a chair, deflated, but she listened closely while Dr. Koener told her that Mary's optic nerve had been pinched when she'd fallen from her horse and struck her head on a rock.

Melissa felt shame that she'd never asked the specifics of Mary's accident, but she pushed it aside to concentrate on what the doctor was saying.

"An operation might or might not relieve the pressure on the optic nerve," he explained. "There is a possibility that her sight will return on its own—in these cases, the body can take considerable time to repair itself. Mr. Rafferty's concern—and I admit that I share it—is this: Surgery could halt the healing process, if it's happening."

Melissa was sitting on the edge of her chair. "You mean it's really possible for Mary's eyesight to come back on its own? It's been a year, after all."

The doctor nodded. "Yes, it's possible."

She turned and looked up at Quinn's face, and in that moment she knew that the subject of Mary's surgery was closed. The risks were too great, and he wasn't willing to take them.

His decision was either the beginning of Mary's hopes or the end of them. Only God could know which.

 *Eighteen*

The big house was quiet at last.

Adam Corbin breathed a contented sigh and spread an ace-high straight flush out on the surface of the small table in his office.

Jeff threw in his cards and muttered, "Damn it, that woman's got me so confounded I can't even play a decent hand of poker!"

Keith laid down two measly jacks and laughed. "Who are you trying to kid?" he asked good-naturedly. "Fancy's the best thing that ever happened to you, and you know it."

Turning in his chair, Jeff glowered at his younger brother but said nothing.

"Don't mind the captain here," Adam said, taking a cheroot from the pocket of his shirt and lighting it with a wooden match. "He's feeling sorry for himself tonight."

Keith coughed as smoke wafted through the cramped, cluttered little room. He ignored Adam's remark. "You ought to give those things up," he said, referring to the cheroot. "They're bad for you."

Jeff rolled his eyes. "Are you going to treat us to a sermon?" he drawled.

Keith drew his chair a little closer to the table and cleared his throat. "As a matter of fact, big brother," he began, "I do feel a need to offer my help in your hour of desolation." He paused and looked back over one shoulder. "It's sure quiet in here. Where are the children?"

Adam shrugged. "We're hiding out from them," he answered with a straight face. In truth, Maggie, the housekeeper, had put the herd of them to bed upstairs.

Jeff glared at Keith. "I don't need your help or anybody else's," he grumbled, as though there had been no break in the conversation. "In fact, I think you've got some nerve even bringing up the subject! What the hell do you know about what I'm going through? *Your* wife is safe under your roof, probably warming your slippers or something!"

Keith sighed. "Tess is as fired up about women getting the vote as Banner and Fancy are," he told his brother patiently.

"But she didn't go to Seattle to the rally, did she?" Jeff asked, looking smug.

"She would have if it weren't for the chicken pox."

Adam was amused to see that Jeff shrank back a little at these words, as though Keith had been in contact with bubonic plague. "Chicken pox?" he echoed thinly. "Tess has the chicken pox?"

Keith chuckled and shook his head. "No, Jeff. The children do. Probably got it from the Bradley children. They came down with it a couple of weeks ago."

"Oh." Jeff looked reflective for a few moments, then horrified. "My God, what if my boys get it? Fancy's going to be away for a week!"

Although Adam certainly didn't relish the idea of a chicken pox epidemic sweeping through the family as well as Port Hastings in general, he couldn't help grinning at the thought of Jeff trying to take care of three itchy little boys. "You've got a housekeeper," he suggested. "Make her look after the kids."

Jeff looked crestfallen. "I can't. She quit."

Adam and Keith exchanged a knowing look that seemed

to infuriate Jeff, and he shoved back his chair and nervously loosened the collar of his shirt. "Hell, what am I worrying about? They might not even come down with anything."

"How about you, Jeff?" Keith asked with a broad grin. "Have you ever had chicken pox?"

"I don't remember," Jeff said.

"You haven't," Adam informed him.

"Good God!" Jeff boomed as the possibility of his own infection struck him. He'd talked with the Bradleys at church himself!

Adam and Keith both laughed, even though neither of them was immune to chicken pox, either.

Jeff scratched the side of his neck. "Don't just sit there," he said to Adam. "Deal the cards."

Adam began to shuffle the worn deck. "Actually," he began after clearing his throat, "it just so happens that Keith and I did want to have a little talk with you."

Jeff looked suspiciously from one brother to the other. "About what?" he demanded.

"Your private business," Keith said bluntly. "We feel the need to interfere in it a bit."

Color suffused Jeff's face. "Is that so?"

Adam set the cards in the middle of the table, and Jeff cut them automatically, even though his dark blue eyes were fixed on his brother the whole time and snapping with fury.

"You're going to lose Fancy if you keep on being so damned hardheaded," Adam said, speaking around the cheroot clamped in his teeth. "Do you really want that, Jeff?"

He seemed to deflate, settling back in his chair and reaching for the glass of whiskey he'd been nursing all evening. Glumly, he shook his head. "This whole thing has gotten completely out of hand. I don't even know how to start making things right again."

"I'd suggest moving back into your own house, for one thing," Keith ventured to say, making a steeple of his fingers beneath his chin. At the defiant look this brought from his brother he added, "You're going to have to give some ground, Jeff. Let Fancy have a little breathing space."

Jeff sighed and idly scratched his left shoulder. "I guess

that means I shouldn't go over to Seattle and drag her out of that rally by her collar," he said with a sheepish grin. "Damn it, a week is a long time."

"Long enough to think about what you want to say to her," Keith pointed out.

Adam was pleased, since this was the first sign of cooperation Jeff had shown since his marital problems had begun. He glanced at Keith. "Shall I deal you in for another hand, Reverend?"

Keith shook his head. "Can't stay. I've got a wife and a warm pair of slippers waiting at home."

"Lucky bastard," Jeff muttered, albeit with a half grin.

"Amen," said Adam.

It was a beautiful, sunny morning, and the steamboat was scheduled to sail in an hour. Quinn was having a heart-to-heart talk with Mary in the hotel dining room, so Melissa set off for the nearby newspaper office.

The place was bristling with excitement, and the huge presses made an ear-splitting racket. People ran in every direction, some of them shouting, and the air smelled of ink and sweat and smoke.

"Can I help you, ma'am?" a clerk yelled, smiling at Melissa.

"I just want to look!" Melissa hollered back pleasantly.

The clerk nodded, but cautioned at the top of his lungs, "Be sure and stay out of the way, now, or you might get hurt!"

Melissa wandered around as long as she dared and left the clamorous building with a freshly printed edition of the *Seattle Times* under her arm. When she met Quinn in the hotel lobby, as agreed, she was full to bursting with what she'd seen and heard.

There were shadows in Quinn's eyes, even though he smiled as he listened to Melissa's accounting. She had chattered on for several minutes before she brought herself up short and said, "I'm sorry, Quinn. I didn't even ask about Mary. Is she going with us, or will she stay here?"

He sighed. "She's staying—going back to school."

Melissa slid her arm through the crook of her husband's. Their baggage was being carried outside and loaded into the boot of a carriage, and in the distance she could hear the sad drone of half a dozen steam whistles. "Maybe Mary will want to come back to Port Riley when the term is over."

Quinn not only failed to answer, he seemed so pre-occupied that Melissa didn't say another word until they'd reached the wharf. Their baggage was being hauled aboard the steamer, and Quinn had just paid the carriage driver.

"Still wishing we didn't have to go back home?" Melissa inquired as her husband escorted her along the creaky wharf toward the boarding ramp.

At last Quinn seemed to really see Melissa, and to hear her. He smiled and squeezed her hand. "No, Calico, I'm not sorry. With you beside me I can handle anything."

Melissa was both pleased and flattered, even though she knew that men often said such things just to distract a woman from a subject they didn't want to discuss. "I can't wait to start my newspaper," she said happily.

Quinn laughed and steered her into the salon, but they didn't remain in that spacious room for long, because the weather was too beautiful. It was only when Seattle was far behind and the midday meal was being served that Quinn and Melissa returned to seat themselves at a table.

Melissa opened her newspaper, the one she'd been given that morning after her brief tour, and immediately a piece midway down the front page caught her eye: "Fraud Uncovered in Seattle Justice System."

A peculiar feeling of dread niggled in the pit of Melissa's stomach as she scanned the short article, as mysterious as the force that had drawn her attention to that particular item in the first place.

"What is it?" Quinn asked, reaching across the table to close one hand over Melissa's wrist. "You're white as snow."

Melissa pulled free of him to rest one hand at the base of her throat. Her heart was hammering there, fit to choke her. "Dear God," she whispered. "Oh, dear God!"

"Melissa!"

She laid the newspaper down slowly on the table, gazing at Quinn and wondering how he could have said such pretty words and made such tender love to her when all the while his heart had been black and shriveled and evil within him. She tried to speak but couldn't, and some calm part of her mind reflected that that was probably a good thing, since there were people around.

Quinn snatched the newspaper up and scoured its front with smoldering brown eyes. "What the—?"

"What a good pretender you are," Melissa managed to get out. Her eyes were brimming with tears now. "When all the time you knew. God in heaven, I don't know how you can live with yourself!"

Quinn looked so explosively frustrated that Melissa stabbed at the headline in question with one finger and half sobbed, "There!"

As Quinn read the piece he looked honestly shocked. What an actor he is! she thought.

"The justice of the peace who married us was a fraud," he said when he looked up, and he sounded like a man talking in his sleep.

Melissa was shaking her head slowly from side to side in an utter agony of the soul. "Don't pretend you didn't know," she pleaded. "I remember how you talked with that man— you called him by his first name, you were friends! Quinn Rafferty, you had to have known that any marriage he performed would be invalid!"

"Melissa," Quinn whispered raggedly, furiously, "you can't believe that!"

Melissa did believe it, and she had initials carved in trees for proof—Quinn's initials, and Gillian's. She had his own admission that he wanted the borrowing power a link with her family could give him. Lastly, there was his first reaction to her suspicion that she was pregnant. He'd been patently horrified.

As he looked at her something changed in Quinn's face. She saw the eagerness to convince her fade away, heard him say with resignation, "I suppose you'll want to get off the steamer in Port Hastings."

Melissa shook her head. "I have no intention of making things so easy for you," she said coldly. "I'm going on to Port Riley, where I intend to publish a newspaper."

His face was drawn, and in that moment Quinn looked far older than his thirty-three years. "I think we've got more important things to discuss than your harebrained ideas about cranking out local gossip on that decrepit old press," he said. Ignoring the angry color blooming in Melissa's face, he went on. "You're so anxious to believe that I deceived you. Why is that, Melissa? Is it because you've decided that being married isn't what you want after all—even though you're probably carrying my baby?"

Melissa had never been more confused or more tormented. The shock of finding herself still a spinster when she'd thought she was a wife left her in a terrible muddle. "This is my baby," she said belatedly, resting both hands on her stomach. "Not yours."

The rest of the journey seemed interminable. When the steamer docked temporarily at Port Hastings Melissa felt a wild urge to run home to her brothers and sob out her sad story. She knew they would take her side and probably even avenge her, but when the ship chugged onward toward Port Riley she was still aboard it.

Quinn had avoided her insofar as he could since their confrontation over the newspaper article. When the ship docked that evening, however, he insisted on escorting her down the ramp and then ordered her things loaded into the waiting wagon.

Melissa was furious, but she was too weary to make a scene in front of the town. She grasped Quinn's arm and whispered, "What do you think you're doing? I certainly have no intention of going home with you, Mr. Rafferty."

"I wouldn't have you," Quinn replied brusquely, his eyes cold. His gaze shifted to the stable hand who had brought the wagon. "Take Mrs.—Miss Corbin to the State Hotel," he finished.

Melissa felt as though he'd slapped her, but she didn't let on that she was hurt. She was far too proud for that. And when Quinn didn't join her in the wagon box but turned and strode off in another direction, she didn't look to see where he might be going.

The telegram trembled in Fancy's hands. The noise of the rally was ringing in her ears, and she couldn't be sure that she'd read the words correctly. She drew a deep breath and started over again.

JEFF AND THE CHILDREN STRICKEN WITH CHICKEN POX. MY HANDS FULL. PLEASE COME HOME. LOVE, TESS.

Although Fancy was worried, she couldn't suppress a little giggle at the thought of Jeff covered from head to foot with calamine lotion. She searched through the crowds of suffrage workers gathered in the Seattle Hotel until she found Banner.

"I'm going back to Port Hastings as soon as I can," she informed her sister-in-law, holding out the telegram.

Banner's green eyes widened. "Thunderation," she said. "I'm going, too—Adam must be working twenty-four hours a day!"

By the time the two women had packed and traveled to the wharf it was dark outside, and the last steamer had sailed. Not to be deterred, Fancy and Banner found a salmon-boat skipper who looked sober and seemed trustworthy and hired him to take them home.

Melissa tried to eat supper in her small, lonely hotel room, but she couldn't get so much as a bite past her constricted throat. If only Quinn had taken her into his arms, she thought mournfully, and insisted that they make right the error and be properly married right away. Instead he'd sent her off to the State Hotel.

It hurt savagely to think Quinn could have rid himself of her so peremptorily after all they'd been to each other. Apparently he was able to pretend that she'd never been a part of his life.

Melissa let out a long, quavering sigh. Quinn was probably with Gillian at that very moment. No doubt the two of them were drinking champagne in their fancy resort hotel and toasting the neat disposal of one used wife.

There was a knock at the door, and Melissa intended to ignore it—until she heard her friend Dana Morgan's voice calling to her from the other side.

"I know you're in there, Melissa Rafferty, so let me in!"

Melissa pulled open the door, and Dana took one look at her and embraced her with a little cry of despair. "Good heavens, what's happened?" she blurted out.

Careful to close the door and to keep her voice low, Melissa countered with a question of her own. "How did you find out I was here?"

Dana dropped her gaze, and her cheeks were flushed pink. "You might as well know that everyone is talking—the whole town saw you brought here in that wagon without Mr. Rafferty."

"And Quinn?" Melissa dared to ask. "Have you heard anything about him?"

Glumly, Dana nodded. "He's in one of the saloons out by the cannery—bent on getting himself drunk."

Melissa suppressed an urge to go and find Quinn. If a man was so stupid as to make a public spectacle, then that was his business and not her own. "I guess he must feel guilty about what he did," she said, but she took little satisfaction in the knowledge.

"What did he do?"

"He made me think we were married when we weren't."

Dana sucked in a horrified breath and fanned herself with one hand. "You're not married! Oh, Melissa, this is terrible! You'll be ruined!"

Melissa was weary to the very marrow of her bones, and she surely didn't need anyone to tell her that she was ruined. She knew that all too well. "Maybe Quinn was right," she reflected. "Maybe I should just go back to Port Hastings and forget I ever saw this town."

"You could go to California and live with your mother," Dana suggested sympathetically.

Melissa shook her head. "No. Mama's just starting a new

life—she doesn't need a woebegone, pregnant daughter underfoot."

Dana's eyes went impossibly wide, and she slapped one hand over her mouth. "Pregnant? Dear heaven, Melissa, you're *pregnant?!"*

Melissa nodded. "I think so."

"Does Mr. Rafferty know?" Dana demanded, and she looked so upset that Melissa was afraid she might faint.

"He knows," Melissa answered miserably, remembering with a stab of pain how dismayed Quinn had been at the prospect, although he'd insisted that was because of his fears for her and the child.

Dana sank into a chair and cried, "I'm going to faint!"

Melissa was quick to say, "Put your head down between your knees!"

It was when Dana had done this and managed to hold onto consciousness that Melissa began to laugh, grimly amused that her friend was near swooning when she was the one who was carrying a child. Only the laughter kept coming. Melissa was gasping for breath, tears streaming down her face, and still she couldn't stop.

Alarmed, Dana rallied herself enough to go downstairs and ask for help.

Melissa was curled into a little ball on the bed, quiet at last, when the doctor arrived. He was a dark-haired, blue-eyed man who resembled her eldest brother Adam, and she was comforted by his presence.

He drew a chair up beside the bed and took her hand in his. "Your friend tells me that you've had quite an upset today," he said gently.

Melissa could only nod; words might start that torrent of tears flowing again.

"I'm going to give you a dose of laudanum," the doctor said after a brief examination. "A good night's sleep is what you need; things will look better in the morning."

Melissa didn't believe that for a moment, but she took the laudanum, and presently she slept. When she awakened things looked no better at all. It was raining outside, and a cold, blustery wind was blowing, and the one dream that remained to her seemed impossible to achieve.

She walked to Quinn's house and knocked at the back door, praying he wouldn't be in the kitchen.

It was Helga who answered, and her eyes were as red and puffy as Melissa's own. "Oh, missus," she blurted out, "it's you! You've come back!"

"I'm only here to get some of my things," Melissa said quietly. "Is Mr. Rafferty at home?"

Helga sniffled. "Yes, missus."

"Then I'll try again later," Melissa said, starting to back out the door.

Helga caught her hand, shaking her head. "Don't go, please," she pleaded. "The master can't do any harm—he's laid up sick."

Melissa sighed. "Some of my notebooks are upstairs in the master bedroom. Could you bring them to me, please, and have the rest of my things sent to the State Hotel?"

Helga's eyes pleaded with Melissa. "Please. Mr. Rafferty's sorry for whatever it is he did—if you'd only see him."

"I couldn't bear to," Melissa confessed.

The maid dragged her to the table and seated her there. "Then you'll have a cup of tea, yes?"

Melissa had to smile. "Yes," she conceded.

Helga put loose tea leaves into a crockery pot, added boiling water, and left the stuff to brew while she went upstairs to fetch Melissa's notebooks.

When she returned her hands were empty, and she was trembling. "Mr. Rafferty says you're to come up to the room," she said. "That's the only way you're going to get those tablets."

With a sigh, Melissa got out of her chair and made her way up the rear stairway and along the hall to the master bedroom. When she let herself in Quinn was sitting up in the mammoth bed. He did indeed look like a man who had dedicated the night to getting himself drunk; he was pale, and there were shadows under his eyes.

Doing her best to ignore him, Melissa edged over to the desk and grabbed up her notebooks. The rest were in the railroad car, and she planned to get them after leaving Quinn's house.

She was scanning the pages of prose she had written when her illicit lover finally spoke.

"It's all there, Melissa. Did you think I would destroy your work?"

Melissa swallowed hard and shook her head. She wanted her novel-in-progress because she needed to take solace in it, not because she'd thought Quinn would burn the pages or rip them up.

Quinn gave a broken sigh. How endearingly decadent he looked, she thought, with his hair rumpled and his beard growing in.

"Before you walk out of here, Calico, I want to say one thing—I didn't know Henry didn't have the authority to marry us. I swear to God I didn't."

Melissa lowered her eyes. "Suppose I believed you, Quinn? What would happen then?"

He was silent for a long time. "I don't know," he finally said.

"I see," Melissa said with soft despondency. She turned and started toward the door, holding her notebooks tightly in her arms. Even as she stepped over the threshold, moved along the hallway, descended the stairs, she hoped in vain that Quinn would call her back.

All he had to do was offer her a real, bona fide marriage, and she would forgive and forget.

But he clearly wasn't about to do that.

Reaching the kitchen, Melissa saw that Helga was waiting to pour her tea. She couldn't bring herself to sit and sip orange pekoe when the universe was crumbling all around her, so she shook her head solemnly and went out.

She had collected her pen and ink and the remainder of the tablets from the railroad car and was on her way back to her room at the State Hotel to write when she encountered Mitch Williams on the street. He tipped his hat to her, but Melissa was too busy staring at his companion to appreciate the gesture.

Standing beside the lawyer, large as life, was Sir Ajax

Morewell Hampton. He was smiling happily, and his fair hair glinted, despite the gloomy weather. He took Melissa's hand and lifted it to his lips. "So you are mine again," he said in a throaty voice. "Imagine my joy at arriving in Port Riley and hearing such news."

Melissa pulled back her hand. She was humiliated, and, suspecting that Mitch had been the one to tell Ajax of her shame, she gave him a cutting look. "I am not yours," she said to her former fiancé. "I never was, and I never will be. Good day."

When Melissa started around Ajax he stopped her, grasping her arm and ushering her along the sidewalk, and then into the relative privacy of a gap between the druggist's shop and the Chinese laundry.

"You don't understand," Ajax said urgently, his smile a little fixed. "I've sent Elke back to Europe for good, Melissa. I'm going to stay in this town until I've won you back."

Melissa wrenched her arm free and nearly dropped her many notebooks in the process. "You're wasting your time!" She spat out the words, furious at his presumption and his persistence. "For the hundredth time, Ajax, I don't love you!"

Ajax looked wounded. "How can you say that? You were willing to marry me not a month ago!" His look of injury became one of maddening pity. "Is it because you've given yourself to that man that you are afraid to start over again with me? Little one, we'll simply pretend that you were never so indiscreet."

That was it. Melissa had reached the end of her tether; her patience was exhausted. She let her writing materials tumble to the ground and slapped Ajax so hard that the imprint of her hand was emblazoned on his cheek.

For a moment Melissa was afraid, for she saw his fist clench at his side, but then Mitch reappeared and pushed past Ajax to begin picking up the fallen tablets. With her own heartbeat pounding in her ears, Melissa knelt down to help.

Nineteen

Frank Crowley, the banker, was obviously trying to contain his excitement, but his pencil-line mustache kept wriggling, and he couldn't seem to sit still in his chair. His catlike eyes flickered over Melissa's simple sprigged cambric dress. "If you don't mind my mentioning the fact, Mrs. Rafferty," he ventured to say, "it does seem strange that your husband is not present."

Melissa bristled and shifted in her chair. It had been a full week since she had even seen Quinn; during that time she had done all she could to expunge his memory from her mind. She had found a building to house her fledgling newspaper, with rooms above where she could live, and now she wanted to go on with her life.

"Please do not address me as 'Mrs. Rafferty.' You must know, as the rest of Port Riley seems to, that Quinn Rafferty and I were never actually married. I was deceived."

Mr. Crowley looked avidly curious, but it must have crossed his mind that he was jeopardizing an opportunity to harbor Melissa's formidable trust fund in his bank, for he immediately sobered. He made a clucking sound to show that he was in sympathy with Melissa's position and then leaned forward in his chair, smiling at her. "How may I help you?"

"I want a loan," Melissa responded forthrightly, "to set myself up in the newspaper business."

"A loan?" The minuscule mustache quivered again. "But Miss Corbin, you have—"

"I know how much money I have, Mr. Crowley," Melissa broke in. "Your bank certainly won't be risking any loss, since my trust fund could easily absorb the entire enterprise many times over."

The little man spread his hands and looked so patronizing that Melissa considered walking out. After all, there were three other banks in Port Riley, although one of them was Quinn's, and she wanted no association with that man. Until the time was right, of course.

"You are quite correct, of course, Mrs.—er, Miss Corbin. Have you written plans for what you propose to do?"

Melissa had been up all the night before preparing. She passed a tidy sheaf of papers across the desk and waited patiently as Mr. Crowley read them.

"Impressive work," he allowed somewhat grudgingly when he'd finished. "Did someone help you?"

At a less harried time in her life Melissa might have taken issue with the suggestion that she wasn't capable of accomplishing such a task on her own. As it was, however, she had enough to worry about without answering every slight, fancied or otherwise. She simply shook her head.

Mr. Crowley aligned the stack of papers neatly and then rested folded hands upon them. He cleared his throat. "You are aware, of course, that the building you've selected to house your enterprise is in the worst part of town."

Melissa was fully aware of that. The structure had once held the Rip Snortin' Saloon, and it was surrounded by other establishments of that ilk. "There aren't a great many empty buildings in town that are large enough to suit my purposes," she said reasonably.

Once again Mr. Crowley was forced to concede the point. He nodded, sighed, and said, "I'll have your funds transferred and ask my clerk to prepare a letter of credit so that you may get underway."

This was the first hopeful thing that had happened to Melissa in over a week, and she felt encouraged. She rose from her chair, prompting the stuffy little banker to rise from his, and they shook hands vigorously. Now she could arrange to have her printing press brought from Quinn's house, along with the remainder of her clothes.

A few hours later Melissa walked into the former Rip Snortin' Saloon carrying a broom and bucket she'd bought on credit at Kruger's Mercantile. Her friend Dana and a young man who served as a stock boy were behind her, carrying other housekeeping items.

The stock boy whistled in dismay as he took in the cobwebs arching like enormous fishnets from the ceiling to the long wooden bar. There was a mirror in back, but it was so filthy that no hint of a human image was reflected.

Dana set her box of groceries and cleaning materials down on a debris-littered pool table, and a cloud of dust rose up to make her sneeze. "You're not actually going to live in this dreadful place!" she wailed, staring at Melissa in disbelief.

"Of course I am," Melissa said, pretending to more courage than she actually possessed. "It only needs a little cleaning, after all."

In the near distance a drunken whoop sounded, followed by shouts of raucous laughter. Melissa hoped that her friend hadn't noticed the slight shudder she'd given.

"You know," Dana began, waggling one finger at Melissa, "sometimes I think Mr. Rafferty is right about you!"

Melissa folded her arms. "Oh? Exactly what is he saying, and how did you happen to hear it?"

The stock boy took his leave by the back way, and Dana watched him slip out of sight before answering. "He came by to see me yesterday, if you must know. It happens that he's planning to build accommodations for wives and families near the lumber camp, and he wants to establish a school."

Melissa was touched by the philanthropy of such a gesture, but she would never have let on. She had to remember what Quinn had done to her and keep her heart hardened

237

against him. "What did he say about me?" she couldn't resist asking.

"That you're stubborn as a blind ox," Dana responded quite willingly, "and that you ought to be given a sound spanking."

Color throbbed in Melissa's face, and she looked away to hide it. "I see," she said.

Dana sighed. "Melissa, give this silly charade up and go home to your husband."

"Mr. Rafferty is not my husband." Melissa bit down on her lower lip in an effort to hold back tears, then added, "He never was."

"He loves you!"

"That must be why he's been maligning me—calling me an ox and saying I should be beaten!"

Dana rolled her eyes. "There is simply no talking to you, is there?" She consulted the watch pinned to the bodice of her blouse. "Well, then stay here and grapple with the dirt and rats. I've got better things to do."

Resigned, Melissa watched her friend march out through the swinging doors. Then, having exchanged her good cambric dress for one of the ugly calicos that had been given to her in Spokane, she covered her hair with a bandanna and set to work.

The first thing she did was sweep down all the cobwebs. When that was done she scrubbed the mirror behind the bar, although it would be taken away as soon as she could make arrangements.

She had just carried the last of the chairs that had surrounded the drinking and gaming tables into the shed out back when Quinn walked in.

The light was poor inside the long-deserted saloon, since many of the windows were boarded up, but Melissa didn't miss the signs of strain that marked his countenance. Quinn looked thinner, there was a haunted expression in his eyes, and, as always, he needed a shave. In some detached part of her mind Melissa wondered why he didn't just grow a beard and be done with it.

"What do you want?"

Quinn was clearly annoyed at the question. His dark eyes turned hot with anger, and Melissa was glad to see that, although she couldn't have explained why. He slammed one fist down on the pool table, and more dust clouded the air. "You can't stay here," he announced, completely ignoring her question.

"I can do anything I like, Mr. Rafferty," Melissa reminded him. "I'm of legal age, and I'm unmarried." Her blue eyes were flashing as she glared at him. "I'm also stubborn as an ox and in need of physical assault, I hear."

Quinn chose to let that last comment pass, but his jawline was tight. He let out a ragged breath and thrust one hand through his hair. "Melissa," he began, clearly struggling for a reasonable tone of voice, "I want you to come home. You can sleep in Mary's room until we figure out what to do."

Melissa would have died before spending a single night under the man's roof, but she didn't want to make things too easy for him by saying so outright. "Until we figure out what to do? About what?"

"About us!" Quinn's frustration fairly reverberated against the dirty but sound walls of the Rip Snortin' Saloon. "About our baby. You're not safe here, Calico, and neither is my child."

Melissa's spine went stiff. "You have no child, Mr. Rafferty—and you never will. Not by me."

He stepped closer to her, and Melissa tried to retreat, only to find that her back was pressed to the long bar. Quinn closed in, resting a hand on either side of her and trapping her within his arms. Although his body was not quite touching hers, Melissa was painfully aware of his hardness, his heat, and his strength, and she felt as if her heart were crowding into her throat.

"I've missed you," he whispered, and then he bent his head and kissed the side of her neck, setting the tender flesh there to pulsing.

Melissa longed to push him away, but she hadn't the power or the will to do it. She trembled as his lips trailed up over her jawline and her cheek to claim her mouth in a tentative kiss.

She could not help responding, and when she did, Quinn took complete advantage. Their tongues sparred, and when the kiss ended at long, long last Melissa was glad of the wooden bar behind her, because it was all that was holding her upright.

"Get out," she ordered, breathless and shaken.

His hands had not moved from the bar; they created a prison of muscle and bone. "If you won't come home with me, Calico," he said against her mouth, "I swear I'll move in here with you. And I'll drive you crazy all night, every night, until you're finally willing to be reasonable."

"I'll have you arrested," Melissa vowed weakly.

Quinn gave a low, gruff laugh and shook his head. "You'd never do that. Shall I prove it?"

Melissa shook her head wildly. "No—please. Just go away and leave me alone!"

Some unreadable emotion moved in his eyes, darkening them. He withdrew, and Melissa felt a tearing desolation at the parting. "Are you planning to spend the night in this place?" he asked.

"No," Melissa answered honestly. She hadn't even started cleaning the room upstairs. The bedroom she'd selected as her own needed painting and wallpapering as well as a new mattress, and the tiny kitchen was inhabited by mice and owls.

He sighed and rubbed his eyes with a thumb and forefinger. "Well, that's something, I guess."

Melissa took up her broom and began sweeping frantically. All she was doing was stirring up more dirt, and both of them knew it, but she had to be busy or burst. "If you wouldn't mind having my printing press delivered—"

Quinn halted the furious progress of her broom with one hand, and Melissa was forced to meet his eyes. "I won't play this game forever," he warned. "I meant what I said before: If you insist on living in this place, you can count on me as a house guest."

Melissa's cheeks were hot, and her knuckles and jawline ached from being clenched. She longed to slap Quinn, but she had a terrible feeling that he would retaliate in kind, so she kept her hand at her side. "I hate you," she said.

He caught a finger under her defiant little chin and lifted. "We'll see about that," he taunted softly, "the first time you lie down under this roof." Having made this pronouncement, he turned and strode away toward the swinging doors, leaving Melissa to stare after him in impotent fury.

When she arrived at the State Hotel hours later she was tired and hungry and dirty as a coal miner coming out of the pit. It seemed a cruel fate that Ajax was lurking around the lobby, waiting for her. She did take some satisfaction in his look of horror, however.

"Hello, Ajax," she said with a sweet smile, offering her filthy hand for a continental kiss.

There was nothing he could do except complete the gesture, and he did, though he looked as though he might retch. "How can you demean yourself this way?" he scolded, shaking his head and clucking like an old lady watching a whores' parade.

Melissa laughed, too tired for a sparring match with Ajax or anyone else. She'd exhausted her supply of emotional ammunition earlier, with Quinn. "I could ask you the same question," she pointed out. "I've told you again and again that there's no future for us, but you still stay in Port Riley, making a pest of yourself."

Ajax smiled his flawless smile, as unmoved as ever. Melissa considered telling him that she was carrying Quinn's child, since that would surely put him off, but the news was too private and precious to share with someone she liked so little.

"Come to supper with me tonight, Cinderella," he said in a smooth, teasing tone of voice. "There's a fine orchestra playing at the new hotel, and we can dance until all the stars have stopped winking."

Melissa was intrigued despite her weariness, but not because she fancied spending an evening in Ajax's arms. What appealed to her was the prospect of being seen in the company of an eligible man by that officious, overbearing rascal who had broken her heart. It was almost a certainty that Quinn would be at the new hotel if there was an event taking place there.

On impulse she nodded her assent, although she felt a little guilty knowing that Ajax was entertaining false hopes.

He kissed her grubby hand again, this time with tenderness instead of revulsion, and said in his autocratic way, "Meet me here in the lobby at six o'clock."

Melissa executed a mocking little curtsy, her mouth twitching at one corner, and climbed the stairs to her room on the second floor. A tub had been brought in for her, as it was every day, and a pair of maids appeared within a short time, each bearing two buckets of hot water.

As best she could under such circumstances, Melissa scrubbed herself clean. She was wearing her yellow silk wrapper and brushing the tangles from her snarled, wet tresses when there was a knock at the door.

Thinking that the maids had come back to carry away the big copper bathtub, Melissa unlocked the door and swung it open without asking who was there. She was startled to find Rowina Brown's daughter, Charlotte, standing in the hallway, looking as though she'd rather be in any one of a thousand other places.

Wordlessly, Melissa stepped back to admit her unexpected caller.

"I suppose you're wondering what I'm doing here," Charlotte began, tossing her blue-black hair, which fell to her waist in a sleek curtain, back over one shoulder.

Melissa only shrugged and went on brushing, though she did close the door.

"I heard you had some crazy idea about opening up a newspaper where the Rip Snortin' used to be. Is that true?"

Melissa nodded distantly. "Yes. Why?"

A beautiful smile broke over Charlotte's face. "My mother was right about you—you've got as much grit as any man."

Although pleased at the compliment—if indeed it *was* a compliment—Melissa was no less confused as to Charlotte's purpose in paying her a visit. "Thank you," she said remotely, still brushing her hair.

Charlotte was pacing, and for the first time Melissa noticed what she was wearing—trousers, a flannel shirt, and a buckskin jacket with fringe. "That was a bad piece of luck you had—Rafferty fooling you the way he did, I mean."

Melissa flushed, hating the fact that Quinn's deception was common knowledge in Port Riley. No doubt the other men secretly admired him for the dastardly trick he'd played. "I've recovered," she lied.

Obsidian eyes refuted the claim in silent challenge for a few moments, then Charlotte said, "I'm sorry I was so rude to you that day when you stopped by our place. I thought you were just another bit of fluff, like Gillian Aires, and I didn't have much respect for you."

Melissa suppressed a smile and waited.

A golden blush showed in Charlotte's cheeks. "Damn it, you're not going to make this easy, are you? I came to apologize and to tell you that you need somebody to help you clean up that old saloon."

"Somebody like you?" Melissa inquired lightly.

Charlotte nodded and ducked her head for a moment. "I'm a hard worker, and I need a job."

Melissa assessed her caller seriously. "I admit that I need help, but before I agree to hire you, I want to know what you have against Quinn."

Charlotte shook her head so that her rich ebony hair flew, and the set of her face was stubborn. "All I'm going to say is that it isn't what you think—Quinn didn't have eyes for anybody besides that Gillian woman until you came along."

The words chilled Melissa's spirit. Now, of course, Quinn was perfectly free to return to his obsession with Gillian. They were probably closer than ever, despite his threats to force his way into Melissa's bed if she ever took up residence above the Rip Snortin' Saloon. She shrugged, letting Charlotte's statement pass without comment or challenge.

The Indian woman looked at her curiously, then burst out, "Quinn and I do have one thing in common, I'm afraid—the same drunken louse of a father."

Melissa sat down on the edge of the bed, her mouth open. "Does Quinn know that?" she asked.

Charlotte shook her head. "I don't think so, and I don't

have any intention of telling him, either. He might think I wanted something."

It was easy to see that that possibility was anathema to Charlotte, so fierce was her pride. "Why did you tell me?" Melissa asked.

Charlotte lowered her head. "It's always been such a big secret. I guess I just needed to say it to somebody."

Convoluted as that reasoning was, Melissa understood it. She thoughtfully changed the subject. "I've seen bears' dens that were cleaner than my building," she said, "but if you really want to work for me, be there at eight o'clock tomorrow morning."

Charlotte nodded, thanked Melissa, and hurried out, leaving her new employer full of wary curiosity about Eustice Rafferty. She had only dimly seen the man that night on the street when Quinn had been prepared to do murder, but she had been able to discern that he was not a comely fellow. For all that, he had certainly cut a wide swath in his younger days.

By the time six o'clock rolled around Melissa was dressed in peach silk. A golden locket Jeff had given her for her sixteenth birthday was her only jewelry, and her hair was braided and wound into an impeccable coronet atop her head. Ajax, who was dressed very formally himself, drew in a breath at the sight of her.

"Ah, Cinderella," he purred, offering her his arm, "I see that the fairy godmother has visited you."

Melissa laughed and shook her head and allowed herself to be escorted outside, expecting to find a carriage waiting, or a horse and buggy.

Instead there was a quivering, chortling motorcar. The pipe by the rear fender made an unnerving popping sound, and a crowd had gathered in the street to look on as Ajax handed Melissa up into the cushioned leather seat. After giving a suave little bow he walked around and got behind the wheel, carefully putting on a motoring cap and goggles that made him look like a very elite insect.

Melissa gave a giggle and then put one hand to her mouth. With a great shimmying lurch that set the onlookers cheering the automobile moved forward.

"Where did you get this?" Melissa cried, delighted, having to raise her voice to be heard over the engine.

"Ordered it!" Ajax shouted back. "Bought the thing purely to impress you, if you must know!"

The machine jostled them over the rutted road that led to Quinn's fancy hotel, and another crowd had gathered on the lawn by the time they rounded the last bend. Foremost in the gathering, with Gillian at his side, stood Quinn Rafferty.

Melissa lifted her chin and was all elegant curves and angles when Ajax helped her down from the conveyance. She smiled at the snapping outrage in Quinn's dark eyes as they passed him, pretending utter fascination as Ajax prattled on about owning the first motorcar ever to grace the roads of Port Riley.

Twilight gave way to night as Ajax and Melissa ate in the huge, beautifully appointed dining room, their meal interrupted intermittently by eager townspeople offering congratulations on the acquisition of Ajax's modern wonder. Quinn was conspicuously absent from their number; in fact, Melissa didn't see him again until dinner was over and the dancing was about to begin in the ballroom.

She knew she was probably the subject of much speculation and gossip. For that reason she entered that brightly lit room with all the regal dignity of a visiting princess.

All through that first waltz in Ajax's practiced arms Melissa could feel Quinn's gaze upon her. It wasn't until they whirled past the massive French doors leading out into the hotel garden that she spotted him standing in the opening, one foot resting on the rim of a fancy marble planter. He held a cheroot between his strong white teeth, and the smoke was like a wispy fog trailing off into the night air.

The next time they passed Quinn was gone, and Melissa felt something twist deep down in her heart. At the end of the dance she excused herself to visit the powder room, and she was there a long time, fighting memories of the hotel. And of Quinn.

He was waiting for her when she reentered the lobby, looking rakishly handsome in his formal suit, and he favored her with a wicked little half smile before offering his arm.

Melissa stubbornly refused to take it, and he chuckled at this, his eyes dancing.

"Here I am," he lamented, mocking her, "trying to help you through a touchy situation. And what do you do?"

"What touchy situation is that?" Melissa asked archly, keeping her distance. She knew what the man could do to her senses and her principles if he was allowed to get too close.

One powerful masculine shoulder moved in a shrug. Another smug grin creased his face. "I hate to be the one to tell you this," he said, "but your—er—friend has left you to take a lady riding in his motorcar. Gillian, as it happens."

Melissa was incensed, but not because she wanted Ajax for herself—far from it. No, it was the humiliation of being abandoned. Again. "I hope they have a very nice time," she said stiffly.

One rusty guffaw of laughter escaped Quinn. "Sure you do, Calico," he said. And then he put his hand on the small of Melissa's back and steered her toward the glittering ballroom.

They danced, and it was a sweet torment for Melissa to be held so near to Quinn when she knew she must never allow him to make love to her again, no matter what.

"Does your friend Ajax have money to lend?" Quinn inquired as they swept through the other dancers.

Melissa smiled up at him. "Why? Do you intend to ask him for a loan?"

Quinn was as furious as Melissa had hoped he would be. Seeing her satisfaction, though, he took obvious care to recover rapidly. "Gillian's the one in dire financial straits. She's been hinting that she might be willing to sell her share of the hotel."

The thought of Ajax buying half of that grand structure and staying in Port Riley forever—and he was just obstinate enough to do it—made Melissa's heart sink. "Why don't you buy it?" she asked, looking up into Quinn's handsome face.

He grinned. "I'm overextended as it is."

Melissa flushed, remembering why he'd pretended to

marry her—for money. "Too bad I found out we weren't really husband and wife, isn't it? Heaven knows what you might have accomplished if you'd just had a little more time."

Quinn's grin faded. "Melissa, that isn't funny," he said.

"I wasn't making a joke," Melissa replied.

The music stopped, and she would have walked away, but Quinn caught her hand in his and held on. When the orchestra began to play he drew her smoothly into another dance. For a time Melissa allowed herself to pretend that that was where she rightly belonged—in Quinn Rafferty's arms.

Twenty

When Gillian returned from her automobile ride over dark roads she was covered with dust and glory. As she entered the ballroom Quinn chuckled at the sight of her, but Melissa was not amused.

Ajax, for his part, looked exhilarated. It had clearly not occurred to him to feel guilty for deserting Melissa. He was beaming as he approached, pulling Gillian along with him.

There was a befuddled look about the woman, and Melissa knew a brief, soaring hope that Gillian had fallen in love with Ajax and he with her.

"Here you are, little one!" he cried, as though it had been Melissa who had slipped away without a word, and not himself. "You must be very tired, and eager to get back to the hotel."

Melissa felt Quinn stiffen beside her and knew a gentle twinge of pleasure at that. She yawned. "As a matter of fact, I am. And I have to be up early tomorrow to work." She turned to Quinn, who had been her escort during Ajax's brief defection, and smiled distantly. "Good night, Mr. Rafferty," she said.

He said nothing, but the dark fire in his eyes threatened to consume Melissa before she could make herself look away.

The April night was chilly, and a fog had rolled in from the water. Even though Ajax's automobile had headlamps, it was nearly impossible to see. Despite this, he insisted on speeding over the twisting road.

"Slow down!" Melissa cried, grasping the seat, frightened for her baby.

Ajax turned to her, laughing at her fear. The look on his face changed swiftly to terror as the machine, making a sound like corn popping in a kettle, careened around the first bend and slammed into a tree with a tremendous, jarring crash.

The impact simultaneously opened the door on Melissa's side and sent her flying through the chasm. She landed, rolling on the grassy ground, a scream of terror trapped in her throat.

When at long last she stopped tumbling, she was lying on her stomach. She grasped handfuls of grass tightly in her hands to anchor herself to the earth and struggled to breathe.

After a little while she was aware of lanterns and voices nearby, and Quinn came to kneel beside her on the ground. "Melissa?" His voice was raspy with fear. "Are you hurt?"

She tightened her hold on the grass. "I-I don't know," she whispered. And she began to cry.

Very gently, very carefully, Quinn forced her to let go of the clumps of quack grass she was crushing into her palms. "See if you can turn over, Melissa," he said.

She was badly bruised and scraped from head to foot, but there didn't seem to be any real damage to muscle and bone. She sat up, pushing her hair back from her face, and mourned, "My gown is ruined!"

Quinn chuckled at this. She would have risen to her feet then, but he stopped her by sweeping her up into his arms. "You're going home with me tonight," he said bluntly. "You can't lie around in a hotel with nobody to look after you."

The truth was that Melissa was still shaken and scared, though not really hurt, and she didn't want to be alone. She let her head rest against Quinn's shoulder. "Is—is Ajax—?"

Quinn was quick to reassure her. "Just a bloody nose and a few loose teeth," he answered.

There were people and horses and buggies all around, but Melissa was only dimly aware of them. When Quinn set her in the seat of a rig and muttered a word of thanks to someone, she yawned and settled against his shoulder, her eyes closed.

It was ironic that immediately after a near miss she felt safer than she ever had before.

Quinn brought her to his house and carried her inside. A slender blond woman met them in the entryway, and Melissa wondered sleepily who she was.

"There's been an accident," Quinn said by way of explanation, and he started up the stairs. "I've sent for Doc Webster. When he gets here, bring him to my room."

Melissa was strangely groggy, as though she'd been drugged, and she felt cold. She whimpered as Quinn undressed her quickly beside the fire in the master suite, then bundled her into a blanket and tucked her into bed beneath the fur spread and silken top sheet.

When the doctor arrived—he was the same man who had given her laudanum the day she learned of Quinn's deception—he examined her carefully and then stepped away from the bed. Although it was a strain, Melissa could hear the two men talking softly over by the fireplace.

"My wife is pregnant," Quinn said.

The doctor sighed in a way that brought both Melissa's hands protectively to her abdomen. She didn't stop to wonder why Quinn had referred to her as his wife when she wasn't, for she was concentrating with her whole being on hearing the physician's reply. "It's important that she rest. If there's going to be a miscarriage, it will happen in the next few days."

Melissa closed her eyes tightly against tears, but they seeped through her lashes anyway. Please, God, she prayed silently, let me keep my baby.

When the doctor was gone Quinn came to the side of the bed and bent to kiss Melissa's forehead. "Go to sleep, Calico," he commanded, his gentle voice tinged with sadness.

"And no worrying. Before you know it you'll be settled in the Rip Snortin' Saloon, publishing recipes, classified advertisements, and advice to the lovelorn."

Melissa sniffled. She would be a fine one to tell other people what to do where affairs of the heart were concerned. There probably wasn't another woman on the face of the earth who felt as lovelorn as she did. "I want this baby," she confided in a broken whisper. "I want it more than anything." Except possibly you, Quinn Rafferty, added a voice in her heart.

Quinn drew up a chair and sank into it, and the expression in his eyes was solemn. "I know, Calico," he answered. "But sometimes things go wrong—"

Melissa shook her head with such purpose that she became dizzy. She closed her eyes. "No. Nothing can happen to this child—I won't let it."

"Sleep," Quinn ordered, offering no argument, no reminders that life can be unmercifully treacherous.

Even though her exhaustion was fathomless, Melissa was afraid to lapse into sleep. She might awaken to find that her baby was gone, and she couldn't take that chance. "Hold me," she said.

After only a few moments of hesitation Quinn removed his boots and his fancy suit coat, now rumpled and dirty, and got into bed beside her in his shirt and trousers. He wrapped his arms around her and held her close, and she drew strength from the scent and substance of him.

When she awakened light was pouring into the room, and Quinn was still beside her. The blanket he had put around her like a cocoon had fallen aside, and one of his hands rested on her belly as if to guard the tiny life within.

Melissa's throat constricted with a jumble of emotions—joy because she knew her baby was safe, despair because she loved its father so desperately and so hopelessly, anger because she'd been so cruelly used that she'd never be able to forgive.

As she cast aside the last remnants of sleep, Melissa became aware of the deep, throbbing ache in her muscles. She hurt from head to foot, body and soul.

Quinn lifted his head from the pillow and looked at her as though surprised to see her there. After a moment he recovered, yawned expansively, and asked, "How do you feel?"

"Terrible," she answered.

His hand rose from her stomach as though it were hot as a stove lid, then fell back to caress her in a gentle way. She was soothed, and the tears that had been welling to the surface subsided without disgracing her. She wanted Quinn, knowing that being possessed by him would be a fierce comfort, and she caught his hand in hers and brought it from her stomach to her breast.

Quinn drew in a sharp breath as he felt a nipple harden against his palm. "No, Melissa," he said firmly. "Absolutely not."

She lifted his hand to her mouth and kissed the rough, callused palm and then the underside of his wrist.

He groaned. "Damn it, you're in no condition. . . ."

Melissa opened his shirt and slid down to take mischievous nips at a masculine nipple with her lips. She felt him rise to straining magnificence against her thigh.

"Oh, God," he gasped, and then, in a violent effort at chivalry, he hurled himself out of bed and stood there gasping.

Melissa's disappointment was cruel, even though she understood his fear. Still, something deep within her said that loving was safe, that no harm would come to the baby because of it. "Please," she said, and her desire was an ache inside her, an ache of the spirit as well as the body.

Quinn glared at her for a few moments, then went into the bathroom. Melissa was afraid that she'd been abandoned, but when he returned he was naked. He came and knelt beside the bed, gently peeling away the blankets that concealed her until she lay bare and bruised and vulnerable before him.

With a strangled cry, he bent and kissed her collarbone where her flesh had been scraped raw, but his hand caressed her breast. Soon his mouth was there, too, tasting the nipple, giving it a tender teasing.

Melissa moaned and arched her back, offering up another part of herself, and Quinn's touch was like rain in a dry garden. She blossomed between his fingers as he pleased her, bringing her nearer and nearer to the treacherous solace she sought.

Writhing, her injuries forgotten for the moment, Melissa whimpered as Quinn propped her bottom up on two soft pillows and then rendered her completely vulnerable with a spreading motion of his fingers. When he came to slake her thirst by drinking of her she gave a lusty cry in welcome and entangled her hands in his hair.

He was gentle and yet ravenous, and he feasted upon Melissa until she'd given all she could give. Then he stroked her with his hand until her breathing was normal and she'd settled into a half trance of contentment.

She saw his desire when he stood and was sleepily amazed when he turned and crossed the room to the armoire. He was getting dressed, preparing to leave!

With tremendous effort Melissa roused herself out of sweet languor long enough to rise up on her elbows and ask, "Aren't you getting into bed?"

Quinn shook his head, ramming his shirttails into his trousers. He had a little trouble buttoning them over his need for Melissa. "Not today," he answered in a clipped tone.

Melissa wondered if he would go to some other woman— Gillian, for instance—for relief and found the idea unbearable. Wide awake now, she sat up, patted the mattress with one hand, and ordered quietly, "Come here, Quinn. Right now."

He came to her as though she drew him by an invisible rope—reluctantly. Even angrily. But he could not defy her, and that knowledge gave Melissa a dizzying sense of triumph.

Kneeling on the bed, she opened Quinn's trousers. He gave a growl of furious submission as she taught him the futility of resisting her commands. The lessons were slow and thorough and completely brazen, and when Quinn had learned them Melissa restored his clothes to their proper order and sent him on his way.

An hour after he'd gone Helga arrived with Melissa's notebooks and a lap desk. "Mr. Rafferty said you might want these," she announced, watching the patient curiously, "so he had them fetched."

Despite her bruises and scrapes and achy muscles Melissa felt strong, and she'd been frightfully bored. She reached out for the writing supplies eagerly.

The first thing she penned was a note to Charlotte explaining her absence. Helga promised to send one of the stable hands to deliver it and was just leaving the bedroom when Melissa stopped her with a question.

"Who was the fair-haired woman I saw in the entry hall last night?"

Helga smiled happily. "Oh, that was Becky Sever, missus. Mrs. Wright's going traveling with her sister, and Becky will take her place."

Melissa shrugged off the uneasy feeling that had gathered around her heart and returned Helga's smile. "How nice for Mrs. Wright. I hope she won't leave without saying goodbye to me."

"Oh, she'd never do that, Mrs. Rafferty," Helga protested, looking appalled.

Melissa didn't bother to correct the maid; just for this day, this safe, cozy, tucked-away-by-the-fire day, she wanted to pretend that everything was proper and perfect.

She wrote industriously until midday, when Becky Sever brought her a tray. The woman was pretty and shy, and she said almost nothing. Melissa, disappointed that Quinn had not returned, was ready for a little conversation.

"What's the weather like today?" she asked as the new housekeeper fluffed the pillows and tucked them back into place behind Melissa.

"Cloudy" was the soft response.

"Are you to be addressed as 'Miss Sever' or 'Mrs.'?" Melissa persisted, undaunted.

"If it's all the same to you, Mrs. Rafferty, I like to be called Becky."

Melissa considered that. "If I'm to call you by your given name, then you'll have to reciprocate. I'm not really Mr. Rafferty's wife, you see."

Becky blushed at this, and her gaze searched Melissa's

face briefly and then dodged away again. "Oh," she said, clearly shocked. Her cheeks were bright with color, and she escaped the room as quickly as she could.

Since it was evident that she wasn't going to be able to strike up a conversation with anyone, Melissa threw herself wholeheartedly into the story she was writing. She worked so hard that by the end of the day she felt as though she'd been cleaning out the Rip Snortin' Saloon instead of just wielding a pen.

All the same, she grinned when Quinn came in because he looked so sheepish and gave the bed such a wide berth.

Melissa deliberately batted her eyelashes and drawled, "Why, Mr. Rafferty! Can it be that you're afraid of little old me?"

Quinn laughed ruefully and squatted on the hearth to build up the dying fire. "I may never be the same, Calico," he confessed. "How are you feeling tonight?"

"Bored," Melissa answered fitfully, making fists of her hands and bringing them down hard on the bedcovers. "Bored, bored, bored!"

He rose back to his full height, setting the fireplace screen in place as the blaze caught and then dusting his hands together. His gaze was comically wary. "Don't count on me for entertainment," he warned. "I'm all done in."

Melissa smiled. "Want to bet?"

With a wondering laugh Quinn thrust his hand through his hair. "You're a brazen little scamp, aren't you? I hardly dare imagine what you'll be like when you've been in that bed a week."

"I don't plan to be confined for that long. My baby is all right, and so am I, and I'm leaving tomorrow."

The mirthful indulgence in Quinn's eyes was replaced by annoyance. "You're not doing anything of the sort." He waggled a finger at her, growing more incensed with every passing moment. "If I have to, Calico, I'll tie you to that damned bed!"

Melissa's resolve weakened slightly in the face of his obvious sincerity, but she still protested, "My reputation will be ruined!"

"Your reputation? My darling, you haven't had one since the day you arrived in this town, so don't start worrying now!"

"I don't want to argue, Quinn," Melissa said softly, and she bit her lower lip and allowed tears to pool in her eyes. She even allowed her chin to quiver just a little.

Quinn was immediately contrite, just as Melissa had intended him to be. "I'm sorry, sweetheart," he said. And then he brought two envelopes from his coat pocket. "I almost forgot. There were a couple of letters for you today."

Melissa held out her hands delightedly and rubbed her fingers together until Quinn brought her the mail.

The first letter, and the fattest, was from her mother. It contained long, heartfelt exclamations of bridal happiness, descriptions of Harlan's ranch and the people who lived and worked within its borders, and comical accounts of her efforts to give the enormous ranch house a feminine touch.

Bittersweet emotions filled Melissa as she read; she was delighted at her mother's joy, but she also envied it. She finished the letter, folded it carefully, and opened the second one. Fancy had written a witty, harried narrative that made Melissa laugh out loud.

"Jeff and all the kids except Caroline have the chicken pox," she paused to explain.

Quinn shook his head, clearly sympathetic to his gender. "That's awful."

Melissa read, then gave a little squeal of delight. "Fancy and Banner are ordering a motorcar so that they can travel back and forth to Olympia and plague the legislature to grant women the vote!"

Quinn laughed at that and sat down on the edge of the bed. When Melissa had finished reading the letter and was staring off into space and biting her lower lip, he took her hand in his. "You miss them a lot, don't you?"

Melissa nodded, though it wasn't just homesickness that was bothering her. She would have to write her mother and Fancy back now and admit to her scandalous predicament. She had no idea where to begin.

Quinn cupped her chin in his hand. His voice was low

and gruffly tender. "I'll take you home as soon as you're well enough to travel, if that's what you want."

"You're awfully eager to get rid of me, Mr. Rafferty," Melissa accused, hurt.

He kissed her in that plying way he had and then murmured, "No. Never."

She slid her arms around his neck and drew him into a second kiss. This one pressed her back into the pillows and brought a hesitant masculine hand to her breast. Quinn was the one to break away, short of breath.

"Damn you," he muttered.

Melissa loosened his string tie and then unbuttoned his shirt to the middle of his chest. "I've been stuck in this bed all day, Mr. Rafferty," she crooned innocently. "What I need is a nice, warm bath."

Quinn groaned as she reached beneath the fabric of his shirt to caress him lightly with both hands.

"Care to join me?" she added saucily.

Quinn laughed miserably and halted her hands by resting his own over them. "No," he said, but his eyes were warm as they lingered on her face.

He got up presently and left, and when Melissa heard water running in the bathroom she knew she'd won again. After several minutes had passed Quinn came back and carefully divested her of the bed jacket and matching silk nightgown she'd been wearing since that morning.

He grazed her taut nipples gently with his knuckles just to tease her, then lifted her into his arms and carried her into the bathroom. He lowered her gently into the massive tub, which was filled with warm, scented water, and began bathing her. His attendance was slow and systematic, and when it was over Quinn had extracted proper vengeance.

She was limp with contentment when he dried her and carried her back to the bed. Someone had been in to change the sheets and lay out a fresh flannel nightgown, and Melissa submitted dreamily as Quinn pulled the garment over her head and tucked her in.

"I think I've learned the secret of keeping you docile," he teased, giving her a kiss on the forehead.

Melissa couldn't resist reminding him of the morning, he was so damnably smug and arrogant. "I know a few secrets myself, Mr. Rafferty," she said.

Becky arrived with a dinner tray and left again. Melissa was so relaxed that she only fed herself half the meal— Quinn had to give her the rest. Soon enough he took the food away and turned out the lamp, and the only light in the room was the mysterious glow from the fireplace. Melissa slipped into a sweet, contented sleep.

Somewhere in the depths of the night sudden passion quickened her senses into a semblance of wakefulness. Bitter disappointment seized her when she realized that she'd only been dreaming. Quinn was not loving her; he was not even in bed with her.

The fire had been reduced to mere embers on the hearth. Melissa sat upright, feeling brutally lonely as the elemental truths of her situation struck her. While she would have her child, she would never be more than an amusement to Quinn, an occasional plaything. If he'd loved her, he would have insisted that they marry.

She lit the lamp and got carefully out of bed to see if Quinn was sleeping on the settee facing the fireplace. There was no sign of him, and Melissa sensed that he was nowhere in the house, so abject was her feeling of abandonment.

She knew that she dared not stay another day, another hour, not even a minute longer than she had to. To linger was to risk permanent loss of her soul.

She had no clothing except for the ball gown she'd been wearing the night of the accident, so she put that on, gathered up her notebooks, and slipped out into the hallway.

By the light glowing in her own doorway she found her way down the hall to the stairs and slowly, carefully descended. She held her breath as she crossed the entry hall and bent to put her tablets down. Rising again, too quickly, she swayed with dizziness.

She'd managed to work the lock and open the door to a chilly, salt-misted wind and was just about to reclaim her notebooks and slip out when the door suddenly slammed shut.

Melissa jumped, she was so startled, and then told herself that the breeze had drawn the door closed. She was forced to give up this theory when light filled the entryway and strong masculine hands turned her around.

The expression on Quinn's face was terrible, but Melissa knew instantly that he was frightened, not angry, and she felt an incomprehensible urge to comfort him.

"I didn't think you were at home," she said lamely.

"That's obvious," Quinn replied, his jawline still taut. "As it happens, I just came in about two minutes ago. Where were you going, Melissa?"

She bit her lip and sagged back against the door, feeling weak. She was forced to admit—to herself, at least—that she probably wouldn't have made it as far as the sidewalk. "Back to the State Hotel," she admitted.

"Why?" he demanded.

"Because it isn't right, my being here. I'm not your wife—this isn't my home—"

He took her by the arm and propelled her into the study, where he promptly seated her in a chair and then turned up a gas jet so that there was light. "It's the middle of the night," he reminded her, turning his back to pour a glass of brandy.

Melissa sighed. I know that, she wanted to say. So where were you, Quinn? Whom were you with?

He was annoyed by her silence; the emotion flared in his eyes. "I'm taking you back to Port Hastings in the morning," he announced with flat, arrogant finality. "Maybe you'll be safe there."

Melissa was shaking her head, amazed. "If you're so anxious to see the last of me, why did you stop me from leaving just now?"

"It's the dead of night, that's why, and you've been hurt. You're still weak."

Melissa could not deny that her strength was depleted, but she needed work and distraction from her troubles, not bed rest. "Please understand," she said softly. "I can't keep giving myself to you as though I were your wife—"

"I'm perfectly willing to marry you," Quinn said without a shred of affection in his voice or grace in his manner.

Melissa stared at him. "What?"

"You're carrying my child, after all," he went on after tossing back the last of his brandy. "You belong in my house and my bed."

Although Melissa had longed for Quinn to suggest marriage—a real, legal marriage—she heard something else in his words that put her off and made her wary. "But, of course, I'd have to give up writing books and forget all about publishing a newspaper, wouldn't I?"

Quinn folded his arms and leaned back against his desk. "Is that too much to ask, Melissa? Raising a child takes a lot of time and effort—were you planning to leave the job to the servants?"

"Of course not." Melissa flared, torn in two. She wanted to have a family of her own and spend the rest of her life with Quinn, but she had other dreams, and she knew she'd be as dull as worn calico without them.

"I want an answer," Quinn pressed.

Melissa lifted her chin. "Very well, then," she replied. "My answer is no, Mr. Rafferty."

Twenty-one

Melissa moved back into her room at the State Hotel the following morning. Knowing that it would be unwise to engage in heavy physical labor too soon, and wanting to avoid Quinn Rafferty, she concentrated on her writing. She was careful to eat properly, and get her sleep, and take a walk in the fresh air every day. At the end of ten days the weakness was gone.

The sky was a soul-wrenching shade of blue that bright spring morning when she set out for the newspaper office, where Charlotte had been working diligently for nearly two weeks. Passing drunks tipped their hats to Melissa as she made her way along the wooden sidewalk and into the building that had once been the Rip Snortin' Saloon.

Even though the progress Charlotte had made came as no surprise to her—she'd visited almost every day—Melissa felt a twinge of guilt as she surveyed the ground floor. Every speck of dirt was gone, the bar and mirror had been removed, and the walls had been whitewashed. Two of Quinn's millhands had delivered the printing press in a wagon just that morning, and Charlotte had already polished it until it glowed.

With a soft smile Melissa approached the ancient flatbed press and touched the handle, dreaming. Sadness filled her because she could not have Quinn and the newspaper, too.

There was a sound behind her at the swinging doors, and Melissa turned, expecting to have to chase away a reveler. Occasionally men wandered in thinking that the Rip Snortin' Saloon had reopened.

The visitor was Miss Emma Bradberry, and she was in the company of a short, rotund man with a flowing white mustache and a hairless pate. "This is my papa," Miss Emma explained bluntly, looking very uncomfortable. "Mr. Wilson Bradberry. Papa, may I present to you Mrs.—er—Miss—"

Melissa took pity on the embarrassed Emma, who was clearly at a loss to explain the scandalous intricacies of the situation, and stepped forward, her hand out in greeting, a smile fixed on her face. "I'm Melissa Corbin," she said warmly. "How do you do?"

Wilson Bradberry cleared his throat, and in that moment Melissa knew that this pleasant-looking little man had not come to bring good news. "My daughter tells me that she's sold you my press and you intend to publish a newspaper."

Melissa nodded, and out of the corner of one eye she saw Charlotte edging cautiously down the stairs.

"What do you know about newspapering, young lady?" Mr. Bradberry demanded, not unkindly.

"Not much," Melissa answered, shrugging her shoulders. "But I did graduate from the University of Washington, and I've published a few—works of fiction."

"I see," said Mr. Bradberry, who was clearly unimpressed. He lapsed into a pensive mood then, seeming to forget that there were other people around.

"Is there a problem?" Melissa was forced to ask when the silence grew interminable. By that time Charlotte had worked her way to her employer's side.

Mr. Bradberry awakened from his reflections with a *harumph* and a small start. "There is, you see, in that I've brought presses all the way from New York and just this morning bought the land and lumber to construct a building to house my newspaper."

Melissa felt as though the floorboards had parted and she was about to drop through. While thriving, Port Riley was not large enough to support two newspapers, and she knew she couldn't hope to compete with Mr. Bradberry. He had years of experience and a reputation in town, while she had only dreams. The disappointment was overwhelming, but Melissa was determined to lose graciously. "I wish you every good fortune, of course," she said.

Mr. Bradberry was staring at her, sizing her up. He harumphed again. "You say you've written fiction. That's different from dealing with good, solid facts, you know."

Melissa nodded. "I meant to learn by doing," she said sadly, hurting as her dream died.

The old man looked around with approval in his eyes. "There's something to be said for plain old bullheaded courage, young woman, and I can see that you have plenty of that. If you still have a hankering to learn reporting when my presses are up and running, you come and see me."

Feeling a faint flicker of hope at this, Melissa bit her lower lip and then nodded. "Would there be a job for my friend Charlotte?" she ventured to ask. "She's the one who did most of the heavy work around here."

Mr. Bradberry assessed Charlotte with the same crisp dispatch with which he'd studied Melissa and then agreed, with an abrupt jerk of his head. He seemed preoccupied now, looking around him. "You know, we could house my presses in here, just until the new place is built. It would be a little cramped, but—"

"Papa," Emma protested, speaking for the first time since she'd made introductions, "this is a saloon!"

"It's got four walls and a roof," Bradberry replied dismissively. His eyes danced with energy and exuberance as he looked at Melissa. "What do you say, miss? Can we come to some sort of arrangement?"

Melissa was beginning to see the positive aspects of the situation. The sooner Mr. Bradberry's newspaper could be published, the sooner she could start learning to be a reporter. "Yes," she said, her chin high. "I think we can."

At that Mr. Bradberry shook Melissa's hand, and then

Charlotte's, promising to return with his presses and other equipment within the next few days.

"Have I told you that I'm a twin?" Miss Emma called back as her father dragged her out of the building.

With a sigh Melissa crossed the room and sank into one of the chairs Charlotte had lined up along the wall.

She put both hands to her face, drew a deep breath, and let it out again. "Well, I guess I'm beaten before I start," she said.

Charlotte came and sat beside her. "Maybe it's better this way, Melissa."

Melissa knew that it was—Mr. Bradberry had a lot to teach her, and she should be glad that he was willing to give her a chance to learn. Still, she'd made plans, and now she was set adrift.

Her eyes widened as she remembered her pregnancy. Mr. Bradberry had not known about that when he'd offered her an opportunity to write for his newspaper. It went without saying that he would not be amenable to the idea of a woman with a watermelon stomach dashing all over town to get a story.

"Oh, Charlotte," she wailed, despondent, "what about my baby?"

Charlotte looked glum. It was enough of a miracle that a seasoned newspaper publisher had been willing to consider a woman for a job; for him to accept a pregnant one would be unheard of. "You have a few months to prove yourself," she said lamely, spreading her hands and looking very sad.

It was time to face defeat, Melissa decided. The only thing to do now was go home to Port Hastings. There she and her child would be surrounded by a loving family, and she could open a dress shop or a candy store.

Completely depressed, she paid Charlotte what she owed her and left.

Her walk carried her past the pretty saltbox houses and the tree where Ajax's motorcar had met its disastrous fate. She skirted the exclusive Seaside Hotel for the rocky beach that fronted it.

Far out on the strait a luxury ship was passing, and its

great whistle droned a greeting to Port Riley. Seagulls chattered and squalled against the skies, and at the top of a grassy slope, on the hotel lawn, people laughed over a game of croquet. Although she had vast sums of money at her disposal, Melissa did not feel like one of the privileged any longer. She was a person meant for mediocrity, a failure, and the knowledge was crippling, for she had been bred to be special.

She stopped there on the beach to struggle against a wave of sheer misery. High on the hill there was a *crack,* and presently a brightly colored wooden ball rolled to a stop beside Melissa's shoe.

With a sad smile she retrieved the ball and turned to see Ajax making his way down the hill, smiling and swinging his arms at his sides. Melissa hadn't seen him since the accident, but he looked none the worse for it.

"Hello," he said, and though he kept a little distance between them, his eyes were gentle. "I'm glad to see that you're well."

Melissa extended the croquet ball to him but didn't speak. She had nothing to say to Ajax these days, which was strange, considering that she'd once chattered at him until he'd laughingly begged for silence.

"I'm sorry, Melissa," he said gruffly, with such tenderness and caring that she wondered if he knew about the newspaper. In the next moment his meaning was clear. "If you'd suffered serious injury because of my stupidity, I would never have been able to forgive myself."

She smiled. It was tacitly understood that Ajax was no longer pursuing her, for whatever reason, and although Melissa was relieved, she was also a little sad. Once she'd expected to live like a fairy-tale princess, taking all her importance from being the wife of this man. "It's all right," she said softly. "All's well that ends well."

Ajax was turning the croquet ball in his pale, graceful hands. "I'll be leaving at week's end, Melissa. Father's ill, so I'm going home to look after the estates." He spoke quietly, watching her with sympathy in his crystal-blue eyes.

She wanted to slap him for daring to feel sorry for her,

but she didn't raise a hand except to offer it in farewell. Ajax kissed her fingers and then turned and climbed back up the slope to the lawn without so much as a backward look.

Melissa suddenly felt an overwhelming urge to see Quinn—just see him. If he was working in his study or the office at the mill, she wanted to sit silently in a chair nearby. If he was on the mountain, felling trees or overseeing the construction of the cabins or the schoolhouse, she would watch him from a distance, never letting on that she was there.

Of course, she reflected, lifting her eyes to the hotel rising before her like a magnificent castle, it was possible that he was inside.

Melissa had no intention of crying on his shoulder, and she'd meant it when she'd turned down his proposal, too. She wanted nothing from Quinn except the strange, silent comfort of his presence.

When she knocked at the door of the office Quinn used when he worked at the hotel, a feminine voice called out a cheerful "come in."

Gillian. Melissa's throat tightened, but she opened the door and stepped inside anyway in the hope that Quinn would be there.

He wasn't. Gillian sat alone at the desk, up to her eyes in ledgers and looking wan and pale. "Hello," she said, as though it were an everyday occurrence for Melissa to approach her.

Melissa's throat felt tight. "I'm looking for Quinn," she confessed. "Have you seen him?"

Gillian gave a rueful chuckle. "If I had, I'd have made him do these dratted books," she said, waving her hand over the clutter before her. After studying Melissa pensively for a few moments she said, "He's probably up on the mountain. Quinn's been working like a crazy man for the last week or two. I can't even pin him down long enough to discuss his buying out my half of the hotel."

Gillian's words, idle as they were, altered something deep down inside Melissa. They reawakened hopes and dreams that had seemed shattered only an hour before.

"He expected Ajax to buy your shares," she said, praying that her eagerness didn't show.

Gillian made a skeptical sound. "How could Ajax and I have any fun together if either one of us were tied down to this place?" she said.

Melissa was wildly intrigued, but she kept her mind on business. If there was any juicy gossip concerning Ajax and Gillian, she would hear it soon enough. "I have some money to invest," she ventured to suggest.

Gillian sat up straight. "That's right! With all the hubbub, I almost forgot you're one of the Corbins!"

Melissa suppressed a smile at being informed of her own identity. "Yes," she replied simply.

"You were all het up to start a newspaper," Gillian recalled, frowning.

"That fell through," Melissa said, unwilling to go into painful explanations.

Gillian was gazing at Melissa through narrowed, speculative eyes. "I want fifty thousand dollars for my half of this place," she warned.

Melissa's heart leapt with excitement, but she allowed nothing to show in her face. "I couldn't give you more than forty," she countered.

Gillian considered. "Cash?"

Melissa swallowed. Even for her, forty thousand dollars was a lot of money. "Cash," she replied after a moment.

Gillian's face was alight. She jumped out of her chair and pumped Melissa's hand exuberantly to seal the agreement.

"There's just one thing, Gillian," Melissa said when she was about to leave the office. "I don't want Quinn to know that I'm his partner until I'm ready to tell him. That kind of news has to be broken gently."

There was resignation in Gillian's smile. "Don't worry," she replied. "Quinn and I don't talk much anymore."

Melissa offered no answer to that. "Is there a place here where I can stay?" she asked, remembering that Quinn had said the hotel was booked solid until Christmas.

"There are some rooms we kept empty in case we need extra people on the staff. Nothing fancy, of course."

Melissa thought of her small, seedy room at the State and of the chamber she'd meant to occupy above the Rip Snortin' Saloon. "Just so long as it has a window and a lock on the door," she said, and once Gillian had assured her it did, she left.

Wondering how she could possibly keep her delicious secret, Melissa started back toward town. She would next look for Quinn in the office at the lumber mill.

As she was passing Kruger's Mercantile, however, Dana ran out and dragged her inside to have a cold drink and a chat.

Melissa told her friend about Mr. Bradberry's return to Port Riley and his plans to establish another newspaper.

Dana, who had been spending time on the mountain overseeing the construction of the lumber-camp schoolhouse, was rosy-cheeked with health. Her color faded, however, at Melissa's words. "How can that be? Miss Emma told us herself that her papa didn't ever want to lay eyes on another printing press, remember?"

Melissa sighed. "I remember," she confirmed. She shrugged. "He's changed his mind, I guess."

Dana reached out to pat Melissa's hand. She was not one to lament a lost cause for long, it soon became apparent. "Everything will be all right, you'll see."

Melissa had just agreed to buy half of a very expensive hotel, and she was dizzy with her own daring. In fact, she could hardly believe what she'd done. "H-have you seen Quinn?"

Understanding flickered in Dana's eyes, and she nodded. "He's on the mountain," she said softly. "You're going to marry him now, aren't you? Oh, it would be so romantic if you did!"

Melissa shook her head and pushed away her glass of lemonade, unable to finish it. Approaching Quinn in an office or even in his home was one thing, but climbing a mountain was another. He might jump to the conclusion that she was willing to agree to his terms if she did that. "I'm going to be a reporter for Mr. Bradberry," she said. She still wanted to keep her forthcoming plunge into the hotel business to herself.

Dana looked singularly horrified. "But you're pregnant!" she cried.

"Shhh!" Melissa hissed as several matrons turned from the notions counter to stare. She sat ruffled and indignant, red to her ears, before going on. "I might have been able to keep that a secret for a few months if it hadn't been for you!" she accused.

"I'm sorry," Dana said with a sigh. "It's just that—well, if a man like Quinn Rafferty wanted to make an honest woman out of *me,* I'd let him. I don't understand you, Melissa."

"I'm not sure I understand myself," Melissa replied, and then she stood, bid her friend a distracted farewell, and left.

There was no point in going on to the lumber mill, knowing that Quinn wouldn't be there, so she returned to the State Hotel, planning to have lunch. After a light meal in the dining room she intended to visit her banker.

Two letters were awaiting Melissa when she stopped by the reception desk. The first was from her publisher; the second, forwarded from Quinn's address, was from Keith. She opened her brother's letter immediately.

Keith's message was typically concise. There was something he wanted to discuss with Melissa—he didn't say what—and he would be arriving in Port Riley by train the morning of the fifteenth.

Melissa's hands trembled a little as she refolded the letter, her brow knitted. She wasn't afraid of any of her brothers, for she knew they loved her, but the terseness of the missive alarmed her. Something must be terribly wrong.

The possibilities were discouraging to consider—probably the family had learned somehow that her marriage to Quinn had been a bogus one. Perceiving their sister as a spinster, humiliated and scorned, her brothers had probably gotten together and appointed a rescuer from among themselves.

Tasks requiring diplomacy nearly always fell to Keith.

Melissa was so deep in thought as she entered the shabby little dining room of the State Hotel that she nearly collided with Mrs. Wright, who was just coming out. The delicately built woman was dressed for traveling, and she was accompanied by a lady taller and sturdier than herself.

"I've come to say farewell, Mrs. Rafferty," Quinn's housekeeper said, taking one of Melissa's hands in her own and drawing her to the side so that the doorway wouldn't be blocked by the small gathering.

Melissa let Mrs. Wright's form of address pass unchallenged, since she'd already learned that no force on earth could dissuade the woman from using it. "You're off to Europe," she said a little enviously.

Mrs. Wright beamed and nodded, then introduced her sister, who was clearly in better circumstances and thus able to finance the expedition. "We're going to have a wonderful time," she promised, her eyes shining. But concern dimmed her happiness a moment later, and the color of conviction rose in her papery cheeks. "I'm an old woman, and I've earned the right to speak bluntly," she said in a moderate tone. "You've got to stop all this nonsense, Mrs. Rafferty, and look after your husband properly. It isn't as if there weren't any other women in the world who'd undertake the task, you know."

Since Mrs. Wright was so dear, and a product of a less modern generation, Melissa overlooked her presumption. "I'm afraid it's not so easy as that," she said gently.

"Oh, but it is," the elderly housekeeper argued politely. "You get yourself up that mountain, young woman, and come to some kind of understanding with your man before it's too late."

Melissa blushed, filled with a mingling of defiance and embarrassment. Mrs. Wright was the second person that day to suggest that she humble herself by trudging up that mountain like some kind of prodigal. She wasn't about to resign herself to a life of surrender, for she knew that her love for Quinn would soon wither and die if she did.

It simply wasn't fair that she should have to make all the concessions while Quinn went merrily on with his life, doing as he pleased.

"You're upsetting the poor girl, Marion," said Mrs. Wright's sister, who had been presented to Melissa as Hattie. "Merciful heavens, you're always trying to boss everybody around!"

Mrs. Wright looked at Hattie indignantly. "Why, sister, I do nothing of the sort!"

Amused by this mild tiff between elderly siblings, Melissa smiled and gave Marion Wright a gentle kiss on the cheek. "Good-bye, my friend," she said softly. "Have a wonderful journey."

Mrs. Wright sniffed, standing up very straight and trying hard not to show undue sentiment. "I will send postal cards," she promised, and then she and her sister took their leave, and Melissa went on into the dining room.

She seated herself beside a window that looked out over the street, ordered a bowl of soup and a glass of milk, and opened the letter from her publisher. They were happy to learn that she was writing again and eagerly awaited her manuscript.

Melissa sighed and set the letter aside to reread the one from Keith. Her feeling of unease grew. Perhaps her brother's plan to visit had nothing to do with her scandalous situation. Someone in the family could be seriously ill, for instance.

Maybe one of the children, or even Jeff, had suffered serious complications from the chicken pox.

Melissa was so distracted by that dreadful possibility that she was caught utterly off guard when Mitch Williams doffed his hat and slipped into the chair facing hers. He smiled and pointed out that her soup was getting cold.

With a sigh Melissa took up her spoon. She didn't ask Mr. Williams what he wanted, for she knew that he would volunteer that information soon enough.

"I talked with Bradberry this morning, Melissa. I'm sorry about your newspaper."

Melissa swallowed, keeping her eyes on the noodles and colorful vegetables in her soup. "Thank you," she answered.

"You don't like me much, do you?" Mitch ventured to ask in a quiet, concerned tone of voice.

Melissa looked up. "I don't trust you," she admitted forthrightly.

He looked wounded. "Why not?"

"Because you told Quinn that I asked you for money that day I couldn't get into the railroad car, when in fact you volunteered it with absolutely no encouragement from me."

Mitch sighed. A waitress approached, and he ordered coffee. When he and Melissa were alone again he confessed, "I may have been trying to put Quinn on his guard a little."

"Why?" Melissa demanded angrily. It wasn't as though she and Quinn didn't have enough problems without other people interfering.

The lawyer shrugged. "He's my friend, Melissa—the first one I had in this town, and the best. I didn't want to see Quinn get hurt."

Melissa smiled and arched one eyebrow. "In other words, you didn't trust me, either."

Mitch smiled winningly. "That's about the size of it, love," he replied. "But you've won me over now."

The wholesome, tasty soup was beginning to restore Melissa's flagging energy. "What a relief," she replied with a wry little shrug.

Her companion laughed at that.

Melissa took a more serious tack. "You've heard about our fraudulent marriage, I suppose."

He nodded, immediately sober of expression and quite sympathetic in the bargain. "Yes. It does seem that you've had an uncommon amount of trouble lately."

Self-pity was a morass Melissa didn't care to slip into. She took a firm grasp on sensible optimism. After all, she would soon be busy reporting the news and helping to run the new hotel. She sipped her milk and took her time in answering. "I'm a Corbin, and it takes considerably more than what I've been through to discourage me."

Respect glimmered in Mitch's blue eyes as he looked at her. He was handsome, in a rough-edged sort of way, and Melissa thought she might have found him very appealing if it hadn't been for Quinn.

There was a short silence, then Mitch cleared his throat and said, "Melissa, there's a picnic at the Seaside Hotel this

Saturday. I wondered if you would go with me. Might give Quinn a few things to think about."

Melissa liked that idea. So far Quinn Rafferty had taken her purely for granted. Still, she was careful. "Isn't there someone else you'd like to take, like Gillian?"

Mitch looked very uncomfortable. "She's—she's got Quinn for an escort."

Melissa was not only shocked, she was wounded, but she kept her pain to herself. It wasn't as though she hadn't known about Quinn's affection for Gillian and hers for him.

For a few desolate moments Melissa wavered wildly between going to the picnic with Mitch and spending all of Saturday hiding in her room. She was nearly finished with her novel, thanks to a lot of hard work, and if she pressed, she could be done with it. . . .

"Melissa?" Mitch prompted.

Just then Melissa spotted Quinn crossing the street. He was wearing the uniform of the woods—oiled trousers, a flannel shirt, and cork boots—and his expression removed all doubt that he'd seen her through the window. Picturing him fawning over Gillian at the upcoming picnic, Melissa reached out and closed her hand over Mitch's.

"I'd love to spend Saturday with you, Mr. Williams," she said sweetly.

🙂 Twenty-two

The look that passed between Quinn and Mitch there in the dining room of the State Hotel was not a friendly one. Melissa almost expected St. Elmo's fire to crackle along the shabby cabbage-rose carpet.

Her hand lingered on Mitch's. She looked up at the father of her child and arched one eyebrow, as if marveling at such a rude intrusion. "Quinn," she said, and that had to suffice as a greeting.

Without waiting to be invited Quinn appropriated a chair from the next table and sat down. Melissa looked for blue flames to consume the tablecloth and the limp lace curtains at the windows.

The tension proved intolerable to Mitch; he slid back his chair, mumbling words that Melissa didn't quite catch, and jammed his hat onto his head. "I'll see you Saturday," the lawyer told her pointedly, without so much as another look at Quinn. A moment later he was gone.

"Saturday?" Quinn inquired.

Melissa smiled brightly. "That's the day of the picnic at

your hotel." She paused to remove her napkin from her lap, fold it in a tidy fashion, and set it aside.

Quinn scowled and pulled an envelope from the pocket of his shirt. He clearly didn't want to discuss the picnic; perhaps he had hoped Melissa would never even learn there was such an event going on. That way he could have cavorted with Gillian with impunity.

"I got a letter from Keith," he said, as though a grievous crime had been committed. "He's coming here."

The alarm Melissa had felt earlier was heightened. She forgot her differences with Quinn for the moment. "What did he say?"

Quinn gave a sigh. "Just that he'll be in town tomorrow. Melissa, he's a preacher, and he's not going to look kindly on our situation."

"What situation is that?" Melissa chimed, secretly thinking that Quinn was right about the reason for Keith's visit. If anyone in the family had fallen ill, she would surely have been asked to come home immediately.

Rich color moved up Quinn's neck. "You know damned well what situation—our marriage was a charade, and here you are pregnant!"

"Shhh!" Melissa hissed, embarrassed. She didn't know why someone didn't just hire a bugler or a town crier and be done with it.

"We've got to do something!" Quinn persisted. Though he tried to keep his voice down, people were still looking.

Melissa sat back in her chair. Her chin was at a regal angle, and she kept her hands folded in her lap. The picture of serenity she presented was a false one. "What do you suggest we do, Mr. Rafferty?" she asked coolly.

He glared at her. "I'm asking you to marry me. Now that that newspaper nonsense has been settled, there's no reason for us to stay apart."

So he'd learned of Mr. Bradberry's return to Port Riley. Melissa was so instantly and completely furious that she hadn't the time to reflect on how fast gossip travels in a small community. "To think," she whispered, sliding back her chair and rising, "that I expected comfort and understanding from you—that I actually went looking for you!"

Quinn got to his feet. "Melissa, wait," he said hoarsely.

She willed herself not to cry. "I'm not in the market for a man to pat my head and wipe my nose, Quinn Rafferty," she told him, gathering up her letters and leaving money on the table to pay for her lunch. "I can take care of myself!"

With that she turned and swept majestically out of the dining room. Quinn caught up to her in the middle of the lobby and grasped her by one arm. Soon Melissa was being propelled out of the hotel.

She knew it would be fruitless, as well as humiliating, to protest or try to break away, so she pretended to be willing. Except for the flush in Melissa's cheeks and the stubborn set of Quinn's jaw, a passerby would have seen nothing suspicious.

They had stridden down the street to the depot and entered the railroad car before Melissa lost control. Filled with disappointment and pain, she began grabbing up the books that covered Quinn's desk and hurling them at him. He dodged the first few, then simply walked through the onslaught to take Melissa by the wrists, forcing her to stop.

"Melissa, listen to me," he said, giving her a little shake. "What I said about the newspaper—I didn't mean that the way it sounded."

She categorically refused to cry. No matter what, she had shed enough tears. "Get out and leave me alone," she said, glaring up into his eyes. "I won't let you hurt me anymore."

Her words seemed to wound him; it was as though he hadn't known that he'd hurt her and found the knowledge shattering.

Melissa turned away, unable to bear the look on his face. "You've got to let me get on with my life," she said. Then she paused, drew in a deep breath, and let it out on a lie. "I don't love you, Quinn. Maybe I never did. I can be fickle— just ask Ajax."

The silence that followed was long and dreadful. Quinn finally broke it by saying, "Let me hold you, Calico. Let me comfort you."

She shook her head, careful to keep her back to him. "I don't need comforting," she answered, and that was another untruth. "I feel perfectly fine."

Quinn turned her around by her shoulders. "You were counting on that newspaper for a way to make some kind of mark on the world," he said gruffly. "Melissa, I'm sorry."

She kept her eyes lowered, fighting a desperate battle against the tears that came too readily these days. "It's a little late for that," she replied.

He curved a finger under her chin and lifted it. "A few minutes ago you told me that you went looking for me. You want me to hold you—why can't you admit that?"

Melissa let her forehead rest against his shoulder, and he made a haven for her within the circle of his arms, linking his fingers together at the small of her back. "I really don't need your sympathy," she said with a little shuddering sigh.

Quinn kissed the top of her head. "Of course you don't," he agreed, with a smile in his voice. His arms tightened, and he felt solid and good, even if he was dressed in oiled trousers, a woodsman's shirt, and cork boots. It was obvious that he hadn't been working, for he didn't smell of sweat.

One of his hands moved from her hip to her breast in a slow, caressing motion with hardly more substance than a whisper.

"You probably don't need this, either," he teased, chafing an eager nipple to attention with the side of his thumb.

Melissa moaned. "You are an unconscionable rascal," she managed to say.

"Thank you," Quinn replied, his lips moving against hers now, soft and warm.

"This wasn't—exactly—the kind of comfort I expected," Melissa murmured just before he kissed her. The torrent of longing he unleashed during that deep and thorough foray left her weak.

Quinn circled her trembling lips with the tip of his tongue. "Surely you wouldn't want me to pat you on the head or wipe your nose," he muttered. "Not an independent, resourceful woman like yourself."

"Assuredly not." Melissa sighed as he held her deliciously close to him and at the same time trailed his lips along the length of her neck. He lingered at the pulse point for a time, deliberately wreaking havoc with her heartbeat, then began unbuttoning the front of her dress and eased the material away from her breasts. Next he led her to the fur-covered bed, sat on its edge, and arranged her so that she was facing him, straddling his lap.

The formidable Corbin will deserted her, as it always did whenever this man worked his magic. She admitted to herself, in those exquisite moments when he was baring her breasts, that this was what she had wanted when she'd gone looking for Quinn earlier. He'd been right, though he wouldn't hear such a confession from her lips if he lived to be as old as that mountain of his.

Instinct caused Melissa to lean back against the hard support Quinn's left hand offered her. His right was busy paying a gentle homage to her naked breasts, preparing them for the work of his lips and tongue. She whimpered as she finally felt the heat of his mouth close over one nipple. Her hands were frantic and strong, gripping his shoulders as she offered up the sweet plumpness he sought.

When he had reduced her to writhing need he gently removed her clothes garment by garment, loving each part of her as he bared it. At last she was naked, and she had never felt more beautiful than she did when he laid her gently on the fur spread and offered caresses of another sort while he removed his own clothes. His dark eyes moved over her, possessing her. It was as though he massaged her with some rich, spicy oil.

At last he stretched out on the bed beside her, running one work-roughened hand over her belly, her breasts, her smooth white thighs. She was desolate; only a complete union with Quinn could appease her, and she pleaded with him as he put her pliant body slowly, methodically, through its paces.

He took her only when she thought she had nothing left to give, when she wanted to sink into the soft fur beneath her and become a part of it. She was totally spent, having reached pinnacle after pinnacle. She would grant him the solace he demanded, and then maybe, when he was satisfied, he would allow her the deep sleep she craved.

The first long, sliding stroke set her afire all over again. Shifting so that he was standing beside the bed, he held Melissa's hands wide apart and kissed and suckled her breasts while taunting her with his hardness. He would give her a few inches, then withhold himself until she searched for him with her hips, trying to possess him.

When at last she was frantic, her neck and back arched in utter surrender, Quinn plunged deep inside her. That single, powerful motion wrung a series of broken cries from Melissa as her body convulsed repeatedly in a primal ecstasy unlike anything she'd felt before.

By the time her fierce spasms had abated, Quinn's were beginning. He grated out her name as both a blessing and a curse while his powerful muscles locked to thrust him as deep inside her as he could go. While he spilled himself into her he prayed to her and he berated her in a tangle of hoarse vows.

She received him joyously, for his seed was precious to her even though it had already taken root in her darkness and her warmth. Her hands moved soothingly up and down his moist back, and she whispered gentle words, as though he'd been injured and needed consolation.

It was only later, when they were both getting back into their clothes and their right minds, that Melissa grew angry once more. "I suppose you think everything is fine now," she spat as she fastened the front of her dress. "You probably expect to do the same thing again right after supper, and then get my brother to marry us tomorrow morning in your front parlor!"

Quinn chuckled and shook his head as he tucked in his shirt and closed his trousers. As he was buckling his belt he said, "Your mind has obviously been working along those lines, Calico, even if mine wasn't."

Melissa went red at the implication that she'd been thinking in terms of marriage when he hadn't. She put her hands on her hips, thrust back her shoulders, and drew in a deep, furious breath, but before she could unleash her fury Quinn gave her an impudent kiss.

"Save the indignation, Your Majesty—I'm perfectly willing to make an honest woman out of you, and your brother is about the only man I'd trust to perform the ceremony. After what happened in Seattle, I'm taking no chances."

Melissa stepped back, incensed. "Do you call that a proposal, Quinn Rafferty?" she demanded. "I certainly wouldn't. Why, you sound like you're doing me a tremendous favor—"

A muscle bunched in his jaw, and the look in his eyes was sharp enough to slice deep. "You'd better thank the good Lord that you're pregnant," he bit out, "because if you weren't, I swear I'd blister your shapely little backside right here and right now!"

She folded her arms and stood her ground. "So that's how you mean for it to be? In between pregnancies you plan to wallop me whenever I step out of line?"

He shoved one hand through his hair in frustration and made a sound that was half growl and half war cry. "Why the hell does this always happen?" he roared, flinging his arms wide of his body. "Five minutes ago you couldn't get close enough to me. Now you're twisting my words to make me sound like my father!" He stood close to Melissa now, his brown eyes scorching hot as they linked with her blue ones and held her prisoner as effectively as if he'd manacled her with his hands. "I'm not like him," he hissed.

Melissa's eyes went wide. Her bravado was faltering in the face of Quinn's anger, and she laid her hands on his upper arms to quiet him, to offer an unspoken apology. "Tell me about your father, Quinn," she said quietly.

He turned from her. "The devil himself wouldn't keep company with that old man," he answered in a low, rough voice. After a few moments Quinn looked back at Melissa over one shoulder, and she glimpsed an old, deep-seated misery in his eyes. "I'm tired of trying to reach you, Calico," he said. "You know where I live. I'll be around until I've met with Keith."

With that Quinn walked out of the railroad car, leaving Melissa to wonder what had happened to spoil the soaring closeness they'd enjoyed during their lovemaking.

Once she could trust her knees to support her Melissa left the sanctity of the railroad car and went to talk with her banker. Frank Crowley didn't say whether he approved of her decision to buy out Gillian's share of the new hotel, and Melissa didn't ask for his opinion. When she was satisfied that the proper papers were being drawn up she turned her efforts to the task of moving from the State Hotel to the Seaside.

Her room was not so modest as Gillian had led her to expect; it was situated in a rear corner of the topmost floor, and the ceiling slanted at a steep angle, but there was a view of the water and a private bath. Of course, in summer the room would be suffocatingly hot, but Melissa decided not to do any advance worrying on that score. She had plenty of other things on her mind.

She had an early dinner in the corner of the huge kitchen downstairs, wanting a chance to watch the chef in action, then retired to her room for a bath. When she'd dried herself and gotten into a nightgown she crawled into her narrow bed with a notebook and a pen, her ink bottle resting on the nightstand.

The story she was writing was nearing its spectacular end, and Melissa felt a certain grief at the inevitable parting that would separate her from her beloved characters for all time. She worked diligently, from her heart, until the hour was late and she could not keep her attention focused. She set aside her work, went to sleep, and dreamed that she and Quinn lived in a tiny cabin in the woods. She had babies hanging from her skirts and sticking out of her apron pockets, and her husband got drunk and beat her with one of her own notebooks.

In the morning Melissa took special care to look her best. She wore a cornflower-blue dress that set off her eyes, and she brushed her hair until it was as soft and glossy as sable. Then, weaving in a blue ribbon as she went, she plaited it into a single braid to trail down her back.

She went to the kitchen, but the sight and smell of frying eggs drove her right out again, so Melissa ended up meeting Keith's train with an empty stomach and a pounding heart.

His smile was gentle as he stepped out onto the platform at the depot. "Hello, brat," he said, and his very presence put a lot of her fears to rest.

Melissa stood on tiptoe to kiss his cheek. "I've been so worried!" she scolded, but she couldn't be angry with him. She'd vented all those feelings on Quinn the day before. "Is the family all right?"

Keith touched her cheek. "The family is fine, sweetheart," he said. The spring sunshine glittered in his longish, dark gold hair, and his eyes, exactly the color of Melissa's, swept her up in a look of affectionate reluctance. He was about to speak again when his attention shifted to someone standing behind Melissa.

He put out his hand and said, "Hello, Quinn."

Melissa stiffened, then looked back over her shoulder and glared at Mr. Rafferty, silently warning him not to blurt out that the two of them weren't married until she'd had a chance to break the news gently. After all, Keith was a preacher, and it wouldn't be right to shock him.

Quinn chuckled as though she'd said something extraordinarily funny and returned Keith's handshake. "Welcome," he said quietly, and then he turned and led the way down the platform steps, onto the sidewalk, and on toward his house. He was deliberately giving the impression that he and Melissa had come to meet the train together, she getting a little ahead of him in her eagerness to see her brother.

Melissa did nothing to correct the misunderstanding, though she knew she wouldn't be able to lie to Keith about her circumstances and hoped that Quinn didn't expect that of her. She would cross her bridges as she came to them.

They had all reached Quinn's house, where Becky and Helga had set out a splendid brunch in the dining room. Keith looked at the food in polite despair, obviously, whatever he had come to say had affected his appetite.

Melissa's was no better. She helped herself to a cup of tea and left the scones and croissants and sliced fruit untouched on the sideboard.

"What is it?" she finally demanded of her brother, too nervous to wait in suspense any longer. When Quinn's hand closed around hers underneath the table she made no attempt to pull free.

Keith sat back in his chair with a heavy sigh. "Someone has probably written and told you that we had a rash of chicken pox in the family a while back," he began.

Melissa nodded, frightened again. "Fancy told me," she said.

After a moment's reflection Keith went on, speaking very softly. "Jeff developed a high fever, and we almost lost him. While he was out of his head he told me something that he and Adam have been keeping from the rest of us for a long time."

Biting her lower lip and fidgeting in her chair, Melissa held tight to Quinn's hand. Strength and balance seemed to be flowing into her through his fingers. "Go on," she whispered.

He sighed. "I'm not sure I'm right to tell you about this—believe me, Adam and I debated it. He thinks it's better to let sleeping dogs lie, that what happened doesn't have any bearing on your life now." He paused, scanning the ceiling as if in search of some wisdom written there. "In my opinion, you have the right to know the truth, just as I did. Whether to tell Mama or not is something none of us has been able to decide."

"Keith!" Melissa blurted out in agony. Quinn's thumb made a comforting circle on the back of her hand.

Keith closed his eyes for a moment. When he finally spoke again his words rocked Melissa to her very soul. "Papa didn't die when he and Adam had that accident on the water, Melissa. He was alive for five years after that."

The room seemed to dip and sway violently, like a wagon careening straight down a mountainside. "No," Melissa whispered. "No—it can't be true."

Quinn shoved back his chair to rise and stand behind Melissa's, his hands resting strong and solid on her shoulders. She'd told him about her father and the boating accident that had taken place when she was thirteen. And the awesome, numbing grief she'd suffered afterward.

Keith got out of his chair and sat on his haunches in front

of Melissa, his hands holding both of hers in a tight, warm grip. "Sweetheart, Papa was sick. Really sick."

Moisture welled in Melissa's eyes. "We would have taken care of him, Mama and I!"

Her brother smoothed away a stray tear with one thumb. "I know that, brat, and so did Papa. There were reasons for what he did—good ones."

Melissa was beginning to recover a little from the initial shock. "Where was he, Keith? Where was Papa all that time?"

"Remember how Adam used to make those mysterious trips up the mountain all the time when Banner first came to Port Hastings? Papa lived up there in a cabin."

Quinn's grasp on Melissa's shoulders was sustaining her. "Why?" she whispered. "Just tell me why Papa hid from us—tell me why Adam kept such a secret!"

"Papa had leprosy, Melissa," Keith said, and now there were tears in his eyes, too. "He was afraid the rest of us would contract the disease, and so was Adam."

Melissa's hand trembled as she reached out for a napkin and dried her eyes. A wild hope possessed her. "Maybe Jeff just dreamed all this. You said he had a high fever!"

Keith shook his head. "I went straight to Adam, and he admitted everything."

"You're not angry!" Melissa breathed, marveling. She wanted to find Adam and scream at him for keeping her papa from her when she'd loved him so much and needed him so badly. "I can't believe you just accepted this! Adam and Jeff had no right to withhold a secret like that from us!"

Keith went back to his chair and sank into it with a sigh. "I was angry, Melissa," he said quietly. "But once I'd thought it through, I understood. I know you will, too, when you get over the feelings you're having now."

Melissa thought of the mourning she'd done, the conversations she'd had with her father after his "death," believing him to be something of a guardian angel looking after her. She threw back her head and screamed in fury and pain, then burst into ragged sobs. Never in all her life had she felt so betrayed. Or so alone.

Quinn drew back, sensing that she didn't want to be touched, and when she leapt from her chair and fled the room he did not follow her.

Quinn felt almost as sorry for his brother-in-law as he did for Melissa. It had been a hard thing for Keith to come and tell his sister a story like that when it was obvious that he'd barely recovered from the shock himself.

"She'll be all right once she's had some time to arrange all this in her mind," Quinn said, taking a cheroot from the pocket of his flannel shirt. He struck a match and drew the aromatic smoke into his lungs.

Keith nodded. "I know." He smiled bleakly. "Melissa looks as fragile as a violet, but she's tougher than your average coal miner."

Quinn chuckled ruefully. "Amen," he said.

"I know it's early, and I'm a preacher," Keith began with a sheepish grin, "but I could use a shot of whiskey."

Quinn brought a bottle and two glasses from a cabinet next to the sideboard. "I've been doing a little drinking myself since I met Calico," he confessed.

Keith laughed at that. "Does it help?"

"No," Quinn responded without hesitation. "Nothing helps. And it just so happens that Melissa and I have a secret of our own."

After he'd taken a sip of his whiskey Keith eyed Quinn speculatively and asked, "Oh? Like what?"

Quinn tossed back his drink and poured a second before answering. "We're not married, and I think she's going to have a baby."

Keith set his glass down with a crash. "What?"

Quickly, Quinn explained the misunderstanding that had taken place in Seattle. He was careful to point out the fact that he hadn't known the justice of the peace was a fake any more than Melissa had.

"But she believes you tricked her?"

"She did," Quinn answered sadly. "I don't know if she still thinks that, because we can't talk without fighting."

To Quinn's surprise, Keith smiled. "You're either loving or doing battle," he guessed aloud, "and there's no in-between."

Quinn nodded.

"It's the passion," Keith said with a shrug. "You and Melissa have got to learn control, that's all. The knack of it comes with time."

Quinn shook his head. He couldn't imagine controlling what he felt for Melissa. It would be like trying to stop a train by stringing thread across the track.

✑ *Twenty-three*

Melissa took refuge in Quinn's study, curling up in a large chair facing the empty fireplace and covering her face with both hands.

"What's the matter, lady?" a small voice asked when Melissa's deep, hiccuping sobs had abated.

Melissa spread her fingers and saw a little girl of four or five sitting on the hearth, playing with a one-eyed rag doll.

"I'm Margaret," persisted the pretty child, clearly determined to strike up a conversation. A tiny, delicate finger waggled at her. "Your name is Calico," Margaret went on, "and the end of your nose is all red from crying."

In spite of everything, Melissa had to smile. She dried her cheeks with the backs of her hands, heartened by the presence of the child. "My name isn't Calico," she said pleasantly. "It's Melissa."

Margaret shook her head solemnly, fragile wisps of blond hair escaping from her braids catching the sunlight as she did so. "Mr. Quinn says Calico," she insisted, and Melissa had a suspicion that the matter was settled in her mind. "Did Mr. Quinn make you cry?"

Melissa shook her head.

"My daddy makes my mama cry all the time," Margaret went on, getting up and drawing close to Melissa, the doll dangling at her side. "He made her nose bleed once. Mama says we don't have to live with him anymore—we get to stay right here in this pretty house."

Melissa's heart twisted within her, and she forgot her own pain to put a gentle arm around the child. "I had a doll like this once," she said, assessing the worn toy fondly. "I found her in a field, and I loved her best because she'd been lost."

Before Margaret could make a reply Becky appeared, looking harried and very much afraid of offending. "Don't bother Mrs. Rafferty," the woman said, shooing the little girl away with her apron.

Melissa would have preferred for Margaret to stay, but she made no protest because it would have been wrong to interfere. Nor did she point out that she was not "Mrs. Rafferty," for she needed the illusion of being connected to Quinn more than ever.

The room was quiet after Becky left, filled with the masculine scents of tobacco and leather and bay rum. Melissa remembered her laughing, handsome father and wept inwardly, even though no tears trickled down her cheeks or swelled in her eyes. How bitterly she coveted those five years that had been stolen from her.

She heard the door open presently and stiffened as Keith bent to kiss her on the cheek. "Ready to talk yet?" he asked.

Melissa let out a sigh and forced herself to look at her brother as he drew up a hassock and sat down facing her chair. She didn't speak or even nod.

Keith reached out and took one of her hands. "I'm sorry, Melissa. Maybe Adam was right—maybe I should have left well enough alone. But I was afraid you'd find out on your own someday and hate us all for not telling you."

She bit her lip. The news Keith had brought had wounded her, and badly, but the hurt was subsiding a little now. Although she had not yet absorbed the whole thing, she was beginning to understand what a dilemma Adam had faced.

She guessed that in his position she would have kept the secret, too.

"Did Quinn tell you about our wedding and—and the baby?" she ventured to ask.

Keith nodded. "Don't be too hard on yourself, sweetheart. After all, you thought you were married. The question is, what are you going to do now?"

Melissa had a headache. She swallowed and made a fitful gesture with one hand. "I don't know."

"What do you mean, you don't know?" Keith asked, with big-brother sternness in his voice. "Any fool can see that you love the man, and you're carrying his child. What else can you do but marry him?"

"If you knew what I should do," Melissa challenged with a lofty sniffle, "then why the devil did you ask, Keith Corbin?"

He heaved a sigh and shook his head. "You're as impossible as ever, brat. Now, are you going to let me perform a new ceremony before I leave, or do I have to go home and tell our brothers what's going on with their baby sister?"

Melissa winced at the thought of their reaction, but, love Quinn Rafferty though she did, she'd had more time to think, and she had her reservations. "Are you aware that Quinn could legally take my inheritance from me, if I were his wife, and throw me out in the street?"

Keith's eyes snapped. "If I thought he was that sort of man, Melissa, I wouldn't be sitting here trying to talk you into marrying him. Besides, Adam and Jeff and I would never let that happen."

Melissa was suddenly and poignantly aware that over the last month or so she'd grown from a spoiled child into a woman. She sat up a little straighter in her chair. "You've all got your own families and your own lives to live," she pointed out. "It wouldn't be fair to expect you to keep on looking after me until the end of my days. As for my marrying Quinn, I'm not going to do that until he proposes properly."

Keith stood up, shoving one hand through his hair in agitation. In the distance a train whistle sounded. "What do you want, Melissa? Does the man have to get down on one knee, spout poetry, and pluck daisy petals?"

"I'll know when he gets it right," Melissa said, folding her arms. "And that's going to take a while, so if I were you, Keith Corbin, I'd hurry up and catch that train home."

Distractedly, her brother took a gold watch from a pocket of his vest and checked the time. He closed the case with a click and reflected for a few moments, then said, "Today's the fifteenth of April. I'll be back in Port Riley in exactly one week." He waved a finger under Melissa's nose. "You, young lady, will either be ready to marry Quinn or come home to the bosom of your family. Is that clear?"

Melissa's temper flared. She shot out of her chair and caught hold of Keith's arm as he would have started toward the door. "Wait a minute!" she cried. "You can't deliver an ultimatum like that and then just walk out of here!"

Keith touched her nose with an index finger. "One week, brat," he repeated, and then he was gone.

Melissa stomped one foot and gave a cry of frustrated fury when she heard the front door slam in the distance. She started after her brother only to run headlong into Quinn at the base of the stairs.

He barred her passing as effectively as a brick wall.

"Feeling better?" he asked solicitously.

Melissa tried in vain to get around him. "No," she answered. And then she sputtered, "Men! Do you realize that that arrogant brother of mine just *ordered* me to be married?"

The set of Quinn's face was solemn, though his dark eyes danced with laughter. "The nerve," he said. "And just because you're having my baby and the whole town knows we're lovers."

Melissa gave another strangled cry of frustration and tried again to pass Quinn. Again he stopped her, this time by taking a hard though painless hold on her arm.

"For once, woman," he said, "I'm laying down the law. I've got to go back up the mountain for a couple of days, and by God, you're going with me."

Mouth open, Melissa simply stared at him. Quinn had been impossible before, but never to this degree, and she didn't know how to respond.

"Get your things together," he said, cupping her face in one hand and sending sweet chills through her by his touch, "and meet me at the depot in an hour. We're taking the railroad car."

Of course, Melissa decided, she would defy him. She would pretend that she was going to fetch her nightgown and her toothbrush and her pens and paper, but then she simply would not come back. If Quinn wanted to drag her up that mountain, then he'd have to find her first.

All these ideas were firm in Melissa's mind, and yet when Quinn stepped into the car some sixty minutes later she was sitting primly on the velvet upholstered bench, her necessities stuffed into the bulging valise beside her.

Quinn smiled at her obedience. "You know, Calico," he said, "I half expected to have to search the county for you."

Melissa gave him a haughty, sidelong glance and squared her shoulders. "Aren't you going to ask what changed my mind?" she queried.

He came and moved her valise so that he could sit beside her on the bench. "Why should I?" he countered. "I already know."

"You do?" Melissa asked, her eyes round. She wished he'd go ahead and tell her, since she'd only been bluffing a few moments before and had no earthly idea.

There was a loud *clang* outside, and the car gave a jarring lurch as the engine hooked up to it. Quinn put an arm around Melissa, ostensibly to steady her. "It's instinct," he said sagely.

"Instinct?"

"Yes." He stroked her cheek ever so lightly with the fingertips of his right hand. "You want to chase down newspaper stories and write books in the daytime, but you need me in your bed at night."

Melissa had never wanted to slap anyone more in her life, and the knowledge that Quinn was absolutely right only made her more furious. "Any man would do, I'm sure," she said, to repay him. And then she got up and dashed toward the door, meaning to make her escape.

The train was already moving, and when Melissa stood on the platform and saw the ground flashing by in a blur she wasn't foolish enough to jump. She reentered the car to find Quinn leaning against his desk, his arms folded across his broad chest, a cocky grin on his face.

"Any man would do, would he?" he asked.

Melissa tried to ignore Quinn, giving him a wide berth as she went around him to reclaim her valise and carry it to the opposite end of the car. She opened it and took out a small box containing pen and ink, along with a fresh pad of paper.

She was once again in an embarrassing position. She could not settle at the desk to write, for Quinn was still standing there, and if she sat cross-legged on the bed he might draw unwarranted conclusions. In the end she went to the bench and sat down, although writing there would be an awkward, if not hopeless, proposition.

Quinn laughed at her quandary and drew back the chair at the desk in a motion so graceful that it was worthy of a maître d' in the finest restaurant.

Melissa didn't trust him for a moment, but she had no idea what she would do if she couldn't take refuge in her novel, so she allowed Quinn to seat her at the desk. Out of the corner of one eye she watched him as he picked up the array of books she'd thrown at him the day before.

After he'd restored the volumes to their shelf he selected one to read and went around the partition to stretch out on the bed. At least that was what Melissa imagined him doing.

Cheeks burning, she kept her eyes on her paper and continued to write. After a while the task absorbed her, as she had hoped it would, and she forgot all her own problems as she created new ones for her characters.

Presently, however, writing became impossible. The train was climbing, and the incline grew so steep that Melissa had to seal her ink bottle and put it away. Once she was sure her pages were dry, she tucked them into the back of her notebook and made her awkward way to the window.

Looking out, she saw a sheer drop and a collection of tiny

rooftops. She staggered backward with a little cry and then lost her balance.

Quinn laughed as she tumbled ingloriously over his prone body to lie beside him on the bed. "Don't fight it," he said, rolling onto his side and looking down into her face with delight. "It's fate."

If Melissa knew anything in that moment, it was that God was surely a man. No female deity would subject a woman to so many indignities. She doubled up one fist and slugged Quinn in the chest.

He only laughed again and kissed her, and Melissa knew she was lost then. An hour later, when the engine came to a noisy stop on the edge of Quinn's lumber camp, she had to scramble into her clothes.

"You can help Wong in the cook shack," he said generously as he handed her down from the little platform at the back of the railroad car.

Melissa gave him a scorching look and walked away on her own to explore. In the distance she could hear the bawls of oxen and the rhythmic rasp of crosscut saws, but the camp itself was quiet.

She sought out the new cabins and the schoolhouse first and was pleased to see that several families had already moved in. She stopped to chat with a plain, friendly-looking woman working at a washboard. The housewife's name was Elsa, and her man was a bull whacker; it was his job to drive the oxen that dragged the big timber down out of the woods.

Melissa was at a loss to explain who she was or what she was doing in the lumber camp. There was really no point in being secretive, however—heaven knew, word would get around camp soon enough when it was learned that she was sharing Mr. Rafferty's fancy railroad car.

She excused herself and, kicking at the dirt, started off for the schoolhouse, which sat on the edge of a little clearing. A creek ran past the front door, and wildflowers bloomed orange and yellow and purple and pink in the deep, sweet-scented grass.

Melissa was enchanted with the place, and she envied Dana her job as mistress of this small kingdom. She loved children for their laughter and their noise and their lack of guile.

She was not surprised to see Dana sitting in the cool, shadowy interior of the building. The young teacher was perched on a child-sized chair at a tiny table, helping a solitary student with a problem of arithmetic.

At Melissa's entrance Dana looked up and beamed, gesturing for her friend to come inside.

Melissa looked at the crisp, colorful maps and ran her hand along the spines of new books while she waited. Finally Dana sent the little girl home to her mother.

"What are you doing here?" Dana demanded of her friend, closing the arithmetic book and rising from her chair.

"Some greeting that is," said Melissa, out of sorts. "I was practically shanghaied, in case you don't know."

Dana smiled and rolled up the world map behind her desk like a window shade. "I would imagine Mr. Rafferty is trying to keep you out of trouble," she said airily. "Well, never mind. Tomorrow is the first day of school—you can help me with the children."

Melissa forgot that she'd been dragged up the mountain against her will and reduced to thrashing about on Quinn's bed like a strumpet along the way. She even forgot that she was hungry and needed a nap. "Really?" she cried, delighted. Then she frowned. "Schools all over the state are about to let out for the summer, and you're just starting?"

Dana nodded, settling in the chair behind her impressive new desk. "Yes. Lots of the children I'll be teaching have never been to school at all. It seems silly to wait until fall just so our school will be out at the same time as the others."

"I suppose this place is a sort of law unto itself," she reflected, going to the window to look out on the spectacle the wildflowers made over beyond the bubbling creek. "Oh, Dana, I'm so jealous I could spit."

Dana came and put a friendly arm around Melissa's shoulders. "Once you and Quinn get the knack of being married, you'll be the happiest people on earth," she promised. "Now come on. I'll show you my cabin and brew us up a cup of tea."

Melissa followed Dana outside into the dazzling after-noon sunshine. The last in the fourth row of cabins, un-painted and still smelling of fresh sawdust, had been set aside for the teacher.

It was a one-room building, although Dana's bed was hid-den behind a thin wooden partition. There was a small stove to cook on, and someone had been building what looked to be a window box at the table.

"All right, who is he?" Melissa demanded good-naturedly, whirling on her friend with folded arms.

Dana, who was taking a shiny new teapot from the stove with a pot holder, smiled mysteriously. "I don't know what you're talking about."

"You've met a man," Melissa accused, beaming. "I can tell it by the sparkle in your eyes."

"I have met someone," Dana confessed shyly as she poured hot water into a crockery teapot that had prob-ably come from her uncle's mercantile. "His name is Paul Wiley, and he's a sawyer. He only comes calling when his sister Constance is with him, of course. For us to be alone wouldn't be proper."

Melissa was the last one to give lectures on propriety. "Do you love him?" she asked, sitting down at the table and running one hand over the neatly planed window box.

Dana shrugged as she carried the teapot to the table and then went back to take two cups, a sugar bowl, and some spoons from a little cupboard near the stove. "I'm not sure. He's very handsome, and he likes books."

"Does he make you laugh?" Melissa asked, for she had her own opinions on what made a man and woman suitable for each other.

Dana gave a happy little giggle as she joined Melissa at the table but did not share the memory that had amused her so much. "Oh, yes," she answered. "Does Quinn make you laugh, Melissa?"

She hadn't been prepared for the tables to be turned that way. In the railroad car Quinn had tickled her until she'd shrieked with laughter, but she wasn't sure it was the same thing. "I guess," she said, her cheeks throbbing.

Dana patted her hand. "I wish I knew what you're remembering that would make you blush like that," she teased, her eyes twinkling.

"No you don't," Melissa argued, pouring a cup of tea for her friend and for herself. "Believe me, you don't."

The two women talked and drank tea for an hour or so, and then Quinn loomed up in the doorway and rapped at the outside wall. Although he exchanged pleasant greetings with Dana, he turned down her offer of tea and cookies and was soon squiring his errant almost-wife out the door.

"Wong needs your help with dinner," he said.

Melissa looked up at him in despair. "Oh, Quinn, you weren't serious!" she wailed. "I don't know anything about cooking for so many people!"

Quinn smiled at her, showing his straight white teeth. "Do you want everybody to say that you're only a bird in a gilded railroad car?" he inquired.

Melissa wrenched her arm free of Quinn's grasp. "Damn you, Rafferty, it was your idea to bring me up here in the first place! Don't you dare stand there and lecture me about how it's going to look if I don't pretend to be a cook!"

Quinn shrugged. "Whatever you say, Calico," he agreed. "But remember, the general consensus will be that you were brought up here to take care of my baser needs."

"Isn't that the truth?" Melissa demanded, glaring at him, her arms locked stubbornly across her breasts.

His mouth quirked at one corner, and his mischievous brown eyes caught the sunlight and turned to flecks of amber. "Of course it is," he mocked in a soft voice. "Don't worry, love. You'll get your chance at me after the sun goes down."

Melissa had a wild urge to stomp both feet and scream in fury, but she didn't indulge it. "Wonderful," she purred in response. "Then the first thing I'll do is slap you silly!"

Quinn laughed and pointed to a long, weathered building with smoke curling out of its chimney. "There's the cookhouse, Calico. Enjoy the afternoon."

Melissa's throat tightened over a shriek of annoyance. She turned on one heel and stormed into the cookhouse, where she was immediately put to work peeling gnarled potatoes. She worked for an hour and escaped when Mr. Wong left the sweltering kitchen to argue with a peddler in the dooryard.

Desperately hungry, she stole the heel of a ham and half a loaf of bread from Wong's supplies before dashing out through the front. Safe inside the railroad car, she wolfed down the food and then, yawning, sat on the edge of the bed to unfasten her shoes and kick them off. Soon she was curled up on the fur spread, sound asleep.

She was awakened hours later by gentle hands rolling down her stockings. "No," she whimpered, "please. I'm too tired."

Quinn chuckled in the gathering twilight. "I know, Calico," he said quietly. "Don't worry."

He undressed her and then helped her into her nightgown before lighting a lamp.

"Don't you want any supper?" he asked.

The ham and bread had worn off, and Melissa was starving. "Do I have to go back in the cookhouse and face Mr. Wong?"

Quinn shook his head and grinned, disappearing around the partition to reappear moments later with a plate.

Melissa reached out for the food eagerly. There was fried chicken, corn, and mashed potatoes with gravy, and she ate hungrily. "I peeled these potatoes," she said between mouthfuls, to justify herself.

Quinn looked mock-stern. "To hear him tell it, Mr. Wong is going to peel *you* if he catches you in his kitchen again. He wanted you to shuck the corn and wash up the breakfast dishes."

Melissa waved a chicken leg at Quinn like a conductor's baton. "Let that be a lesson to you. You should never shanghai people and drag them off to lumber camps. It just isn't done, Mr. Rafferty."

He only smiled at her and waited patiently for her to finish eating. When she had, he disappeared for the better part of ten minutes, returning with buckets of steaming water. While Melissa watched, he dragged a copper bathtub around the partition and then began filling it from the buckets. "I'd have made you carry my water, but you're pregnant," he said reasonably.

Melissa swung her legs over the side of the bed. "That seems to save me from any number of indignities," she remarked.

Quinn was taking off his clothes. "Most, but not all," he agreed, and when he was naked he stepped into the water and sat down with a lusty sigh of contentment. "Come and wash my back," he said.

Pushing up her sleeves, Melissa walked over to the tub, knelt beside it, and took up soap and a washcloth. "When are we going home?" she demanded, scouring his grimy back.

"Don't worry," he replied magnanimously, "we'll be back in time for you to waltz off to the picnic with Mitch."

Melissa had forgotten all about Mitch and the social gathering that would take place at the Seaside Hotel on Saturday. Being reminded of Mr. Williams naturally brought Gillian to mind, and she struck the back of Quinn's head with the washcloth. "While you escort the lovely Miss Aires, of course," she said.

His powerful, sun-browned shoulders moved in a shrug. "If she's there. Gillian's leaving town as soon as she can unload her half of the hotel on some poor sucker, you know. She's in love with your English friend, Calico."

Melissa was glad that Quinn couldn't see her face and read the varied emotions reflected there. She was overjoyed that Gillian was going away, but she was also troubled by the prospect of telling Mr. Rafferty exactly who his new partner was. "I think whoever buys Gillian's share is getting a bargain," she said.

"I just hope they want to run the place," Quinn said with a tired sigh. "I hate being cooped up in that office with all those little old ladies running in to tell me that I ought to plant petunias by the front door or get the chef to fix some cherished family recipe they just happen to have brought along from home."

Melissa laughed and tossed the washcloth into his lap. "I think it would be fun managing a hotel," she said.

"Don't get any ideas," Quinn grumbled.

Melissa thought it was a fortuitous time to change the subject, and besides, she had an almost unbearable craving for something sweet. "Do you suppose Mr. Wong would be angry if I took some of that cherry pie I saw hidden away in the pantry today?" she asked.

"Yes, but help yourself anyway," Quinn replied.

Melissa bit her lower lip and cast a look at the darkened windows, thinking of bears and snakes and marauding lumberjacks. "Will you go with me?"

Quinn nodded. "As soon as I finish my bath, Calico," he promised.

He took his time doing that, but presently he was dressed and following Melissa through the moonlit night toward the cookhouse. They hadn't gone twenty feet when an awful explosion sounded behind them and the railroad car splintered into a million flaming pieces.

Twenty-four

The blast hurled Melissa forward; she smelled and tasted pine needles, and small stones embedded themselves in her flesh. Quinn sheltered her with his body until the fiery debris had stopped falling down around them, and then he rolled away, looking back at the holocaust with a muttered curse.

Melissa was trembling as she turned over and sat staring at the inferno that had almost claimed both their lives. She dusted the pine needles and dirt from her nightgown and got shakily to her feet. Meanwhile, men and women alike came running from every corner of the camp.

The immediate danger was that the fire still consuming the bulk of the railroad car would spread through the camp and then into the timber.

Quinn grasped Melissa's shoulders with such sudden force that she was startled. "Are you all right?" he rasped.

Melissa nodded, still too shaken to speak.

He issued his orders clearly, and in a tone that brooked no argument. "Stay out of the way until the fire is out, but don't wander off by yourself."

Again Melissa nodded. The lumberjacks were already starting up a steam-powered compressor; soon water was spewing out of hoses connected to a special tank. She ran barefoot through the camp, zigzagging around hot embers that glowed on the ground until she reached the schoolhouse.

There, after some foraging, she found paper and half a dozen sharp pencils and then hurried back to the scene of the fire to scribble hasty notes as she watched the lumberjacks battle blazes that threatened the nearby woods. She had lost several chapters of her book in the explosion, but there was no time to grieve.

When the fire was finally out she went to the cookhouse, following the other women. She sat alone at the end of one of the tables, reading over her notes and making changes with quick strokes of her pencil. Her lower lip was caught between her teeth, and she looked up, startled, when someone laid a blanket over her shoulders.

Quinn was standing there, his face, hair, and clothes black with soot. With a glance at her papers he sat down on the bench beside her and gave a weary sigh. "I thought I told you to stay with the others."

The women of the camp had gathered at a different table, where they were drinking coffee and chattering excitedly about the events of the night. Melissa was tired and shaken, and she didn't feel like doing battle. She changed the subject. "What happened out there tonight, Quinn? That car didn't just blow up and burst into flames all by itself, did it?"

Quinn shook his head and ran one hand through blackened, greasy hair. "It was dynamited, and some kerosene had been tossed around for good measure."

Melissa's eyes were wide. "Then someone tried to kill us?" she asked, horrified.

A muscle in Quinn's jaw twitched. "They were probably after me," he said, not looking at her.

She laid a hand on his arm and for the first time realized that her own skin was smudged with soot, too. She knew that he was trying not to frighten her further, and to save her embarrassment, but there was no sense in pretending that everyone in camp hadn't known of her presence in that car.

Quinn's hand rested over hers, and she was reminded of the way he'd sheltered her after the explosion. A wild sort of tenderness filled her. "Who would do a thing like that, Quinn?" she whispered. "Who wants to see you dead?"

"I can think of a couple of people," he replied, gazing off into space. His Adam's apple moved along his grimy neck as he swallowed. "Melissa, you've got to go back to Port Hastings until I find out. You're not safe here."

She scooted a little closer to him on the bench and lowered her voice. "I'm not going anywhere, Quinn Rafferty," she argued. "Why, I wouldn't have a moment's peace for wondering if you were all right!"

He turned and smiled briefly at her, his teeth startlingly white against his dirty face. There was sadness in his eyes, though, and a stoop to his shoulders. "I wonder if you'll still feel that way after I've told you the whole truth."

Before Quinn could elaborate one of the women approached to say that she had fixed up a bed in one of the new cabins. Her eyes carefully skirted Melissa, making her feel like a pariah.

"I guess we'd better try to get some sleep," Quinn said to Melissa after he'd thanked the woman and she'd gone away. "I've got some people to track down in the morning."

Melissa didn't like the sound of that. "You should let the sheriff handle this, Quinn," she objected, holding the blanket around her with one hand and clutching the notes for a newspaper article about the fire in the other.

Once they were outside Quinn noticed that Melissa's feet were bare and unceremoniously hoisted her up into his arms, "Now you'll have to rewrite part of your book," he said, in a transparent attempt to distract her from the subject at hand.

Melissa pulled an arm out of the blanket and curved it around Quinn's neck. "Right now I'm just happy not to be dead," she replied. Horror possessed her again as she thought of all the things that could have happened. For instance, she might have left the railroad car by herself, instead of making Quinn go along. . . .

She buried her face in his neck and thanked God that he'd been spared.

It was only when they'd entered the cabin that had been prepared for them that Melissa asked, "What did you mean earlier, about hoping I'd still care for you when I knew the whole truth?"

Quinn waited until Melissa was settled in the makeshift bed of blankets and sheets that had been arranged on the floor, then blew out the lamp and began stripping off his clothes. "We'll talk about that in the morning," he said. "Right now I need you to hold me so I won't forget that you're alive."

Melissa was so touched by this revelation of vulnerability, and so much in need of holding herself, that she didn't press for an answer to her question. Morning would come soon enough, and she and Quinn were both damned lucky to be around to see it. When he stretched out beside her and drew her into his arms, she went willingly.

Their lovemaking was slow and methodical that night, an affirmation of life and love that reassured Melissa and comforted her in a very profound way. When Quinn stiffened upon her and cried out in abandon she didn't care that the walls were thin and the other cabins close by. If everyone in the world knew that she'd given her man solace when he needed her, that was fine with Melissa.

The morning brought hectic activity. Although he'd promised to confess some secret sin to her when they awakened, Quinn had already gone when Melissa opened her eyes. She saw that someone, probably Dana, had brought her a set of clothes and a pair of shoes, and she was grateful. Running around camp in a nightgown was fine when it was dark and there was a major disaster going on, but in the broad light of day it would naturally have been another matter.

When Melissa reached the cookhouse, where breakfast was being served, she hesitated on the step, shy about going inside. It wouldn't be easy to face all those men, aware that they'd seen her in her nightgown and knew she'd shared Quinn's private railroad car. It was only the golden band on her finger, which she'd refused to take off, that gave her the courage to step through the open doorway.

A silence fell when she entered, and then someone dared to whistle. Melissa couldn't discern who the culprit was and didn't care. She had one priority, and that was to find Quinn.

She scanned the shadowy interior of the cookhouse, the smoke from Wong's stove stinging her eyes, but saw no sign of her mate. After drawing a deep breath she approached a large man with a bushy red and yellow beard and a toothless grin.

"Pardon me, sir," she said formally, "but I'm looking for Mr. Rafferty. Have you seen him, please?"

The lumberjack's grin broadened, and Melissa was beginning to suspect that he was the scalliwag who had whistled at her minutes before. "I reckon you've probably seen a lot more of the boss than I have, ma'am," he replied.

The men howled with laughter at this, and Melissa charitably supposed that they had little merriment in their dreary lives and must therefore seek amusement where they could. "Thank you," she told him, with her chin high. She was just about to turn and walk out when Quinn came in.

The look in his eyes fairly pinioned her to the floor. She had obviously committed a serious breach of etiquette by entering the cook shack when the men were there, but she was in no mood to apologize. After all, her motives had been sterling.

His jawline clamped down tight, Quinn gestured with one hand toward the door. Breaking her paralysis took deliberation on Melissa's part, but she managed to precede him out into the dazzling new day with dignity.

"I was only looking for you!" she burst out in a defensive whisper before he could begin the inevitable lecture.

Quinn curved one arm around her waist and propelled her toward a team and wagon waiting near the burned-out hulk of the railroad car. "Well, you found me, Calico," he said flatly.

Melissa dug in her heels. She knew he meant to take her down the mountain, and she was eager to go, but she wasn't leaving without her notes, and they were still in the cabin. "I've got to get my article," she protested.

Quinn pulled folded sheets of notebook paper from the pocket of his shirt.

"Here you are, Nellie Bly," he said dryly. With that he lifted Melissa into the wagon seat and then climbed up beside her to take the reins. She noticed a shotgun lying on the floorboard within easy reach, and a chill shivered up and down her spine at the incomprehensible idea that someone actually wanted to take her life, and Quinn's.

They'd traveled some distance down the harrowingly narrow mountain road before she ventured to present the question that had been chewing at her on one level or another since the night before. "What's your terrible secret, Mr. Rafferty?"

He looked at her out of the corner of one eye. Although he'd washed up that morning, as Melissa had, he was still essentially dirty, and his clothes were the same ones he'd been wearing when the car exploded. "Before I answer that I want to tell you something else, Melissa. What happened last night put a lot of things into perspective for me. You're the most important person in my life, and I want you to remember that."

Melissa bit her lower lip. Nearly losing Quinn had changed some of her attitudes, too, but she wasn't ready to define those new feelings yet, so she kept her peace.

Quinn drew in a deep breath and let it out again. "Mary isn't my sister," he said, keeping his eyes on the twisting, rutted trail before them. "She's my daughter."

After what she'd learned about her father and the life-and-death trauma of the explosion, Melissa was hardly moved by this revelation. In fact, she realized that she'd known the truth all along in some corner of her heart. She put her hand out slowly and rested it on Quinn's leg. "And Gillian is her mother," she guessed softly.

Quinn nodded. "You're not angry that I didn't tell you?"

"I'm not sure you've ever had a chance to. Ever since we met, things have been happening so fast that a body can hardly catch his breath."

He bent to kiss her temple. "Thanks, Calico."

Melissa's brow furrowed in a concerned frown. "Have you told Mary?"

Quinn shook his head. "Not in so many words. Sometimes I think she already knows."

After that they fell into a reflective silence. Quinn concentrated on the road and his own thoughts, and Melissa wrote and rewrote her newspaper article in her mind. At the same time, on another level of her being, she worked at accepting the painful knowledge that someone else had borne Quinn a child.

Whenever Melissa's mind turned to thoughts of Gillian and Quinn making love, she renewed her efforts to concentrate solely on the article. By the time they'd reached Port Riley, in midafternoon, she could have recited the piece word for word. It was only a matter of writing it all down.

She waited until Quinn was in the bathtub, and thus relatively helpless, to announce that she was going to the newspaper office to talk with Mr. Bradberry.

Quinn was outraged, knowing he'd been outmaneuvered, but there wasn't much he could do. He'd have to find fresh clothes and wrench them on before he could stop Melissa from leaving the house, and by that time she'd be halfway to her destination.

His outburst was still stinging her ears when she hurried into the shell of the Rip Snortin' Saloon, where Mr. Bradberry had set up his presses. At the sight of Melissa's bright, excited eyes he knew she had a story and led her to a typewriting machine.

Melissa had learned to typewrite in college, although she was not skillful or fast. She pecked out the story of the explosion and fire as rapidly as she could, making a number of mistakes, and ripped it from the machine to hand to her editor.

Mr. Bradberry nodded as he read and then informed her that the piece would appear on the front page of the first edition of the new Port Riley *Testament*.

Melissa was delighted. "Does this mean I can be a reporter?" she asked, unable to contain her enthusiasm.

The elderly man cleared his throat. There was hubbub all around as clerks and printers prepared for the first run of news, and Melissa had to strain to hear his words. "I understand that you may be—er—in the family way, Miss Corbin," he said, his cheeks turning bright red. The contrast with his white hair and mustache was striking.

Melissa lowered her eyes. It was no marvel to her that something so private was so generally known. She'd grown up in a town only slightly larger than Port Riley, and she understood that gossip got around faster than a head cold. "I'm a good writer, Mr. Bradberry. If you'll only give me a chance, you'll see."

"I'll be glad to, young woman," he replied, "but it's fiction I want from you. Long stories that I can publish in serial form. That way, you don't have to be running around town poking your nose into everybody's business."

"But that's a reporter's job!" Melissa argued. She was tired of always having her plans circumvented.

Mr. Bradberry was equally adamant. "We'll discuss that after your child is born. In the meanwhile, it's fiction I want."

Melissa sighed. At least she hadn't been told that she could never again write for the paper, and her piece on the fire *had* made the front page. "I'll be at the hotel picnic on Saturday. Don't you want my account of that?"

The old man's fingers tapped rhythmically against his upper arm. "You are a stubborn little snippet, aren't you?"

"Yes, sir." Melissa beamed proudly.

Bradberry laughed at that. "It just so happens that a good reporter has to be stubborn. You bring me whatever pieces seem pertinent to you, miss. If I like them, I'll print them."

The deal seemed fair to Melissa, and she offered her hand to seal it. She was leaving the building, her mind racing over possible topics for articles, when she saw the man leaning against a hitching rail. His shape and something else about him were familiar, and it was obvious, even though he tried to be subtle, that he'd been waiting for her.

Melissa decided to be bold, since she was a real reporter now, and she walked right up to him and put out her hand. "Hello, Mr. Rafferty," she said.

Eustice looked at her in surprise, unsettled at being recognized. He was an ugly man, but not because of his scraggly beard or hawk nose; it was the plain evil that emanated from him that made him unattractive. The only trace of Quinn that Melissa could see in that dissolute face was in the dark, brazen eyes, and she suppressed a shudder, at the same time keeping her smile fixed to her mouth.

He ignored her hand until she let it fall back to her side, then said, "Say hello to my boy for me."

The words were innocuous, and yet they chilled her. She turned and walked away from Eustice Rafferty without looking back.

In her room at the hotel Melissa took a hot bath, shampooed her hair, and had an early supper in the kitchen. She was on her way back upstairs when she encountered Quinn in the lobby.

"Where have you been?" he demanded after he'd dragged her into the office he shared with Gillian.

"Right here," Melissa responded cheerfully.

Quinn turned away and slammed his fist down on the desktop in frustration. He immediately gasped in pain, and Melissa smiled, thinking he'd gotten what he deserved for losing his temper. "Damn it," he barked out, "last night you were almost killed. I bring you back to Port Riley to protect you, and what the hell do you do? You disappear!"

"I had a story to turn in," Melissa answered, widening her eyes innocently.

"'I had a story to turn in,'" mimicked Quinn, infuriated. "You could have damned well come back to the house when you were through!"

"Whyever would I do that?" Melissa asked guilelessly, gazing up at him. "I don't live there."

"And you do live here, I suppose?"

"I do indeed," Melissa replied, savoring her moment of impending triumph. "You see, I own half interest in the place."

The starch drained out of Quinn. He groped for the desk chair and collapsed into it. "Oh, no," he groaned.

Melissa nodded. "Aren't you going to welcome me to the business, partner?"

Quinn folded his arms on the desk and dropped his head

onto them, still groaning. Melissa was beginning to think his appendix had ruptured when he finally rallied and sat up straight again.

"You don't know a damned thing about running a hotel," he pointed out reasonably.

"Since when has that ever stopped me?" she countered.

Quinn had no answer for that. "Melissa, I forbid you to do this. You are my—"

"Your what?" Melissa interrupted. "I'm not your wife, so what am I, Quinn?"

He rose slowly, ominously, to his feet, glowering at her, bending forward. "You would be my wife if you'd stop this foolishness long enough to let me drag you in front of a preacher," he said in a voice that was all the more unnerving for its softness.

Melissa retreated a step. "Your utter lack of romantic refinement never ceases to amaze me, Mr. Rafferty," she said coldly, reaching behind her for the doorknob. "If you want me for a wife, you'll damned well have to court me."

"Court you, hell," Quinn hissed. "In another five seconds I'm going to carry you out to that lobby and throw you into the fountain!"

Melissa patted her heart as though to still its hammering beat. "My hero!" she sighed. While Quinn was standing there looking volcanic she whirled, wrenched open the door, and made a dash for it.

She was in her room, gasping for breath with the door locked behind her, when she realized that Quinn hadn't pursued her. She was both relieved and disappointed as she settled herself at the small desk she'd had brought in and began rewriting the pages of her novel that had gone up in the explosion of the railroad car.

That night she dreamed of fire and fear, and at first she thought, in that detached way of dreamers, that she was reliving the near-disaster that had taken place on the mountain. Instead, she soon learned, she was in hell, having been consigned there for writing trashy novels and sharing Quinn's bed without benefit of clergy.

When she was brought before the devil, kicking and fighting every inch of the way, she was not surprised to find herself looking into the face of Eustice Rafferty.

The final preparations for the picnic had been going on since dawn, and Melissa was in her element, bossing everyone from the chef to the lowliest chambermaid. Special poles had been set up, linked by thin wire, and she was making sure that the Chinese lanterns and paper streamers were hung properly. Just as she turned, satisfied, to go inside and see that André had chosen the best caviar, Quinn opened the French doors and stepped out of the dining room.

Melissa hadn't seen him at all the day before, and she felt as though he'd just returned from a long absence. Hiding her eagerness, she strolled toward him. "Good morning, Mr. Rafferty," she said. "It's good to see that you're taking an interest in the festivities."

"It ought to be almost as much fun as a hanging," he observed.

Melissa gave him a winning smile. "That would depend, of course, on who was being hanged," she said.

He glared at her. "Enough is enough, Melissa. We're going to Port Hastings today to get your brother to marry us."

Melissa shook her head. "No poetry, no daisies." She sighed, thinking of her conversation with Keith a couple of days before.

"What?" Quinn demanded, glaring at her.

"Never mind," Melissa replied airily, starting around him.

He stopped her, as she had known he would, but before either of them could speak the unmistakable noise of an automobile engine sounded, along with an insistent horn. Both Quinn and Melissa went to investigate.

Pure joy bubbled up inside Melissa when she realized that the motorists approaching the hotel at breakneck speed were Fancy and Banner.

They came to a flourishing stop just short of a forsythia bush beside the front walk and were engaged in a lively conversation, made up mostly of hand gestures, when Quinn and Melissa approached.

The two women exchanged places so that Fancy was at the wheel, and the vehicle sputtered and popped as it shot into reverse and zoomed backward.

Quinn squeezed his eyes shut and Melissa winced as the rear bumper came perilously close to a brass hitching post, but Fancy stopped the motorcar in the nick of time.

Melissa ran, laughing, to greet her sisters-in-law. "Why did you change places like that?" she wanted to know as Quinn cautiously approached.

Banner smiled broadly, her face coated with the dust of the open road. "I drive when we're going forward, and Fancy takes the wheel when we reverse our direction."

Quinn looked baffled. He opened his mouth to say something and then closed it again.

"Jeff and Adam are coming to the picnic, too," Fancy said brightly, "but they were afraid to ride in the motorcar, the cowards."

Melissa thought of Keith and his ultimatum and wondered if he'd told the family about her pregnancy and sham marriage. She glanced warily at Quinn. He must have been thinking along the same lines, for he looked arrogantly pleased. "How about Keith and Tess? Will they be here?" she asked.

Banner shook her head. "Tess's mother and father are visiting from back East, so they couldn't get away. She paused and frowned. "Keith did ask me to tell you that he'll see you on Wednesday as planned."

Melissa swallowed and glanced at Quinn, who looked downright smug. Deciding to ignore him, she put an arm around each of her sisters-in-law and led them toward the hotel, where they could wash and have cold lemonade.

When the morning train was due Quinn went to meet it with a wagon. He returned twenty minutes later with a sheepish Adam and Jeff.

The moment Melissa saw her brothers she knew they hadn't come because of her situation; they were there to find out if she'd forgiven them for keeping the secret concerning their father.

Looking at them, Melissa found she couldn't be angry.

Jeff was still a little pale from his recent sickness, and a streak of silver had appeared at Adam's right temple, a sharp contrast to his ebony hair. Reminded that life was fragile and family was precious, Melissa hurried down the front walk to greet her brothers with exuberant hugs and kisses on the cheek.

Jeff's eyes were suspiciously bright as he grinned down at her. "It's good to see you, brat," he said gently.

Adam glanced over at the motorcar, parked within a hair's breadth of the brass hitching post, and shook his head. "You should get one of those for Melissa," he said to Quinn.

Quinn rolled his eyes at that, and Melissa's brothers laughed in sympathy.

"Where are those two thrill seekers of ours, anyway?" Jeff wanted to know.

At that moment Fancy answered his question by bursting out of the hotel and running across the lawn, beaming. Melissa's heart swelled and grew warm within her, because the look that passed between her brother and his wife was proof that everything was all right with them again.

⟡ Twenty-five

Eustice Rafferty sat in a shadowy corner of the Blue Pig Saloon, his hands cupped around a whiskey glass, his gaze fixed on the wiry, grudge-filled little man in the chair across from his. It had been a mistake, he reflected, to try to kill both Quinn and that fancy woman of his. If that whore's son had died in the railroad car, the agony would have lasted only minutes. Eustice wanted him to live another fifty years, suffering every moment of that time, but convincing Sever to let Quinn live was going to take some doing.

Jake shifted in his seat. He could never sit still for long, because some injustice, big or small, was always chewing at his middle. His eyes glowed as if he had a fever, and even his voice was quick and whispery. "All of 'em gathered out there for a party," he muttered, reflecting. "We ain't gonna get a better chance than that, Rafferty."

Eustice settled back in his chair. He was no more patient than Sever, if the truth be known, but he liked the illusion of being superior in some way. "Just the woman," he said.

Sever wet his lips with the tip of his tongue. His wife, Becky, had left him recently to work in Quinn's house, and

Jake believed he'd been cuckolded. "No," he said. "It's your boy I want—I ain't got no quarrel with the girl."

It occurred to Eustice that what folks said about Sever was true; his hot temper had burned up his mind a long time ago. He just wasn't right in the head, and there would be no reasoning with him.

Eustice nodded and smiled. "Whatever you say, Jake," he said. "We'll do whatever you say."

The two men spent another hour laying plans and then left the saloon by the back way. This was Eustice's suggestion. He told Sever that there was something he wanted him to see.

The afternoon sunshine glinted on the blade of Eustice's hunting knife. With a smile on his face he plunged it into Sever's middle, pushing until he felt the hilt lodge against the man's ribcage.

Sever made a bloody, gurgling sound and toppled to the ground, a look of surprise etched into his features for all time.

Eustice pulled his knife out of his friend's belly. There was a rain barrel beside the back door of the saloon, so he went over and washed the blade clean, drying it carefully on his shirt before sheathing it again. By the time he reached the street he'd convinced himself that he'd done the poor bastard a favor by putting him out of his misery.

Gillian swung her violet gaze from Mitch and Melissa, who were participating in the croquet tournament, to Quinn, who was standing with his back to a cedar tree, scowling at the couple. His tie was loose, the top three buttons of his shirt were unfastened, and his hair was rumpled from repeated combing with his fingers.

She went to the man who had loved her so long and so well and stepped between him and the woman he had been watching all day. "There's still time for a—private farewell," she said, gripping one end of his string tie in each hand.

His brazen brown eyes flashed with such reproach that she let her hands drop to her sides. "We said good-bye years ago, Gillian," he told her.

She had to lower her gaze to protect herself from the searing contempt in his. "Years?" She choked out the word. "We were engaged until a few weeks back, Quinn, when you met Melissa. You loved me, you wanted to marry me."

"No," he answered. "I was only playing out a part—and so were you. If we'd really wanted to be married, we wouldn't have found so many excuses to put off the ceremony."

Gillian swallowed. She couldn't deny what Quinn was saying because she knew it was true. She had delighted in his companionship and his lovemaking, but she'd never wanted to be his wife, because that would have made her a Rafferty, and the name was a taint to her. Quinn's father was a dreadful man, and his mother had been a timid, snuffling little creature who took in other people's wash.

She looked up at Quinn and saw that he was smiling. "You'll be happy in England," he said. "You were born to be the mistress of some manor."

Gillian felt a little better. While her affection for Quinn was not and had never been strong enough to sustain a lifelong partnership, it was a very real emotion, and she could not bear his fury. "What about her?" she asked, turning slightly and gesturing toward Melissa. "What was she born to be?"

Quinn laughed. "The bane of my existence. The walking, breathing punishment for every sin I've ever committed or even considered committing. And I've got no idea how I ever lived without her."

Rising to her tiptoes, Gillian gave Quinn a light kiss, then turned and walked away. She was looking ahead now, to meeting Ajax in New York and sailing on to a new life. She had a lot of packing to do.

Jeff cornered Melissa in the relatively barren area that would soon be a lush garden. "All right," he demanded, "I want to know what's going on here."

Melissa pretended puzzlement even though she knew Jeff was wondering why she was spending the day with Mitch Williams instead of the man he believed to be her husband.

While she was trying to think of a reply that would satisfy her brother two strong arms closed around her from behind.

She jumped, startled, and turned her head to look up at Quinn. He gave her a very forward kiss, and she was blushing when he finally released her, but when she glanced at Jeff she saw that her problem had been solved. At least temporarily.

"I was beginning to think the two of you were here with other people," Jeff boomed, pleased, as he rarely was, to find himself in the wrong.

Quinn was still standing behind Melissa and still holding her close. He gave her a husbandly swat on the bottom. "I like to give the little woman space to breathe," he said, smiling magnanimously.

Melissa wanted to kick him. He was deliberately baiting her, knowing that she didn't dare tell Jeff the truth about their situation, and there was nothing she could do. She blushed, frightfully embarrassed, and averted her eyes.

That made Jeff laugh. He walked away to find Fancy, probably thinking that he'd done Melissa a favor by leaving her alone with her "husband." She whirled, meaning to slap Quinn soundly in payment for that smack on the backside, and found herself swept up into a kiss that threatened to consume her.

Lively fiddle music was struck up inside the ballroom, and Quinn and Melissa were forced to draw apart. Couples were starting to wander in from the lawn, hand in hand, to dance.

In the distance lightning severed the sky and dark clouds were gathering. Melissa gave a little shiver that had nothing to do with rain coming to spoil a picnic and allowed Quinn to lead her inside for a dance.

One dance followed another until Melissa was breathless. Such close contact with Quinn made her want him, and she was embarrassed at having such feelings with so many people around.

When she could, she made an excuse and disappeared, thinking that a walk in the cool and windy outdoors would restore her sense of balance.

The hot springs exerted a mysterious pull. She got the key from a hook just inside the kitchen door and made her way to the gazebolike building that housed the natural pool. She unlocked the enclosure and went inside, dropping the keys on one of the benches that faced the water and kicking off her slippers.

The water looked so inviting. Melissa slipped out of her Spanish off-the-shoulder blouse and brightly colored skirt, laying them carefully on a bench along with her petticoat, drawers, and stockings.

She was in the pool, swimming in slow circles and delighting in the release of tension the steamy water brought her, when she heard the door open and close. She smiled, expecting Quinn, but it was Eustice Rafferty who stood on the pond's edge watching her.

Melissa opened her mouth to scream and knew in the same instant that it would be useless to cry out. Everyone was dancing in the ballroom, and they would hear nothing but the laughter and the music.

"You're intruding," she said, trying to hide her nakedness by hunkering down in the churning water and keeping her arms crossed over her breasts. "Please go away immediately."

The old man laughed at that and stood his ground. "He'll grieve for you," he mused. "Yes, indeed, he will."

A shiver passed over Melissa despite the warm water, leaving goosebumps in its wake. She watched in round-eyed horror as he took a knife from his battered leather scabbard.

Melissa began easing backward toward the opposite side of the pool, but Eustice only rounded the edge, smiling at her with gruesome relish. "Step out of there," he said after a few moments, "and let me get a look at you."

Melissa shook her head. She wanted to scream now, but she couldn't. Her throat was closed so tightly that it would have been impossible to make any sound. Papa, she thought wildly, help me. You owe me that.

The hulking man made a grumbling sound and lunged into the water feet first, making a horrendous splash that freed Melissa's vocal cords. A scream tore itself from her throat, so primal and powerful that it left rawness in its wake, and she scrambled frantically to escape.

Eustice caught her before she reached the other side of the pool and pressed the blade of his knife to her throat. Standing behind her, he grasped her waist and dragged her back against him. Melissa was afraid to struggle or scream with the blade at her jugular, and her mind was running wildly through a very limited list of possibilities.

When she felt one of his great, groping hands close over her breast she was so repulsed that she turned her head slightly and sank her teeth into his wrist.

Eustice bellowed in rage and pain, and the knife toppled from his hand into the water. Melissa lunged for it, found the weapon, and grasped it in both hands.

"Don't touch me," she warned as Eustice approached, his grizzled hair and beard streaming, his clothes sodden. His movements were slow and laborious in the water, but he was coming closer and closer, and he didn't look afraid.

He kept coming, and he reached out for her, and Melissa shrieked in mingled fear and horror as she raised the knife and plunged it into his chest. Eustice fell forward, blood staining the water that bubbled and gurgled around him, and Melissa was still screaming when Quinn came and gathered her into his arms.

The next few hours passed in a haze for Melissa. She was wrapped in a blanket and taken to her room in the hotel, and Banner gave her a bath and a shot that made her sleep. When she awakened night had fallen, and she was not alone on her narrow bed.

The terror returned, and she stiffened violently, a scream rising in her throat. But the scent and substance of the man holding her were Quinn's, and she settled against him and wept with relief.

Quinn's lips moved gently at her temple. "It's all over now, Calico—there's no reason to be afraid."

"I k-killed him," she whispered.

His hand rose to smooth her damp, tangled hair. "You

did what you had to do," he said. "I've already talked to the sheriff, and he agrees that it was obviously self-defense."

"Why? Why did he want to hurt me?" Melissa fretted, shuddering as she remembered the look in Eustice's eyes.

"It was me he hated," Quinn answered, and there was pain as well as resignation in his voice. "He was so full of venom that it eventually ate away his soul."

Melissa shivered. If she had learned one thing from the incident, it was that life could be snatched away without warning, at any moment. She might have been parted from Quinn forever.

"I love you," she said, her lips moving against the hairy flesh of his chest.

Quinn poised himself above her, studying her face in the moonlight. "Do you mean that, Mrs. Rafferty?"

Melissa nodded, loving the sound of the name even though it wasn't rightfully hers yet. "Yes," she answered solemnly, "but I still want to write articles for the newspaper and help run this hotel, and I'll make your life miserable, Quinn Rafferty, if you try to make me sit home and knit!"

He gave a raucous burst of laughter. "Loving you is going to take all the energy I can spare, Calico," he told her, his lips only a breath away from hers. "But you'd better be prepared for one hell of a lot of that."

Every instinct Melissa possessed cried out for union with Quinn; survival demanded celebration. She wriggled beneath him, delighting in his groan of need and immediate physical response.

She was wearing a nightgown, but he removed that with the deftness of an ardent lover, and they were soon resting on their sides, face to face on the slim mattress, the heat of their skin bonding them one to the other. Melissa, raising herself on one elbow, began by kissing Quinn's shoulder and soon progressed to his neck.

He trembled and uttered a low moan as she caressed his hip and thigh with her hand. Her fingers brushed his manhood, her touch as soft as velvet, and she laughed with joy when he grew even harder and hotter. When she caught him in her strong fingers and trained him to the rhythm she wanted, he threw his head back in a primitive gesture of surrender and submitted.

Melissa trailed her lips slowly down over his torso, stopping to pay proper homage to his nipples before kissing the hard muscles of his stomach. When she took him he cried out and turned onto his back. She parted his legs so that they hung down over the sides of the bed, and she freely enjoyed his vulnerability.

He tossed his head from side to side as she pleasured him, a man in delirium, but when he would have given up what she sought to draw from him he suddenly thrust her away. Quinn was gasping as he fought for control of his body and his mind. When he had achieved that, long minutes later, he placed Melissa beneath him and told her, in gruff, gentle tones, exactly what he meant to do.

She was pliant and responsive under his hands and his lips, letting every sweet sensation have free rein, and when he took her she was exalted. Her release was immediate, piercing, and seemingly endless, and Quinn's ran parallel to it. She gloried in the way his powerful body buckled over hers, and in his low cries of desolate satisfaction.

When he collapsed beside her she touched his face and felt tears there. "Don't ever leave me, Melissa," he said when he could speak. "I can handle anything but that."

She kissed him and snuggled close, and they slept.

When Keith arrived on the Wednesday morning train, looking stern and determined, Melissa was there to meet him. She smiled and stood on tiptoe to kiss him on the cheek.

He embraced her, his eyes filled with tenderness. "Are you all right?" he asked, referring to the incident at the picnic the previous Saturday.

Eustice was nothing but a bad memory to Melissa; with characteristic resilience, she'd put the vicious old man out of her mind and concentrated on being happy with his son. "I'm fine," she answered, linking her arm with her brother's. "You didn't tell the family that Quinn and I aren't married yet, did you?"

Keith shook his head. "No. None of us is in any position to lecture on the proprieties," he said, and Melissa wondered what he meant by such a statement.

There was a buggy waiting in front of the depot, and Melissa climbed in and took the reins. In a few minutes they reached the house she and Quinn meant to fill with children.

The parlor had been decorated by an excited Helga. Becky, a widow since Jake Sever's body had been found behind a saloon on Saturday, had taken her small daughter and gone back to her cabin on the mountain. She would earn her living by raising vegetables and helping Mr. Wong with the cooking at the lumber camp.

Keith took in the streamers and paper bells decorating the parlor, and he was relieved. It was plain enough that he'd been expecting Melissa to stage some kind of rebellion.

Quinn appeared in the doorway, dressed formally and already pulling at his stiff collar, and Mitch Williams was at his side, looking almost as uncomfortable.

Melissa excused herself to go upstairs and change clothes, kissing Quinn on his freshly shaven cheek as she passed him and making a scandalous promise with her eyes.

In the master bedroom Dana, Mary, and Quinn's Aunt Alice were waiting. Alice and Mary had returned on Monday for Eustice's burial, out of propriety rather than grief, and stayed for the ceremony. Melissa had confessed to them that the first wedding was not legal, and they'd taken the news with equanimity.

If Quinn had told Mary the truth about her identity, he hadn't confided as much to Melissa, but there was an air of relief about the girl that made Melissa wonder if she knew, or whether it was simply due to Eustice Rafferty's no longer being a threat.

With Dana to stand up for her and Mitch to give her away, Melissa was legally and rightfully wed to Quinn Rafferty that afternoon of April 22, 1891, with her brother saying the holy words.

When the ceremony was over she flung herself at Quinn with a cry of joy, kissing him before he had an opportunity to exercise his groomly rights and kiss her. After that she embraced Keith.

"Be happy," he said, kissing her forehead.

Melissa turned to her husband and looked up into his dancing brown eyes. "I love you, Quinn Rafferty," she said clearly, and he put his hands on her waist and responded with a declaration of his own. They were to leave on their honeymoon, a journey to Victoria by steamboat, in a little more than an hour, and Melissa could hardly wait to be alone in their stateroom.

They ate cake and had their pictures taken, and all of that was a happy blur to Melissa. When they were aboard the steamer, however, Quinn refused to take her to their stateroom right away.

"Be patient, Mrs. Rafferty," he chided, tucking her hand into the crook of his elbow and patting it solicitously. "We have the rest of our lives to do that. Let's take a walk on deck and enjoy the fresh air."

Melissa flushed, feeling chagrined. There were several things she wanted to enjoy, and fresh air wasn't one of them, but she walked the deck with Quinn until they were well on their way out onto the Strait of Juan de Fuca. Victoria, a lovely city with an English flavor, would be a marvelous place to honeymoon.

Finally, when Melissa was beginning to think that Quinn had already tired of her—had indeed married her for her money and not because he loved her—he squired her to their private chamber.

In that spacious room, with its round bed covered in velvet, champagne awaited them, cooling in a silver bucket. But it was the small, beautifully wrapped package on the pillow that caught Melissa's attention.

She went to it and was already ripping it open when she demanded, "It is for me, isn't it?"

Quinn laughed. "Oh, yes, Calico. It's all yours."

Inside the fancy paper and ribbon was a framed pen-and-ink drawing of a railroad car. Melissa didn't understand at first, and she looked up at Quinn with questions in her eyes.

He smiled. "I'm having it built because I want you with me as much of the time as possible," he said. "That is, whenever you can leave the hotel and the story-writing and all that." An uncertain look crossed his face. "You will come with me, won't you?"

Melissa's eyes were filled with happy tears. She set the photograph gently aside and went to Quinn, wrapping her arms around his middle and looking up at him. "You just try keeping me away, Mr. Rafferty," she said.

He gave her a thorough kiss and then casually removed the broad-brimmed picture hat she'd put on after the wedding. When he'd tossed it aside he unbuttoned the many fastenings of her blue traveling coat. Melissa was trembling by the time he'd removed her dress.

Quinn undid the ribbons that held her camisole closed and bared her breasts, drawing in his breath as he admired and then caressed them. When he bent his lips to them Melissa was utterly content, though wilder needs were starting to gather like a storm inside her.

She stopped Quinn and undressed him. He bore her kisses, caresses, and teasing nips in stoic silence until she'd driven him far beyond the line where a man's patience would normally end. Then, kneeling on the floor, he made Melissa kneel, too, astraddle his thighs. He took her in a slow, tantalizing glide, supporting her with his hands as she leaned back in proud submission.

His mouth teased and tempted one breast and then the other as he exerted his rhythmic possession, taking her, giving her up, taking her again. Melissa began to plead with him, but he withheld satisfaction, making its price dearer and dearer with every leisurely motion of his hips.

Finally Melissa was forced to battle him for what she needed. In a wild flight to fulfillment she moved with fierce, furious speed, rising and falling upon his manhood. The friction caused him such excruciating pleasure that he had no way of escaping.

When it was over he laughed breathlessly and gave her a swat. "I'll have my vengeance for that," he promised, easing her back so that she lay on the soft rug, still connected to him.

Melissa whimpered as he caressed her breasts and belly and then rolled her nipples between his thumbs and forefingers. She was exhausted and wanted only to crawl into bed and nap for an hour, but it was obvious that Quinn wasn't going to allow that. He continued to toy with her senses, and soon he was as hard and powerful within her as he had been before.

"Oh, God, Quinn," she whispered, "please don't make me wait—please."

He shifted so that he was poised above her and kissed her once before granting her plea by thrusting deep within her. The culmination came to them both at the same time, and it was volcanic, wringing the last bit of strength from each of them.

They climbed into bed and slept, and since the trip from Port Riley to Victoria was not overly long, they had to hurry to be dressed in time to leave the ship.

Tuesday, December 29, 1891

Dearest Mama,

I know you and Harlan have been waiting and watching for this letter, so I won't keep you in suspense any longer. Your eleventh grandchild has arrived: Our baby girl was born the day after Christmas, and we plan to christen her Katherine, for you. Katie is very healthy, and so am I, thank you very much. The doctor wants me to stay in bed for another week, but I'm getting up tomorrow.

Needless to say, the holiday season has been a very happy time for us, and, we hope, for you as well. We spent Christmas Day in Port Hastings, where Maggie made a huge and delicious dinner for us all, and there were lots of presents, as always. Adam grumbled that the tree was nothing but a fire hazard, as usual, and we all ignored him.

Thank you for the beautiful set of silverware to go

with the china you gave us as a wedding gift. It's a perfect match.

Anyway, we were on the way home from Port Hastings in the new railroad car when Katie decided to join us. You should have seen Quinn's face when he realized what was happening! He ran to look for a doctor in the passenger car, but all he came back with was a conductor. Between the two of them they brought your granddaughter into the world. Need I say that I've never gotten a better Christmas present?

I was glad to read in your letter that you had forgiven me for writing all those books without telling you. I cried for joy when you said that what made you furious was that you hadn't gotten to read them. I've been clipping out the episodes of my newspaper saga about Harriet, the circus woman, and I'll send them along soon.

It's strange, but I'm beginning to find my work at the hotel almost as challenging and exciting as writing. (I imagine both pursuits will pale in comparison to being a mother.) Quinn lets me have a free hand at the Seaside, concentrating most of his efforts on the lumber operation and our investments.

We hear from Mary often, and she visits whenever she can. Her eyesight seems to be returning in stages, and we all have hopes, although one can never be completely certain how far the process will go. In any case, Mary is engaged to a nice young man who attends the university and is very happy.

You asked me for a report on the boys, and I can honestly tell you that they were all well and happy when I saw them over Christmas. Jeff has not only accepted Fancy's work in the suffrage movement, he's proud of it. Adam is working too hard, but you know how he loves that, and I suspect that Keith is writing a book, though he won't admit to anything. (Quinn says you can bet it isn't about a woman bound for destruction.)

I'm tiring now but will write more next week.
Please give Harlan our love and esteem.

Your loving daughter,
Melissa

P.S. I want to have another baby right away, and
I've told Quinn, too. Whispered it right in his bad ear!

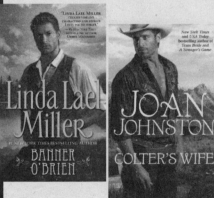